The LADY AND DOC HOLLIDAY

By PRESTON LEWIS

DIAMOND BOOKS ☆ Austin, Texas

FIRST EDITION

Copyright © 1989
By Preston Lewis

Published in the United States of America
By Diamond Books
An Imprint of Eakin Publications, Inc.
P.O. Drawer 90159 ★ Austin, TX 78709-0159

ISBN 0-89015-727-8

For Harriet,
my best

FALL

1876

ONE

Into his clenched fist he coughed once, twice, three times, each throbbing convulsion gouging out tiny bits of lung tissue mixed with bloody mucus. Today the excruciating attack had started earlier than usual, but then he was up earlier than normal. The Fort Griffin stage left Jacksboro at seven o'clock on Saturdays and John Henry Holliday planned to catch it.

His cough hacked through the cool stillness as light chased away the faint stars in the western sky. A stinging scorpion, seeking a hiding place from the emerging daylight, scurried from a crack in the gray clapboard sidewalk toward the leather medical satchel and maroon carpetbag on the weathered planks outside Dan Brown's General Merchandise. With the toe of his boot, Holliday crushed the arachnid, grinding it into the splintery wood well beyond the lethal requirement. As he slid his right hand inside his black broadcloth frock coat, his nimble fingers brushed against the .38-caliber Smith and Wesson pocket revolver in the clipspring shoulder harness, then skirted the sheathed dagger in the breast pocket before pinching a splotched handkerchief free. After wiping his hand of phlegm, he jammed the blue cloth to his mouth to shut off another cough, or at least catch consumption's debris.

Over the handkerchief in his balled fist, his blue eyes, deep and foreboding like an unfilled grave, focused on a cavalry officer marching toward him with steps army-precise, uniform new and crisp, face handsomely chiseled beneath a brown mane and brown eyes curious but pleasant.

John Henry Holliday wondered if he should kill the captain.

If he must, Holliday could blame only himself. He had violated his rule for survival: Never return somewhere you are unwelcomed but wanted. Just fifteen months ago, in a Jacksboro saloon, Holliday had wagered a token of lead against an identical bet from a cocky Fort Richardson lieutenant no luckier at gunplay than at cards. The bullet which had rearranged the lieutenant's chest cavity could have hurt no more than the tuberculosis in his own lungs. But Holliday had not lingered that night to inquire. He had grabbed the disputed pot and by the time the white smoke of black powder had cleared, so had Holliday.

Jacksboro had numbered one less gambler among its population that night — and would have still, except for Lottie.

Some faro dealers were better; none were prettier. Lottie Deno, she called herself, was a lady, no saloon harlot available for the taking. The same auburn hair, gray eyes, downturned lips, and sexual aloofness attracting Fort Richardson soldiers and Jack County cowboys to her faro table in swarms had drawn Holliday back to Jacksboro, like a bee to honey.

As Holliday fought the recurring cough, the captain sidestepped a puddle spotting the street from last night's shower and preserved the shine on his new boots. If this officer asked about the lieutenant's murder, he would die with a nice pair of boots on, Holliday thought. Turning slightly away from the captain and switching the handkerchief to his left hand, Holliday unbuttoned his frock coat and hooked it behind the 1851 Colt Navy revolver holstered at his waist. His empty gunhand tensing for business, Holliday twisted to meet the erect soldier. Between coughs, Holliday noted the captain lacked a sidearm but wore the insignia of the Tenth Cavalry. Holliday's late card partner had ridden with the Sixth Cavalry. Holliday's gun hand relaxed slightly.

The captain marched toward him with the martial precision of a soldier who remembered what it was to be a lieutenant. His step crisp, his uniform fitted to his lean frame like bark on a tree, he betrayed neither fear nor recognized danger. Holliday's thin lips, fringed by the bottom of his handlebar mustache, twitched at the corners into a sinister scowl.

Perversely amused that this inscrutable captain might spoil his clandestine return to Jacksboro, Holliday remembered his precautions, faultless except for this chance encounter. He had timed his arrival for Friday afternoon and his departure Saturday morning. Between the two, he had scoured the saloons where Lottie once dealt faro. Holliday had stabled his horse at Harrell and McLeod's Livery at the northwest corner of courthouse square and paid for three days in advance. As long as the horse remained in the livery yard, Sheriff Crutchfield or Marshal Bingham, should they learn of his arrival, might not so soon discover his departure. Holliday would buy time with his horse and saddle, for both were well worn. At the Horton House, he had paid for three days in advance for a ground-floor room. Then this morning, while it was still dark, he had climbed out the room window with his medical satchel and carpetbag. Clinging to the back of buildings, he had walked to the store of Dan C. Brown, general merchandiser and agent for C. Bain and Co. stage lines, and paid his Fort Griffin fare to a spindly, bespectacled clerk more interested in reading the paper than attending customers.

Now as he stood idly anxious, his fingers curving to fit the ivory grip and trigger of his nickel-plated revolver, Holliday tilted his head toward the street. The cavalryman approached the clapboard sidewalk and stopped. Holliday ruptured into a coughing spasm, covering his mouth with the handkerchief in his left hand. Despite the cough's quiver, his steady gun hand froze an inch from the Colt's ivory grips.

"Good morning," the captain said, his voice no more threatening than the call of a quail.

"Depends on what kind of night you had."

"Sounds like you've had better."

Holliday ground out a harsh word under his breath and relaxed his gun hand. Talkers weren't fighters. He unhooked his coat from behind his revolver and shoved his dirty handkerchief back into his pocket.

The captain extended his hand. "Heading for Griffin?"

Holliday bent and unlatched his carpetbag. From among

the spare change of clothes and the fresh decks of cards, he pulled a quart bottle, half-full. Uncorking it as he straightened, he paused, then drowned a budding cough with two cheek-bulging gulps of bourbon. "Medicine," he sneered. He dropped the re-corked bottle into the carpetbag. Turning before the captain could reply, he stalked inside Dan Brown's store and shoved the door shut, its windows rattling as he advanced past the valise on the dark varnished plank flooring and down the slick whitened path between mounds of darkened merchandise. As Holliday advanced toward the lone clerk standing in the halo of a single lamp on the back counter, his step fell silently on a floor that usually creaked with weight.

The spindly clerk glanced up indifferently from behind yesterday's edition of *The Frontier Echo*, advertising Brown's wares purchased in New York, Philadelphia, and other eastern cities, then turned to the back page.

"When's the stage leaving?" Holliday demanded.

Frowning, the clerk cocked his head and eyed Holliday through the smudged lenses of his spectacles. "On time."

Holliday admired economy with words, except when he wanted information. He leaned his arms on the counter's glass case and drummed his fingers. "Any other passengers?"

Grimacing at the smudges Holliday was tapping onto the glass, the clerk folded the paper in half. "The soldier out there. His fare's paid. His bag by the door."

"Damn," Holliday shrugged, "my ears'll be worn out from his chin music before we get out of town."

"Next stage departs for Griffin on Wednesday. Same time of day," the clerk offered as he placed the paper on the neat rolltop desk against the back wall.

"How about your paper?" Holliday asked. "Reading beats talking."

"Only one I got," the clerk replied, his shoulders drooping with boredom.

"Fellow like you shouldn't have trouble getting another. Easier than me trying to find one between here and Griffin."

"This one's Mr. Brown's, not mine. He likes to see his advertisements in print. I best save it for him."

A commotion outside closed the subject. A bottle-green

5

Concord stage rumbled to a stop, its four dry wheels screeching with thirst, its trace chains jingling from each bump remembered, its six mules bawling at tight harnesses, and its driver cursing the start of another run.

The clerk bolted through the swinging counter gate for the door. "If you're going to Griffin, better be fast about it," he snorted. "Chuck cares more for his mules than his passengers, and his mules are impatient." The clerk grabbed the officer's valise and flung the door open. "Probably got one more coming, Chuck," he yelled.

"He'd best hurry," Chuck answered, spitting a muddy stream of tobacco over his scuffed boot on the brake lever.

Holliday tugged the wide lapel on his tailored frock coat and stepped past the batwing gate and around the counter to the rolltop desk. Picking up Mr. Brown's paper from the neatly organized desk, Holliday folded it twice more and stuck it inside his coat. His unhurried gait then carried him outside, where the braying mules complained as much as they broke wind.

"Decided to go after all?" the clerk taunted as he bent over Holliday's satchel and carpetbag. "Want your bags in the boot?"

"I carry my own," Holliday said, grabbing them from the clerk and stepping up to the stage. He planted his foot on the folding step and leaned easily inside the coach, tossing his bags onto the rear seat. The captain lounged in the preferred seat, his back to the front of the stage. Holliday skirted him and the middle bench, sliding onto the cushioned leather of the back seat. As the clerk slammed the door, Holliday poked his elbow out the window and jerked from his coat the purloined paper.

The mules pulled against their harnesses, tugging the coach against the brake, as the clerk lifted the folding step. "Let 'em loose, Chuck," he called.

The stage lurched forward. Holliday stuck his head and the unfolded paper out the window. "Tell Mr. Brown thanks for the reading material," Holliday called. The clerk kicked at the street and shouted epithets Holliday could not hear. A laugh tumbled roughly out of Holliday's throat, then erupted into an uncontrolled cough that he spit out the window.

The stage rumbled down the street, accompanied by the noise of clinking trace chains, rattling double-trees, creaking har-

6

ness leather, and the popping of the driver's whip — like firecrackers celebrating the departure. Skirting the courthouse square, then turning wide around the corner, the coach leaned heavily into the thoroughbrace support, rocked gently as the team gathered speed in front of the crumbling sandstone courthouse, then passed the string of lesser stores and saloons and headed out the road toward Fort Richardson.

A half mile south of Jacksboro, Holliday could see oaks, pecans, and cottonwoods growing in clumps along Lost Creek. Across the creek stood the buildings of Fort Richardson. The fort awoke slowly this morning, as it did most days now that the Comanche and Kiowa threats had diminished. The soldiers moved singly or in pairs between breakfast and their chores. By the creek a laundress was building a fire under her black washpot. And further upstream two soldiers were filling the post's water wagon. The soldiers, once in numbers great enough to make twenty-seven saloons profitable between the Jacksboro square and the north bank of Lost Creek at the edge of government property, were gradually being decimated by War Department reassignment rather than Indians. Extinct or soon to be were the Island, First National, Union Headquarters, Little Shamrock, and Last Chance saloons.

The road, still damp from yesterday's shower, pulled away from Lost Creek and Fort Richardson toward Belknap and Graham. An economical landscape — not given to the frills of mountains or giant trees — stretched out westward in rolling, grass-covered swells that gently waved with the dry breeze at the ever distant horizon. Holliday stared a while, then picked up the paper from his lap as a shield from the captain who seemed to be dozing. Gradually, though, the pain returned to Holliday's lungs. His troublesome coughs grew more frequent. Dropping the paper, he opened the carpetbag for another boost from his bottle. He popped the bottle's cork, startling the officer, whose eyes opened for an instant, then drooped shut.

"Medicine," Holliday said quietly, then erased the word from his lips with a gulp of the jaundiced liquid. *The Frontier Echo* slipped from his lap to the floor. As he picked it up, his gaze fell across a bold black headline over two paragraphs at the bottom of the front page. He snapped the paper to his face and, despite the bouncing of the coach, read the dispatch quickly, then again.

Wild Bill (James B. Hickok) was murdered in a mad cowardly manner by one Jack McCall shooting him in the back of the head while he was playing cards.

McCall claimed that Bill murdered his brother several years ago. McCall, after standing a sort of mock trial by the miners, was acquitted.

Occupational hazard, Holliday thought. A gambler created his own justice in this world and if the deck was stacked against him in one town, he'd best clear out and stay out. Holliday had violated that credo but once, and only then for Lottie.

He studied another story about the luckless cavalry still chasing Sitting Bull and the Sioux across the northern plains. Almost three months had passed since Sitting Bull had made news of George Armstrong Custer and his Seventh Cavalry command. Sitting Bull, evidently pessimistic about his future, had been kind enough to pass along to the *Boston Transcript* his "last words" now reprinted in *The Frontier Echo*. "Wah-wah, munkgooro, nix-any," reported the reprint, "which freely translated means 'Don't let 'em write any dime novels about me.' "

Holliday threw the paper on the middle bench seat, braced himself with another swig of whiskey, then watched the West Texas countryside wither as it passed before his eyes at eight miles an hour. Now and then he spotted bleaching bones left by the buffalo hunters. Fortunes had been made off those bones, and Holliday had collected a cut of his own from them at Jacksboro's faro tables. But the buffalo slaughter and the killings at the gaming tables had moved west to Griffin, the westernmost town in Texas before El Paso.

The officer stirred, stretched, and then yawned his eyes open. Holliday, sensing the captain's eyes sizing him up, returned the favor. The officer was a cleanly made man, lean and tightly muscled on a medium frame the way General Sherman (who on this very road four years ago had avoided an Indian ambush only by the whim of a Kiowa medicine man) liked his cavalry troopers. His wavy brown hair, parted down the middle, matched his brown eyes, squint-wrinkled at the corners from too many months in the field searching for water and Indians but finding little of either. He was narrow-jawed, broad-nosed and thin-mouthed, but his features lacked a military hardness, as if he were more at ease following orders than giving them.

8

"Conversation bother you?" he asked.

"Not one for idle talk with a blue belly."

The captain's eyes narrowed. "You sound south. Some memories don't fade."

"Georgia was home," Holliday answered. "Thanks to General Sherman, it's been a long time since I took a liking to blue uniforms." He drew a swig from his bottle, then exchanged it in his valise for a pack of Hart's Linen Eagle cards. Pulling the cards from the box, he manipulated them adroitly between his nimble fingers. "Care for a friendly game?" he offered.

"Not much for gambling."

"Then I'm not much for gabbing," Holliday said, tossing the cards from hand to hand, then returning them to his grip.

The captain motioned toward *The Frontier Echo* on the seat between them. "Mind if I read your paper for a spell?"

"Go ahead."

The soldier retrieved the paper and settled back into his corner. For miles they rode without words, hearing only the stage sounds, Chuck's affectionate blasphemy for his mules, and Holliday's monotonous cough.

"Well, I'll be." The captain whistled, bending down the corner of the paper and staring at Holliday. "Somebody killed Wild Bill Hickok. Been a bad year for gamblers, wouldn't you say?"

"A worse year for blue-belly soldiers. Ask General Custer."

The captain shook his borrowed paper and said nothing more until Belknap, where a gate salesman with a squeaky voice and jittery eyes climbed aboard the stage and quickly began a conversation with the captain, returning periodically to the merits of the gates he was willing to sell the army.

A heavy stench drifted across the prairie. Before Holliday could see the town, he could smell it. The fetor discomforted him so, he jerked the bottle from his carpetbag and drained it. Instantly, he felt better. Bourbon solved many problems.

The Flat, as the town was called, lay in a broad valley carved by the waters of the Clear Fork of the Brazos, a river traversing Texas from the High Plains to the Gulf. Beside the Clear Fork,

Fort Griffin the town had sprung up, a parasite at the foot of Government Hill, the terraced plateau where the military post had preceded the town. Now both fort and town shared a name and a deathly odor, the breeze reeking of rotting flesh still clinging to thousands of buffalo hides. For Holliday, it was the perfume of money.

The gate drummer squirmed in his seat, wrinkling his narrow nose. The captain sensed his perplexity. "First time to Griffin?"

"Yeah," the drummer replied, covering his nose.

"You're smelling it."

"Bad as a gut wagon!" The drummer shifted uneasily.

"It's not bad now, not like it was. The weather's cooled some. Fewer hides now. You'll grow used to it."

"I don't plan on staying long."

"Just as well," the captain said, staring at Holliday. "Griffin's not easy to like. More vagabonds and temporary trash in the Flat than any town I've ever seen. Maybe five or six hundred permanent residents and twice that number of thieves, gamblers, prostitutes, and vermin of that breed." As his words emerged from behind a West Point smile, the captain's eyes locked on Holliday's.

The gambler's hardened jaw cracked in front of a cough. Holliday averted his eyes from the officer and reached inside his coat. With cat quickness he jerked his revolver from hiding. His cough died instantly as he leveled the .38 at the captain's heart.

The officer's brown eyes never blinked.

The drummer squirmed forward in his seat, his gaping eyes fixed on the revolver. His voice, edgy as a crosscut saw, broke the sullen silence. "Gentlemen."

"Shut up," Holliday said softly, but his voice carried a steel edge. The drummer shrank back into his seat as if the steel were at his throat. "Unless you plan on making this your business . . ." Holliday dropped the statement unfinished but understood.

The captain folded his arms slowly across his chest. Beyond that, he showed no emotion, least of all fear.

Holliday thumbed the hammer back on the single-action Smith and Wesson revolver. "By your words," Holliday said softly, accentuating his Georgia drawl, "you have called gamblers vermin. You got enough grit to call me that to my face?"

Slowly, the captain lowered his arms and leaned forward, resting his hands on the center bench. "I hold gamblers as you hold soldiers in the United States Army — with contempt. Nothing you have said on our journey has changed my estimation. I may be a fool, but I'm no coward or liar."

Holliday's lips curled slowly into a cynical smile. He eased the hammer down on the pistol and casually opened his coat to shove the revolver back into its clipspring harness. "You're no fool, Captain."

"And you're not fool enough to shoot an officer of the U.S. Army this close to Fort Griffin."

"Never bet against a gambler's foolishness, Captain."

The drummer loosed a heavy sigh, as if he had saved each breath since the pistol had appeared. Then he chuckled. "I see it now," he stammered. "It takes me a while to catch on to the humor you people pull on us city folks. Good joke, mister."

Holliday cut his icy blue eyes toward the salesman. His voice carried softly, but menacingly like distant thunder. "I was serious. Dead serious."

The drummer sank deeper in the seat, sullen as a scolded child.

Holliday leaned toward his stage window. On the plateau ahead he spied the Stars and Stripes waving atop a fifty-foot flagpole at the military post. The stage lurched down then up a smooth gully, the driver Chuck cursing the tired mules for their awkward footing. Slipping forward in his seat, Holliday grabbed the strap handhold and studied the countryside just in case he should need to leave Griffin as he had Jacksboro, on the run.

The valley was broad and long. The Clear Fork twisted like a huge, shimmering serpent in the late afternoon sunlight. Beside the river were stands of pecans, oaks and cottonwoods, their leaves not yet yellow with fall. Cradled in one giant curve of the river was a fine grove of trees surrounding a gigantic cottonwood with no competitor growing in its shade. The length of the stream was tinted a sharp green, the grama grass still thriving on the moisture of a summer flood. Beyond that ribbon of green all the way to the slope of Government Hill, the Flat melded in with

11

the gray of the distant grass, the tan of the ground, and the dark brown splotches of buffalo hides piled as high as a strong man could throw them from the bed of a freight wagon. Holliday noted a strand of some thirty tepees strung out along the creek a half mile upstream from town.

"Looks like Sitting Bull's found you, Captain," Holliday scowled.

"Tonkawa. They're harmless," the officer offered. "The army uses them for scouts."

Holliday nodded. "Between the buffalo hides, the Tonkawas, and the blue bellies, no wonder Fort Griffin stinks."

"Don't forget the other vermin, mister."

"Yeah," Holliday grinned. "We discussed them earlier." Holliday twisted in his seat to better view the Flat. More tents than buildings sprouted from the clay soil, but even so some sixty structures were scattered up and down the creek. Outnumbering the buildings and tents, great bundles of deep brown buffalo hides were stacked in piles hehind the merchant houses and in less imposing but more numerous stacks beside many tents. Baled and ready for shipment like cotton on a Galveston wharf, the hides welcomed the coach with their rancid odor.

As the stage drew closer to the creek, Holliday observed the flotsam of a summer flood. Brush and debris hung like Christmas decorations on the low branches of trees rooted in the bank, bundles of grayed grass queued up behind every stump or rock that poked from the earth, and pieces of driftwood, like bloated corpses, lay half submerged where they had snagged along the bank. This flood had reached into Griffin.

When the stage hit the creek crossing, the shouts of the driver flushed a trio of turkey buzzards from atop the naked limbs of a dead cottonwood. Emerging from the water, the stage was enveloped by a buzzing swarm of flies, big ugly blowflies sensing in the autumn air the end to a prosperous summer of proliferating on rotting buffalo flesh. Holliday swatted at the pesky insects, then disgustedly spit one from his mouth. "Damn flies," he sputtered, jerking his whiskey bottle to his mouth, then remembering he had drained it half an hour ago at the first smell of Griffin. He tossed the empty out the window and it cartwheeled by the roadside, startling a mangy hound scrounging about for a

12

meal. The dog snarled at the glass intruder, sniffed at it, then turned toward the creek and a string of cribs where whores on cornhusk mattresses allowed men to spend their money and themselves between female legs.

The road, hardpacked from the tons of hides it had carried, led straight through the Flat and up Government Hill toward the post. Flanking the road, widely spaced buildings were laced together with myriad footpaths and wagon trails among the vast stacks of buffalo hides. A few buildings were masked with false fronts and even fewer were built of roughcut native stone, but most were an unpretentious cross between the functional and the intolerable, the bastard offspring of pickets chinked and painted with sand and lime and adobe.

In the late afternoon sunlight, the street boiled with Saturday activity, the horses, wagons, and pedestrians reluctantly parting for the stage to pass. Holliday, more interested in spotting old enemies than in renewing friendly acquaintances, searched for familiar faces. Seeing none among the stew of human leftovers mixing on Griffin Avenue, he looked next for saloons which might hire a good faro dealer, or serve good liquor. He preferred the latter, but there were eight, maybe ten, saloons which might suit either need.

Ahead a knot of cheering men blocked the road. The stage stopped shy of the Bee Hive saloon, which spewed patrons into the street to see the finish of a fight started inside. Holliday opened the stage door and leaned outside to see the commotion. The shouting men jeered as one pugilist, ducking too late to avoid an iron right hand, dropped like a ball of lead in front of the stage's mules.

The stage driver popped his whip at the dispersing crowd. "Damn you all, somebody jerk his tail out of the street before I decorate him with muleshoe and wagon tracks."

"Do it yourself, you old coot," yelled a cowhand made eloquent by liquor.

Glimpsing the insolent spectator before he could meld into the crowd, Chuck snapped his twenty-foot whip. The drunk's hat flew off like a felt duck.

"If you don't want me to pick your nose with this whip, you'd better move your friend," Chuck threatened.

The cowboy ran his fingers through his exposed auburn hair. "He ain't my friend," he answered, bending to pick up his hat. The whip flashed like lightning through the air and cracked thunder at the cowhand's ear, drawing blood. The lanky cowpuncher slapped his ear and shot straight up.

"Unless you want your other ear to match, move that jackass from in front of my mules."

Convinced of both the driver's sincerity and his skill with a whip, the hatless spectator struggled to drag away the defeated fighter, twice tripping over his unconscious load. The instant the wobbly but humbled cowhand was clear of the mules, the driver threatened the animals forward, right over the cowhand's hat. Holliday drew himself back inside the stage, but before he could sit, the stage stopped at the building beside the Bee Hive.

Instantly an agent was opening the door and welcoming the three passengers to Griffin, even calling the captain by name. Holliday grabbed his medical satchel and grip, emerging from the stage first, his thin frame aching from every jolt between Jacksboro and Griffin. He tramped to the back of the stage, working loose the knots in his legs and shaking the kinks from his arms, then stepped toward the plank walk, where the aroma of food piqued his nose.

He felt a cold gaze upon himself and looked beyond the passing faces toward a broad-shouldered man leaning casually against a hitching rack, rolling a smoke in his massive hands and returning Holliday's stare. Depositing his cigarette fixings in a tobacco tin under the sleeve garter on his left arm, the man straightened from the hitching rack and shoved the cigarette into his harelipped mouth, his thumbnail flicking a flame from the match in his hand. His eyes were deepset and dark. Even the match tipped to his cigarette failed to penetrate those brooding eyes for their intent. As the big man inhaled deeply, the cheeks of his broad face deflated, then regained their normal shape as a stream of smoke flowed out of his flat nose over the ragged mustache which failed to hide his harelip. Holliday eyed the stranger's brawny frame, taking in his starched white shirt with sleeve garters, his bulky gabardine britches tucked in Napoleon leg boots, his wool hat and, most importantly, his suspenders. Without a belt, the stranger lacked a sidearm.

From among the passing throng, a woman jumped off the plank walk and rushed by the smoker toward the stage. Holliday admired the fair cut of her narrow-waisted figure, the bounce of her freshly washed blond hair, the glimmer of emeralds in her eyes. As the captain pulled his grip from the stage's boot and stood erect, she threw her arms around him and her lips upon his, bringing a cheer from an envious buffalo hunter.

She came close to being a widow today, Holliday thought.

The captain, breaking from his wife's kiss, seemed to sense Holliday's thoughts. Turning from the wetness of his woman's lips, the officer squinted at Holliday, his narrow jaw and thin lips tight like his hand on his wife's arm.

Holliday laughed. "Enjoyed our conversation."

"Your kind will welcome you to the Flat," the officer replied, his voice tight with sarcasm.

"I'll bet." Holliday stepped on the dilapidated walk, looking for the stranger at the hitching rack, but the big man had disappeared into the crowd. He heard the soldier's wife ask who Holliday was.

"Just an acquaintance, just an acquaintance," the captain answered.

The aroma of food tickling his nose, Holliday stared through the smudged window of the stage stop, otherwise known as Uncle Billy Wilson's Eatery, then shoved his way inside. The long narrow room smelled of fresh food and stale men. The room, its unlit lamps and low ceiling accentuating the dwindling afternoon light, lacked frills. Roughhewn benches carried the weight of two dozen appetites. Hunters, cowhands, even a couple of soldiers, shared the benches and a common like for the cooking. A huge buffalo roast in the middle of a long table was being attacked by the mob. Platters of fried salt pork and sweet potatoes and bowls of canned tomatoes and corn cakes were scattered on either side of the roast or were circling the table for extra helpings. A chorus of spoons and forks hitting the tin plates rang out over the conversation subdued by stuffed mouths.

Though Holliday's craving was generally for liquor, the slight meaty smell wafting toward him stirred his stomach and he moved to the near end of the table where the bench was less crowded. As he dropped the carpetbag by his feet and placed his medicine satchel atop the bench, a fellow talking with an Irish brogue approached, wiping his hands on his ankle-length, stain-splattered apron, smiling through his unkempt beard like he'd just won a poker hand or found a new customer.

"Me name's Billy Wilson, Uncle Billy mos' folks call me, and I run this place. Just off the stage, are ya, mister?" The words rolled off his tongue like the alphabet in an avalanche. "'Tis a good ride from Belknap, maybe e'en Jacksboro, eh? 'Tweren't President Grant on the stage with ya, 'twas there?"

Hell, no, thought Holliday, but he only shook his head.

"Okay, boys," Billy Wilson boomed across the room, "the president's not arriving on today's stage. Ya table manners ain't so importan' now 'cause ya be spilling something on me table-cloth and I'll 'ave time to wash and iron it 'fore the next stage. Jus' don't spill something I can't wash out."

The other customers ignored Wilson, who confided to Holliday that President Ulysses S. Grant wasn't really coming to Fort Griffin, the lie being perpetrated only to preserve among these ravenous men the virtue of his only white tablecloth.

"I can serve ya the bes' meal on the Texas frontier or regale ya with true tales of what 'twas like to pan for gold on the Yuba River in the Rush of Forty-Nine out in Californy." He unhooked his wire-rim glasses and dabbed at the lenses with a patch of his dirty apron.

"A plate and fork will do," Holliday answered.

"Tell ya, sir, I'd be rich today 'ad I gone prospecting up the middle fork of the Yuba River instead of the north fork," Wilson continued, replacing his glasses and squinting his eyes back into corrected focus. "Why, I'd reside in a gingerbread mansion on Nob Hill in San Francisco and spend a couple months a year back in Ireland, showing my distant cousins how a gentleman lives. And, I'd have . . ."

"Stop your palavering," ordered a stern woman who wad-dled up beside Wilson. Her eyes were bloodshot and sweat-rimmed from her work in the kitchen and her shoulders drooped from bending too much over a hot stove. "Only one gentleman in this conversation and he's a customer. Fetch him some grub," she scolded.

"If I'd gone up the middle fork," Wilson murmured, "I'd a

had me a wife that'd let me finish a conversation." He strode off swatting at a fly like it was his wife.

"Don't mind my husband none," Mrs. Wilson apologized. "He always is a talking when others just want a bit of grub. Uncle Billy'll get you a plate. Help yourself. There's plenty or I can fix you an omelet for a nickel more. We got fresh eggs."

"That'll do," Holliday said, pointing at the roast, "if I can get a plate."

"Uncle Billy," she yelled, spying her husband halted in conversation, "hurry up with that plate 'fore you lose a customer. I slave back in that hot kitchen and all you do is talk and collect their money."

A sheepish grin crossed Wilson's face and he moved on, but too slow to satisfy his wife, who waddled after him. From any angle, both looked like they enjoyed her cooking. Shortly, Wilson returned with a plate and eating utensils, collected a quarter, and indicated he'd return with a cup of coffee.

Holliday slipped down the table, squeezed between a pair of bearded buffalo hunters needing baths, jerked the sticky carving knife from the roast, and cut off a generous portion. After serving himself with fried sweet potatoes, runny canned tomatoes, and a pair of corn cakes, he reclaimed his seat and took an occasional bite. Mostly he toyed with the food. The meal wasn't bad as vittles went, but the realization failed to match the expectation. Holliday figured most of life was like that, except for bourbon, good or bad. It never let him down. He wondered if Lottie would have been like bourbon or like everything else.

After a while he gave up on ever getting coffee, as Uncle Billy tied himself up in another conversation, reliving the Gold Rush. Holliday stared at his plate, then felt the bench sag as a big man claimed a berth uncomfortably close. An uneasiness grated down Holliday's back like chalk on a slate. Out of the corner of his eye he recognized the harelipped man who had eyed him off the stage. The table trembled when the stranger dropped his clenched fists, one holding a smoldering cigarette, on the white cloth. Holliday reached with his right hand inside his coat, then twisted his neck to study the man with the unhealthy curiosity. Their eyes met, Holliday detecting caution but not fear in this stranger's deepset eyes. The man turned his face away and stared across the table.

17

"Not meaning to spook you, mister," he said softly, as if revealing a secret. "Just watched you off the stage. Generally, I meet the stages looking for fools to part from their money. I don't take you for such as that, but you do look like a man that might know of a good card mechanic, say a fellow that knows how to squeeze the pips just right."

Holliday's tight muscles loosened and he pulled his hand from the butt of the revolver under his coat. He didn't speak at first, just stared at the big man's clenched paws. They were rough and the knuckles were scarred. Holliday took a bite, in no hurry to respond. He wanted to consider the possible angles, if he were being set up. The big man betrayed no impatience as Holliday slowly chewed his food. Holliday liked that. Patience was a virtue among swindlers.

"By gosh and by golly, 'tis Shawn Chancey," Uncle Billy Wilson said, stepping up beside Holliday. "As good an Irishman to ever dirty a boot in Fort Griffin. What brings ya to me eatery on a Saturday evening? The slop ya serve in ya saloon not as good as Mrs. Wilson's cooking?"

Chancey glanced over his shoulder. "Uncle Billy, sometimes I like to visit the other establishments in Griffin and steal their business. Take, for instance, this gentleman by my side. I'll have no trouble persuading him to eat a bite down at the Cattle Exchange. Granted my food's not as good as Mrs. Wilson's, but he's almost finished and you've yet to set a cup of coffee before him."

Uncle Billy shrugged, then turned around to see if Mrs. Wilson had discovered his forgetfulness. "Sorry, mister," Wilson offered. "Ya should have reminded me. I'll be back with a cup of mud for ya."

"Obliged," Holliday said as Wilson scampered away.

"Uncle Billy," called Chancey, "bring me a cup too. We don't serve much coffee in my place." Then to Holliday he whispered again, "Wilson's a good man, talks too much, but he's trustworthy. Can't say that about a lot in Griffin."

"Can you say it about yourself?" Holliday asked, lifting a fork to his mouth.

Chancey took his time about answering. Holliday liked a man who chose his words carefully and didn't lower their value by flooding the market with them. Wilson returned with two cups

18

of hot coffee, the heat clouding up around the edges of the tin-ware, then retreated to find another conversation.

"I run a saloon. I'm no gambler, not with cards at least, though I do use gamblers to improve my take. I don't know that you can say I am trustworthy. If I were, I wouldn't watch the stage arrivals or be here with you now."

Holliday pushed his plate toward the middle of the table. He smothered the cup with both hands for a sip of the burning coffee, swallowing it hard like bad liquor. At least it was real coffee, not some of those bad imitations they tried to sell in some places. But real coffee wasn't bourbon, good or bad. Holliday decided to hear Chancey out.

"I may know a good card mechanic for you," he offered, "if I can find him. What's the best hotel in town? That's where he would be."

"Planters House's better than most. It's away from the saloons and maybe a little quieter than the others."

"If I find this gentleman, what should I tell him?"

"If he has enough money to get in a fifty-dollar house stakes poker game . . ."

"He does."

". . . tell him to come to the Cattle Exchange Saloon around ten o'clock. Sit at the poker table furthest from the door. The dealer will be tooled. Your friend will win, splitting the proceeds thirty-seventy, with me getting the big end, of course."

Holliday mused over the offer. "Double the average take at thirty percent. Generous terms for a man you don't even know."

Chancey drained his coffee, then spoke. "You have to take risks to make money. I need someone not recognized locally. Several cattlemen returning from Kansas with full pockets think they can fatten their money rolls at my tables. Looks funny if the house dealer wins it all."

"I'll pass along the message," Holliday said. "Anything else I should tell my friend?"

Chancey stood up, crushing his cigarette stub in the empty coffee cup. "Tell him to stay out of the Bee Hive. Just yet."

TWO

From the frameless poster tacked into the stark adobe wall, a bengal tiger silently snarled, its paws upraised to fend off the clouds of cigar and coal oil smoke. The tiger, its comic orange and black stripes as gaudy as its circus broadside kin, hawked the Bee Hive's faro tables. Except for the splattered remnants of spittoons missed and the pockmarks of bullets gone awry, only the tiger decorated the wall. Faro was the lord among games of chance, and the tiger was faro's deity.

Only in the great cat's green eyes smoldered a semblance of life, but they were forever stilled in ink, staring down upon a dealer beginning another shift in the Bee Hive. The dealer shuffled the cards from hand to hand in the fashion of the day, two dozen sets of eyes joining the tiger's, all transfixed upon the swift motion. Back and forth the dealer pitched alternate portions of the deck between soft, agile fingers. Bee Hive proprietor Mike Fogle, rearranging the house's neat stacks of chips on the check tray, admired the faro dealer's fluid grace almost as much as the dealer's luck. Faro was more than just a game in the West, it was a religion. And this table was the most popular — and profitable — altar in his house of worship. After a final shuffle, the dealer squeezed the cards into a neat stack and placed them on the table.

Lottie Deno was ready for work.

"Gentlemen," she purred, the word floating like a downy cottonwood seed on a spring breeze "and you are gentlemen for I allow only gentlemen to take my money . . ." She paused, a delicate smile lingering like a kiss upon her lips, ". . . if they can."

Her customers laughed and she softly with them, an auburn ringlet shaking free from under the brim of her ribbon-spangled Parisian hat. She brushed the curl back in place.

Fogle felt the corner of his lips quivering against a smile. That damn curl. He'd seen it fall a hundred times, as if on cue, and a thousand times more he had watched her beguile her customers and dislodge the money from their pockets.

With Lottie behind the faro layout, the nobility and the serfdom of West Texas lined up to buck the tiger. They gawked at her silky white hands, her delicate neck, and her softly rounded face — the only flesh peeking from her long-sleeve, high-necked, floor-length dresses. Her pale skin captivated the men, all more accustomed to the wind-chapped, reddened faces of their wives and sweethearts or the thick skins of the prostitutes. Her alluring gray eyes suggested liaisons that would never be. Her narrow lips, downturned at the corners, always said "no" more sensually than the downstairs whores could say "yes." And her soft auburn hair, peeking from under her broad yellow hat, invigorated men accustomed to the drab colors of the fall prairie.

Lottie's beauty and charm, Fogle knew, deceived her customers, who sensed a vulnerability existing only in their minds. Fogle knew that within the folds of Lottie's soft yellow dress she packed a revolver, and in her hat she wore a hatpin as dangerous as any stiletto.

"Gentlemen," she said softly, "let us begin." Picking up the cards, Lottie inserted them face-up in the dealing box, a metal rectangle with an open top exposing the identity of the top card. On one side, the box was open to admit the cards between the spring-pushed tray which kept the deck tight against the top window. The opposite side was covered, except for a narrow lengthwise slit wide enough for a single card to pass.

Lottie surveyed her domain, a rectangular table covered with green billiard cloth worn from activity. Thirteen spades were acid-stained into the cloth in two rows of six, the odd seventh card offset between the two rows. She leaned over the deal-

21

ing box and the discard squares tatooed into the cloth and rested one hand on the nearest row — the ace running from the left to the six on the right. With her other hand, she flicked tobacco ashes from the upper row, running from the king on the left to the eight on the right. Looking up, she smiled. "I see some new faces at my table. A couple of you look a little too young for my game. You, in particular, cowboy," she said, pointing to a blushing youth, embarrassed further by his guffawing companions. "Promise me you won't bawl to mother when I take all your money."

The cowboy shrugged sheepishly. She was setting up another cowboy for a fall, Fogle thought as he unfolded an abacus-like device in front of the chips. From his wide-eyed looks, the cowboy was no match for Lottie's luck, Fogle guessed.

"Ma'am, I . . ." the cowboy struggled to complete his sentence, taking off his hat and running his fingers through his stringy auburn mop as if feeling for the words.

"He'd be pleased," shouted one of the red-faced cowboy's companions, "to tell his mother about this instead of what he plans to spend his money on downstairs later."

Everyone laughed, except Lottie. "If this is your first time, cowboy, good luck. What's your name?"

"Jimmy," he answered with a gulp.

"I'll explain how we play, Jimmy."

"Somebody should've explained to Jimmy how to play with that saloon girl downstairs," interrupted the embarrassed youth's companion. Again everyone laughed, except Lottie.

"It's a simple game, Jimmy." She pointed at the faro box. "The first card is soda, which doesn't count for anything. You place your bets on the cards you think will come up. You beginners just bet on one card at a time by placing your money atop it on the felt. When I pull the soda out of the box, the card that shows is a loser. I take everything on that card. The next card is a winner and I pay those who've bet on it. Every two cards after soda is a turn and we repeat the procedure until we get down to the last three cards. The final card, hock, doesn't count. But, if you can pick the order of the final trio, I pay you four to one for calling the turn. Say you're better at picking losers than winners, place your bet on a card and place one of these coppers atop it," she said, picking up a handful of hexagonal tokens. "If that card comes up, I lose and pay you for coppering it. Of course, if you bet to lose and the card comes up second, I win. Any questions?"

The bettors crowded closer to the table, shaking their heads and saying nothing.

"Okay then, place your bets." She paused a moment as the men smelling of the prairie dropped their money all over the board. "One more thing for you still wet behind the ears at this, if on any turn two cards of the same denomination shows up, I take half of all bets," she smiled. "That's how I win money for the house. And," she added, "for myself."

The cowboys chuckled.

"I know you gentlemen are good at counting buffalo hides and cattle, but keeping up with cards is not so easy. To help you out," she said, motioning to Fogle and his abacus-like device, "each game uses a casekeeper. Tonight, we are lucky to have Mike Fogle keeping case for us. He owns the Bee Hive and usually doesn't handle such chores." She winked and leaned across the table. "But he thinks I cheat the house." She tilted her head closer to her customers and in a mock whisper, continued. "I'd rather monkey with the house's take than cheat you gentlemen."

The bettors laughed as Lottie straightened and Fogle held up the abacus. "Like on the layout, we have a set of thirteen cards and four beads opposite each one. As a card is played, the casekeeper moves one of the beads opposite that denomination. A glance can tell you what cards remain. But it won't do you any good because Lady Luck will outsmart you all. Let's play."

The men, including Jimmy, squeezed their bets on the layout.

"Okay." Lottie pulled the soda from the dealing box, exposing a seven of clubs, the house winner. Then she pushed the seven through the slot, revealing a queen of hearts.

"Whoopee," exulted Jimmy, lifting his sweat-stained felt hat and running his fingers through his red hair, "A winner."

A narrow smile broke across Lottie's lips, like a crack in ice. "Evidently, the ladies have all been good to you tonight," the words rolled provocatively off her tongue. "But I never knew a first bet to lose. It's the way Lady Luck traps you."

It wasn't just Lady Luck setting this cowboy up, Fogle nodded as he drew in the house's share and paid the lucky cowhand from his check tray. Fogle settled back for a long night. The yellow light of naked kerosene lamps swinging from the ceiling beams cast an unhealthy glow through the smoky haze about him. Tobacco odors and the stench of men who worked more than they bathed mingled with the aroma of his high-priced cheap liquors the barkeeps hauled from the bar downstairs to quench the thirsts and deplete the money rolls of his customers. Fogle called a barkeep to bring a glass of iced lemonade for Lottie — she drank nothing stronger — and a whiskey for himself.

With the drinks from downstairs came the strains of music. A piano, fiddle, and horn struggled to be heard over voluble drunks, brazen dancehall girls, and braggarts seeking a Saturday night's refuge from their hard lives. The music making it up the stairs came as song fragments, choruses severed from stanzas, stanzas dismembered from songs. As Lottie paused in dealing to sip her lemonade, Fogle stretched his legs and surveyed the room. Two competing faro tables, a half dozen poker games, and a keno operation in the corner drew respectable business but neither the crowd nor the profits that centered around Lottie's table. He glanced at the check tray now overflowing with chips and bills that two hours ago had been tucked inside the pockets of the men around him. The Bee Hive, thanks to Lottie, drew more customers and made more money than any of the nine other saloons or three dance halls in the Flat. Fogle needed the money to cover his own gambling debts. Thank God for Lottie, he thought, as he slipped back into his chair.

"Shall we resume, gentlemen?" Lottie began, after a final sip of the cold lemonade. She inserted the cards into the dealing box and pointed at Jimmy. "Maybe some of his luck will rub off on the rest of you."

Unlikely, Fogle thought. Had it been a man, Fogle might have called it cheating — the turns falling too often against her opponents, the splits coming too frequently to be mere chance, but with her he simply named it "Lottie's Luck" and enjoyed his share of the profits. Her finesse at blind shuffles, jogging cards, and blind cuts made the manipulation hard to detect. And with her, no man really tried.

"Hot damn," the young cowboy called at another winner.

Then a blushing smile drifted across his reddening face. "Sorry ma'am, my language, I mean, not about winning."

Lottie nodded her acknowledgment.

Fogle estimated the cowboy had increased his roll by a hundred and fifty dollars at the house's expense, but still he figured the kid would leave this game disappointed. Fogle detected a glint of mischief in Lottie's gray eyes each time he won.

As Fogle pulled the knot from his string tie and unbuttoned the stiff paper collar around his sweat-moistened neck, he glanced about the gaming room. Business downstairs must be slowing because he observed two whores defying house rules by wandering among the gamblers, drumming up business. Fogle stared at the pair until they glanced his way. With a jerk of his head toward the stairs, he flushed them away. Their frivolous trade must not interfere with gambling's more serious calling. He pulled in the losing bets on Lottie's next hand, then glanced back at the stairs, thinking for a moment he had also glimpsed Big Nose Kate, ducking behind a pot-bellied stove. If it were Kate, it would take more than a glance to send her back downstairs.

Lottie seemed oblivious to everything but the game and the bettors. Her concentration, Fogle guessed, might be a large part of her success. Just as Lottie inserted the cards into the dealing box for another game, a strident harlot voice grated over the cacophony in the room. Damn, Fogle thought. It had been Kate dodging behind the stove. Kate elbowed her way through the knot of men watching Lottie.

"Get out of my way, dammit," Kate screamed, holding the skirt of her scarlet dress in her hands. "Where is he? Heard he was having a run of luck. Jimmy, where are you?" The young cowhand winced at her voice. Big Nose Kate, well-endowed at both places men tended to watch and pay for, bulled her way nearer the table. "Hey," she shouted, turning to slap an offender, "who pinched my fanny? You pay to play with this merchandise." With too many potential perpetrators, all looking equally guilty and equally amused, she lowered her hand to her face and pampered her rouged cheek. "Manners, hell. Don't anyone here know how to treat a lady?"

"When we see one," answered a buffalo hunter behind her.

"You boys've spent too long herding cattle or chasing buf-

25

faloes to know a lady. It's affecting your manners. If you want a night with a lady instead of a few heifers, you best recall your damn manners." Kate fluffed the black satin bow at her belt and then plowed through the men to the betting edge of the table. She belched. "There you are, Jimmy. You told me you'd be back in an hour so I could teach you a few things. You're late. Let's get to my cabin."

Lottie slammed the dealing box into the table, knocking over two tall stacks of chips by Fogle's check tray. The men turned from the amusing spectacle of Kate to Lottie.

"Mike," she said to Fogle, all the time cutting her icy eyes straight at Kate, "you make the rules, now enforce them. She and the other girls belong downstairs, not in the gaming room."

Kate turned up her hooked nose, rolled her green eyes, and gave a sweeping gesture with her arms. "Pardon me, milady, but this young man and I have business to attend," she said, bringing one arm around his reddened neck and brushing her free hand across the crotch of his work pants. Jimmy shifted uncomfortably away, but Kate stuck to him like a leech.

"As long as he stands at my table, you'll not pester or embarrass him with your loose ways. Conduct your business downstairs, or I'll come to your crib and interrupt your customers with an offer to play cards."

Fogle stood up. "You know the rules, Kate. Now move."

Kate jerked her arm from around the cowboy's neck. "Jimmy, all she'll do is take your money. I'll give you something to remember."

"Yes, sir," Lottie said softly, "something the doctor will remember too."

Kate's eyes flared like sap in a burning pine knot. Screaming like a wounded mountain lioness, she lunged across the table, scattering the chips and money. Three men grabbed her flailing arms before she reached Lottie with her clawlike nails. Lottie's steady hand flew to a waist-high fold in her dress. Seeing the men had restrained Kate, she brought her empty right hand back out to the table.

"Okay, okay," called Mike Fogle, "you boys that's got a hold of Kate, escort her back downstairs. She won't charge you for pressing her flesh, now will you Kate?"

"You horse's ass, Mike Fogle, I can well make my own way."

"But Kate, this is probably more men than you had feel you all night. I'd hate to deprive you of the sensation. After you boys deliver her, tell the barkeep I said to set you up with a couple free drinks."

The three men jerked her from the table. Kate struggled against them, her flailing legs clearing a wide path through the spectators. "Jimmy," she called as they dragged her away, "don't forget our agreement."

"How can I?" he said meekly.

"Then I'll see you later," she smiled.

"I guess." He answered, his eyes downcast, his face a red deeper than before.

Lottie picked up the cards and resumed shuffling. "Please excuse the interruption, gentlemen. It was a most inopportune display. Despite what that vile woman may have said, I have never dealt faro with more mannered gentlemen. My sincerest apology, if you were offended by my response. Shall we continue?"

The men grunted their approval as they picked up the scattered chips and money.

"Perhaps I should reshuffle," Lottie said, taking the cards from the dealing box and remixing them.

As Lottie inserted the deck into the faro box, Fogle spotted the soda card, a three of hearts, the card the fortune teller would read as sorrow or poverty. Fogle watched Lottie's eyes; the glint of mischief for Jimmy was gone.

"Okay, gentlemen, place your bets," Lottie said. "I hope the woman's intrusion fouled no one's luck." She looked at Jimmy without smiling.

By hock, Jimmy had lost his winnings plus the bankroll he had started with. Now he couldn't afford Kate, cheap though her price may have been.

Lottie's Luck, Fogle thought.

THREE

Refreshed by a bath and by the aroma of shaving tonic, John Henry Holliday snapped the corners of his four-ply linen collar over a black silk cravat pierced by a gold stick pin. Staring into the cracked mirror nailed over the washstand, he adjusted the collar with his nimble fingers, invigorated by the feel of a fresh shirt.

Suddenly, with a quick catlike motion, he plucked the pocket Smith and Wesson from its clipspring shoulder harness, aiming at the furniture. After dispatching the bed, the washstand, the chair, the table with lamp and the simple bureau, he sighted in on the seam of the mail-order-house wallpaper puckered from washbasin spills, squeezing off a final imaginary round, then checking the load. He repeated the process with the Colt sidearm. A man could never practice too much with cards or guns.

From the iron bedstead opposite the washstand, he lifted his vest, slipping it on and immediately covering it with his frock coat. He glanced again in the mirror, nodding his approval and tugging on his lapels. The suit had cost him plenty, but damn if good clothes didn't make even a lunger feel better.

He patted in his pants pocket a money roll that was down to three hundred and fifty dollars and then slipped his hand inside his coat. As his gaze fell on the wallpaper blister above the wash-basin, his hand flashed free of his coat, the thud of steel striking wood following instantly upon the motion. Holliday's dagger, dead center of the paper bubble, still vibrated as he grabbed the hilt and jerked it from the wall. Bending over as he slipped the gleaming weapon back into its sheath, he blew out the lamp and stepped out the door.

When Holliday emerged from the Planters House, it was past ten o'clock, but he was in no hurry to keep Chancey's sched-ule. Patience was a virtue among gamblers, and Holliday avoided partnerships with men so anxious to steal a pot they became care-less. Holliday would test Chancey's gambling mettle.

Holliday noted the convenience of Pete Haverty's Livery Stable across the street, should he need to steal a horse, then strolled north toward Griffin Avenue and Chancey's saloon. The cool air was loaded with stench that smothered the shaving ton-ic's aroma. Nearing Griffin Avenue, Holliday joined the throng of men and loud women wandering from sin to sin or watching a drunken Tonkawa squatted in the middle of the street, chanting incomprehensible songs and trying to start a fire with a handful of twigs.

Holliday spat at the boots of three approaching soldiers, linked arm in arm and singing a bawdy tune. "Damn blue bel-lies," he called, his curse drowning in their verse. Holliday crossed Griffin Avenue just ahead of two racing horsemen, one brushing by the Tonkawa pyromaniac. Wobbling to his feet, the Indian shook his fist and yelled, "Eating shit white man."

Shortly, Holliday spied the Cattle Exchange and sidled up to a saloon window, the imperfect glass swarming with flies drawn by the seepage of a fetid yellow light. Brushing away the flies, he peered inside. Chancey towered behind the bar, serving drinks and glancing often at a back table. Holliday's gaze fell on that table, a dozen spectators gathered around it like the flies cir-cling his head. Swatting at the buzzing pests a final time, Holli-day, plenty tardy to gauge Chancey, surrendered the window to them.

As Holliday straightened his coat, a drunk teamster one jig-ger shy of spending his night on the clapboard sidewalk bumped into him. Holliday swung around, his hand darting instinctively for the Colt riding ready on his hip.

Staggering backward a step, the whiskey-addled teamster slurred a warning. "Watch where you're standing, fellow." The drunk raised his fist, clenched around an empty bottle.

"Watch it! Behind you!" Holliday called, pointing to the chanting Tonkawa in the street. "Comanche. Run for cover."

Screaming "Charge," the befuddled teamster broke toward the Indian, misjudging the step from the walk. The empty bottle, like the teamster, tumbled to the ground to stay a while.

Letting his fingers slide off the ivory grip of his Colt, Holliday readjusted his coat and pushed through the saloon's swinging doors into a long, narrow room with a bar running along the entire wall to his right. From the back, a roulette wheel telegraphed its invitation to suckers. Money lay on three poker tables, a faro layout, and the rail of a billiard table rooted before a rear office door. Beneath the drooping horns of a mounted steer head (the taxidermic masterpiece among six longhorn heads hanging on the opposite wall) spectators had clumped around the money game. A pot-bellied stove midroom and a silent piano against the far wall divided the gaming tables from the front tables dedicated to drinkers. As he eased up to the bar, Holliday observed a dozen tables, full but not crowded, and, weaving among them, a pair of prostitutes and a banjo player who overvalued his talent.

Understandably, Chancey ran an orderly saloon. He stood half a foot over six feet, his bullish shoulders the breadth of an ax handle, his powerful arms protruding from his rolled sleeves as threatening as a bear trap, his thick fingers when clenched more sledge than fist. Deepset in his forehead, his black eyes were dull like twin caves in a mountain too great to climb. From the harelip his jagged mustache failed to hide, Holliday guessed a few unwise men had tried besting that mountain. Except for Samuel Colt's invention, Chancey might have had few equals in all of Texas, but damn if his size didn't make him a better target, Holliday thought.

Chancey glanced toward Holliday, offering no sign of recognition. Without emotion, he pulled his cigarette makings from the tin strapped around his left arm and constructed a smoke. Damn if Chancey wasn't patient, Holliday decided. Too patient. Holliday propped his boot on the bar's brass footrail and

30

rested his arms on the walnut bar, noting in the backbar mirror reflected paintings of bulls, their testicles prominent testament to their virility. He coughed into his fist, then wiped his hands on the soiled towel in the nearest handhold as Chancey, his cigarette smoldering, advanced toward him.

"Mind handing me that towel when you're done?" Chancey asked through a cloud of smoke. Silently, Holliday obliged. Chancey tossed the used towel into the corner and offered Holliday a fresh one from under the bar. "What'll it be, a beer?"

"Whiskey," Holliday replied. "Good whiskey. Jigger first, then the bottle if it's good. No barreled house liquors."

"Ever try Silver Star sour mash whiskey?" he queried, reaching to the backbar for an amber bottle and the glass atop a pyramid of its mates.

Holliday shook his head.

"Many around these parts like it. Comes from Clark and Tollant, the liquor dealers in Weatherford."

"Yeah, Weatherford's known for its great whiskeys."

Uncorking the fresh bottle, Chancey shrugged, then poured.

The gambler grabbed the brimming jigger, gauging the vile color of the liquid against the lantern light, then drained it. He grimaced. "This the best you got?"

"Didn't say it was the best. Just a lot of people like it."

"Your neighbors've never had good whiskey."

Chancey offered a harelipped grin. "I keep some good stuff for special occasions." He bent over the backbar, slid a door open, and pulled out a virgin bottle. "Monarch Bourbon. Best I can get in these parts." He uncorked it and refilled the glass.

Lifting the glass slowly to his lips, the gambler sniffed, then emptied its amber contents, savoring the taste before swallowing hard. "Don't give any of this to the locals. They won't appreciate it. I'll take the bottle."

Chancey shoved the bottle to him. "Two dollars."

Holliday pulled the wad of bills from his pants pocket, dropping his payment on the counter.

"Mister, you look well-heeled for the card game going on in back," he offered dispassionately, wiping the bar.

"From the observers, I'd say it's a money game," Holliday

said, his eyes aimed straight at Chancey's. "Only problem is I don't feel too lucky tonight."

For an instant Chancey's eyes, flaring like a powder flash in those dark caves, betrayed his stake in the game. But that sign passed so quickly, Holliday wondered if he had imagined it.

Holliday leaned closer to Chancey. "With a fifty-fifty split of the winnings, I'd feel luckier," he said, tucking the bills into his pants pocket.

Chancey nodded, smiling broadly. "Well, sir, it's a pleasure serving you. Remember next time you get thirsty, I'm the only one in the Flat who carries Monarch," he said, picking up his wiping rag and Holliday's two dollars.

Holliday grabbed Chancey's wrist, feeling the strength coiled in Chancey's tightening muscles. "Thirty percent's fine," he whispered. "I like playing for a man that don't bluff easy."

When Holliday loosened his clasp, Chancey spit his cigarette to the floor, crushing it with his foot. "You won't need luck tonight," he said softly as he resumed polishing the bar. "First hand after the dealer calls for a new deck, run up the biggest pot you can. It'll be ours."

Chancey retreated up the bar and Holliday lingered, letting the bourbon dull the pain rising in his chest. A cough exploded from his throat and he spewed bloody phlegm at the nearest spittoon, missing. He jerked the bottle to his lips and gulped at the liquid, swilling the final mouthful to deaden the taste of sickness. With the clean towel beside him, he wiped his face, beading with sweat. Damn consumption. A rigor convulsed through his slight frame as the liquor settled. Holliday shook it off, tossed the towel over his shoulder and ambled toward the money game, carrying his bottle, a third of its contents emptied.

Past the clicking roulette wheel and the faro game, he squeezed between the observers and stared across the chip- and bill-littered table at the dealer, flat-nosed, broad-mouthed, and wide-jawed like a frog. His fleshy face melted into a short, bulging neck which lapped his stained and frayed collar like rising dough out of a breadpan. His moldy shirt, a virgin to washtub and soap, strained at the buttons against his paunch, which peeked at his cards through the bowed gaps in the placket. As dirty as his shirt, his coat may once have corralled his girth but no longer. A gambler who ignored his clothes, Holliday believed, ignored his craft. He coughed in disgust.

The dealer, sensing the disdain, lifted his bushy brown eyebrows and stared through muddy eyes at Holliday. Baring his yellowed teeth, stained from the silver-inlaid pipe he clenched between them, the dealer tossed his cards on the deadwood — the discards — and grunted his distaste for them and for Holliday.

A lanky cowman won the hand. "Keep giving me hands like that, Ed," he said, raking in a modest pot. While the dealer gathered the cards, Holliday's eyes focused on his stubby fingers protruding from small, plump hands. The best card manipulators had broad hands, long supple fingers. Ed was no card mechanic.

Holliday watched Ed place his smoldering pipe beside his money on the table, then toss the cards from hand to hand, his movements jerky, uncertain. Then Ed passed the cards to his right for the cut, waited for the slice, then stacked the bottom half on top. No blind cut there. The players anteed, then Ed. Fifty-dollar floor. Methodically, Ed dealt five cards slowly around the table, too slow, Holliday decided, for bottom dealing or dealing seconds. The players picked up their blue-backed cards emblazoned with an anemic eagle and fanned them out cautiously. The cowman in front of Holliday glanced suspiciously over his shoulder at the spectators behind him. After tossing their rejects into the pile of deadwood, the players took their replacements and Ed picked up his pipe, drawing heavy upon the silver mouthpiece, smoke boiling from the pipe's shiny bowl.

The pipe. The damn pipe, it dawned on Holliday, was a reflector, the laziest way to cheat. These cowmen had stared at longhorn butts too long to catch Bailey watching the reflection as he pulled each card over his pipe. A dealer relying on so simple a ruse lacked the skills Holliday preferred in a partner. He shrugged. You never knew how deep the water was until you waded the creek. Holliday dug into his pants for his money. As Ed was gathering the deck for another hand, Holliday tossed the wad on the table. "Room for one more?"

Ed glanced at Holliday, jabbing a finger in his tight collar for relief. From his neck, Ed's hand went for Holliday's money.

Holliday bent over the table and plopped his liquor bottle atop his cash, nicking Ed's stubby fingers as they retreated.

"This is a fifty-dollar floor game, mister," the dealer spit out. "You got enough greenbacks for those stakes?" His words were tinged with doubt.

Cocky son of a bitch, Holliday mused. "Enough to last a while. Just how much, I keep to myself," he said, lifting the bottle and using it to sweep the money his way.

The dealer licked his aching fingertips. "What you boys think? Is present company adequate? Walt?"

"If he's got the money, let him play a while," the man answered from under the brim of a sweat-stained hat.

"Hell, we've been at it more than an hour with nobody doing much damage," another added. "What you think, Blackie?"

"No matter," Blackie said, his words caustic as acid, "as long as there's more card playing and less jawbone diarrhea."

"Okay, mister," said Ed, "we'll be glad to take your money." Holliday settled into the vacant chair, placing his bottle and towel at his side on the table.

"Ed Bailey's the name," the dealer said. "Yours?"

"John," Holliday replied.

Bailey waited for the rest, but Holliday just coughed. A gambler's name, like bad news, traveled fast.

"Okay, John," said Bailey. "To my left here is Blackie, on your other side is Beck and between him and me is Walt."

"Shuffle, Ed, this ain't a goddam social," Blackie growled.

Holliday liked Blackie's attitude. Bailey mixed the deck, passed to Walt for the cut, deposited his pipe on the table, then dealt out five around as the others anteed their fifty dollars.

"Make the pot right, Ed," Holliday said as the dealer finished. Their eyes met, lingered, and clashed until the dealer tossed in his entry fee. The scowl embedded on Bailey's face offered no favors, and Holliday knew he was on his own until the dealer called for a new deck. His three hundred and fifty dollars wouldn't go far against these stakes.

Holliday gathered his cards, drew them to his chest, and fanned them enough to read the corners. A pair of kings and three throwaways. Holliday glanced across the table at Bailey and his pipe, resting beside the deck. Walt raised the pot fifty dollars, Bailey dropping out, everyone else staying. Out of the corner of

34

his eye, Holliday watched the taciturn Blackie separating three discards from his keepers. Holliday pulled two cards from his hands, then squeezed three back together. As Blackie tossed his discards to the middle of the table, Holliday pitched his rejects — two cards — beneath them.

Blackie took three. So did Holliday.

He added the new trio to the three cards in his hand. His nimble fingers stacked and restacked them twice, his left wrist twitching when he finished. Then he pulled the cards to himself, slowly exposing the corners of an ace, king, ten, eight, and seven. The sixth card — the king of diamonds — had disappeared up his sleeve.

Holliday, feeling Bailey's icy gaze upon him, hesitated a moment after Blackie upped the pot another fifty dollars. Did Bailey suspect the card up his sleeve? If he did, Bailey would draw the deadwood in now and count the discards before anyone else threw in a hand. Bailey leaned forward, but only to pick up his pipe. Puffing on it, he leaned back in his wooden chair as ignorant as the others. Holliday pondered the raise a moment, stacking and restacking the cards between his nimble fingers.

"Too much for me." Holliday shook his head.

"Thought this might be a little out of your reach, John," Bailey said, the satisfaction warming his eyes.

You cocky son of a bitch, Holliday thought, a sinister smile slithering across his thin lips. He examined his cards again, shaking his head. His nimble fingers snapped together, the cards disappearing in his palm for an instant. His left wrist twitched as he tossed the cards — one shy of five — onto the deadwood. Now he had a pair of kings up his sleeve, but his money roll was skinnier by a hundred dollars. Could he last?

With three deuces Walt claimed the seven hundred dollars in the pot. As Bailey put down his pipe and pulled in the deadwood, everyone anteed another fifty, Bailey remembering to add his promptly this time. He dealt Holliday a sorry hand, an ace high, but nothing else above a nine. Holliday, with only two hundred dollars remaining, folded and watched.

Blackie laid his cards on the table and tugged at his waxed mustache. "I'll go fifty dollars," he said.

Beck tossed his cards on Holliday's. "No sense wasting any

more money on this hand," he said, digging in his shirt pocket for his cigarette papers and tobacco pouch. As Beck rolled his smoke, both Walt and Bailey sweetened the pot.

Blackie took one card. Holliday watched a glint of a smile, as out of place as snow in July, speed across Blackie's face. His hand dropping to his money pile, Blackie had been dealt his prayer's request. Walt took two, revealing no emotion. Bailey took one, then picked up his pipe.

If the dealer stayed long, Holliday knew the pot was Ed's. Blackie bet a hundred, Walt and Bailey following, but the dealer upped it two hundred. Walt frightened, but not Blackie. He matched Bailey's raise, then revealed a queen high straight.

The dealer shook his head. "Close, Blackie, but mine's a full house." Bailey revealed three eights over kings, the two kings Holliday lusted for.

Blackie's smile soured. "Damn, Ed, you always seem to know when to stay in. How is that?"

Bailey swallowed hard, his ruddy face flushing even more, and acknowledged the god of gambling. "Just good luck."

"I've heard of Lottie's Luck, but you're not in that class."

Holliday felt his throat tighten at the mention of Lottie. Could she be in Griffin? But he must not think of her now.

"Just good luck," Bailey repeated, dragging deep on his silver good-luck piece and pulling in his winnings. His yellow teeth flashed at Blackie. "Just good luck."

Bailey left his pipe beside the fresh winnings, then mixed the discards with the rest of the deck. With Blackie suspicious, the dealer was stupid to leave the pipe on the table, Holliday thought. If Bailey blundered again, Chancey's plans might fall apart before the first hand of a new deck.

Adding fifty dollars to the pot, Holliday's fingers slid over the new cards Bailey had tossed his way. Slowly, he spread them, his fingers tacky from perspiration. Damn. No king. He stared at a pair of nines over an ace. The two kings not up his sleeve hid somewhere else. Three kings would be hard to beat, if only he had a third sovereign, but his money was shrinking fast. He must make a move soon or he'd be broke. Perhaps he should risk it with two pair.

No one upped the pot until the bid reached Bailey. "Doesn't

appear anyone's too certain of their cards, does it?" Bailey said, poking his finger between his neck and the noose of a collar. "I'll go fifty dollars to keep it interesting."

Goddam him, Holliday thought. If Bailey's raising, he's setting everyone up. Holliday, joining the others in the pot, was down to a hundred dollars. He followed the deal around the table, guessing at each hand. Blackie took three cards, a good sign he only had a pair. Holliday asked for three and, when they came, stacked them unseen atop his keepers as the deal went to Beck. Beck lifted a mug of hot beer, pondering his play. He discarded one and picked up its replacement without emotion. Both Walt and Bailey took three, so they were staring at a pair themselves. But what about Beck?

Holliday's pulse quickened as he lifted his cards and spread their corners. Nine of spades, nine of hearts, he knew of them. Then came the six of spades, ace of diamonds and six of diamonds. Damn. Two pair with no chance of three of a kind. It would be risky, especially if Bailey stayed in. Blackie passed the bid. For bluff, Holliday added fifty dollars, half his remaining funds. Each opponent, including Bailey, matched him.

"First time we all stayed in after the draw," Bailey noted.

With Bailey meeting the raise, Holliday knew the dealer figured to win. With more money, Holliday could bluff the cowmen, but Bailey and his damn pipe would never fold. Holliday coughed loudly as Blackie passed the bid again. Looking at Bailey as he wiped his mouth, Holliday spoke. "I'm fine."

Bailey grinned widely as the bid went to Beck. "Well, John, I'll go up another fifty." Blackie folded, but Bailey and Walt contributed to the growing puddle of money.

Holliday, his wrist twitching twice, stacked and restacked his cards, then eyed them coldly, nodding his satisfaction as nines over sixes had become kings over nines with the diamond ace throwaway. The creek was getting deeper, Holliday thought, pushing the last of his roll to the middle of the table.

Bailey chuckled at Holliday. "I'll raise you two hundred and fifty."

Beck and Walt folded instantly. Holliday stared hard at his cards, but he was broke. The others knew it and, most galling, Bailey could take the pot without showing his hand. Now all

Holliday could afford was a lie. "I've got a fine horse in Haverty's Livery Stable. What's he good for?"

"He's good for getting you out of town," Bailey laughed. "This game is cash or gold. Your goddam horse ain't worth a shit at this table. Same goes for any pigs or chickens you got." The crowd laughed.

Holliday squeezed his cards together, considering how much pleasure it would give him to kill Ed Bailey.

The dealer reached for the pot, his hands freezing at the sound of two icy words.

"John's in!"

Everyone turned to Blackie as he tossed two hundred and fifty dollars onto the growing pile and then made a return trip with more. "He'll raise you five hundred dollars."

The spectators shuffled their feet and moved closer to the table as Bailey grated his teeth against the stem of his pipe. A yellowish grin formed around the pipe. "Blackie, you don't want to lose your money on a hand you can't even see."

Holliday turned to Blackie. "Obliged."

Blackie clenched his fist. "Damn tired of seeing you win every time you stay in, Ed."

"I'll see your five hundred and raise you two-fifty more," Bailey spit back, counting the money from his dwindling pile.

Holliday turned to Blackie, who automatically pitched another two hundred and fifty dollars onto the pot. "We call you," Blackie said.

"Two pairs," Bailey said, "Queens over jacks." The dealer reached for the pot.

Holliday nodded and the crowd groaned. "Two pairs here," he said, "and the pot's mine."

Bailey's hands flinched as Holliday exposed kings over nines. Bailey's eyes widened and his broad mouth gaped. "But, you . . ." he stammered.

"But I what?" Holliday asked, leaning forward, his elbows on the table, his right hand draped over the edge near the gun under his coat.

"You didn't have, I mean . . ." Bailey caught himself.

"Just surprised your luck soured?" Holliday goaded him. "Why's that? You care to explain? Maybe you just better suck your pipe this next deal and think about it."

The dealer's eyes burned with rage, the fire flaring his nostrils and reddening his cheeks with defeat. Bailey was stumped and Holliday knew it. To accuse Holliday of cheating would expose the dealer's own artifice. Bailey had been outwitted at cheating on a crooked hand.

Holliday spoke. "Blackie drag in the pot for me. Take your money and an extra hundred for the stake."

Blackie pulled the money in. "I'll take what I risked. You keep the hundred. Seeing Bailey's face fall was worth it."

Bailey ignored the comment. Twisting in his chair toward the bar, he called, "Chancey, bring us a fresh deck."

Instantly, the owner of the Cattle Exchange towered over Bailey's shoulder and tossed an unopened deck on the table. "Things not going your way, Ed?"

"Luck frowned at me the last hand," Bailey offered, the pipe still clenched between his teeth.

Holliday felt the hard edge in Bailey's voice and saw in Chancey's deepset eyes doubts that his plan would succeed. A coughing spasm attacked Holliday's spare frame. He grabbed the towel, spit into it, then wiped his face, hating himself for his infirmity, and wondering if Bailey would pull a weapon now that he was not in command of his body. The thought quickly strangled the cough.

Instead, Bailey gathered the old deck and handed it to Chancey. "Save those cards for me, Chancey, I'll count them later. Perhaps I can learn a little about John's skill." Bailey nodded his froglike face at Holliday. Then Bailey broke the seal on, to all appearances, a virgin deck, but Holliday knew better. It was a cold deck, altered or stacked to the dealer's advantage, then repacked to appear unmolested. Extracting the cards Bailey crushed the box, dropping it on the floor.

Chancey, doubts clouding his face, fumbled for his cigarette makings in the tin on his sleeve. "Don't let one bad hand ruin you for the night, Ed," Chancey said. "Play your normal game. If the house dealer bellyaches each time he loses a big pot, dammit, it'll cost me customers."

Holliday stacked his winnings and eyed Bailey, the tiny red veins popping in the dealer's fleshy cheeks. He toyed with the money, annoying Bailey, then took up the whiskey bottle to soothe the recurring pain in his chest. Bailey split the new cards to shuffle.

"Just a minute," Holliday said. "Let me inspect the deck."

"What?" yelled Bailey, leaning back in his chair like he might be going for a weapon.

Instantly, Chancey clamped a hand on the dealer's shoulder. "Easy, Ed."

"Give me the deck," Holliday said, extending his left hand, his right-hand gun ready. "Just to make sure she ain't marked."

"Dammit, Chancey," shouted Bailey, shaking his shoulder against Chancey's iron grip. "We've got a troublemaker accusing us of cheating. Thinks you brought in a marked deck."

Holliday slapped his hand on the felt table. "No accusations now and no reason for any later — if I see the deck." Holliday lifted his palm at the dealer. "The cards."

"Go ahead and do it, Ed," Chancey ordered, his knuckles whitening on Bailey's fleshy shoulder. "We've nothing to hide. And we don't want trouble, not tonight."

Bailey slapped the deck into Holliday's hand and instantly Holliday was studying the red ink splattered in triangles on the card backs. He examined for markings, but if the cards were coded, Holliday knew he'd not likely decipher them. Instead, he wanted a feel of the deck, his fingers stroking the deck's edge, pressing the cards together from side to side. Just as he suspected, the cards had been stripped, the edges of some — the bottom four especially — shaved so that practiced hands could discern what calloused hands could not. Holliday tilted the deck enough to see the bottom card, an ace. He nodded his head, offering the cards to Blackie.

"Look good to me," Holliday said. "You fellows care to look see?" When everyone declined, he dropped the cards on the table. "I'm ready to play."

"The rest of us were ready before," Bailey answered.

"Ease up, Ed," Chancey commanded, loosening his hand on Bailey's shoulder. "An angry dealer doesn't pay attention like he should. Don't lose a hand because you weren't thinking."

Bailey shuffled the deck as Holliday, finishing a drink, banged the bourbon bottle on the table, drawing the stares of the cowmen and distracting them from Bailey's inept blind shuffles.

Finishing, Bailey crimped the deck at the spot he wanted the cut and shoved the cards to Walt. Taking the pipe from his mouth, Bailey started to the table, then thinking better of it, returned it to his lips. He crossed his hands, picking up Walt's cut which had fallen naturally at the crimped cards, uncrossed them, and stacked the cards in their original position — a blind cut.

"Is anybody going to ante before I pass out cards?" Bailey griped, tossing fifty dollars on the table to make his point. The others followed suit.

This was it, Holliday thought as he studied Bailey's moves. He observed three faultless rounds of the deal. No tricks so far. Then on the fourth round, Bailey's fingers paused a fraction of an instant as they came to Holliday and then continued. Again on the fifth round, the dealer's fingers stilled for the blink of an eye. Holliday hoped the cowmen missed Bailey's pauses — and the two cards he'd dealt from the bottom. As Bailey finished, Holliday gathered his cards in a single stack, running his fingers along their edges, discerning two strippers by their slighted widths. Perhaps the scam would work after all.

Holliday slowly fanned his cards. Two aces, a king, a four, and a five. The aces were shaved. They were keepers. The king perplexed Holliday. How was the cold deck stacked? For four aces? Full house, aces over kings or kings over aces? If he kept the king and called for two, he might worry away a cowman. If he discarded the king, he might wreck the prepared hand. Safer to keep the king, he decided.

To his right, Blackie twisted his mustache and stared at his cards. Beck lit a cigarette, but it smoldered between his fingers like wet timber afire, and Walt glanced from player to player, trying to read his opponents' cards as he would the pages of a closed book — by guessing. No one offered any clues. Only one man wasn't guessing. Bailey sat simmering behind his cards, his eyes glowing hot like the fire in his pipe. He drummed his fingers on the table and glared at Blackie, who pondered for a moment, then moved a hundred dollars from his funds to the pot.

"Cost you a hundred to stay in," he said. Everyone anteed.

"Raise you a hundred fifty," Walt challenged, and again no one backed down.

"Damn," Bailey said, grabbing the deck, "someone's gonna

put in a fine night's work when this hand's done. You ready for cards, or you gonna price me out of this hand?"

"I'll take one," Blackie snapped, his words as taut and prickly as newly stretched barbed wire.

Could be trouble, Holliday thought. The cattleman might have two pair, four of a kind, or even a shot at a straight flush. Blackie snagged his new card the instant it hit the felt, inserted it among the others, and let his left hand fall to his money. Blackie, Holliday nodded, was ready to back up his hand.

Holliday tossed his two rejects on the deadwood. "Two," he said, studying Bailey's fingers as the cards flew from the deck and across the table. Two more from the bottom. Sliding them in with his three keepers, Holliday knew he had two more strippers. When he spread them out, he stared at four aces and a king. Bailey had played straight, provided Blackie didn't have a straight flush.

Then Beck asked for two. Maybe three of a kind, Holliday thought. Walt took three cards. A pair to begin with and maybe a full house at best, Holliday figured. Bailey took three.

Without waiting for Bailey to look at his hand, Blackie fattened the pot. "Five hundred," he called, the bet echoing from mouth to mouth among the encircled spectators. Holliday matched Blackie before the murmur subsided. Without hesitating, Beck added his five hundred dollars. Walt was a little slower but stayed in.

Bailey eyed Blackie suspiciously. "I think you're bluffing, Blackie. I'll match you and raise you five hundred." Bailey counted out more sweetening for the pot.

All matched the raise, then Blackie spoke. "I'll see you another five hundred bucks," he said, staring at the dealer.

Bailey sputtered a moment, sucking hard on his pipe, and counted his bills. As Holliday and Beck matched Blackie, Walt folded, then Bailey tossed his cards to the table in defeat.

"Now who was goddam bluffing, Bailey?" Blackie laughed. "You can't buffalo me."

Unwisely, Bailey reached for his coat pocket. Before he could withdraw his hand, he stared at the gaping mouth of Blackie's Colt .45. Bailey's trembling hand emerged slowly from his pocket, clamping between his thumb and forefinger a tobacco pouch the way he would hold a dead rat by the tail.

"Wasn't a smart move," Blackie said, reholstering his gun.

"All I'm after is more tobacco," Bailey answered. "You're a mite jumpy tonight, Blackie."

"Just suspicious, Bailey, of you monkeying with the deck."

"I'll call you," Beck challenged in a friendly way that cut the tension.

Blackie grinned. "Queens over tens, full house."

Beck nodded. "Four nines."

"But it doesn't beat four aces," Holliday said, showing his cards.

Beck sat stunned, disbelief etched on his face as if it were carved out of stone. Blackie picked up his cards and tossed them on the deadwood. Turning to Holliday, he shook his head. "Mister, how do you do it, winning the night's big hands?"

"Bailey," Holliday said, staring across the table, "deals me rigged hands."

The dealer's eyes flared like a flame doused with good liquor, doubt and uncertainty racing across his face like a prairie fire.

Blackie glanced from Holliday to Bailey, then slapped the table, his mouth erupting with laughter. "Like hell he does," he gasped. "Bailey wouldn't do no goddam favors for anyone but himself. I like your humor, mister, I'd just like to see how funny you are when your luck is as sour as seven-day milk."

Chancey bent his large frame over the table, leaning on his doubled fists. "Gentlemen, I think there's been enough for one night," he said. "We're tempting trouble. Free drinks for the lot of you."

Shortly the cattlemen stood and stretched their cramped muscles, then ambled to the bar. Holliday lingered, wrapping his winnings in his handkerchief and stuffing the wad in his pocket, making sure that those watching saw the gun hanging from his hip, just in case any had ideas about waylaying him. As Bailey slipped away, Holliday corked his liquor bottle, picked up the towel, and marched to a vacant section of the bar.

"Another bottle of Monarch," he called to Chancey.

Chancey obliged. "Anything else?"

"Yeah," Holliday said, shoving the towel to Chancey. "Under there you'll find a pair of sixes. Add them to Bailey's deck. I'll settle with you tomorrow afternoon in my room, last door on the left, upstairs in the Planters House."

Chancey nodded. "Just one more thing."

"Yeah."

"Stay out of the Bee Hive."

Holliday shrugged, his left hand grabbing the necks of the two liquor bottles, his right falling to the ivory grip of his Colt. In the wash of jealous stares of the less lucky, he strode from the Cattle Exchange.

Then he was lost in the darkness of the Flat and in his single thought. Was Lottie in town?

FOUR

The light of an afternoon sun bounced off the Clear Fork's rippled waters like reflections from a thousand shards of broken crystal. Like a mirror flawed, the ribbon of water distorted the forms of the giant pecan trees which gathered in clusters along the stream. A soft wind came from the north, the tall prairie grass waving as it passed, the leaves murmuring among themselves about the winter not long away. Husks of pecans thousandsfold had darkened, dried, and split open, a few dropping their nuts like scattered jewels on the grassy carpet lining the stream.

Under a sky stained with meandering white wisps of clouds, the animals rested during the heat of the day, reserving their strength for winter's stealthy approach. The long-eared jackrabbits hunkered within the sweep of grass, nibbling at the plants within reach. Squirrels, lords over more nuts than they could ever collect, sunned themselves on the highest branches of the pecan trees. Quail huddled in coveys under squatty bushes, prairie dogs — except for the occasional lookout — reclined in their dens, while turkeys hid behind the brush scattered in patches along the river. Overhead, a solitary orange-breasted hawk circled effortlessly, floating on unseen air currents, surveying the land below and spotting an occasional fish leaping from the creek long enough to defy gravity then disappear in a splash.

It was Sunday and it was peaceful, the countryside at ease with itself. Even the dead man hanging from a pecan branch seemed grotesquely tranquil, his suspended presence no longer concerning the animals at rest. Screened from distant eyes by the surrounding trees, the dangling body attracted only flies. As lifeless as another husk-sheathed pecan, the corpse waited to fall to the ground, the harvest of a savage reaper.

The ears of a jackrabbit twitched, then stood at attention. A prairie dog sentinel squeaked an alarm that brought the heads of a hundred chattering rodents peeking above the mounded ramparts of their earthen burrows. The quail sent up their whistling call to warn others, then darted headlong through the grass. From upriver came disconcerting human sounds, peals of laughter tumbling across the still prairie. Man was dangerous. He even killed his own kind.

Stretching the full reach of her lithe frame, Rachel drew back the buggy whip and snapped it toward the pecan cluster clinging to a twisted branch. The whip cracked but missed its target and Rachel lost her balance, the slick bottoms of her button-up shoes slipping on the thick grass growing along the sloping stream bank. She slid slowly toward the water. Like windmill blades in a stiff breeze, her arms spun for equilibrium, but inexorably she skated toward the water, too slow to fall, too fast to stop. "Help me!" she giggled.

Dropping her basket of pecans, Lottie lunged for Rachel's whipping arms, but stumbled over the basket and plopped down brusquely on her seat, her hat at a rakish tilt. "Oh my," she laughed as Rachel threshed her arms against gravity and an unscheduled bath. Gathering her full skirt in her hands, Lottie hurried to stand, but Rachel was beyond reach and help.

Then Rachel's thick heels dug into the mud at the stream's edge, her legs braking quicker than her upper torso. For a moment she teetered precariously over the water, but her flailing arms pushed against the sky and she, too, settled roughly on her rear, dropping the buggy whip half in the creek. At the jolt, a startled laugh wrenched itself from Rachel's slender throat, followed by an embarrassed cackle at her awkwardness.

"Some help you are, Lottie," Rachel said, twisting her head to look at her companion. Then she laughed in torrents and laid back on the grass, her head almost touching Lottie's shoes.

Lottie snickered, then leaned forward until her eyes met the green of Rachel's. "You're laughing at me, Rachel?"

"Such a fine hat you wear, Lottie," Rachel started, then broke into more laughter. "But it's not as pretty on the side of your head."

Lottie's nimble fingers raced to her auburn hair and the broad-brimmed hat which dangled limply by her ear. In the fall, her hair and her hat had shifted — like her balance downward. She patted her mane, mussing it further, drawing peals of laughter from Rachel. Exasperated, Lottie finally extracted two giant hat pins and tossed the hat toward the rented buggy. Her laughter, like her long auburn locks, fell loose and free. "Such grace befits ladies of the plains like ourselves," Lottie said.

"If you can call an army wife and a gambler ladies," Rachel shot back.

"Indeed we are, madam," intoned Lottie. "Have we both, in our younger days, not read *Miss Leslie's Behaviour Book?*"

"It's true, but I confess I've forgotten so much."

"Me too," answered Lottie, "especially the chapter on falling on your fanny."

"Perhaps we could borrow a copy of Miss Leslie's book from a harlot in the Flat."

"Indeed, my dear Rachel, they might have forgotten other chapters, but they'd certainly be familiar with reclining on their fannies."

Both women giggled like schoolgirls, unconcerned that others might hear their silliness for they were five miles from the Flat. Lottie enjoyed these Sunday afternoons with Rachel as if they were sisters. Her life was spent too much among gambling men and the wrong kind of women.

Lottie grabbed the upturned basket. "Care to knock down any more pecans from that high branch?" she asked, adding the scattered pecans within reach to her basket.

Rachel tossed one pecan at the basket, a second at Lottie, then stood brushing the seat of her sky blue muslin dress. When she bent to attend the splattered hem, she groaned. "Grass and mud stains! Can't afford this, not on an army captain's pay."

"Rachel, my dear, I shall buy you a new skirt."

"I could never allow that," she answered, releasing the folds of stained cloth from her fingers and grabbing the whip.

"Then perhaps you should take up gambling and enhance Richard's meager earnings," Lottie teased as she stood.

"At the cost of my marriage?" Rachel questioned without offense. "No, Lottie I should never do that. Richard is a fussbody. Why he even worries about me seeing you. Fears I might get the gaming urge."

"You could get worse urges, Rachel."

"That's what Richard fears. Anyway, he thinks I ought to get you married to someone who'll take you away from those saloons." She moved up the incline toward the buggy, Lottie walking with her. "Why," asked Rachel, "have you never married? You could have your pick of many a decent man."

Lottie stiffened, her lips tightening, her knuckles blanching tightly around the basket handle. There was an answer, but the words were buried too deep within her to uncover.

"Why haven't you married? The war?"

Lottie coughed, but the knot lingered deep in her throat. "Sometimes, you show your hand. Other times you don't." Lottie smiled. "Do we have enough pecans, or should we try to knock a few more down?"

"Lord knows Richard will put enough away that if I don't bring home plenty, I won't get any for myself or for baking. Both Richard and I love pecan pie. And the pecans are so full for this time of year. Must have been the summer flood."

Lottie gathered another handful. "Then perhaps, Rachel, we shall be fortunate enough this afternoon to meet a teamster with an empty wagon we can fill for your Richard. A teamster I can marry, of course."

Now Rachel cleared her throat. "Lottie, forgive me for prying. I would hate for my curiosity to harm our friendship."

"My dear Rachel," Lottie said, "promise me but one thing."

"Anything."

"At the next pecan tree, I'll handle the whip."

Rachel laughed and nodded. "Race you to the wagon." She darted up the creek bank, bending over to scoop Lottie's hat from the grass.

"You're crazy," Lottie called after her. "I'm saving my energy to gather all these pecans you and Richard can eat."

At the top of the embankment, Rachel waited for Lottie.

"Just one more stop, Lottie. There are several pecans in those trees," Rachel said, pointing to a copse of trees downstream. "We'll get what we can there and head home."

They walked together toward the buggy, its black piano box body glistening in the sun, Rachel shading her face with Lottie's hat. At the buggy, Lottie dumped the pecans into the back as Rachel untied the reins to the grazing bay mare.

Lottie leveled the new pecans over those they had gathered earlier, the nuts coming within an inch of the shiny black sideboard's top, and crowned the haul with the basket.

"We may wish later we had run into a teamster with an empty wagon, Rachel. I'll bet we've a hundred pounds of pecans here. Your Richard can't eat that much, can he?"

"Not in a single sitting," Rachel said, tossing Lottie's hat on the green body cloth seat and climbing into the buggy beneath its three-bow top. She fluffed the folds of her skirt, knocking a layer of mud from the bottom flounce. "More mud, and would you look at my shoes?" she said, the disgust distorting her voice. "And the grass stains, doubt they'll come out."

"But," said Lottie, coming up on the other side of the buggy, "at least Richard will have plenty of pecans."

"And a wife that dresses like a field hand."

Lottie lifted her skirt to her calf — a sight men at the Bee Hive would have paid plenty to see — and placed her foot on the wagon's Brewster green step. Taking Rachel's hand, Lottie stepped up into the buggy and settled in beside Rachel on the cushioned tufts of upholstery, adding the hat to her lap.

At the snap of the whip, the mare pulled the buggy toward the copse of trees downstream. The buggy plowed through the grass which bowed down behind it. Game skirted ahead, with an occasional jackrabbit popping its head from the grass to watch. The mare pranced in the sunshine as if she knew she were pulling the best buggy from Pete Haverty's Livery.

Then, unexpectedly, the mare stopped, jarring both women forward in their seat. Rachel cracked her whip, but the horse reared on its hind legs and whinnied, coming down hard on its front hooves at a buzzing patch of grass.

"Rattlesnake," Lottie shouted, grabbing the reins and tugging them savagely to the right, her hat tumbling to the floorboard. The mare reared up against its harness just as the rattlesnake darted for her legs. "Hold the animal, Rachel," Lottie commanded, tossing the reins to Rachel's lap, jumping from the buggy and landing as gracefully as a cat in full stride. She circled behind the buggy and, while out of Rachel's sight, pulled from the folds of her blouse a revolver. Gun in hand, she moved cautiously forward until she spied the serpent.

The snake was coiled around its uplifted tail, which buzzed ominously. Beady eyes stared at Lottie, and a slithering tongue darted out at her. Inching forward, ever careful to stay out of striking distance, Lottie lifted her hand and the gun exploded in an angry fit of lead and smoke. And then the prairie was hushed, except for Rachel's sobs. The snake convulsed in the grass, its white belly turning to the sun, its rattle flopping limply on the ground.

"Oh, Lottie," cried Rachel, "are you okay?"

With her back still to Rachel, Lottie nodded, straightening her blouse. When Lottie turned around, neither hand carried a gun, but Rachel seemed not to notice the difference. Lottie walked to the mare, patted the animal on the neck to calm her, then bent to examine her forelegs. Lottie lifted each leg and ran her hand over the short hair perfumed with perspiration.

"No bites," Lottie called to Rachel. "We're lucky."

"Lucky to have you, Lottie."

Lottie walked around the rattlesnake, still writhing in death, and guessed it more than five feet long. And it had an impressive rattle. "You want the rattle for Richard? Or maybe for your future children to play with?"

"Oh no, Lottie, I wouldn't want that disgusting thing in my house. Never!"

"Suits me, because you'd have to get it yourself. I'm not touching that filthy thing, either."

They enjoyed the sound of each other's nervous laugh as Lottie climbed back in the buggy, retrieving her hat from the floorboard. "My hat isn't fated to survive this outing." Lottie punched the trampled crown back in place.

"Your hat and my dress, I might add. Maybe we should head back for the Flat, Lottie?"

"And let the day end on such an unpleasantry? No ma'am, my dear Rachel. We've one more stop to fill our wagon."

Rachel slapped the reins against the jittery mare's flank and pointed her toward the trees just ahead. "Lottie," Rachel said quietly, "where'd the gun come from?"

"Rachel, in my business I always carry one."

"That's why I worry about you so and would like to see you out of that life. It's dangerous. Why just yesterday when Richard returned from Jacksboro, another stage passenger, a fellow Richard took to be a gambler, pulled a pistol on him for no good reason. I saw the man — thin, evil-looking fellow — when I met Richard. It's dangerous around that type of people."

"You worry too much, my dear Rachel. There's no more danger there than, say, a Sunday afternoon ride through a rattler-infested prairie. Everything's chance, happenstance in life. I just happen to make money off chance."

"Precarious living, though."

"Beats working in a harlot's crib, rutting like hogs."

"But it's not like having a husband." Rachel stopped suddenly and shook her head. "There I go preaching another sermon. Forgive me, Lottie. I am concerned, that's all."

"Forget it," Lottie said, reaching over and squeezing Rachel's hand. "Someday I'll give it up. That's a time off, though. Now, we've got pecans to gather."

The buggy neared the clump of pecan trees, flushing a flock of turkeys from nearby brush. Rachel flinched. "Oh, me," she said, "that rattler sure made me jumpy."

"It made both of us nervous." Lottie patted Rachel's knee.

At the trees Rachel tugged the mare to a halt and tied the reins around the brake lever, but the animal seemed skittish, pawing at the ground instead of eating the tall grass. "What's a matter, girl?" Rachel asked. "Please not another rattler."

A faint odor drifted on the slight breeze, the festering smell of death. Lottie caught the aroma, but its source was screened behind the huge trunk of the nearest pecan tree. "Dead animal must be near. Makes the mare nervous," Lottie said, adjusting her hat. "Let's be quick. I'll knock the pecans down this time and maybe you won't fall on your fanny, Rachel."

Both laughed as they climbed from the buggy. "Oh, look, Lottie," Rachel said, pointing at the grassy carpet beyond the nearest tree. "Many pecans have fallen here. Our best find today." Handing Lottie the whip, she said, "We may not need it here." Rachel raced down the sloping earth, which bled into the creek, and fell upon her knees scooping handfuls of pecans onto her skirt for a basket. "Hurry, Lottie, with the basket."

Lottie tossed the whip onto the seat, grabbed the basket, and followed Rachel's trail until she passed the massive tree trunk. She stopped cold, her mouth gaping. "Ahhh" — she caught herself before her surprise turned into a scream. Hanging not six feet behind the kneeling Rachel was a dead man.

"Just look at all these pecans," Rachel called, glancing back toward Lottie. "Unlike anything we've found before."

And Lottie knew why. As he had struggled for a foothold in midair, as he had fought for his last breath, and had thrashed madly in death's throes, the dead man had shaken the pecans to the ground. Lottie held her breath a moment, fearful her voice might break, then called. "Come, Rachel, we've enough by now."

"Oh, Lottie," she replied, "I've just started. There are many, but it won't take long, not like this."

"Rachel," Lottie implored, a tinge of panic in her voice, "suddenly I feel sickly."

Rachel stood, holding in the lap of her skirt a mound of pecans. Almost within reach behind her, the corpse swayed slightly toward Rachel as if she were death's magnet. "I'm sorry, Lottie, you feel faint. Then we must go, but I should remember this place so I can bring Richard." She turned around.

"No," cried Lottie, but too late.

Rachel screamed, both hands flying from her skirt to her mouth, the pecans tumbling to the ground, some rolling into a sticky stain of body fluids beneath the dead man. Rachel stared in horror, too disgusted to look, too fascinated to turn her face from the hideous corpse: bulging eyes like glassy walnut shells, bloated tongue twisted like driftwood between two rows of teeth tombstone white, the flesh puffy and purple, nose strangely contorted, and neck decorated with torn flesh and dried blood on either side of a hemp rope.

Rachel's thin frame went limp. Lottie dashed for her, discarding the basket, grabbing Rachel under the arms and easing her upright. Lottie's touch seemed to revive Rachel.

"It's okay, Rachel. We must go." Lottie's voice flowed calmly. She patted Rachel's pale face and looked into her innocent eyes, learning from them that Rachel had never before seen a victim of violence. "We must go."

Rachel nodded. "Please, let's do," she said, her voice calm with desperation, her face swathed in terror's paleness. She broke from Lottie's grasp and walked steadily toward the buggy. Lottie started behind her, turning a second to retrieve the dropped basket, then deciding to leave it. They must depart. Now. For Rachel's sake.

Lottie caught up with Rachel at the buggy, her face regaining its color but her eyes still vacant. Rachel's hands shook as she jumped on the seat and untied the reins. As Lottie fought against her skirt to get in, Rachel grabbed the buggy whip. Lottie had just lifted her leg over the sideboard when Rachel popped the flank of the nervous mare. The buggy lurched ahead. As the horse turned a sharp circle back toward the Flat, Lottie struggled her other leg in. Then she collapsed into the seat beside Rachel, who still beat upon the frightened mare. Lottie wrenched the buggy whip from Rachel's white-knuckle grasp. Rachel slapped the mare with the reins, hollering at the animal, as the buggy bounced over the terrain, scattering in its wake dozens of pecans.

"It's okay, Rachel. No matter how fast we get back to Griffin, it won't do him any good."

Rachel seemed neither to hear nor to comprehend, as if her mind had been seared by naked death's terrible torch. She screamed at the horse again and drove harder until Lottie held onto her seat. Finally fearing Rachel would overturn the rig, Lottie lunged for the reins. Rachel struggled against her. "No," she shrieked, but Lottie's resolve outweighed Rachel's terror and she let go. Rachel burst into uncontrollable sobs as Lottie gradually slowed the mare to a lope.

"I can still see him, Lottie. Even when I shut my eyes," she struggled with her words. "He's . . . oh . . . he's still there, his eyes bulging, his tongue sticking out at me. I know I will dream about him forever. He won't go away, Lottie. He won't go away."

The contorted face lingered, too, with Lottie, but she had seen other men dead. Their faces had all dissolved hazily in her memory except for one. The first. Though it had been more than twenty years earlier, she remembered a trip with her father on a steamboat. Just up from Cairo on the Ohio River, there had been an altercation over a card game. A handsome man, fashionably dressed, was sitting in a chair, but the chair had fallen backward on the floor from the impact of the bullet which had turned the back of his skull into a bloody pulp. She recalled a single drop of blood, crawling down the dead man's face from the hole in the forehead. She remembered the blue eyes empty of life, glaring at her, asking why. She could still see a paleness on his lips which grinned into eternity at a fatal card hand. "Sure, you'll forget it," Lottie assured Rachel, knowing it was all a lie. "One day you'll have a story to tell your grandchildren."

Rachel gasped, her sobs louder. Lottie regretted her well-meant words. Nothing could change them now, just like they could never erase what Rachel had seen. Not now, not ever.

"I'd never tell my grandchildren something that horrible. I just couldn't. I don't even think I can tell Richard."

"You'll forget it, Rachel," Lottie said, the sincerity in her voice as lacking as prairie mountains around them.

The somber music of Rachel's sobs accompanied them for better than a mile, their minds dulled to their surroundings until a rider was almost upon them.

"Someone's coming, Rachel."

With the edge of her sleeve, Rachel dabbed at her eyes.

Straight and lean, the rider carried himself like one accustomed to miles in the saddle. As he drew nearer, Lottie recognized the set of his head, even though the broad brim of his hat cast a shadow over his face. Coming closer, he took off his hat and Lottie smiled. She patted her hair and pushed the stray curls she could under her hat.

"It's Jack Jacobs, Rachel."

"The sheriff?"

"Not now. He was until April, when Vernon Trickus replaced him. Jacobs is a good man, too good a man for this wicked county to keep long as sheriff. He's a man we can trust."

Lottie stopped the buggy as Jacobs met them, his hat over his heart, a genuine smile over his broad face. "Good afternoon, Lottie, ma'am. Good day for a Sunday ride."

Rachel sniffed twice, as if she might cry again. Jacobs, his smile evaporating into a mask of concern, dismounted.

"Jack, there's been trouble back down the river." Lottie said, handing the reins to Rachel. "Hold onto these."

Lottie stood in the buggy, lifting her skirt enough for the pale flesh of her calf to show. Taking his extended hand, she smiled as Jacobs turned his blushing head away from her leg's exposed flesh. "Pardon my looks, Jack," she said as she stepped onto the ground. "My hair's a mess."

"You look fine, Lottie, I promise you."

"Let's take a walk, Jack," she said, nodding toward Rachel.

Jacobs replaced his hat, took his mount's reins, and walked hand in hand with Lottie twenty yards behind the buggy. "There's been a lynching back down the river."

"Vigilance committee?"

"Don't know. Didn't stay long enough to look for a warning. Finding him shook Rachel up too much."

"Back in the spring, the vigilance committee made rope meat of four men. Guess the law's coming to Shackelford County."

"I preferred it when you had something to do with the law."

"Thanks, Lottie. More folks been like you, I might still be sheriff, but a man here has enough troubles of his own without taking on those of everyone else's making. I'll ride downriver, bury the fellow. Did you recognize him?"

"Don't know I could've if I'd known him, face like it was. When you go, Jack, would you do me a favor?"

"Name it."

"We left a basket there near him. Bring it in the next time you're in town?"

"Sure. Now get your friend back to Griffin," Jacobs said, mounting his horse. He nudged the animal away from the river.

Lottie pointed downstream. "He's that way."

Jacobs pulled up on his horse and nodded. "I'll need a shovel to bury him. There's a ranch house a mile this direction. I'll borrow one there. You two just forget about this."

"I wish we could."

FIVE

Clad in red flannel underwear, Holliday doubled over the bed's edge, convulsed with coughing. Sweat drenched him, dark stains growing like a cancer down the chest and around the armpits of the undergarment. Fumbling for the whiskey bottle on the plank floor, he squeezed the glass neck between trembling fingers and lifted the muzzle to his parched lips. He spit out curses as he drew air from the bottle's dryness. The empty slid from his fingers, clattering on the floor, useless against the pain raging deep in his chest. Where was his extra bottle?

"Damn it to hell!" He stood, the pain settling deeper in his lungs, squeezing a gasp from his frail chest, and kicked the empty aside. His watery eyes struggled to focus. Shaking his head to clear sleep's cobwebs, he batted his eyelids against the afternoon sunlight bursting through the open window and stumbled around the bed to draw the curtains. Dropping to his knees by the bed, he searched beneath it, his quivering fingers following his gaze, touching cold glass and extracting his fresh bottle.

Twisting around on the floor, he sat back against the bed and stretched his legs out until he could feel the wooden coolness prickling his flesh through the undergarment. As he jerked the stopper free from the bottle, his arm brushed against his holstered Colt, hanging from the bedpost. He swallowed his medicine in quick gulps, the alcohol gradually numbing the agony in his lungs. In damning consumption for another night without rest, he began this day like most, with a drink and a curse.

Above the consumptive gurgle of liquor in his throat, he heard heavy footsteps halting outside his door. He slipped his Colt from its holster and cocked the hammer at the slight rap on the door. Pointing the barrel just above the chair wedged under the doorknob, he held onto the bottle. "What do you want?" he called, his weak lungs mustering but a whisper.

"It's Chancey," came a whisper back.

Holliday slipped catlike to the door. His bare foot nudged at the chair until it came free, the door slitting open enough for Holliday to confirm Chancey, then widening to admit him. Holliday uncocked his gun and began to speak, until his throat clogged with phlegm.

"You look like warmed over shit. Gambler's disease?"

Nodding, Holliday coughed in his fist, retreated across the room, tossing his pistol on the bed, then falling onto the mattress and wadding the sheet at his mouth. Tears moistened his eyes as the cough shuddered through his frame. "You came for the money, not to check on my health," he said, his words muffled by the sheet. His heart hammering from the strain of tuberculosis, he pointed limply to the overturned washbasin. "Money's there, two stacks."

In two strides, Chancey was uprighting the washbasin, uncovering the bills, thumbing through the thicker stack.

"It's all there," Holliday said, his voice squeezing through the tightness in his throat, "split like we agreed, though I figure I deserve a bigger cut for putting up with that son of a bitch you call a dealer."

Chancey, counting the winnings, shrugged. "Most folks get along with Bailey."

"I'm not most folks. If I hadn't swapped kings for sixes, he'd skinned me of my money and everything you hoped to win." Holliday picked up his Colt and cocked the hammer. "I don't like being double-crossed." He aimed chest high at the saloon owner.

Turning around at the metallic click, Chancey's stony black eyes glanced from the gun to Holliday. His heavy voice, weighted by pause, challenged Holliday. "Nor do I."

Holliday's thin lips curled into a smile that was not reflected in his steely eyes. He eased the hammer down. "Less my stake money, I had seventy-six-fifty when play ended. My cut comes to a little over nineteen hundred dollars. You keep the difference for cutting me in."

The saloon owner nodded, tucking his share in his britches pocket, then extracting his cigarette makings from his tobacco tin. "You ever thought of owning a share of a saloon, mister?" He dripped tobacco onto a slice of paper, then lifted the result to his mouth, closing the cigarette paper with his tongue.

"I like to take my assets with me, if I leave in a hurry."

Chancey exchanged his tobacco fixings for a match, scratched it to life on the washstand, and stuck the flame to his cigarette, blurring behind the cloud of smoke. "Another deal for you. If you win I'll give you a table in the Cattle Exchange."

"Bailey's table?"

Chancey drew hard on his cigarette. "Local folks like him. Bailey brings in a regular clientele. What if I say no?"

"Bailey's table or the conversation's over."

"Bailey's table then. I want a share of the Bee Hive. Mike Fogle runs the place, makes the best profit in the Flat. I can't get a run at him, but a stranger with my money can."

"Let me think on it a day or so."

"No time for that. It's tonight or never, with you anyway."

"Don't like to be rushed," Holliday said, raising the whiskey bottle to his lips.

"You're new and unknown here, but word's getting around after your winnings last night. And today's Sunday."

"And tomorrow's Monday," Holliday shot back.

"There's a dealer at the Bee Hive I want to avoid," Chancey started slowly, wrapping his words in a ribbon of smoke. "This dealer doesn't work Sundays."

"A mean fellow?"

"Not mean at all, best manners you'll ever see. No fellow, either."

Holliday felt a tightness in his throat and it wasn't from consumption. He swallowed hard. He had found her.

"Ever hear of Lottie Deno?" Chancey asked.

Holliday nodded, thinking how much simpler his life might be if he hadn't.

"I don't want her involved in a turn of the cards," Chancey said, matter-of-factly. "Her luck's too queer. I don't want to buck Lottie's Luck. You gonna play my hand or not?"

"Bailey's table if I win?"

Chancey nodded, drawing the cigarette fire down to his lips as he inhaled.

"I deal faro and that's what I'll play."

Chancey dug into his pocket for last night's winnings and tossed the wad on the bed in front of Holliday. "I can come up with two thousand more, if you need it."

"Be a shame to lose all your money," Holliday grinned.

"Mr. Fogle," the dealer called across the subdued gaming room, "I need you here a moment."

Fogle felt a sinking in his stomach and glanced from behind three sevens. Benson was in trouble.

"Damn, Benson," Fogle shouted. "I'm in the middle of a good streak."

"Not at my table, you're not," Benson replied, a wash of panic rising like floodwaters in his voice. "There's a gentleman here who wants to remove the house limit on bets."

Damn, Fogle wondered why every time he hit a lucky streak, something went awry. This time the trouble was a thin man with ash blond hair, a walrus mustache, hollow cheeks, thin lips, pasty complexion, and unhealthy cough. Fogle slammed his cards onto the table. "Excuse me, gentlemen," he apologized as he shoved his chair away from the table. He could feel anger's flame rising within him, stoked by the narrowed stare from the slender wisp of a man standing at the faro table opposite Benson. By the gambler's natty dress, Fogle took him for a professional, one of the leeches who sucked blood out of the Bee Hive. "What's the problem, Benson?" Fogle asked as he stepped to the table, all the time staring at Holliday.

"I'm the problem," the emaciated man spoke, his words ringing of the south, his insolent eyes watering with insult.

Fogle nodded, observing the gray frock coat hooked behind the gambler's sidearm, knowing another gun would be inside the man's coat. Fogle noted the bottle of Monarch bourbon in the man's left hand. Only Chancey at the Cattle Exchange sold the Monarch brand locally. Was Chancey behind this? "Now, what is it, Benson?"

The dealer pointed across the table. "He wants to lift the house betting limit."

"That true, mister?"

Holliday nodded, as he struggled to trap a cough, but it escaped from his lips, chased by a rasping gasp for breath.

"Your gambler's disease sounds bad, mister."

"I'm here to gamble, not discuss my health," Holliday answered on the tail of another cough.

Fogle leaned over the table toward Holliday and rested his weight on his hands. "Then maybe you'd just better live with a hundred-dollar limit."

Holliday nodded, stacking his winnings. "I'll take my business elsewhere, someplace more accommodating."

"You just do that," Fogle said. "Go to Chancey's, he probably sent you here. Just stay away as long —"

Benson pointed at Holliday's winnings. "Mr. Fogle, he's about five hundred ahead."

"What?" Fogle straightened to face Benson. "Damn, you should have called me before now."

"Thought my luck would change," Benson defended himself.

Now Holliday leaned across the table toward Fogle and the dealer. "You can't afford to settle up? By god, I will take my winnings elsewhere, if you can even afford to pay them."

"I can pay," Fogle bulled, clenching his fists, "but first, I want a chance at you. You want to play no limit, then by god, we'll play it that way. I'll deal the box." Benson backed away and Fogle stepped in his wake.

Holliday grinned, though his eyes remained as emotionless as a rattlesnake's. "Whose dealing doesn't matter as long as we continue the deck as is."

"The deal will continue as is, mister," Fogle said loudly, "once you place your bets."

Holliday took his time, surveying the casekeeper, absent-mindedly dropping a dozen of his chips from palm to palm.

Fogle drummed his fingers on the table and tapped his

booted foot on the floor. He wished for Lottie to play his hand; she would never let this tinhorn gambler anger her. Fogle studied the casekeeper closely. Twelve turns had been completed, thirteen turns remaining until hock. The cards had split fairly evenly between the highs, eights through kings, and the lows, aces through sixes. Already three aces, three kings, and three sixes had fallen. No splits were possible on those three cards when play resumed. A knowledgeable gambler would bet heavily on those, unless he were superstitious, Fogle thought. Three fives, three sevens, three eights, and three nines remained in the dealing box, plenty of chances for splits, if the stranger was fool enough to bet on them.

The gambler pushed a stack of chips — Fogle counted five hundred dollars' worth — onto the ten. Fogle, his hands growing clammy, hoped his luck had accompanied him from the last table.

"That all?" Fogle sneered. He pulled back the exposed card to reveal a ten, a loser. Fogle laughed. "All that thought on a loser." As he revealed the next card, his smile evaporated. A split. Instead of taking all of the gambler's money, he'd draw only half. Fogle split the stack of chips, raking his share to the check tray. Before Fogle had stacked his winnings, Holliday doubled his own two hundred and fifty dollars on the ten and moved the stack between the queen and jack, so either card would win or lose. After a turn without result, Fogle revealed a losing five over a winning jack.

"You owe me five hundred," Holliday said under his breath, his thin lips barely quivering beneath his mustache.

Like steam building in a fired boiler, anger gathered inside Fogle. He knew what he owed without being reminded. As Fogle slapped a matching set of chips beside the gambler's bet, Holliday pushed the entire stack across the queen until it rested between the lady and her man; either a king or a queen would win. Fogle pulled two turns without a result, then uncovered a losing four and a winning king.

"Add another thousand dollars," Holliday commanded smugly.

Propelled by the steam rising within him, Fogle reached for a moment menacingly across the table, but his hand froze when

Holliday's slipped inside his frock coat. Fogle sighed as the gambler extracted a handkerchief. Fogle's outstretched hand dropped to the table and counted out the loss as his opponent coughed decorously into the cloth. "Damn luck," he said, dropping his loss in front of Holliday's chips.

"Or damn unlucky," Holliday challenged.

Fogle winced and stared at the casekeeper, trying to calm himself. He could do little to change the tide of misfortune washing across his table. The stranger must make a mistake. Though only a single queen, jack, seven, five, four, deuce, and ace remained uncovered, three nines and three eights were still to be turned. It might not matter until the last turn because the gambler would avoid eights and nines in fear of splits. But on the last turn, if the gambler could call the order of the final three cards, the house paid greater odds. If the cards were all different, the odds were four to one. But if two of the last three were the same, odds were only two to one. That might be meaningless if the gambler stumbled before then, but offered a glimmer of hope in case he didn't.

Holliday pushed his chips back across the face of the queen and stopped between her and the jack for either to win. Fogle slid the top card out of the box, revealing an eight to lose. Then came a nine to win. Fogle cursed to himself. The next turn revealed the same two cards only in the opposite order. Damn. Now only nine cards remained, all of them singles. Fogle shook his head and stared at the casekeeper to make sure he hadn't miscounted. He hadn't. When he turned back to the layout the gambler was moving his hand away from his bet. Fogle's own hand trembled as he pulled away the top card. His eyes widened and he slapped the table at the sight of a losing jack. Both hands instinctively reached out to drag the pot in as a mother would pull a child to her bosom. But his fingers stopped just inches shy of their target. A copper token rested atop each stack. Had the gambler placed a copper there before the turn? Fogle's eyes blinked twice. Was he mistaken? He now saw clearly what he had missed while studying the casekeeper. The gambler had coppered his bets, played the queen and jack to lose, which they had.

"Two thousand dollars," the gambler declared softly.

"Benson," Fogle said, "did he copper them before the turn?"

"You're damn right I did," Holliday interjected. "Now pay up. You're not playing with a damn schoolboy so don't try to sucker me." Holliday stared at Benson, who was slow to respond.

"Well, Benson, did he?"

"Yes," Benson nodded. "I warned you he was lucky."

"Shut up," Fogle ordered as he emptied the check tray of money. Lacking some nine hundred dollars to square his loss, Fogle shoved chips and money across the layout toward Holliday's stack. "There's eleven hundred. That clears out my check tray."

"Where's the rest?" Holliday demanded, his hands counting Fogle's settlement against being shorted further.

"When the deal's over, you'll get all that's yours," Fogle answered. "You gonna let that ride the next turn?"

"All of it, plus the nine hundred you still owe me," Holliday replied. "Four thousand total on this turn. The money'll stay where it is, less the coppers." Holliday removed the tokens.

Fogle stared at the casekeeper, his nerves taut, the plinky piano music drifting from downstairs grating on his nerves. Another win by this emaciated gambler would break him. And if that weren't enough, the whores were beginning to climb the stairs and test his rules again. A queen, nine, eight, seven, and four were the final five cards, yet this gambler left his bet between the queen and jack. Damn insulting, Fogle thought. With no jacks remaining, the gambler was actually betting on the queen alone, yet he had not pushed his bet atop the black lady on the layout. Fogle felt his neck burning at the contemptuous gesture.

"We gonna play?" The thin man pushed him.

Fogle slapped the dealing box and pulled away the top card, revealing a losing seven, then a winning eight, resulting in no action on that turn. Three cards remained hidden — a queen, nine, and four. Fogle felt his jaw tighten and the blood pulse from his neck to his temples. He knew the odds, four to one if the gambler named the order of the final three cards. If the gambler succeeded, Fogle had lost the Bee Hive. Six possible combinations meant the odds lay with the dealer, but Fogle's intuition suggested odds no longer mattered with this foe.

The gambler gulped a mouthful of bourbon, then wiped his lips on the back of his hand. "Odds four to one on the turn?"

Fogle nodded.

"I'm going the entire four thousand," Holliday said. "Four, queen, nine."

Fogle swallowed hard, but his throat was dry and he almost gagged. He slid his hand over the dealing box, delaying the pull of a card and spotting Big Nose Kate making her way to the table. Damn, his luck was running bad now.

With his free hand, Fogle wiped the sweat from his forehead. A four, queen, and nine hid beneath the top card, he just hoped not in that order.

Sliding the top card out of the box, Fogle felt his breath hang in his throat. It was a four. If the next were a queen, he'd lose the Bee Hive. Fogle looked across at Holliday and despised the man for his imperturbable face, his contemptuous manner, his damnable luck.

Fogle pulled away the four and a queen surfaced. The gambler had called the turn. All was lost. The Bee Hive was under new ownership.

He stared at the queen with glazed eyes, then slid it out of the dealing box. As should be, a nine came up hock.

"Sixteen thousand dollars," Holliday smiled coldly.

Fogle nodded at the vagaries of luck, then turned the dealing box on its side, a gesture akin to a defeated general surrendering his sword to the victor. "I'll bring what money I have. There's not sixteen thousand."

"Plus the nine hundred you already owe me."

"There's not sixteen nine, either."

"The saloon will make up the difference," Holliday grinned.

"You Chancey's man?" Fogle questioned.

Holliday nodded.

"I figured as much, but knowing that didn't change my luck," Fogle replied, watching Big Nose Kate move up to the faro table. "Kate, peddle your ass downstairs, not up here."

"Way I figure it," Kate strode forward, her hands on her wide hips, "you don't own the Bee Hive now so I don't take your orders no more." She winked as she walked up behind Holliday. "I want to be on good acquaintance with the new proprietor of the Bee Hive," she said, placing her hand on Holliday's shoulder.

The gambler twisted instantly toward her, his hand reaching for the gun under his left shoulder, then relaxing.

Her hand fell away. "Jumpy one, isn't he boys?" she said.

"A lady keeps her hands to herself," Holliday scolded.

"Mister, you and me aren't gonna fool anyone here into believing you're a gentleman, much less me a lady. All I care about is you're the new owner of the Bee Hive, the way I see it," Kate said, baring her teeth to Fogle like a wolf moving in for a kill. "I want to get to know you better."

She touched his shoulder again and ran her hand down the front of his shirt.

Disgusted, Fogle backed away from the table. "I'll be back to settle up."

"If you can," Holliday answered, his words salt in Fogle's open wound. Holliday shoved Kate's hand from his chest.

"By damn, I'll settle one way or the other," Fogle said, turning his back on Holliday and Kate, then walking slowly down the stairs. The music still played downstairs, but it lacked jauntiness to Fogle's ears. Tomorrow, Fogle thought, he might be tending bar, if someone would hire him.

At the foot of the stairs, Fogle, lost in his thoughts, bumped into a perfumed woman. "Watch it, you whore," he called as he glanced into the soft gray eyes of Lottie Deno. He shook his head, but could not rid the flush from his face. "I'm sorry, Lottie, I didn't expect you, this being Sunday."

"Had an unsettling experience on my afternoon ride, Mike. Found a man hanging from a pecan tree. Thought I'd come in and play a little to ease my mind." "What's troubling you?"

"I've lost the Bee Hive."

"Oh, no."

"Chancey put up a lucky one to make a run for it. Never seen luck run that deep except at your table."

"You can't cover the losses?"

"Sixteen thousand dollars."

Lottie whistled. "How can I help?"

Holliday swigged on the bottle of bourbon to cut the edginess tingling through his body. The tubercular pains had subsided and now he drank out of impatience with Fogle and the whore hovering over his shoulder. As he put the bottle on the table, Kate grabbed it and poured a manly mouthful into herself.

"Damn, woman, you don't drink with me unless you're invited," Holliday said, jerking the bottle from her lips and spilling some of the amber liquid across her dress.

"My favorite perfume," she said, rubbing the wetness from her dress onto her fingers and daintily transferring it behind her ears.

"You don't drink with me unless you're invited," Holliday repeated.

"Well, well," Kate mocked. "Don't think you can screw me without an invitation." She primped her hair and walked around to Holliday's other side.

"Nobody's talking screwing, woman. I want no part of you."

"Sure you do," she answered, licking her bourboned lips. "I won't even charge you."

"I can find better free."

Kate laughed. "But will it have you?" She turned and walked away, the scarlet hem of her dress sweeping a clean trail through the sawdust on the floor.

Holliday reached across the table for the dealing box, but Benson made a tentative gesture to stop him, then held back.

"Customers usually don't fool with our dealing boxes," Benson said uneasily, "but I guess you're more than a customer now."

Curious about Benson's concern for the box, Holliday wondered if it were rigged. Crooked dealing boxes were easy to come by if you had the money. Holliday remembered ordering one out of San Francisco, but after killing the Fort Richardson soldier, he had had to leave Jacksboro before it had arrived. Holliday pushed the box back and forth on the felt-covered table. With some rigged boxes such a movement would release a spring allowing two cards instead of one to slide out of the slot. On other rigged boxes, one of the pins holding the metal frame together was a dummy. By pushing the tiny rivet, the slot would widen enough for two cards. Without success, Holliday tried each tiny rivet. Maybe the box was honest after all.

66

A crooked box was operated in conjunction with rigged cards. Unless a cold deck was used after a blind shuffle and blind cut, the cards had to be altered in some manner, to give the dealer an edge. Holliday reached for the cards, then inspected them by sight and touch. Some gamblers punched tiny holes in the cards to see what followed the top card. Others roughed the backs and the fronts of selected "tell" cards so their perceptive fingers could read where the next card was high or low, for instance. The game was only as honest as the dealers it attracted, and the gambling fraternity was seldom honored for its integrity. Holliday shuffled the cards from hand to hand, examining them closely, his soft fingers detecting nothing. Damned if he hadn't stumbled into an honest faro game, Holliday thought. Best, though, to always assume and play otherwise.

Waiting for Fogle to return, Holliday dealt out a game of solitaire, turning over to begin with the three of hearts, a card he hated to see. It supposedly indicated sorrow or poverty arising from indiscretion. Holliday thought himself no more superstitious than any other gambler, but still the three bothered him. He quickly played the game, losing handily. At least no money was riding on the game, Holliday thought.

As he dealt himself another game, he heard a commotion of several men coming up the stairs, Fogle's voice among them. Holliday tossed the cards onto the table, his hand slipping to his belt, nearer his sidearm. Holliday tensed as Fogle marched opposite him, throwing a money bag on the faro layout.

"There sixteen thousand there?"

"I'm six and a half shy."

Holliday's mustache lifted atop a smug smile. "Then the Bee Hive ought to make up the difference."

"If I don't get a chance to win it back."

"Brash talk for someone that can't match his losses."

"I've found someone to cover my losses. You'll get full pay. Are you a sporting man, or should I pass the word you and Chancey don't give a man a chance to recoup his losses? Won't be none too good for your reputation or Chancey's business."

"One time through the deck, no more," Holliday offered.

"Agreed. No limit?"

"I'll return the favor."

"Someone else is playing for me," Fogle stated.

"Benson wasn't any luckier than you."

"Not Benson, someone else."

"Seems you want to be nursemaided, if you can't call your own turn."

"Agreed or not?" Fogle demanded.

"Okay, dammit, let's get on with it."

Fogle smiled broadly for a man with sour luck. "Lottie," he called.

Holliday could feel the heat rising in his face. He had wanted to find her, wanted her badly, but not like this, not across the card table. He watched the stairs and saw her appear, step by step from under the broad brim of a yellow hat covering her auburn curls. Her face was as soft as he remembered. Damn Lottie. She was beautiful. As she stepped full before him and walked across the floor, the hem of her pale yellow dress swept away the trail made by Kate's dress. He felt her gray eyes sweep across him and he hoped for some glimmer of pleasure, but there was none. Several men tipped their hats as she passed, but she ignored everyone until she reached Fogle. To him she extended her delicate hand and Fogle bent to kiss it. She never missed a trick, Holliday thought, his blood boiling with envy. She rattled an opponent any way she could. Before Holliday, she stopped with a modest curtsy.

"John Henry Holliday," she said softly. "How long's it been since Jacksboro? Eighteen months? Two years?"

"Been a long time, Lottie, too long," he said, removing his hat.

"It's never too long, John Henry. Not among thieves."

"But among admirers, yes."

"No, John Henry, not even among admirers."

"Guess there's no sense in discussing old times, huh?"

Lottie nodded, a curl falling across her forehead.

"I suppose you're here to play for the former proprietor of the Bee Hive."

She nodded again.

"You got enough to cover sixteen thousand?"

"Not with me, but I can cover it. My word's good. You know that."

68

"I do," Holliday said as he shuffled the cards from hand to hand several times. He inserted them in the box as he looked at the circle of men gathered around. A nine showed as the soda card.

"Place your bets, Lottie, unless you've changed your mind."

"I owe it to Mike for keeping me on at the Bee Hive."

Holliday laughed. "Hell, we all know he owes more to you for the crowd you bring in." Holliday glanced at Fogle, who nodded slightly at the one thing both men agreed on.

"Eight thousand," Lottie said, "on the low cards." She picked up a copper token and placed it behind the row of low cards. "That'll do for my money. I'm betting to win."

Holliday thumbed the nine soda card from the dealing box and stared at a naked jack, the loser. Slowly, he pulled the jack from the box and grimaced at the sight — the tray of hearts. He pitched Fogle's unopened money bag to Lottie. "The money should be there, if your man's honest."

"He's more honest than most," Lottie answered, leaving the sack where Holliday tossed it. "I'm playing the low cards to lose."

As Holliday pulled the winning three of hearts out of the way, the crowd cheered. A six of clubs had taken its place. Lottie had won. Holliday's only chance to hang on now was a split, but the next card turned up a ten. The Bee Hive had changed hands again. Holliday turned the faro box on its side. "How do you do it, Lottie?" he asked.

"I work at it."

"Damn, you must," Holliday answered, turning away from her and toward the stairs.

Holliday heard Fogle's laughter following him down the stairs. "God bless Lottie's Luck," Fogle kept yelling.

SIX

At the poker table beneath the stuffed head of a mottled long-horn, one horn twisted wickedly back around toward its eyes, sat Holliday, toying with a tin plate of salt pork, red beans too salty, and dark bread too stale. The food's saltiness clung in his mouth like the bitterness of last night's loss to Lottie. The thought of her stirred in him an emptiness he could not fill, a pain he could not drown even with a barrel of bourbon. Failing to hold the Bee Hive was Chancey's loss, Lottie his.

Since killing the Fort Richardson soldier and escaping Jacksboro, Holliday, longing to find her, had wondered if she shared his desires. Many times he had imagined finding her, perhaps in a hotel lobby, maybe on the street or during one of the Sunday excursions she relished so. Always she had welcomed him with a smile that overflowed into the depths of her gray eyes. But last night, her shallow smile never reached her eyes. Herding a bite of beans onto this fork, Holliday wished cards and money had not passed between them. For a life with her, Holliday would renounce gambling for dentistry. Damned if it wasn't foolish, this schoolboy fixation on her, but damned if he could shake it. No doubt he could manipulate luck, but never this.

Listlessly, Holliday jabbed a piece of salt pork and sopped up a puddle of bean juice with a hunk of bread. Glancing up from his plate, he scanned the bored room calmed by the midafternoon doldrums, the dozen customers as silent at their tables as the mounted longhorns on the wall. A pair of buffalo hunters shot pool nearby, but they played without talking. A lethargic, barrel-shaped bartender squeezed between the mostly vacant tables as he followed a broom around the floor. Behind the counter a thinner barkeep emptied and polished the Cattle Exchange's spittoons, stopping occasionally to dump the fetid black liquid into a battered bucket or to pour another round of liquor for the lone patron belly up to the bar. Holliday wondered if Chancey cut his house whiskey with those chaw fixings in the dented bucket. He shuddered and mopped up a final bite that turned sour in his mouth when the saloon doors swung inward with Ed Bailey behind them.

"Howdy, Ed," said a pair of men leaning back in their chairs near the door.

"Afternoon, boys," Bailey answered, then helloed the barkeeper dancing with the broom and the one riding herd over the spittoons. Bailey approached the counter, taking off his bowler with both hands and aiming for the opposite wall. "Free drink if I make it," he called to the bartender wrist deep in a spittoon, "I buy a round if I don't." As the bartender grunted approval, Bailey flung his hat at the nearest mounted longhorn. The dust-discolored bowler twirled twice around the horn's point, almost hanging on, then falling away, the bartender with the broom catching it before it littered the floor.

"Well, gentlemen," Bailey bellowed, "looks like I buy drinks around." The patrons nodded agreeably as Bailey twisted his kettle belly in a full sweep around the room and glanced from face to face. "Pleasure to buy my friends a . . .," he started, but stopped, his eyes burning toward Holliday.

Holliday stared back.

". . . a good drink," Bailey continued, "including you in the back." He nodded at Holliday.

Holding up his bottle of Monarch bourbon, Holliday shrugged. "I'll stick to my own," he said, impassively. "It's better than the cheap stuff you'd buy." Holliday watched Bailey's fleshy cheeks redden and his eyes bulge with more hatred.

"You should try my liquor before you insult it, mister." Bailey accepted his bowler from the rotund sweeper.

"Way you play poker," Holliday answered, "I doubt you can afford anything but the bucket of spittoon juice."

Bailey clenched his fists, turned to the counter, and slammed them on the bar. "The best in the house." The saloon's patrons cheered. "On me." His voice quivered with rage. Turning back to Holliday, Bailey leaned an elbow on the bar, his tight coat puckering between buttons until he undid them and freed his abundant stomach. Cautiously, his hand inched inside his coat and just as slowly reappeared with the silver inlaid pipe in his fingers. "From what I hear, John, Lottie Deno stripped you of your winnings last night in five turns of the cards."

"Three" he corrected, "and she didn't use a shiny pipe."

Bailey, straightening from the bar into a more defiant stance, pointed the pipe stem at Holliday. "You misread me," he answered. "One day I'll teach you a few things about cards."

"You couldn't teach shit to stink." His words sliced through the humorless air like the clink of unsheathed swords.

"One day, John, one day," Bailey replied, shaking the cold pipe at Holliday.

"What's wrong with today?" With catlike quickness Holliday stood, his hand by his waist, his fingers curled to fit the ivory grip of his Colt, his every muscle tensed with the exhilarating expectation of conflict. Bailey drew his pipe back to his chest with startled suddenness and the two pool players, quitting their game, backed away from Holliday. In the rounds of Bailey's eyes Holliday could see a thread of fear unraveling. "One day, what, Bailey?" Holliday challenged.

His eyes widening above fleshy cheeks that quivered like spilled jelly, Bailey swiveled around on his heels and stared blankly into the backbar mirror at Holliday. "Drinks around the house," Bailey repeated, his voice breaking into heavy panting. "The good stuff."

"Bailey," Holliday fairly spit out the name, "don't load your mouth with more than you've guts to back up." Bailey's mirrored eyes averted Holliday's, so Holliday slid back into his chair, disappointed there would be no fight.

The bartender quit his spittoons long enough to offer a jigger of Monarch bourbon to everyone but Holliday. Bailey downed several jiggers, one after the other, then, his courage recovered, asked the bartender for a deck of cards and led three customers to a table in the corner opposite Holliday's perch.

The two pool players chalked their cue sticks and picked up their game. Holliday watched Bailey open the fresh deck, fire up his pipe, and draw deeply on his larcenous companion until his face was enveloped in a veil of smoke. Damn brazen of him to still use the pipe, Holliday thought.

Gradually, the saloon filled. The piano player came in and his music seemed to draw customers like flies to a gut wagon. A few prostitutes straggled in to cut the horny ones from the herd, and the cadre of drinking customers grew with those desiring to cut the dust from their throat or the monotony from their day. With the company of his bottle, Holliday waited at his table for Chancey and when his companion was drained he motioned for the bartender to bring him another bottle of bourbon.

Midway through the second bottle, Holliday saw Chancey scurrying through the swinging doors, a scowl on his face. The prostitute called Big Nose Kate was on his tail. Holliday groaned. Chancey marched brusquely through the room, Kate jabbering at him every step of the way. The pool players stepped aside as Chancey strode to his office door, jerked a thong of keys from his britches pocket, and fumbled for a moment against the lock. "Damnation, woman," he blurted out, "give my ears a break."

"Then let me work your place." Her voice screeched like chalk on slate.

"Okay, dammit, okay," he said, shoving the door open and quickly following it inside.

Kate trailed him as close as his shadow, then retreated back out, her ungainly step quickened by a sound shove.

"Don't damage the goods," she screamed with the compassion of a wounded mountain lion. As customers twisted their heads to watch, Kate nonchalantly smoothed a ruffle on her black blouse and dusted an unseen speck from her matching skirt. After fingering the kinks of her mussed brown curls when only a brush could help, she surveyed the room. "Kate's here and ready for business," she called, then swaggered forward.

Holliday glanced away, pulling his hat lower over his head, but too late. She had seen him. He could tell by the broad, toothy grin which chilled him. Marching with big, manly steps, Kate was beside him before Holliday could move.

"Well, well," she said, "remember me?"

"How could I forget?"

"My looks, they do that to men."

"Not your looks, your damn manners."

"Well hell, fellow, my manners are no worse than your gambling, as I recall things last night."

"My luck was running right well until you showed up."

"Don't blame me," Kate said, sucking in a deep breath, then cutting loose on him. "Seems like another woman changed your luck. Your eyes as big as twin moons the way you were looking at her. And it wasn't the big pot you were gaping at, but them tits of hers. But don't think you or anybody else is gonna get a piece of Lottie Deno. You may fondle her cards, but by god that's all of hers you'll ever touch." With her foot, Kate shoved a chair closer to Holliday, brushing her skirt from around her full hips as she plopped down beside him.

Holliday retreated to his bottle.

"Anyway," she continued, "I'm not here to discuss Lottie or to accept your compliments on my manners. I'm due an apology!"

Holliday stared blankly across the room at Bailey's table.

"I said you owe me an apology." She smoothed more wrinkles from her skirt, pulling the hem to her knee, as she waited for a response. She smiled broadly at his indifference. "Sometimes, mister, I can be rather loud and it don't embarrass me to call attention to myself. It's how I make my living, if you know what I mean. Are you gonna apologize or not?"

"Damn," Holliday grumbled, "why in hell should I apologize?"

"You got me run off from the Bee Hive."

"Why you female fool, just how in the name of hell did I manage that?"

Kate cleared her throat and straightened her back like a schoolgirl called upon to recite in class. "It looked to me you were the new owner of the Bee Hive," she started. "Mike Fogle didn't like me sassing him when I was ordered back downstairs. Of course, he wasn't the owner when I got sassy with him, but by the time Lottie finished whipping your butt, he was back in charge. Way I see it, if you hadn't screwed up, I'd still have roaming rights in the busiest saloon in Griffin."

"More curves in your thinking than in a ball of rattlesnakes, and probably as much venom." Rubbing his chin as he spoke, Holliday felt his cheek twitch and he could not stop the grin that pried at his lips. Kate's pose lost its stiffness like a corpse coming back to life and Holliday, for the first time, took in her features. She had weathered the storms of many men's lusts well. In her silence reposed a softness unusual among women in her trade. When she was quiet, her doelike brown eyes hid behind the flutter of her long lashes; her patrician nose, slightly hooked, stood guard over full, inviting lips; her rouged cheeks melted into a defiant chin; and her brown hair, though mussed, hung soft and shiny around her head like an expensive curtain. But when she spoke, the red lips uncaged a biting tongue, the eyes flared with sparks, her nose drew deep masculine breaths, and her hair seemed like a low flame over the glowing coals of a bad disposition. Whether speaking or quiet, she could appeal to men with her breasts pressing tight against her blouse, her midriff funneling in on a narrow waist, the waist blossoming into broad hips that swayed invitingly when she walked.

"You'll be working the Cattle Exchange now?" he asked as he pushed his empty plate and bottle toward the middle of the table.

She nodded. "He doesn't do the land office business like the Bee Hive, but there's enough pickings here to keep me busy." Kate leaned toward the table, resting her forearms on the worn felt, her hand tentatively reaching for his. When he did not retreat, she clasped it gently. "My offer last night still stands, if you ever get the itch."

"One screw, no charge, the best I recollect." He pursed his lips, as if mulling the offer, then withdrew his hand from hers.

"You know how, don't you?" She grinned. "If you need some practice, I'll find you a low stump and a sick cow nearby."

Holliday leaned back in his chair, the front two legs rising off the floor, and rocked leisurely, scratching his mustache and tugging at the corners. "What you lack in manners you make up for in gall, woman."

75

"Kate's the name, Big Nose Kate," she answered, sparks flaring anew in her eyes. "And what I lack in manners I make up in a lot of ways. You've just got to let me show you."

"Lot of things I may need to be shown, but that's not one of them." Holliday stretched his arms, then massaged a leg cramp.

"Let me rub it for you." She reached for him.

"Damn, woman . . . Kate . . . whatever the hell your name is. What's it take to get through that thick skull?"

"Way to get to me isn't through my skull."

"I'll be damned. You want to do something for me, I've got something you can do," Holliday said as he eased his chair down.

"Name it."

Reaching toward the table, he pushed his half-full whiskey bottle aside, then leaned forward like a man bracing against a strong headwind. He shoved his dirty plate and empty bottle toward her. "Return that to the counter for me," he commanded, tensing for her explosion.

A cloud of disappointment fleeted across her face and left in its wake a smile, like the sunshine following a thunderstorm. Her smile surprised him. He relaxed. She was so unpredictable.

"My pleasure," she answered, arising slowly from her chair like a gentle dowager at a tea. Picking up the tin and the bottle by the neck, she suddenly spun around and sailed the plate through a crack between two customers at the bar, the tinware clattering from the bar against a newly polished spittoon.

Not that unpredictable, Holliday decided.

Kate twisted around at Holliday, striking the empty bourbon bottle on the edge of the table, shattering the glass into a hundred noisy pieces. "I'm not your goddam servant," she screamed, waving the jagged glass at Holliday's nose.

Like a trap sprung by the breaking glass, Chancey's office door flew open and he lunged into the gaming area, dropping behind the pool table and leveling the business end of a double-barreled shotgun across the room. Customers dove to the floor.

"Easy, Chancey," called the thin bartender. "No trouble. Just that hussy throwed a plate and bottle." He pointed to Kate.

Chancey glared at her, while customers picked up themselves and their conversations. "Dammit, Kate, you keep on causing trouble in my saloon and you won't have a place to peddle

76

your ass unless they'll take you on at one of the stables." Chancey broke the breech of the shotgun with a loud metallic click.

"Just an accident, Chancey," she said, the hand holding the bottle shard hidden by the hips of her widespread legs. "I dropped them."

"All the way across the room? Hell, you're not smart enough to drop anything but your drawers." A cackle of laughter spread across the room.

Holliday stood, cursing at the glass fragments that dotted his new suit like crystal insects. As he brushed them off, Kate stepped toward him, pointing a crooked finger at his nose and cutting loose with that stinger of a tongue. "His damn fault, Chancey," she called. "He's responsible for my bad luck. And for some of yours."

Holliday clenched his fists and took a half step toward her. He wondered the penalty for strangling a woman. If the jury knew Kate, Holliday suspected they'd reward him handsomely for his service to humanity.

"I'm telling you, Chancey," she said, flinging the bottle neck at Holliday's approaching boots. "He got me kicked out of the Bee Hive and now he's ordering me around like I'm his wife."

Chancey glanced at Holliday, a glint of recognition flashing across his eyes for a brief instant, then shook his head. "Kate, you're an ass. Otherwise, the rest of us wouldn't have to put up with so much crap."

A wave of laughter lapped across the saloon, but Kate turned to face the gaiety. Her back to Chancey, she bent forward and flipped her skirt up over her hips.

"Now that's an ass," she said, "in case you didn't know." The men laughed louder, a couple clapping. As Kate straightened and herded her skirt into place, she whispered at Holliday. "I'll still screw you any time free." Her skirt primly in place, she marched away, proper as a virgin at Sunday meeting.

Holliday missed her like a toothache. She had this way of making him nervous as a long-tailed cat in a room full of rockers. He picked up his bottle, spotting the flush of amusement in Bailey's face, and followed Chancey into his office. The room was small and windowless. On a rolltop desk to one side, a single lamp with low flame pushed a ball of light against the dimness.

Chancey laid the shotgun atop the desk's clutter and adjusted the lamp for a higher flame. "Close the door," he ordered Holliday.

The thick plank door shut with the lock's metallic firmness and in the growing light Holliday noticed a peephole. He turned and took in the room, observing first the strongbox bolted to the floor by the desk and chair, then numerous cases of liquor stacked along the opposite wall, three barrels of beer along the back wall, three rawhide-bottomed chairs, and two outdated calendars still tacked to the wall.

Chancey settled into his chair and propped his feet atop the desk corner. "I ought to shoot you for taking up with Kate."

"Seems she's taken up with me," Holliday answered. "I didn't have much say in the matter."

"You never will with her, John Holliday. I don't know what she wants, but you best let her have it or she'll pester you from now until hell freezes over."

Holliday wanted to forget about Kate. "I've got business with you, best we get on with it before someone thinks we're big friends." Holliday dug into his coat pocket and pulled out a wad of bills, tossing the roll into Chancey's lap. "There's your money, fattened a little by my early luck at Fogle's table."

"Yes, sir, John Holliday, I came close to owning the Bee Hive." Chancey thumbed through the bills for a total. "A month of Sundays and Lottie Deno wouldn't show her pretty face inside a saloon. Then some damn peckerwood gets his neck stretched when my luck's running good and she's there in time to change it. There's something to Lottie's Luck. But I'll make another run at it one day," Chancey added, as he finished counting the money. "I like your honesty in returning my stake."

"I like your patience in waiting for me."

"I had your hotel watched," Chancey said, digging for his cigarette fixings. "Caution helps my patience."

Holliday nodded. "Good day," he said and turned to leave.

"Wait a minute," Chancey called. Standing, he leaned over the lamp chimney until his cigarette took to flame. "Don't you want a table at the Cattle Exchange?"

"The deal was if I won the Bee Hive. You still don't have it," Holliday answered.

"But I didn't lose this, either," Chancey said, holding up

the stack of bills in his paw of a hand. He kneeled at the end of the desk by the strongbox and pulled a rawhide thong rattling with keys from his britches pocket. Working one of the keys into the iron, heart-shaped padlock, he popped the lock and lifted the heavy lid far enough to admit the bills.

Chancey dropped the iron lid with a clang and snapped the padlock back in place, giving an extra tug. He unfolded his big frame and stood erect, his black eyes drilling right into Holliday. "After the last two nights, word's gotten around you're a gambler. You won't be surprising anyone now," Chancey began. "I need a faro dealer. Lottie'd be my preference, but you'll do. I'll give you seventeen percent of your winnings. That's a fair proposition, more than I pay anyone else."

Holliday stroked his mustache. "Good money, but working in the same saloon with Bailey don't appeal to me. I'd spend as much time looking out for him as I would for your money. That'd be unhealthy for both of us."

Chancey scratched his head, drew hard on his cigarette, then exhaled a heavy ribbon of smoke. "Bailey's got a lot of friends, local men that give me a steady business between cattle drovers and buffalo hunters. Can't say I want to get rid of him. Had we hung on to the Bee Hive last night, I'd a had two saloons to keep you apart. I don't favor Bailey much, too loud, too careless sometimes, but he draws business. I more than make up in drinks what he loses at poker."

"There are other saloons, by my count," Holliday answered. "I'll make out."

"I know you will, that's why I want you here."

"I'll remember that, but I've got money to last a while."

Chancey grinned. "If you work another saloon, see if that damned Kate will honor it, instead of the Cattle Exchange, with her charms."

Holliday shuddered and walked out the door. He scanned the room quickly, looking for Kate, but she had disappeared. He breathed easier. Skirting the pool table, Holliday eyed Bailey's table, the reflecting pipe prominent upon it as Bailey dealt. He felt a cough rising in his chest and took a quick swallow from the bourbon bottle he still carried. Drawing about as much air as whiskey, Holliday stopped at the bar, bought another bottle, enough to last the night, then emerged into the street.

The sun was burning low in the west, like a candle about to die, and the street dozed in the suppertime quiet. He marched down Griffin Avenue toward the Clear Fork and stopped to lean against the false-fronted wall of Shifflet's Tannery. Resting there, he could smell the bittersweet odor of unpleasant chemicals mingling with the aroma of raw and finished leather. He stared across the street at the adobe front of the Bee Hive, reposing before another frenetic night.

The biggest and gaudiest saloon in Griffin, the Bee Hive stood two stories high, the tallest structure between Fort Worth and El Paso. On the Bee Hive's plastered and whitewashed front was the most famous sign on the Texas frontier. Painted in natural colors on that wall, two prominent hives trailed streams of bees flitting among the honeysuckle branches in bloom and lettered in the fresco was the crude poetry of a frontier muse:

> Within this hive we are all alive,
> Good whiskey makes us funny,
> And if you are dry, step in and try
> The flavor of our honey.

As the long shadows merged between buildings and distant stacks of buffalo hides, Holliday waited, swigging on his bottle, swatting at the buzzing flies. He lost track of time before he caught a glimpse of Lottie approaching the Bee Hive. She carried a small carpetbag, empty now, but by night's end it would hold her winnings, a couple hundred dollars or more. He admired the cut of her frame as he pulled his pocket watch from his vest and held it close to his eyes. Lottie was a beautiful creature, nonetheless, one of habit. She would begin her turn at the table each night at the same time. It was eight o'clock. Holliday turned and walked toward the Planters House, wishing she were beside him, her arm in his.

Damned if he wasn't a noisy lover, Kate thought. Lying atop her he moaned and grunted like a rooting hog and he smelled just as bad. Buffalo skinners generally stank like they had bathed in a cesspool and this one, lunging wildly, noisily between her legs, was certainly a credit to his profession. Kate rubbed his chapped back and forced perfunctory moans, a professional courtesy. But he kept snorting and grunting and ughing and gasping and groaning and whooping and farting. Kate shuddered and then cried out as she struggled to disguise the guffaw building within her. Kate wondered if her paying lover had taken his lessons from copulating buffaloes. The thought tickled her and she laughed, softly at first, then almost maniacally, as the spent buffalo skinner collapsed around her in a sweaty, sticky embrace. He grabbed her head and turned it to kiss her. Running his fingers through her hair, he pressed his rough lips against hers. Kate returned his lust with the passion of a corpse. His breath smelled of cheap liquor and his mouth of strong chewing tobacco. Kissing a buffalo's behind couldn't be much worse, Kate decided, then sniggered, wrenching her lips loose from his.

"Let me breathe, fellow, let me breathe," she gasped for air, disguising the laughs, each growing harder and harder to control. Finally, with too much to restrain, she cackled out in his ear.

"Funny is it?" he scowled.

Kate unwrapped her arms from around his back and spread them until they drooped over the head of the cornhusk mattress and her breasts were thrust even tighter against the man's scaly chest. "You must've enjoyed me, 'cause you made more noise than a pack of dogs mooning over a caged bitch in heat."

"You're the bitch. You weren't worth what you cost."

"You haven't paid me yet. Next time, though, do me a favor and sit in the damn creek for a week so you don't smell like a buffalo's butt. Hard enough to keep my sheets clean without a walking turd rubbing off on them."

The buffalo skinner pushed away from her, as if he were picking himself up from a dung heap, and roughly tweaked her upthrust breast. "Won't be a next time with you."

"No matter, just do a favor to whatever girl you screw and use something other than buffalo innards for tonic water."

Her customer stood bedside in the darkness, groping for his clothes. "My pants? Where'd you throw them?"

"Hell, I don't know and when I took 'em off you didn't care what in tarnation I did with them. You were too anxious to get out of them and into me."

"Light a lamp, dammit."

"Lamp? Fellow, you don't need a lamp. Crawl around and sniff 'em out. A dead hound could smell them at half a mile."

The skinner kicked around the floor for a moment. "Dammit, I can't find them. Light the lamp."

"Then your nose is broke. Maybe the pants rats carried them off."

"I don't have lice, bitch."

"Why not, can't they stand the stink?"

"You gonna light the lamp?"

"You need it, you light it."

The hunter eased along the bed to the wall and the small table within reach of Kate's pillow. He fumbled for a tin of matches, knocking over the lamp's dome. It clattered on the table.

"You break my lamp, you're gonna owe me more than for one screw."

"Shit, woman, don't you ever give a guy any peace?"

"You just got a piece."

"Oh, hell." The skinner found the match tin, opened the container lid, and spilled several matches into his hand. He pinched one between his fingers and let the rest fall with the tin to the table. Cursing indecipherably, he flicked it against the rough adobe wall. The flaring match bled sulphur fumes as the skinner lit the wick and adjusted the lamp until a jaundiced light contaminated the room.

The crib was small and dominated by a bed, Kate spread-eagled upon it. In addition to the bedside table, a washstand at the foot of the bed, an eating table and two chairs near the door, a trunk for her clothes, and a small stove were crammed into the room. A stack of newspapers littered the dirt floor by the woodbox and a dozen books were lined up on a rough shelf resting on two pegs protruding from the wall over her bed. The room functioned well for paid sex, but for little else, including ease of movement.

Finding his britches under the washstand at the end of the bed, the buffalo hunter worked them quickly up his legs. He stared at Kate, enjoying the sight of her undulating breasts and the curly triangle between her pale legs. Kate, fearing another manly rise within him, sat up and reached for the sheet at her

82

feet, then reclined, pulling it to her neck. Angered by her false modesty, the buffalo skinner spit on the hardpacked dirt floor as he buttoned his britches. He pulled his shirt over his head, wrestling his arms through the sleeves. After hitching his suspenders over his shoulders, he bent to retrieve his boots, then sat roughly on the bed, almost on Kate's leg.

"Damn, that's what the chairs are for."

The skinner ignored her, pulling worn boots over dirtied socks. He stood up, slapped at Kate's leg, and walked to the chair where he had hung his holster and hat.

"Say, fellow." Kate sat up, holding the sheet around her neck. "Aren't you forgetting something? Like my pay?"

The skinner whirled around, a grin flashing across his face. "Now it's my turn to laugh. This screw was on the house."

"No, it wasn't," she answered instantly. Kate let the sheet fall down from her neck, exposing her rounded breasts and a .35-caliber revolver in her right hand. "Don't move for your gun, fellow, or I'll plug your pecker," she ordered, holding the gun menacingly toward his crotch. "Then you'll have no cause to pay a woman for anything but sympathy. Now pay up. Three dollars like we agreed."

The buffalo skinner stood frozen, the grin exposing his tobacco-rotted teeth like dirty icicles. Kate pulled back the hammer on the revolver. Slowly, the grin disappeared like melting snow. The skinner reached cautiously for his right pants pocket. Now Kate smiled. He was going for his money. She knew it was in the right pocket because she had already stripped the roll of two bills while pulling down his pants. The skinner jerked three soiled bills from the others and stepped toward her.

"Just drop 'em on the floor and come no closer," she commanded. The skinner obliged then backed to his hat and holster. "Pick up your hat first." He obeyed. "Now with your right arm, take up your gunbelt by the buckle. If I even think you're gonna try something funny, I'll start shooting."

His eyes rolled in anger and the pink flush of liquor reddened his cheeks. Perhaps rage boiled within him, but he was not too drunk to let it overflow. The gun barrel pointing at his crotch promised more excitement than he had bargained for. Holding his hat over his privates, as if the greasy felt shield might save his manhood, he inched backward to the door, lifted the handle, and slipped out into the darkness, leaving the door ajar. Kate jumped quickly from the bed, blew out the light, and stumbled naked for the door. Sticking her hand through the doorway, she squeezed a shot into the ground to hasten his retreat. From somewhere down the creek, another gunshot answered hers, but that was all. She stepped across the opening and shoved the plank door shut, quickly barring it for the night.

It was midnight, maybe later. Though time remained to find another customer, she had amused four already, skinning two of them of a few bucks more than they thought. That was enough for the night. Through the narrow darkness she made her way to the bed and relit the table lamp. From the box of cartridges beneath the bed she replaced the wasted hull, then slipped the revolver into the holster nailed into the wall inches below the mattress top at the head of her bed. Holding the lamp close to the bed, she satisfied herself there were no lice from the skinner, then sponged herself with the cold water from the washbasin. The water sent a pimply chill over her body and muted the smell of the men who had used her. She dried quickly with the towel hanging over the bedstead and picked up the money the buffalo skinner had dropped on the floor. Like him, the bills smelled. She tossed them in the wash basin's murky water. "Wish I could do that to all of them that come in 'fore we screwed," she said to herself.

Though she had had four men in as many hours, she thought about another as she pulled the newest book from the shelf over her bed. As she tugged the sheet to her chin, she wished she were drawing the covers over the new gambler, the one they called Holliday. She knew he wouldn't smell. He dressed well and shaved daily, unlike many of her professional acquaintances. She would like to feel his soft, slender fingers caressing her body. She wanted to run her hands through his ash blond hair and look into his blue-gray eyes which glinted danger like the edge of a finely honed saber. Behind those eyes, Kate sensed a vulnerability which drew her to him like a mother to a hurt child. She fluffed the cover at her neck and opened her book, Mark Twain's latest, a volume called *Tom Sawyer*. Kate had enjoyed it so far, its story of young and innocent love, a kind she could never have, if she ever had love at all. She settled into her bed and read ponderously but steadily until her eyelids grew too heavy. After dropping the book on the floor and blowing out the light, she dreamed peacefully. In her sleep she was Becky Thatcher, and her Tom Sawyer had eyes the blue-gray of tempered steel.

SEVEN

A naked ace of spades fell boldly onto the hemstitched white linen tablecloth covering the gateleg breakfast table. In rapid order its nearest relatives of spades dropped by rank — king, queen, jack, and ten — in a perfect deal. Lottie smiled, amused by her manipulations. Every time she touched the pasteboards, she remembered her father and herself, a girl in lace and bows, nestling in his lap during the gentlemanly poker games he enjoyed with other wealthy planters. Oh, how he had loved gambling. Lottie, too, had been infected with its permutations, never thinking it would become her living. But that was before Fort Sumter led to Appomattox. Before the war, little seemed more secure than being the eldest daughter of a Kentucky legislator. After the war, little was more useless than her kinship to a dead man. Lottie had had nowhere to turn but to cards.

Except Sundays, Lottie practiced daily an hour or more on card table artifice runs, dealing seconds, palming, bottom dealing, blind shuffles, blind cuts. Like other gamblers, she practiced more than she used, but when Lady Luck needed a boost, Lottie assisted. Satisfied with the day's effort, Lottie placed the cards in a tiny drawer in the table's side. Yawning and stretching in her chintz robe and muslin nightgown, she stood and walked to an imposing walnut bureau that somehow had been squeezed through the adobe cabin's tiny door. She pulled a tortoise-shell brush from a vanity drawer and attacked a tangle of auburn hair.

Standing in a window-squared shaft of western sunlight, she stroked her glistening auburn hair and hummed a gentle ballad — her father's favorite — about love gone awry. Outside, the mockingbird she fed each day took up its grating cry as a pack of taunting school kids passed on their way home from class on Government Hill. Such a beautiful creature, the mockingbird, to squawk such horrid music, she thought. As she acknowledged her fine looks in the bureau mirror, she knew the song of her own life — at least since the war — was no prettier.

Finishing her hair, she opened the bottom bureau drawer and extracted a small maroon carpetbag, placing it on the adjacent bed. Sitting on the mattress and unhooking the latch, she freed a revolver, then dumped out the carpetbag's remaining contents, last night's winnings scattering upon the quilted cover. As she always practiced cards before combing her hair, so too she always slept before counting the previous evening's take. Perhaps it was superstition, but impatience bred bad luck. Wait long enough and Lady Luck would treat you kindly. Now, though, she quickly counted the money, totaling only forty-seven dollars and some assorted change. Not a good haul, even for a weeknight, but still she had come out ahead. Things would slow now with the buffalo hunters refitting for another winter season when the hides were thickest and most valuable. Most cattle outfits had already passed Fort Griffin with their trail drive profits. It would be spring before they passed again and late summer before they returned from Kansas with any money.

Gathering her money, she slipped into the back room, dark from the shuttered windows, depositing the stack of bills on the cold cookstove. A rough-hewn table with a box of groceries and a stack of dishes atop it, a washtub, and a woodbox also hid in the dimness. Standing sentry by the door was a loaded double-barreled shotgun. After checking the latches on the window shutters, Lottie bent over the woodbox and removed its kindling. The woodbox emptied, her index finger slipped knowingly into a small knot hole, lifting the false bottom. Even in the dimness she could make out the stacks of bills and coins. With her other hand, she reached atop the stove.

A loud rap at the front door startled her. She shoved the money into hiding, fitting the false bottom in place and tossing kindling over it, the wood clattering around the lip of the box. The kindling still rattled as she grabbed the double-barreled shotgun by the door and cocked both hammers, the dual triggers going deadly stiff. Slipping into the front room, she addressed the door. "Your name and business?" Her throat held her breath.

"Jack Jacobs," answered a welcomed voice. "This a bad time, Lottie?"

Easing the hammers down on the shotgun, Lottie released her breath. "No, Jack, just a moment." She raced to the bed, threw the revolver in the carpetbag, then shoved it and the shotgun under the bed. She smoothed the slight ruffle in the quilted spread, glancing as she did in the mirror. Retrieving her brush, she ran it through her hair a couple times, pinched her cheeks to give them color, and retied her loose robe to cover her nightgown. She unbarred and unlatched the door, swinging it open.

Jack Jacobs stood before her, a hat in one hand, a basket of pecans in the other. "I came to return your basket."

Lottie smiled, giving a toss of her head, her auburn hair rippling with pleasure. "Come in, Jack, won't you? But forgive my appearance."

Shuffling his feet, Jacobs cast his blue eyes downward. "You look fine, Lottie, just fine." Jacobs was tall and lean without an ounce of nonsense on his frame. He wore working clothes — denim pants and flannel shirt, old but clean — without shame for he had frayed the cuffs and frazzled the knees from honest labor. When he smiled, his grin came narrow under a broad nose, but his eyes danced under arched eyebrows. By the set of his jaw and the challenge in his eyes, he feared no man and respected all women, though around the young and pretty ones he might bite his lower lip.

"Come on in, Jack, and quit biting your lip. It's always a pleasure to have a gentleman visit me."

His tanned face colored, gratifying Lottie that she could still make a decent man blush. Jacobs extended the basket awkwardly. As Lottie's hand touched his on the basket handle, her robe parted, exposing a sliver of gown. His gaze passed by without lingering there and stared beyond her.

As he stepped inside, Lottie carried the basket to the back room. "You shouldn't have filled the basket."

Shifting his hat from hand to hand, Jacobs took in the precise neatness of the room. A walnut bedstead, bureau with mirror, and dress cabinet spoke well of Lottie's gambling success. An eight-day clock in an enameled case with gilt designs ticked its displeasure at sharing the bureau top with a lamp. At the end of the bed she shared with no one reposed a huge traveling trunk on a rag carpet that covered most of the wooden floor. The quilted bed cover was as free of wrinkles as the sky and so, too, the linen cloth on the gateleg table. Two walnut chairs by the table, a store-bought cane-bottom rocker and small divan offered more seats than Lottie ever had visitors. For a moment the heavy silence was broken only by the irksome clock.

"I'd offer you some coffee, but my stove is cold and it would be a while," Lottie said, emerging from the back room.

Jacobs waved her apology away with his hat. "No matter, Lottie."

She motioned to the divan and he settled down on its edge, dropping his hat at his side and leaning toward her. Lottie sat in the rocker opposite him. "Thank you for returning the basket, filled with pecans at that. I'm not sure, though, that Rachel has any appetite for pecans yet."

Jacobs rubbed his calloused hands together. "Shame she had to see that," he answered, biting his lip after he spoke. "You, too, for that matter, Lottie." His face flushed again.

His embarrassment was contagious. "I understand what you mean, Jack," she reassured. "I've seen unpleasantries before. It wasn't a pretty sight, but it hasn't haunted me. Did the sheriff know who he was?"

"The sheriff never saw him. I buried him with a borrowed shovel and without a prayer. I let the sheriff know, but he'd rather polish his badge than find the killers. I suspect Sheriff Vernon Trickus knew more about the lynching than he let on. Hell, Trickus . . ." Jacobs looked up full into Lottie's eyes, "Pardon my language, Lottie."

"I've heard worse."

"But you shouldn't in your own home."

"Your apology's accepted, though unnecessary. Now go on."

"Sheriff Trickus may be a member of the vigilance committee, maybe not. Several ranchers and merchants around Griffin aren't above stretching a neck to civilize Shackelford County."

"This is a hard country, Jack, but it'll change. My likes won't be around then, but yours will and things'll settle down."

Jacobs appeared lost in a tangle of his own thoughts and Lottie, sharing in his discomfort, shifted in the rocker. He spoke. "Your kind?" He bit his lip. "Lottie, a lot of men around here would favor your kind for a wife."

Lottie felt a blushing heat in her cheeks and stood. "My kind?" she said, walking to the unshuttered west window. "My kind is no different from the girls selling themselves in the back of the saloons or in their cribs. I just take men's money by a different method." She stared out the window and spotted her mockingbird hopping through the grass, pecking at insects.

Jacobs cleared his throat. "Not a man in Shackelford County and maybe in all of Texas would think you that type."

"The less men know of me, the more they flock to my table. They come to see this female outcast with startling beauty, but it's an illusion, like a card trick. They don't know my past and I'd tell no one of it." Lottie, smiling softly, turned to Jacobs. "Except maybe you." She watched him bite his lip. "At San Angelo," she laughed, "they called me 'Mystic Maude' when I dealt faro there. Now Maude's an ugly name . . ."

Jacobs nodded. "It's several steps down from Lottie, or even Charlotte, I'd guess. But here they call you 'Lotta Dinero.' "

Puzzled, Lottie shrugged.

"It's Spanish. Means lots of money."

She giggled.

"Don't know that it's that funny, Lottie. Seems a lot of men, men I'd trust with my life about as far as I could throw my horse, have been noticing that you tote away more money than you lose. Word's gotten around you were covering Fogle's losses Sunday against Chancey's man. Some men might be tempted to look around your place."

Lottie stepped to the rocking chair. "Nobody knows where I keep my money."

"But they know it's here somewhere. They know you don't spend much so you're bound to stash it here," he said, tapping his boot on the rag carpet, "or there in the kitchen."

Lottie glanced away from Jacobs to the woodbox. If an honest man like Jacobs could figure it out, no doubt a lot of men with fewer scruples could too. Her lips tightened.

Jacobs stood, reaching for Lottie's hand. "Everyone in the Flat knows you can take care of yourself. But one day some fool might want to test his luck at finding your stash. One of the storekeepers in town, Frank Conrad, has a new safe, the only one this side of Jacksboro, I hear. He's putting up valuables for a lot of people with less to worry about than you. Don't know that you ought to put your money there, but you ought to put something in for show."

Lottie stirred, her limp hand finally moving in his. "How's that, Jack?"

"Cut some wedges from a catalog or newspaper the size of bills, wrap them in paper, tie it up with twine to leave in the safe. Occasionally carry a bundle like that to the safe. Make people think your money's there, even if it's not."

Lottie laughed, her hand squeezing his. "You've got it all figured out, don't you, Jack?"

"Everything but what your type is," he grinned, his smiling lips unable to hide the burning curiosity in his eyes.

"Just a wayward woman in an untamed town, making my living at the expense of a lot of fool men. I wish I were your kind." Her lips lifted slightly in a smile of remorse and her eyes avoided his.

"You make it sound worse than it is, Lottie." Jacobs released her hand and bent over the divan for his hat. "But why the gambling? And what do you save the money for?"

"To bury a past and buy a future, a better life, Jack. One day, I'll get away from this, not in shame nor in pride. That day will come when what few looks I've got will survive only in a daguerreotype or two and the men will no longer notice me."

Jacobs adam's apple bobbed deep when he swallowed. "You're most becoming, Lottie." Pausing, he bit on his lip. "It makes it hard for a man not to notice you."

Lottie reached for his free hand and lifted it to her lips. Such a good man, she thought, as she kissed the back of his hand, then looked up into his eyes which held onto hers. "I know I can depend on you, but we can be no more than friends."

"I'm not your kind," he answered.

"Oh, Jack," she stepped toward him and closed her arms around him, resting her head softly on his hard chest. "I'm not your kind."

"I would do anything for you."

Lottie nodded half-heartedly against his chest and she felt his arms tightening as her eyes moistened. A single tear rolled down her cheek. There was something he could do, but would he misunderstand? Perhaps she should do it herself.

"What's the matter, Lottie?"

"Jack, there is one thing."

"Name it."

"There's a man in town I should see."

His arms loosened and he backed gently from Lottie's embrace. Lottie, dabbing at her wet eyes, looked into his face, wreathed in hurt. "It's nothing like you think," she said.

Jacobs nodded. "I'm not thinking, Lottie. It's too hard to figure."

"Would you deliver a message for me? His name is John Henry Holliday. He's a gambler, probably find him at the Cattle Exchange. Slender man, walrus mustache, half-eaten with consumption."

"The one Chancey set up to take the Bee Hive? He your kind?" He asked without malice.

"Ask him to come here tomorrow at five."

"Nothing else?"

"That's all."

"What if he won't come?"

"He will. Wouldn't you?"

Jacobs nodded without emotion, then left.

The stiffness in his new shirt crinkled as he straightened his string tie, then tugged on his freshly ironed frock coat. Holliday coughed, a dry, empty hack borne less of consumption than nervousness. Though a betting man, he didn't care to make odds on what Lottie wanted. Holliday rubbed his smooth-shaven chin, then twisted the bottom of his slightly waxed mustache as he stepped to the door of a modest adobe dwelling in front of several

92

huge cottonwood trees near the Clear Fork of the Brazos. As he knocked on the doorjamb, he felt the warm rays of the sun seeping through the black wool of his coat and into his back, heating his flesh and blood not nearly as much as thoughts of this meeting had. Receiving no response, Holliday knocked again, louder, the noise provoking a mockingbird resting in a cottonwood rooted just beyond the house. The bird's shrill cry taunted Holliday, ridiculed his infatuation, tested his patience. Holliday vilely cursed the bird just as the door opened.

The world, including the mockingbird, suddenly quieted as Holliday looked into the puzzled gray eyes of Lottie Deno, a flush of color rising in her cheeks.

Folding her arms across her breast, she spoke. "John Henry Holliday, never have I had a caller greet me with a more vulgar word." She spoke softly, her Kentucky accent lifting the words seductively from her lips. "Was that meant for me?" she asked, the trace of a smile softening the corners of her mouth, as if she were amused by his discomfort.

"That, ah, mockingbird . . ." Holliday stumbled over his words like a blind man over scattered firewood, ". . . I mean, not you."

"What mockingbird?" Lottie cupped a hand to her ear.

Damn bird, he thought. Instead of roping himself tighter in his bind, he stared silently at Lottie. Never before had he seen her with her hair down, a soft auburn river flowing from the top of her rounded face, falling down her shoulders and lapping across the full breast of her blue silk taffeta dress. Lottie tossed her head with a laugh which rippled gently down her hair. Holliday smiled at the sound, as flawless as a crystal bell.

"Come in, John Henry," she said with a sweep of her hand, her dress rustling as she stepped aside. "That mockingbird serenades me all the time."

"I'd call it noise," Holliday answered, his hand going for his hat. "Maybe I should use him for target practice when I leave." Fear flashed through Lottie's eyes and he regretted his words, his hand dropping empty from his head.

"Oh no, not that," she answered, a trace of panic in her voice. "He keeps me company. I feed him scraps and even got him to take a few from my hand last week. Please don't harm him."

93

Holliday nodded as he lowered himself onto the small divan. He wished she would join him, but instead she brushed a wrinkle from her pale blue dress — a becoming color on her — and paused in front of the cane-bottom rocking chair opposite him.

"A gentleman takes off his hat indoors, John Henry." She smiled and extended her hand.

Cursing silently, Holliday removed the derby, thinking she seemed to enjoy his vexations. Why did things never go right with Lottie? Was it her own roguish temperament, or was he so taken with her that he was as foolish as a schoolboy carving his beloved's initials in a favorite tree? He wondered if he would ever know, because he could never read her. He offered the hat to Lottie, who deposited it on the gateleg table beside a small wooden box.

"Care for coffee?" she offered. As Holliday shook his head, she gathered the pleats of her dress and sat in the rocker. "Thank you for coming, John Henry."

"The invitation surprised me after our game, quick though it was, at the Bee Hive."

"Professional encounter there," she smiled, her perfect teeth sparkling like gems in a jewel case.

"I was a mite perplexed, though, by your messenger."

"A good man, Jack Jacobs," Lottie said, brushing her hair behind her shoulder and tossing her head like a frisky filly. "He doesn't frequent saloons like some of us." Her crystal laugh followed on the tail of the self-deprecating words.

"The way he eyed me before extending your invitation worried me, like he was the law."

"Intuition, John Henry. He was sheriff until this spring, but he was too honest for the job."

"Never met an honest sheriff before, like I never met an honest gambler," Holliday continued. "This Jacobs, though, should be more careful how he approaches people or he'll be with a few honest saints. By the time he finally came up to me in the Cattle Exchange, I had my pistol out under the table, pointing at his gut." For a moment, Holliday thought he saw a flush of paleness sweep across Lottie's face, but perhaps he was wrong. "This Jacobs special to you, Lottie?"

"He is, John Henry, he is. Nobody else in the Flat I can trust like Jack Jacobs."

"Then tell him to be careful around me. The law makes me nervous since killing the soldier in Jacksboro . . ."

"If I'd known I'd endanger Jack, I'd never sent him after you, John Henry. The reason I sent for you —"

"I will take that cup of coffee now," he interrupted. He coughed nervously, stalling for extra time. He knew what he wanted to ask, but not how. And, he wanted to ask before she explained her invitation.

Lottie excused herself, returning directly with a single coffee cup and saucer. Holliday accepted the steaming drink from her soft hands, then swallowed hard, a gulp of hot liquid burning no less within him than the words he wanted to speak. As Lottie seated herself, he spoke before she could resume. "Lottie," he began tentatively, "there's something I would like to know about you." He watched her eyes narrow, her brow furrow, and her lips droop at the ends. "Your name. What's your name?"

"Why, Lottie Deno. You know that, John Henry." The words came as cold and pointed as icicles.

"No, your real name, Lottie." Holliday's confidence withered under her cool response. "Not your saloon name."

Lottie stood and walked behind her rocking chair, folding her hands across the rocker headpiece, building a wall between herself and Holliday. "You wouldn't ask that of a man in these parts. Too many with an unflattering past to hide or a recent reputation they wouldn't want to get back to their families. Why ask me?"

"I thought if you told me you might . . ." Holliday faltered, his voice fading with the last word.

"Might what?"

"Might consider . . ." Holliday stumbled again over his speech, the words being lost between his brain and his tongue.

"Consider what?" Lottie asked again.

"Marrying me," he blurted it out. The words exploded across the room like a cannon up on Government Hill, and the moment he had said them Holliday felt foolish instead of relieved. An ashen look clouded Lottie's face. Holliday thought he saw a glistening veil drop over her gray eyes. "I figured if you thought enough of me to reveal your name, you might consider marrying me," he said.

Lottie caught her breath and walked around the rocking chair to the table, picking up the small wooden box by his hat. She tossed it from hand to hand, shaking her head.

"John Henry, I'm surprised and flattered." Her words came slowly, deliberately, and even sympathetically, Holliday thought, but for whom he could not tell. "But marriage is impossible. You or anyone else." Then she laughed softly. "Two gamblers marrying. Nothing I can think of would be any unluckier."

"I could give it up," Holliday answered. "I've had training as a dentist, even practiced in Dallas. I could start over."

Lottie carried the wooden box to the rocking chair, falling into the seat without gathering her skirt. "You're like me, John Henry, you might know other occupations, but gambling's in your blood. You might give it up, but it won't be for another occupation or a woman. It's an evil neither of us can root out until our blood runs thin with age or bullet lead."

"Then you won't tell me your name?"

"No, John Henry, neither you nor most anyone else."

"When I got your message I hoped we shared the same feelings for each other."

Lottie stared at the floor. "John Henry, I'm surprised, you letting your feelings get the better of you. That's not healthy among gamblers." She held up the wooden box. "This is why I asked you here. It came after you left Jacksboro. I thought I might run into you later, seeing how flies like us always find the busiest dung heap, so I kept it for you."

Holliday sipped at the coffee, but it was bitter in his mouth as he remembered the crooked dealing box he'd ordered.

Reading the peeling address label on the box, Lottie smiled, a hint of sympathy in her eyes. "From Will and Finck, Leading Cutlers and Bell Hangers," she said, then clucked her tongue. "John Henry, I never realized you liked fine knives — or is it bells? — so well." She laughed. "Will and Finck, I swear John Henry," she said, extending the box to him, "these purveyors of cutlery and bells sure go to great lengths to hide the fact they are a sporting house dealing in crooked gambling equipment. Please pardon me for having opened it, but I was curious if its contents were square."

Exchanging his half-full coffee cup for the box, Holliday nodded. "You should have known I'd bought a crooked box. Helps on days like this when I'm short on luck. Cost me a hundred dollars." He pried the lid from the box, the tiny nails giving way easily. It was just as he had ordered. He replaced the lid and stood. "Your name, Lottie?"

"No, John Henry, though it flatters me you ask." Her words came softer now. She placed his coffee cup on the gateleg table.

His thin lips curled into an defeated smile beneath his mustache. "Just one more thing."

"Yes, John Henry."

"Not a word of this to anyone."

"You have my word," she said, extending her hand.

Holliday held her fingers as she arose, then lifted them to his mouth as if for a kiss, but released them instead and picked up his derby. Hat in hand, he edged toward the door, before turning to look at her a final time. "Should you ever . . ." he began, then stopped and merely nodded.

He saw Lottie's lips tighten at the unfinished sentence. Stepping outside, he heard her close the door softly behind him.

The mockingbird picked up its taunting call as Holliday strode from the house. Holliday paused, scanning the cottonwoods behind Lottie's dwelling. Finally spotting the bird on a low branch, Holliday drew back his arm and heaved the faro box at the feathered pest. Neither his aim nor his strength threatened the bird, though the missile did flush him, grousing, from the tree.

Holliday tramped away from Lottie's place, losing track of time and place. Realizing the lateness of the day, he walked through the Flat with fast, exaggerated steps until his lungs screamed from the exertion. In minutes he shoved through the swinging doors of the Cattle Exchange and headed for the bar, buying two bottles of Monarch bourbon as Big Nose Kate swaggered by. She smiled as she passed, then Holliday spun around and grabbed her arm.

"So you want to screw, do you?" she asked, loud enough for others to hear. "I told you you'd come around, now didn't I?"

97

"I'm not in the mood for talking," he answered, "are you going with me?"

Before she could answer, Holliday jerked her toward the door as many in the Cattle Exchange watched. At the door, Kate shook herself free, turning her back to Holliday to straighten her dress and to wink at Chancey's customers. Then with proper decorum, she linked her arm in Holliday's and stepped with him outside.

"Where's your crib, Kate?"

She pointed toward the creek, and the two walked silently into the night.

WINTER

EIGHT

Holliday rolled atop Kate and rode her, caring neither who had preceded him nor who would follow. Outside, a December norther beat its fury against the thin wooden walls of the Planters House, the chill whining into the room. It was cold and she was warm. Nothing else mattered. Many times they had slept together since that first night in September, but never in Holliday's room or for the entire night. Until now, he had spent his lust in her crib, which reeked with the smell of other men, and never did he lie with Kate that he didn't wish she were Lottie. But Kate was accessible and free, at least to him, so Holliday had wasted himself in her at will.

His body rocked against her hot flesh, then convulsed in a spasm of spent ardor, followed by a riveting cough which echoed off the walls and seemed, for a moment, to drive back even the winter winds. He felt her arms locking around his back, then, as her body held his final thrust, squeezing tightly as if to strangle his cough. He pried himself from her embrace and rolled off beside her, watching the flickers cavort on the ceiling from the feeble flame in the coal oil lamp.

The bed shivered as Kate pulled her muslin chemise down over her legs, then snuggled closer to him, her head leaning softly on his shoulder, her hand playing in turn with each button on his full-length underwear. Reaching his groin, she tucked him back into his drawers. "I want all of you to stay warm tonight," she said, wiping the stickiness on her chemise.

Holliday turned his head away from hers as she kissed his stubbled cheek. A racking cough vibrated from his body to hers before he jerked his shoulder from beneath her head and twisted away. Kate inched over the sheet into his vacated warmth and molded the front of her body to the back of his. Her fingers annoyed Holliday as they slipped down his front, a couple finding the slit between two buttons and playing with the hair on his chest. Holliday coughed again, his hand swiping hers away as it flew to his mouth.

"You ever thought about marriage?" Her words fell as softly as her hand settling back on his chest.

Damn this recurring notion of hers, Holliday thought. The silence stretched taut.

"Don't play possum on me." Her rigid words passed through clenched teeth. "Have you ever thought about marriage?"

"No!" Holliday felt the anger rising in him.

"Not even after all the time we've spent together?"

"Kate, you bringing it up is one thing." He struggled for a breath. "Me thinking about it is another."

"But you do enjoy my company," she said, wriggling her fingers between his buttons.

"A man's gotta relieve himself somehow."

"Just like taking a piss, is it?" Kate's words spewed like venom. "You're as romantic as Huckleberry Finn." Her fingers dug like fangs into his chest.

He slapped at the pointed pain beneath her nails. "Who the hell is Finn, buffalo hunter?"

"Tom Sawyer's friend, that's who. You got any friends here but me?"

"None, so marry this Finn or Tom Sawyer and make us both happy."

"Dammit, they ain't anybody, just a couple characters I've been reading about. Boys on the Mississippi River. Tom's got a girl, but Huckleberry's as vinegary as you toward females."

"Hell, woman, you're educating the wrong end with all

101

your book reading. If you'd spent less time behind books and more time under customers, you'd have enough stashed away so you could quit frequenting saloons and seedy men like me."

"Hell, yourself." As she spoke, Holliday felt her knee in his back and before he could brace himself, he was grabbing for the covers on the way to the cold floor. Shivering, he scrambled for the mattress. Her words, icy as the floor, noted his return. "If I'd charged you for all my free favors," she yelled, "I'd own every damn saloon in this town, and I'd kick your ass out every time you walked through the door. Chancey made a mistake finally cutting Ed Bailey loose and letting you take over his table."

Holliday launched his palm for her cheek, but Kate's upthrust pillow deflected the blow onto the mattress. In an instant she rolled upon his arm, harmlessly, Holliday thought, until he felt her teeth sinking into his flesh through the sleeve of his long johns. "Damn you, woman." He grimaced, then rubbed the wound as she broke free. "Your mouth is lethal. Between your words and teeth, I can't decide which is worse."

"And you get your bristles up at every mention of Ed Bailey." Kate fluffed her pillow, then straightened the covers over herself and Holliday.

Holliday shook his arm of its subsiding pain, then rearranged the blankets to his satisfaction. "He's a cheat."

"Now, hell, you're a gambler, not a circuit-riding preacher, so don't tell me you've never cheated."

"Chancey brought me in to win a cold hand and skin a couple cattlemen of their money belts. I won the big hand but had to outcheat the bastard and his damn reflecting pipe. When Bailey played against me, he was playing against the house."

"Then why'd Chancey wait until last week to cut him loose?"

When Holliday spoke, a growl gathered in his throat. "Chancey's loyal to a dollar, nothing more. As long as he figured Bailey was bringing in more business than he was costing, he let it go. But then he caught Bailey cheating the house, losing too much to his friends and taking better care of them than the Cattle Exchange."

"Seems to me, firing Bailey won't make Chancey popular with Bailey's friends." Kate slipped her hand in Holliday's. "But that's not our worry."

102

Holliday laughed. "Chancey blamed me. He told Bailey I'd offered him a thousand dollars and would take a lesser cut of the winnings if I had a table, his table. Smooth, that Chancey, he even offered to let Bailey keep his table if he could match my deal." Holliday settled deeper under the covers and rolled onto his side. "It'll be the death of one of us."

Kate answered with a sigh and the soft touch of her hand along his back. He squirmed closer to her warmth and felt her moist lips and her warm breath upon the nape of his neck. What an abominable name, that Huckleberry Finn, whoever the hell he was, Holliday thought just as he sank into the haze of sleep. And outside it was cold and she was warm and nothing else mattered.

Softly Kate hummed a saloon song as Holliday fell asleep beside her, his breath wheezing like a bellows worn from overwork. She massaged his back gently at first, then harder as if she could exorcise the demon consumption within him. As her hand tired, she rested her ear to his back, her saloon melody exhausting itself, and listened to each breath drawn like a dull saw through dried wood, rasping and grating. Maybe he was more Huckleberry Finn than Tom Sawyer, but it was the tuberculosis that put the vinegar in his veins. She felt a tear roll down her cheek. Damn him, why did he have to have consumption? And why did she have to fall for him? What was the cure for him? And for her? She remembered reading of patent medicines in the *Frontier Echo*. Perhaps she could get him well and one day they could marry.

A sharp gust of wind rattled at the window pane and whistled its fury at the impediment, the wicked melody sending a chill down her spine. She pressed tighter against Holliday, wondering if any woman could ever win him, and then, remembering Lottie Deno, Kate stiffened and her face soured. Lottie could, if she wanted. Kate had seen a flame deep in Holliday's blue eyes for Lottie and she felt as helpless to extinguish it as a woman without water at a fire. Holliday was like the other men, all enamored of her beauty and the virginal vestige she made out to be among a horde of local prostitutes. But pure though Lottie pretended, for her living she still slopped at the same trough as the dirtiest whore in the Flat; she still wallowed in men's wallets for money and gave less in return. Fearing that the coals burning behind Holliday's blue eyes could only be stoked by Lottie, Kate drew herself closer to him, her arm around his chest, as if by proximity she could change his heart. Only the wind moved until Kate worried herself asleep, without releasing him.

Time dissolved in her sleep, the minutes passing as a mist into hazy hours untotaled. How long she had dozed, she could only guess. At first she believed herself caught in some inexplicable dream, a trance alternating between heated shivers and cold sweats. Slowly her mind cut through the fog of drowsiness. It was Holliday. She shook the haze from her head, moaning at the cramp in her arm, still locked around his body. His nightclothes were drenched with perspiration's dew, and through them she could feel a fevered heat fueling his shivers. He was dying. "No don't," she heard herself say, her trembling hand sliding to his simmering forehead, then stroking his cheek. His breaths came as dying whispers instead of great gasps, and Kate nudged him for a spark of life, gently at first, then harder, the flame within him burning low like the bedside lamp. He groaned, his head shifting slightly, then falling limp again. "You'll be okay. I'll take care of you," she whispered. She parted from him, pulled him over onto his back, tossed her covers away, careful not to expose him to the chill, then stepped onto the floor, her feet arching to the cold.

Kate scurried from the bed to the washstand and grabbed the clean towel, folding it into a sponge. She slipped beside Holliday and held the towel above the lamp chimney to absorb heat from the feeble flame. With the warmed towel, she knelt bedside and planted a kiss upon his cheek, then meticulously wiped away each bead of sweat glistening on his leathery skin. Alternately she mopped his head and then, to evaporate the absorbed sweat, held the towel over the lamp. His breath gradually gathered sickly strength and finally exploded in a horrid hack. Kate's eyes misted at the cough and a dozen times more she swabbed his face. Though she shivered on the floor, his sickness bothered her more than the cold.

Never moving from his side, she lost track of time until she could see through the window layers of darkness peeling away from the sky. Her body numbed with the cold, and still she could not pull herself away from Holliday in his helplessness. Leaning her head against the mattress, she almost dozed off until she was jarred from her rest by a hammering hack that pried Holliday's eyelids open momentarily. He rolled toward Kate, a yellow mucus with tiny threads of blood throughout it dribbling from his mouth onto the pillow. Kate wiped the phlegm from his chin.

Then the coughing came in torrents too great to stop. For this, he must have medicine, she thought, glancing around the room, now bathed in the gentle wash of sunrise. Except for the empty bourbon bottles, there was nothing. As she sighed, her gaze rested at the foot of the washstand where a small satchel — like a doctor carried — hid. Medicine? She blinked her heavy eyelids, expecting the illusion to disappear, but the bag remained. Leaving Holliday for the first time since she arose, Kate crawled to the bag, jerked it from its hiding place, and spread the case's leather jaws. She dug beneath a flask of whiskey, a faro dealing box, and two decks of cards to the bottom, covered with metal tools. Jerking a handful of the cold metallic instruments from the satchel, she held them to the light of the window — odd-shaped pliers, metal probes, a tool with a round mirror on the end, and other implements — but did not understand. Finding no medicine inside the bag, she flung the instruments back inside and closed the case. Maybe he had stolen the bag from a doctor.

For a perplexed moment, she sat on the floor until Holliday coughed. Fighting her exhaustion, she struggled to her feet and staggered around the bed, crawling in beside him, her teeth chattering. She felt a scratchiness in her tight throat and wondered if that was how consumption felt. She guessed not. Even her bone-deep weariness failed to lessen her worry for him. Turning on her side, she propped her head up on one hand and rubbed Holliday's bony chest. So strained was his breath, she instinctively lifted her hand as he inhaled and pressed down on his chest as he exhaled. How could he live with himself each night if consumption meant this?

Finally, her body forced upon her the sleep her mind tried to refuse. Kate rested her head beside his and dozed as Holliday's fever drained away with the lingering shadows. The room was fully lit when she awoke to a gurgling noise. Holliday was strangling, she thought, spinning over toward him. Holliday held a bottle to his lips and was pouring bourbon down his throat like he hadn't had a drink of anything in a month.

"Slow down," she chided. "You've been too sick to polish it away that fast."

Holliday broke for air. "It's like that most nights," he answered, then kissed the bottle until it was empty.

Kate watched him drain the liquor into his anemic frame undermined by consumption and reached for his chest as he finished. "That much liquor that fast can't be good for you. You need medicine."

Holliday laughed and coughed at once. "Nothing but death cures consumption."

"But I've read about cure-alls in the *Frontier Echo*."

Holliday ignored her. "The whiskey eases the pain. It's worst when I wake." He reached for a handkerchief in the frock coat hanging on the bedpost at his head, but started coughing before he could retrieve it, his spare hand flying to his mouth. Finally wresting the handkerchief free, he wiped a wad of bloody mucus from his palm. "See that," he said, holding the stained handkerchief to her grimacing face, "that crap, the bloody stuff, is my lung. Every day I lose a bit more and I'll keep losing it until I can't breathe."

Kate sighed when he folded the cloth over consumption's litter. "Every night you fever and sweat so, how do you sleep?"

"This strong body," he mocked, "tires easily. Exhaustion," he coughed, "overcomes distractions like pain."

His body shook with a paroxysm of coughing as more of his lungs came to rest in his handkerchief. "Damn it all."

Kate withdrew her hand tentatively from his chest. "I didn't know it was this bad."

Holliday controlled his cough for a moment. "It's like this every day. Damn, it's cold."

"You sure all that liquor helps?"

He nodded. "If not for my lungs, then for the rest of me. I may drink a lot, but you'll never see me drunk."

"That's what worries me, like it's unhealthy for you."

"Consumption isn't?"

"No, the liquors. There are medicines. I've read about them in the *Frontier Echo*."

"Hell, Kate, you believe too much of what you read, like that damn Cuckleberry Ben."

"Huckleberry Finn," she corrected.

"Whatever. Damn, you'll find about as much truth in the damn newspaper as you will in your books. None!"

"But the medicine, the advertisements say, will cure consumption. It'd beat all that whiskey."

"Kate, dammit, you've been known to get drunk so get off of me about the liquor."

"But the medicine?"

"It's all alcohol, nothing more, just not as good as bourbon. Hell, a keg of beer or a case of whiskey has as many curative powers as those damn cure-alls and wonder tonics."

"They say, though . . ."

"I don't care what they say. Hell, woman, I don't want to argue about it all morning. I'm not accustomed to arguing my way out of bed each day, and I don't want to start now."

"A woman tries to take care of you during the night and all you do is argue about me arguing."

"I've cared for myself many a night worse than this. I don't need you pawing over me like a mother hen. If that's what you have in mind, you better find somebody else to warm your bed." Holliday threw back the covers and slid out of bed, coughing as his feet touched the floor.

"With your goddam fever, doubt I can find anything short of a live ember that can warm a mattress as good as you," she shouted, grabbing for the covers. "This was the last night I'll ever freeze my ass off for you."

"Nobody asked for your favors. I'd been better off dealing more faro than coming back here to screw last night. Hell, I probably lost money by splitting the crease between your legs," Holliday answered, as he struggled his pants on.

"Well, I damn sure did lose money by coming here," Kate shot back. "I could a had me a couple fellows before sunrise, no doubt about it, you son of a bitch."

Holliday lunged at the bed and slapped Kate full force across the cheek. "Don't you call me that ever again."

Kate rubbed her cheek. Holliday's snakelike quickness had startled her, but his palm had only stung her face. She laughed. "That as hard as you can slap?"

Holliday nodded, pulling on his shirt and hooking his suspenders over the shoulders. "The disease eats away at my lungs and withers my shoulder strength away. You'd been a man, I'd a shot you. Doesn't take too much strength to pull a trigger."

"I've been hit by breezes harder than that," she shook her head. "Now I know why you got the scrawniest chest and arms I ever did see. All these fellows about town worried about your meanness, and you're not strong enough to knock a fart out of a bean-eating schoolboy."

"You don't ever call me that again," Holliday replied.

"And you don't treat me like a whore, even if I am one. Agreed?"

Holliday turned silently away.

"You know your problem, Mister John Henry Holliday? You don't like yourself enough to let anybody else take a shine to you, and you're too damn proud to let it bother you."

"Not another proposal, Kate."

"You have any friends in Griffin? No, just me and you don't claim me. Dammit, I'd gladly be your wife. But who else is there? Not Chancey. He just uses you to bring in money. Who else is there?"

"Ed Bailey," Holliday said sardonically.

"You have any doctor friends?"

"Kate, dammit, last night you jawed about marriage and then your cure-alls. This morning you blabber about marriage and lecture me on my health again. I know what's the matter with me. I'm not going to any doctors and I'm not taking any damn cure-alls you've read about."

"That's not what I mean. When you was fevering I looked for medicine. I found a doctor's bag, I guess that's what it is, by the washstand. Thought you might have some medicine in it."

Holliday picked up the medicine bag and extracted his flask. "This is the only medicine that works."

"Where'd you get the bag and all the funny tools in it? I figure you stole it."

Shrugging and dropping the bag to the floor, Holliday turned to the washstand and picked up his strap and flat razor. He worked the shiny blade back and forth across the leather until the metal seemed to sparkle even more.

"You best answer my question," Kate threatened, "if you

108

want to keep on living here in Planters House. Otherwise, I'm gonna scream words that'll curl the hair on the owner's butt."

He glanced in the mirror at her. "Kate, your charm is so damn persuasive. Those are dental instruments, that's all," he said, then splashed his face with the frigid water.

"You got a dentist friend?"

"I'm a dentist," he answered.

Kate sat up in the bed, the covers falling to her waist. "You're a dentist?" she mulled. "Doctor John Henry Holliday. Well, I'll be damned myself. I like the sound of that, Doctor Holliday. Doctor Holliday," she mused. "Doc Holliday." Then she lay back and stared at the ceiling. "I've never thought how nice it might be to marry a dentist. Doctor and Mrs. John Henry Holliday. I like the sound of it."

Holliday spun around, his intent hidden by the lathery mask over his face, the straight razor held menacingly in his hand. The crease of a scowl split through the lather. "Damn, Kate, do you ever give up?"

"Not when I'm after something I want, Doc Holliday, not when I'm after something I want."

NINE

Standing in front of the only safe in Shackelford County and rocking slightly on the heels of his polished shoes, Frank Conrad wore the look of prosperity, his thumbs hooked in his suspenders. Like the hair on his head, the buffalo of the Great Southern Herd were thinning out, and no man was more responsible for the decimation than Frank Conrad, the merchant. His eyes as sharp as his business sense, Conrad bought lead and gunpowder by the ton at the Kansas railheads, freighted it by wagon to Fort Griffin, and sold it by the pound in the Flat.

With the best selection in Griffin, his mercantile would prosper this season. In one day alone during the fall, hunters and townsmen doing four thousand dollars in business — guns and ammunition accounting for almost two-thirds of that — had passed under the sign "Conrad and Rath, General Merchandise." Just ten days away, 1877 held equal promise when the hunters returned with their hides and the freight wagons lined up by the hundreds to take the bales to the railroads in Kansas or Fort Worth.

The arrival of his chest-high, chilled-steel safe earlier in the year had all but made Conrad the acknowledged banker of the Flat. Behind the back counter in the main room jammed with goods and provisions and smelling of newness and coal oil, he displayed the safe as a symbol of security in an insecure town. Like Conrad's reputation for honest dealing, the safe's visibility was good for business. With a proud flick of the wrist he would twirl the combination dial, pull the heavy twin doors apart, swing open the inner steel plate, and deposit or retrieve a customer's money or gold from among the stacked tobacco sacks or envelopes or wooden boxes filled with valuables.

Though Conrad insisted on knowing the contents and value of each addition in case a shortage was later claimed, Lottie Deno always refused. And today she had done so again when Conrad added her sixth deposit — another saloon brand cigar box wrapped in newspaper and tied with twine — to the safe. Lottie knew Conrad suspected money in each, paper bills in the four light ones, gold pieces in the two heavier boxes. She had only smiled in the face of his request, saying the risk was entirely hers. His curiosity thwarted again, Conrad shrugged, then rocked proudly on his feet, his close-trimmed beard jutting confidently forward. "It's been a good year, Miss Deno. As long as the buffalo hold out, a man can't ask for more."

"Good years, like good cards, come in streaks, but I've had a fine run of luck here," Lottie said, loosening her heavy wool cloak in the stifling warmth of Conrad's store, his stoves always burning the hottest in Fort Griffin because he had the money to haul in abundant firewood, the local quantity being scarce.

Conrad popped his suspenders with his thumbs and glanced over his shoulder at the locked safe. "Yes, Miss Deno, I'd say you'd done quite well for yourself." His lips pursed like a pair of fallen question marks.

"Odd-numbered years have been unlucky for me, Mister Conrad, since the War ended in sixty-five. Of course, being a merchant, you wouldn't believe luck blows like the wind — sometimes with you and sometimes against you — and you never know when it's about to change. Until it's too late!"

"You're too superstitious, Miss Deno. It doesn't take luck to make money, but it does to hold onto it. I'd say you've managed right well, guessing by our few dealings."

Frowning, Lottie folded her arms across her breasts. "Have you been peeking?"

"No, no," he said, waving his arms. "I didn't mean that,

just that everyone in these parts has heard of Lottie's Luck. No, your deposits are safe. My business is based on square dealing and I shall never misplace the trust of my customers, especially one as pretty as yourself." He smiled, obviously proud of his compliment.

Lottie lowered her hands and mirrored his smile. "There is one thing more," she said, stepping to him. "Should something ever happen to me . . ."

"Well, your fears seem —" Conrad started.

"If it does," she continued, waving aside his interruption, "give all my packages to Jack Jacobs. He'll know what to do with them. And if he ever asks for my boxes, give them to him, do exactly what he says. Remember, the risk is mine."

"I shall abide by your wishes," Conrad intoned, "but I worry that you fear 1877 without reason."

"Perhaps, Mister Conrad, but I am a gambler. Not quite the same as running a respectable business, now is it?"

Conrad anchored an arm across his chest, rested the other on it, and swept his steady hand across his beard. He grimaced like a judge pondering the arguments of a starch-shirted lawyer, but his pronouncement was interrupted by the approach of clerk George Wilhelm, who each week delivered to Lottie's cabin a standing order of provisions, always throwing in an extra apple, bag of nuts, or some other gratuity for which Lottie always insisted on tipping him well.

"Miss Deno," greeted Wilhelm, doffing his hat. "Pleased to see you, I am. I didn't by accident forget anything on your last order, did I?"

"Certainly not, George. In fact, I was just telling Mister Conrad what fine service you've provided me these past months."

"You were?" Conrad's lips said without the words passing them. "Yes, she was, George, as a matter of fact," he recovered.

George grinned broadly. "Why thank you, Miss Deno. The pleasure is always mine. Nobody around here gives a better tip than you. Those that are monied enough are too mean and those that are nice enough are too poor, except you."

Wilhelm bent over and tucked one leg of his ducking overalls back into his boot. Tall and lanky, George appeared almost too gangly to navigate the crowded aisles of Conrad's store.

"Besides that, George, I've suggested that Mister Conrad up your pay so you won't have to deliver the provisions yourself just for the tip."

Conrad shrugged.

"Oh, I don't do it just for the tip, Miss Deno," George said, then wiped the sleeve of his blue flannel shirt across his lips, too late to cover an embarrassed grin. "Miss Deno, is there something I can get you?"

"Thank you, George, but I've business matters with Mister Conrad. If I decide otherwise, I'll call."

"Thank you, Miss Deno, I best attend some others then," George responded, refitting his hat and retreating to a grizzled patron.

Lottie tied her cloak and braced herself for the walk back to her cabin. "Always a pleasure, Mister Conrad, doing business with a gentleman," she said, extending her right hand.

Taking it, he bowed his head toward her. "My pleasure."

As she turned toward the door and wove her way to the front, Lottie could feel every man's gaze upon her. She was glad to get outside. The cold slapped at her face and pricked her bare hands like a thousand pins as she stepped onto Conrad's boardwalk. A wintry haze shrouded the town like a gray garment. The late afternoon street was deserted except for a knot of men outside the Bee Hive and the horses shivering at the hitching posts. Lottie could hear the men down the street laughing and jeering, probably at an overflow fight Fogle had swept outside or maybe a drunken Tonkawa. The damn fool men were outside by choice, so Lottie pitied the animals who had no say in the matter. They whinnied and nickered, sympathizing among themselves over the misery wrought by the norther.

The only person in town profiting from this bitter cold spell which had frozen the creek was Uncle Billy Wilson. Lottie could hear the grating bite of his hired men's saws cutting through the ice. Wilson would stock his substantial ice house near the creek with now worthless chunks of ice. When summer came he would turn that frozen water into money, gambling being the only thing closer to alchemy than that, Lottie thought. Carried by the wind, the sawing noises were as plain as the shouts of the crowd down the street.

Drawing nearer the Bee Hive, she ignored the taunting circle of men and would have passed, one fight or drunk being the same as another, except for a high-pitched voice as desperate as the wind. "Come on, Pa," it came. "You've got to get up and make it. I can't carry you and you'll freeze."

Other voices deep and male mocked the plaintive cry. "Get up, Pa. Get on home. You can't carry your liquor and your girl can't carry you." Then laughter.

Lottie darted from the windbreak of the buildings toward the throng of men. She reached the tight knot and shoved her way through, a couple of men raising their fists to swing until they realized it was a woman. Their laughter trailed off as Lottie elbowed her way into the center of the circle. There a coatless girl no more than seven was bent over as drunk a man as ever lived. His legs were stretched straight out and his torso was propped up by his arms behind him, his hands sliding more and more from under him each time the girl tugged at his coat. An empty bottle lay equally helpless beside him. Near the bottle a bleached buffalo skull inexplicably stared with hollow eyes at the spectators.

"Please, Pa, come on. Ma will switch me if I don't get you home soon."

The girl glanced up at Lottie, her big, blue eyes meeting the gambler's and expressing her silent frustration more eloquently than words. Understanding that Lottie now dominated the quieted crowd, the girl glanced down at the dirt, toeing it with her scuffed shoe and kicking a few pebbles toward the buffalo skull. "He's not a bad man, ma'am. Just sometimes takes a drink. Ma can't do nothing about it. Me neither." Then her father collapsed backward, slamming into the dirt. One of the men, himself reeking of liquor, laughed, "Beddy bye." Lottie cut her icy eyes at him and untied her cloak. From beneath the cloak, Lottie pulled her revolver.

"That funny, fellow?" she said, aiming the revolver squarely at his head. His laughter evaporated like the color in his face. "If my finger was to twitch, fellow, you'd go straight to hell. That's where you belong, that's where all of you men belong for not helping this poor child. God have mercy on a place as callous as this. What do you have to say for yourselves?"

She waited, but only the rasping ice saws on the creek and the cold wind moaning answered.

"That's what I thought. None of you have enough gumption to apologize to this child." A couple of men with downcast eyes mumbled embarrassed words, directed more at Lottie than the girl. "What's your name, child?" Lottie asked.

"Sophie."

Two men were inching away from the circle when Lottie looked up. She raised her gun and fired it into the air. "I'll shoot the next snake that tries to slither away." The retreaters froze in their places. "Now, Sophie, where do you live?"

She pointed toward Government Hill. "Cabin on the creek side of the far slope, ma'am. It's a good walk from here. Pa's horse being lame, we all walk, my ma and sisters."

"How many sisters?"

"Three, ma'am, all younger." Sophie's voice rang with girlish pride. "I'm oldest. That's why my ma sent me."

Slipping her gun back under her cloak, Lottie looked from Sophie to the men. "Anyone know where Sophie's cabin is?" Two men nodded and stepped forward. "Good, you two and a couple more take him home. Walk him if you can, carry him if you can't. I'll be there later with Sophie, you tell that to her mother. When I get there, I'd better find you've tucked him in bed or I'll come after you." Lottie revolved slowly around, studying downcast faces and averted eyes. Four men bent over Sophie's unconscious father and lifted him groaning from the ground. "All of you should help out," she shrugged, "but four's enough." Most nodded as they slipped toward the warmth of the Bee Hive.

"Thank you, ma'am," Sophie said meekly as the volunteers stood up her father, then draped his arms around two of them and started him toward home, his feet dragging on the cold ground.

Sophie picked up the empty liquor bottle and flung it at the Bee Hive, watching it bounce, then skitter between the legs of two nervous horses and break against a hitching post.

"Come with me, Sophie," Lottie said, trying to put her arm around the girl, but Sophie dodged her embrace and stepped beside the buffalo skull. Taking a deep breath, she grabbed it, a hand on each horn, jerking it to her waist.

"Okay," she answered, the skull's weight pulling her off balance until she stepped forward into Lottie's skirt.

"My goodness, child, is that awful thing yours?"

"It is, ma'am. Sometimes I find 'em or they'll fall off a wagon along the road, they will," she huffed under the load.

"Pray tell, you collect them?"

"Oh, no ma'am, I sell 'em. One this big might bring a penny, enough to buy my sisters candy for Christmas. Pa says plenty of nothing is all we'll get Christmas."

Lottie dropped her arm around the girl's shoulder and drew her tightly to her side, then rubbed her hand through the girl's muddy brown hair, its tangles frequent from infrequent brushing. Lottie felt a shiver race through Sophie and the cold pimpling her flesh. "My, what are you doing without a coat is beyond me, Sophie. I'll carry the skull. You wrap this around you." Lottie removed her heavy cloak and draped it over Sophie's trembling shoulders. "You and I are going to Conrad's stores."

"Oh, but I've never been there," Sophie squealed. "Pa says there's too many things in that big store that we might want and could never have."

Lottie, taking the prickly skull and aiming Sophie toward Conrad and Rath's, walked rapidly but could not outdistance the cold piercing her blouse. Sophie, her legs churning with excitement, kept pace despite the cloak dragging the ground. At Conrad's Lottie shoved open the door, Sophie darting in under her arm, then stepped into the warmth. Lottie slammed the door in the face of the cold and dropped the skull at her feet. The clattering noise brought hushed stares from Conrad's customers.

George Wilhelm, looking up from a grizzled buffalo hunter, excused himself and strode to Lottie. "Miss Deno, what brings you back?" Shaking his head as he studied Sophie, half-hidden within the cloak, and the buffalo skull on the floor, he grinned. "Been buffalo hunting and brought us a Comanche child prisoner?"

Sophie's back arched and her head jutted forward, the cloak sliding to the floor. "I may be poor, but I ain't no stinking Tonkawa or any other kind of injun," she challenged.

"By goodness you're not, are you?" George said, rubbing his chin. "Have you come to bring us your trade?" Then he swept his hat from his head and bowed before her.

Sophie giggled at the theatrics. "I've got trading goods."

Lottie toed at the buffalo skull and winked at George. "We're trading a buffalo skull for all she needs."

"So we are," George mused, replacing his hat. "Tell you what, princess, you go look around and see what you want. Holler for me, George, when you need help," he instructed.

Sophie grabbed the cloak from the floor, half tossed it to Lottie, then scooted among the merchandise until she was hidden by the stacks.

George laughed. "Excited little booger, isn't she? How'd you get hooked up to her?"

"It doesn't matter, George," she said, pointing to the buffalo skull. "Do you ever buy these?"

"Bones? Not here, though some stores in town do. Not enough money in it for Mister Conrad."

"Whatever the girl wants, let her have it. I'll pay. And for sure, I want you to include a big coat she can grow into." Lottie draped her cloak over her shoulders.

George snickered as he watched Sophie dash through the store." Shame all the kids around won't have much of a Christmas. Does me good to see a little one get excited like this. Some of these old buzzards may build a town, but it takes little ones like that to keep it going."

"How many days until Christmas, George? I've lost track."

"Today's the twenty-first. Four days."

"George, maybe four days wouldn't be much time, but if you'd help arrange it, we could have a party for anybody that came."

"That'd be a fine idea."

Lottie pointed toward the ecstatic Sophie. "Maybe a few more people could share her excitement."

TEN

Rubbing his hands together for warmth, Holliday leaned up to the frosted window, then scrubbed a peephole in the frozen condensation and stared. Snow covered the Flat like a new sheet, white and unwrinkled, and the cold slipped inside around the window and through the plank walls. He shuddered, then coughed into his fist while retreating to the stove. There Chancey rocked on the back legs of his chair, having abandoned his office's seclusion for the stove's warm embrace. On either side of him sat his two bartenders, the stocky one whittling on small sticks of firewood before condemning them to the hell inside the stove. The thinner barkeep sullenly chewed a wad of tobacco, occasionally spitting the results onto the stove and listening to it crackle and sputter. A cowboy who had ridden through the snow to spend his Christmas in a saloon minded his own business and his newly purchased bottle at a nearby table.

"It still snowing?" Chancey asked, without seeming to care.

"It's stopped, clouds seem to be breaking up." Holliday yawned. "Few more people out and about now. Maybe business will pick up. Say, there are a number out there, wagons, horses." He opened the door and stuck his head outside for a look. "Big crowd down at the Bee Hive. What the hell's Fogle doing this evening?"

"Hadn't you heard?" Chancey punched his palm with a wadded fist. "He's rented the saloon to 'Lotta Dinero' tonight. She's throwing a Christmas gathering for anybody that didn't have any place else to go. Whores, hunters, families, soldiers, even us, I guess, though I didn't receive a personal invite."

"Now why the hell would Fogle let her do a thing like that?"

"Way I hear it, Doc, Fogle's run into a little bad luck and he's got some debts he don't know how to get rid of. He gave Lottie the saloon tonight for a couple hundred dollars."

"A Christmas social in the Bee Hive. Doesn't quite seem proper, now does it?" Holliday rubbed his chin.

"Tonight the Bee Hive's gonna be as pure as a sober Baptist. No drinking, no gambling, no whoring. Women, good and bad I guess, men, kids and young ones. As I hear it Lottie had Jack Jacobs out in this snow finding a good tree and shooting some turkeys for grub. Uncle Billy's been cooking them and everything else, and women are bringing their own foods. George Wilhelm over at Conrad's has been gathering gifts for the kids. Supposed to be several musicians there tonight."

Holliday took his hat from a peg and pulled it down over his head, then stepped out the door into the cold, but not in time to shut out Chancey's final words.

"Hell, Kate might even be there."

Holliday hoped not. He hadn't seen her for three days.

Her breath labored so that each gasp was more a conscious effort than a natural reflex. Her body was wracked with fever and she was covered with every quilt in the small crib. She had even unfolded some of the stacked newspapers she kept and layered them between the quilts for additional warmth. Still, she shivered, her teeth chattering.

She could no longer comprehend if the cold pulsing through her body stemmed from the fever or the weather. It had been hard to keep a fire going in the small corner stove and she had finally given up.

Big Nose Kate could not remember feeling so miserable. Her throat burned like it held hot sand. She longed for a sip of water, but the water pail was frozen. She hungered for a warm meal, but she had just as well wished to be a virgin again, her will for food unable to muster the strength either to fix a modest plate much less walk through the snow to an eating house in the Flat. She had subsisted for two or maybe three days on dry soda crackers, a flask of whiskey, and a bottle of Allen's Lung Balsam. After spending the night with Holliday in his room, she'd purchased the balsam at Conrad and Rath's for him. She'd seen it advertised in the *Frontier Echo* and figured it might ease his pain, but she'd not seen him since that night. Instead she'd used it, but the balsam hadn't helped; it tasted like coal oil and she despised it, but it was wet and it lubricated her throat when she swallowed.

Damn him, she thought. She'd stayed up with him in the cold that night, planting within her body the seeds of her malady, and he'd never even come by to check on her. She could be dead for all he cared, Kate thought. The son of a bitch. Only one sympathetic whore had stopped to check on Kate, stoking the fire in the stove and helping Kate attend her body functions before tucking her back in bed. Twice she'd come by — at least that was all that Kate remembered. Something nagged in Kate's mind. The whore had said she wouldn't be by on Christmas Day. Was this Christmas? Kate strained her mind to recall the chronology of her illness. The whore hadn't been by today, at least not that Kate recollected through her feverish haze. Maybe it was Christmas.

Something else stuck in her mind. A party at the Bee Hive. It seemed out of character for Fogle. But hadn't the whore said Lottie Deno was throwing the social? Maybe she had said that, but then Kate had been delirious for several hours. Lottie Deno, damn her. Christmas Day, damn it. Doc Holliday, damn him most of all. If it were Christmas Day, he could have called her, maybe even given her a small remembrance. She'd planned to do the same for that bastard. He's probably trying to screw Lottie Deno or wishing he was or fawning over her charming manners. Kate wished that Doc were beside her and that she had a knife she could plunge deep into his gut like he had stabbed her belly so often with his manhood. Her anger fevered with her. Maybe she was just imagining about Doc and Lottie. After all, she hadn't been thinking straight the last few days. Seems she did recall at some point drifting down the Mississippi River on a raft, she wearing a bonnet and full petticoat dress and listening to the lies of a skinny Huckleberry Finn who looked like Holliday without a mustache. Nothing made sense anymore.

Kate tossed about in her bed, trying to escape her thoughts and to find relief from the pain. She reached for the whiskey bottle on the floor and sat up long enough to swallow a mouthful. She smacked her parched lips and fell back upon her pillow, staring at the ceiling. The room glowed in an unnatural, ghostly light. It wasn't day, but it wasn't night either. Then she heard the crunch of a horse approaching the cabin. It must have snowed and the white was reflecting the moon's spectral glow. For a moment she smiled, thinking, hoping, that Holliday had rented a horse to come check on her. If he just visited her, however brief, it would be the best Christmas she could ever hope to have. But the noise of the horse breaking through the icy crust of snow grew louder only to fade away eventually into the distance. Kate could feel the tears gather in her eyes then slide down her cheeks. She dropped her arm off the side of the bed for the whiskey. She felt alone and sick, hungry and morose, and most of all, unloved. What a pitiful Christmas. Perhaps what was left of the bottle would ease the pain of her tears, which suddenly hurt more than her sickness.

ELEVEN

At first they gathered quietly, almost reverently, the women talking in whispers, the men staring at sanitized surroundings devoid of liquor bottles, painted nudes, and splattered spittoons. The children fidgeted at their parents' feet or gazed with mouths agape at the cedar tree alight with candles and tapers and crowned with a tin star. The men, freshly bathed, scrubbed, shaved, oiled, combed, waxed, and splashed with tonic, stood stiffly in newly washed, starched, ironed, and brushed clothes. Men with reason to fear anything snug around their necks wore ties, and others who never went unarmed came without visible weapons. The single men, without wives to poke them in the ribs when they misbehaved, snickered at one another's cleanliness and at the saloon's transformation.

Two breeds of women — those who had worked the Bee Hive and those who hadn't — mingled with their own kind, sharing only the female instinct to bring food. Each carried a kettle or a pan or a platter and added a pie, a cake, fresh bread, pickles, canned fruits, a cut of beef, and even a dish of rare deviled eggs to the bar where Uncle Billy hovered over his own vittles.

The decent women clumped together, discussing babies, recipes, sewing, and their husbands' bad habits. Laced in their best dresses, the powdered, rouged, and perfumed women of the lesser breed tittered at the sober lunacy of celebrating Christmas in the Bee Hive.

So many had come. Through an ice-blurred window pane Lottie watched dozens more converging upon the Bee Hive across a fairy-tale landscape. Outside on the clapboard walk she could hear the noises of people stomping their shoes of snow and laughing gaily despite the cold. Though the merriment came loud from outside, inside the visitors shed their gaiety like their coats at the door and conversed in hushed tones, uncertain what to do or how to act. Sensing their discomfort, Lottie gathered the skirt of her yellow dress and marched to Uncle Billy, who was arranging dishes of food on the bar.

"Uncle Billy, do something!"

"Do somethin'? What in tarnation ya think I'm doin', Lottie Deno, takin' an afternoon snooze?"

"No, no, tell these folks it's okay to talk aloud, to have fun. Tell them anything that'll loosen them up. Anything!"

Wilson took a pot of beans from a new arrival, placed it on the bar, then backed away from the food. Wiping his hands on his stained apron, he thrust out his chest. "Okay, Lottie," he said. Stepping to the room's center, he raised his hands above his head, waiting for every whisper to die, then he lowered his arms. "Those of ya that don't know me, I'm Billy Wilson — Uncle Billy to me friends, and all of ya are me friends even if I don't know ya." He arched his bushy eyebrows as he unhooked his glasses to wipe them on his apron. "Now those of ya that don't know me won't know that I'm not much of a talker."

Those that knew Billy Wilson laughed and he raised his arms again for silence. "I've been asked by Miss Lottie Deno, whose generosity has brought us together this Christmas evenin', to say a few words." He inhaled deeply. "She says ya can talk."

Everyone laughed and Lottie, regretting her garbled request, joined them.

Wilson refitted his glasses over his ears. "Let's everybody warm up by the stoves and get acquainted. We've pitchers of hot apple cider for those of ya that wanna be warmed up on the inside. That's as strong a liquid refreshment as we're gonna have tonight, fellows, so don't go expectin' anythin' else."

A couple of male groans drew stern stares from the wives.

"Shortly we'll sing Christmas songs, then have treats for the children and dance a while. When me and me wife finish preparin' dinner, we'll eat. So ya start talking."

The guests applauded Wilson and a rising tide of voices quickly drowned the quiet. Now, Lottie thought as she looked around the room, the Christmas celebration was as it should be with people talking and laughing. Spotting Sophie and her family by the Christmas tree, Lottie started that way until she felt a tap on her shoulder.

"Miss Deno." The voice was familiar. Spinning about, she stared into the uniform of a U.S. Cavalry captain and lifted her eyes until they met Richard's.

Lottie giggled. "I'm glad to see you, Richard, but Rachel?"

He smiled, offering his hand. "By the food."

Lottie clasped his hand and pulled him through the mingling crowd. By the bar she spotted Rachel, releasing Richard's hand when she did and hugging Rachel. "You've made me so happy by coming. I feared you might not."

Rachel nodded. "I had second thoughts about a saloon. Oh, Lottie, I've been such a fool after the hanging and all."

"It takes a while to get over those things." Lottie's voice was soothing. "No, child, let's not talk about that day."

"I can talk about the hanging now, Lottie. It no longer haunts me. Look what I brought." She stepped to the bar and lifted a towel from two pans.

Lottie laughed. "Pecan pies. And I've been wondering if you'd ever look at another pecan." Lottie stared at Rachel, noting the sparkle in her eyes, the roundness in her face, and the fullness of her breasts. Perhaps Rachel had gained a few pounds, her waist not quite as narrow as it once was, but she looked better, happier than Lottie remembered. Richard must be good to her, for there was a lift in Rachel's voice. "I'm glad for you two," Lottie said, knowing the words seemed appropriate, but not understanding why.

Lottie turned to Richard. "Thank you for bringing her tonight. Except for a little girl and her family, you two were the only ones I invited by name."

"Looks like somebody did some inviting," Rachel observed.

"It's nice, isn't it?" Lottie answered, crossing her arms across her breast.

"It is indeed, Miss Deno," Richard said, offering an arm to both his wife and Lottie, then escorting them to the tree. "I think Rachel, despite her concerns, was curious to see inside the Bee Hive."

"Richard," Rachel cried, jerking her arm from his and stopping with both hands on her hips. She held her head at a rakish angle, her chin aimed defiantly at him. Then a quiver she could not control broke her wholesome lips into a slight grin. "He's right." She shrugged, inserting her arm back into Richard's. "Oh, I wanted to see you tonight, but I'll admit I was curious."

"It's not as fancy as the Cattle Exchange, but the Bee Hive's the biggest saloon in the Flat," Lottie explained. "The liquor and the spittoons have been put away and the floor swept for the first time I can remember." Lottie tapped her toe on the plank flooring. "And we brought in extra lamps to brighten it."

"I expected," Rachel paused, her white skin tinting pink, "naughty pictures and gaming tables."

Lottie covered a grin with her hand. "Are you disappointed? The pictures, there are some, but I had them taken down and locked upstairs with the gaming tables." Lottie pointed to the staircase. "Care to go upstairs, Rachel?"

Blushing deeper, Rachel stumbled over her tongue to say no. "I fear not, just being inside the Bee Hive is more than I should do in my . . ." The words blurred incomprehensible and Rachel turned away, dabbing at her eyes.

Pretending not to notice, Lottie pointed to a trio of men edging toward the piano, two picking up guitars, the third dragging out his fiddle. The players tuned the strings of their instruments long enough for a man, rain-barrel squat, to raise the piano stool and take up his perch behind them.

Uncle Billy Wilson climbed atop a rickety chair that trembled under his weight. He lifted his arms high and pious like a circuit preacher. "Will ya listen to me?" The noise continued. "If ya wanna eat, ya best listen to me." Slowly, quiet settled into the room. "We'll sing Christmas songs first, then ya children'll get a toy from Miss Lottie Deno and after a few dances we eat. Play the music," Wilson commanded.

Everyone sang "O Come All Ye Faithful," "Silent Night," and "Oh, Tannenbaum," and then each again. And when it was done, the people gathered around the tree while Lottie passed out wooden tops, tin airwheels, magnets or little tin trumpets to the boys and rag dolls or little tin dishes to the girls. Lottie handed the biggest doll of all to Sophie, who reached up for Lottie and hugged her.

By the time she had finished handing out gifts, Lottie had lost Rachel and Richard. She stepped from the tree, studying the room until she spotted them at a table along the opposite wall. Though she planned to join them, she was intercepted midway across the room by George Wilhelm, who asked for a dance. Though she preferred otherwise, she accepted his invitation in gratitude for all he had done to make this night possible. Together they stepped to the dance floor as the musicians called out a waltz. When they struck the song, George stepped awkwardly toward her, his timing off a half count. This improvisation he managed was not the waltz she had learned as a young lady courted by some of Kentucky's finest gentlemen. Step, step, close — she could do it from the memory of a hundred dances. But George danced step, close, step, pausing on the wrong beat and several times trampling her feet.

The days she had danced a true waltz seemed like another life. Once she had waltzed on grassy lawns beneath Chinese lanterns and on the mahogany floors of Kentucky's finest hotels instead of on the roughhewn planks of a dingy saloon. Once her partners had been the well-groomed sons of senators, great merchants, vast property holders, steamboat owners, and generals. Now she danced with a merchant clerk who still wore his hat. If the war had not come, she wondered how different her life might have been. Perhaps she might have borne the son of a senator or even a president; the ambitions of those who had courted her made it seem possible. But maybe the war changed nothing. Like her father, she had loved gambling on cards or horses. Perhaps every road she could have taken would have led to this dirty saloon in Fort Griffin. But like the cards of an opponent's discarded hand, she could never know what might have been.

When the music stopped, she danced a step more, grazing George's boot. She asked his pardon, though he had sought no forgiveness when he had trespassed on her toes, and thanked him profusely for the dance. She thought George pleased by her words and excused herself to join Richard and Rachel, vowing not to dance again. The three watched and talked while the children played all about them with their new toys and the adults careened across the dance floor doing their versions of waltzes and the schottische. People around her laughed, and she was glad. Several times she refused dances and was prepared to say no yet again when she looked up at the latest man standing beside her. Jack Jacobs, his hat over his heart, his upper teeth nicking his lower lip, offered her his calloused hand. Without a word, she lifted her hand to meet his. He dropped his hat on the table and accompanied Lottie to the dance floor.

As the music began, Lottie felt his hand fall gently upon her waist and saw the softness in his blue eyes. "Dancing's not something I'm good at. Though I'm glad enough to have a dance with you, that I'll risk the embarrassment." He stepped to the music in an unadorned two-step, his motions unpolished but their simplicity covering his shortcomings.

"Thank you for coming, Jack," Lottie answered, once she'd picked up the rhythm of his step. "I must pay you for fetching the tree. You should have seen the children's eyes widen at it. And the turkeys, how many did you get?"

"Six, one about as big as I ever saw. Uncle Billy says he's cooked many a gobbler, but never one that size."

"Then I shall pay you a good price, Jack."

"You're paying me now with this dance. That will do."

"Now, Jack," Lottie argued around the dance floor, "this is not your payment. I'd dance with you, no matter." Lottie pleaded with no hope of convincing Jacobs of her debt. "At times I don't understand men. No shame in a woman paying you for what you've done."

"And there's no shame in doing a friend a favor. Now, you are returning the favor." A barrage of applause ended the dance. Jacobs smiled. "I've been repaid."

"But I must owe you another dance," Lottie protested, as Jacobs steered her back to the table.

"One dance will do. More, and I might forget what a poor dancer I am and what a fine lady you are," he answered.

"Thank you, Jack," Lottie squeezed his hand. "This has been a magnificent evening for me and I think for many others too."

When they reached the table, Jacobs pulled Lottie's chair out for her as Richard stood to assist. She took her seat and Jacobs picked up his hat just as Uncle Billy's voice called out above the chatter.

"Everybody, listen up," he said, moving into the dance area. As he walked, he sharpened a carving knife on a whetstone, the rasping of metal against stone sounding like the whispers of old maids. "One more dance, everybody. Then it's time for eats. I'm about to carve up the biggest turkey ya ever saw." Everyone clapped as Wilson retreated to the bar to attack the turkey.

Lottie twisted in her chair. "Jack, will you join us for . . . Jack, Jack Jacobs," she called, but he had disappeared. She looked from Rachel to Richard. "Where'd he go?" They shrugged. "He should've stayed for the meal. He provided a good share of it. He's a good man too."

"The kind that would make a good husband," Rachel suggested.

Lottie ignored Rachel's remark. She stood, taking in the crowd, but Jacobs had gone. Near the door John Henry Holliday stared back. So much for Lottie's Luck, she thought. "Perhaps we should start for the food line," Lottie suggested to her table mates. Still Holliday stared, like a predator stalking prey.

Without waiting for an answer, Lottie marched toward the piles of food, Richard and Rachel joining her just as the music ended. Lottie grabbed a tin plate and eating utensils and worked her way along the line, helping herself to modest portions of boiled potatoes, hominy, dried beans, and a deviled egg. Using the carving knife and a serving fork, Uncle Billy dropped a thick slice of white turkey meat on her plate. After picking up a sourdough biscuit, a slice of Rachel's pecan pie, and a cup of hot apple cider, she angled back to her table and waited until Rachel and Richard rejoined her, then nibbled silently at her food.

Finally, Rachel spoke, a hurt in her voice. "I'm sorry for meddling about a husband. I should be a more gracious guest."

"Please, Rachel, let's forget that and enjoy the evening."

They talked between bites, Lottie learning about Richard's duties at the fort and the latest Comanche troubles and about the fun Rachel had shared on their Sunday afternoon rides. Lottie relished the conversation until she felt the awkward presence of someone beside her, an eavesdropper, an intruder. She frowned.

"Pardon me, ladies, sir," John Henry Holliday said. "Might I join you? Chairs are scarce now that most have been served." Holliday placed his plate on the table.

Lottie could smell liquor on his breath and could see the disgust in Rachel's eyes, but she smiled to Holliday. "Certainly you may join us. It's Christmas," Lottie said, glancing from Holliday to Rachel, her face flushed with fear. "This is John Henry Holliday. John Henry, this is Mr. and Mrs . . ."

"We've met," Richard interrupted her. "We rode the stage from Jacksboro to Griffin back in the fall."

"A good memory, sir. I recollected the face, but not the occasion." Holliday slid into a chair and up to the table.

"I don't forget people who pull a gun on me."

A sinister scowl worked its way snakelike across Holliday's lips and he turned to Rachel, his voice harsh as a winter wind. "Yes, ma'am, that's true. You don't realize how close you came to being a widow that day."

Rachel dropped her fork, her hand flying to her mouth. "Perhaps we best be going, Richard."

"On no, ma'am," Holliday's voice turned soothing. "I promise you no harm, nor your husband. I wasn't much for talking that day, especially with a blue belly cavalry officer, no offense, sir. But this is Christmas and I will ignore my prejudices against the U.S. Army."

"John Henry is a dentist," Lottie interjected to change the subject. "And, in his way, a gentleman, though ruined by the gambling urge in his blood."

Holliday took a bite from his meager plate, chewing it like a kid taking medicine. "It's something Lottie and I have in common."

"I'd say it's all you and Lottie have in common," Rachel answered.

"A noble heritage, ma'am," Holliday corrected, "is something we also share. Our blood may be tainted by gambling, but it is a noble southern blood. Nothing personal against you, ma'am, or your husband, but the sight of his uniform brings back unfortunate days and events." His voice had hardened.

"John Henry, this is Christmas, so show your upbringing and put aside these unpleasantries," Lottie said.

129

"Accept my invitation to dance, Lottie . . . not just any dance, but a waltz." Holliday's voice was soothing again.

"Perhaps, though I am growing tired."

"I understand your reluctance, your toes likely still aching from your two previous trips across the dance floor."

"They were decent men, John Henry."

"Not decent dancers," he shot back. "Say yes, and I will excuse myself so not to offend your friends." He stared coldly at Richard and Rachel. "Then when I collect my dance, I'll behave as a choir boy."

"Then we shall dance, John Henry. A waltz. And now, will you allow us to finish our meal?"

Holliday nodded, then turned to Rachel. "Ma'am, it's been a pleasure to converse with you. And sir, you have a charming wife." Rachel turned up her nose at the compliment and Lottie watched her face color. Standing, Holliday gathered his plate and eating utensils, then wandered away.

"That man," Rachel wrinkled her nose, "upsets me. Lottie, how can you dance with him?"

"There are many things a gracious hostess must do, Rachel. You should know that. But I am anxious to dance with him."

"You continue to surprise me, Lottie," Rachel said.

Lottie laughed at Rachel's awkward smile. "And you never let me forget it."

They talked an hour away while about them people finished their meals and their seconds and their desserts. At length Rachel's shoulders drooped and her eyelids grew heavy. "What time is it, Richard?" she finally asked, stifling a yawn.

Her husband pulled his watch and snapped it open. "Eleven fifteen," he said, closing the cover.

Rachel raised her hand to her lips and tried to shake the next yawn away, but her mouth contorted widely to let it pass. "It's well past my bedtime, Lottie. In the army, men get up early and their wives rise with them, at least this wife does."

"In saloons," Lottie replied, "we stay late without worry of the bugler. Perhaps you should stay long enough to watch me dance with Mister Holliday. Then you will see why I accepted his invitation."

"I'll never understand you, Lottie. You could have any decent man here, but why you choose to dance with him is beyond me. I'm too tired to figure it out," she said, rising slowly from her chair. "Richard, I need my rest."

Arising with her, Lottie realized something about Rachel had changed. Lottie studied her a moment, the roundness in Rachel's breasts and the slight tightness of her dress around her stomach finally making sense. Rachel had not taken a dance all evening, and Richard had been most attentive.

"Lottie, thank you for a most pleasant evening."

"Except for Mister Holliday?"

Rachel nodded. "I hope you have an enjoyable dance," she said, turning to her husband. "Would you find my coat, sweetheart?" He smiled and excused himself.

"Rachel," Lottie whispered as Richard moved away, "are you with child?"

The startled grin, mixed with equal doses of joy and concern, answered Lottie's question. Her eyes lit up with a maternal glow which she could not hide. Rachel nodded. "I told Richard this morning. The news was my gift to him."

Lottie leaned to hug Rachel.

"Oh, Lottie, how I wanted to tell you, too, tonight, but not in a saloon, not with news this holy and joyous."

"Yes, Rachel, but this day celebrates a birth, not in a saloon, but a stable. I'd prefer a saloon, but no matter. You have made good my Christmas, by your news and by your presence."

Rachel squeezed Lottie tightly. "This has been my best Christmas ever, Lottie, and I am glad I shared it with you, even in a saloon." Rachel snickered against her tears.

Richard returned wearing his coat, Rachel's over his arm. "Rachel, I told you that Miss Deno would figure it out."

"Well, Richard, just how do you know what we've been discussing?" his wife shot back, dabbing at a stray tear. "You can't even think, much less talk about it, without your eyes fogging over. And I do detect a mist about them."

Rachel squeezed Lottie a final time, then stepped into Richard's open arms and hugged him. "We must go, Richard, before I make a complete fool of myself around Lottie's guests. Good night, Lottie." Rachel started for the door without looking back. Richard followed her, draping her coat around her shoulders, then glancing back at Lottie and smiling.

"Good night," Lottie called softly after them. Lottie watched as they wove their way through the crowd to the door.

"A touching sight, a man and his wife, Lottie."

Turning around to the voice, Lottie stared at Holliday. She failed to decipher his tone as either sincere or sarcastic. "They make a fine couple. You should be ashamed for scaring them so."

"I have come to collect my dance, not discuss my manners."

"Seems I am repaying everyone with a dance tonight," she said, hooking her arm in his and moving toward the dancers. "I prefer a waltz."

"And I as well," Holliday answered, an unusual note of jauntiness in his consumptive throat.

"But that's not what they're playing."

"Just wait," Holliday said, as he maneuvered Lottie among the dancers. He released her arm, faced her and bowed, the music stopping instantly.

Lottie curtsied. "How'd you do that, John Henry Holliday?"

"Bribery. I passed a few dollars among the musicians, Miss Deno, gold dollars, not those foolish greenbacks."

Then the music began again, a new tune, a waltz. "The song reminds me of Kentucky." Lottie smiled as Holliday put his hand upon her waist and she her hand upon his shoulder. Their free hands united, and at once they stepped to the music.

"I thought perhaps it would make you sentimental and you'd tell me your name, Miss Deno."

"And marry you here tonight?" Lottie said, smiling at his gliding step. "You may be a good dancer, but never that good."

They circled around the floor, like one agile figure, molded at the hands and moving precisely in an ever widening ring, like ripples from a stone thrown upon a pond. Step, step, close; step, step, close. Holliday danced the way a waltz was meant to be danced. Except where they held each other, their bodies never touched; only the hem of Lottie's dress ever brushed Holliday as she twirled about in his arms. He was wonderful on his feet, light and agile, like a cat. Lottie relished the vigor that pulsed through her body as her feet obeyed Holliday's around the floor, both dancers moving as naturally as branches in a breeze. Lottie saw in his blue eyes a smile unnoticed before, like a gold coin at the bot-

132

tom of a clear blue pond, invisible in the sand except in a perfect light. About them, other dancers stopped and abandoned the floor to their superiors. When they alone waltzed, Holliday nodded his head to Lottie, acknowledging her skill. And his.

Circling about the floor as easily as skaters on ice, she lost track of time and of people, as if she lived only to waltz, like a tiny figurine atop a spring-wound music box. Lottie savored the precise and fluid steps of Holliday, recalling not a single man his better. Through several refrains they danced and when the music stopped, they waltzed to the applause twice more around the floor, as if they could dance forever. Then they stopped as they had danced — in perfect harmony, Holliday stepping back and bowing to Lottie, she responding with a curtsy, then both acknowledging their audience. The men and women clapped louder and cheered in a simultaneous convulsion of approval. Lottie could see admiration etched in the faces of the matrons and jealousy trapped in the smiles of the young women. The spectators called "More, more, once more" and applauded harder.

Holliday took Lottie's hand and looked into her eyes. "Shall we?"

Lottie could not help but smile. "I promised you but one."

"But this one is for them. Agreed, Miss Deno?"

"Agreed, John Henry."

The spectators cheered as Lottie curtsied to the four directions. She could see joy in their faces and she could not hold back her smile. It had been a long time since she had enjoyed such a dance.

And then as she curtsied the fourth time, Lottie saw Big Nose Kate. Lottie's smile stiffened.

Kate stood on a chair by the bar, blindly stuffing handfuls of turkey in her mouth. She was eating like a savage and she looked like one, her hair matted and uncombed, her eyes wild and distant, her skin splotched red, her shoulders sloped and trembling. She seemed to be wearing a chemise instead of a dress. Something was wrong with Big Nose Kate, but Lottie could find no sympathy in her soul for the whore.

To Lottie's back the musicians cranked up another waltz. Holliday slid easily around to face Lottie and proceeded to glide across the floor. He moved like before, but Lottie knew she was a fraction of a beat behind him, not enough for others to notice but plenty for Holliday to seek the reason in her eyes. Now, her eyes avoided his, and with every twirl around the floor she glanced at the bar, Kate towering sinisterly above it, stuffing her mouth with food. Kate seemed to be without understanding, staring blankly back, even when she blindly wielded the carving knife to slice another chunk of meat from the turkey carcass.

This dance lasted and lasted almost endlessly for Lottie, and when it finally did stop she glanced immediately to where Kate had stood. But she was gone. The crowd applauded again, louder, but Lottie could not feel the enthusiasm.

Holliday turned Lottie to face the musicians and he gave a deep and long bow, disguising a rugged cough. Lottie curtsied beside him. Everyone cheered.

A blood-curdling scream cut like a knife through the merriment. The applause disintegrated into a terrified outcry. Lottie twisted around, jerking her hand from the coughing Holliday. She froze at the gleam of a carving knife drawn high in the air and starting toward her. She saw Kate's contorted face as the knife came at her. And then she was knocked to the floor as men from all sides rushed in like water after a splash.

Stumbling forward as the men surged around him, Holliday crashed into the piano, a discordant chord announcing his arrival at the worn keys. The noise was lost in the confusion of heavy boots, husky shouts, and horrified women, screaming for their children. Holliday bounced off the piano with a gun in his hand and swung around in a tight arc to face the attackers. His sweaty finger quivered with uncertainty on the trigger and his mind raced with the memory of a dozen enemies, Ed Bailey foremost among them. Everyone else stared at the knot of men writhing on the floor like a ball of snakes, Lottie sitting just beyond the flailing legs, holding her hands over her mouth and shaking her head. Whoever started the commotion, Holliday thought, was under control at the bottom of that pile. He shoved the Smith and Wesson back into the holster riding under his sweaty armpit. As he stepped to Lottie, a straining voice from the floor called out, "I've got the knife. Get up easy."

Assisting Lottie up, Holliday felt her arm tremble. Her lips quivered and her face had whitened. Holliday led her to the piano, a sweep of his arm commanding the piano player to abandon his stool. Lottie sank down upon the seat. Her gray eyes were hard like granite. She glowered at the men unraveling from the floor as she strained for each breath, her bosom heaving from fear. Then she spoke in phrases. "That whore . . ." Lottie pointed, ". . . she tried . . . to kill me."

Holliday stared as the men peeled themselves away. One came up holding a carving knife, another sucking the blood from a slight cut on his hand. Then Holliday recognized Kate, pinned by the last two men. Damn her.

"What do we do with her now?" called one of her captors. Kate lay motionless, her eyes closed. "Something's wrong. She's burning with fever, must of addled her mind." He looked around the room, his gaze stopping at Lottie and Holliday. "Miss Deno, you want us to save her for the sheriff?"

"Just get her out of here," Lottie answered softly, her voice composed now, as calm as water in a rain barrel, but Holliday noticed a slight shaking in her fingers.

The two men holding Kate nodded. "Anyone know where she lives?" one asked, but drew no reply. "Surely somebody has an idea where she sleeps." He shrugged at the quiet.

Holliday looked around the room, recognizing several men who had paid for Kate's favors, but not one would admit it.

"Just dump her in the street," Lottie spit the words out, "but get her out of here so our Christmas can continue."

Holliday swallowed hard, a bitterness stinging in his throat. He watched Lottie's gray eyes. "I know her place." He felt Lottie's cold stare and saw her mouth drop open, then slowly close until her lips puckered with distaste. She looked from him to Kate, then slowly shook her head, an auburn curl falling across her forehead. "Thank you, Miss Deno," Holliday said, "for the pleasure of your dance." He backed away.

Lottie nodded, brushing the curl back in place. "You are quite a man on your feet and, evidently, off them as well," she said without looking. "Good night, Mister Holliday."

Holliday, coughing away his nervousness, looked to Kate. She lay as limp and lifeless as an empty flour sack upon the floor. "I can't carry her home. Somebody with a wagon give me a hand," he ordered. Another whore and a man in a plaid shirt joined him as a path parted through the crowd toward the door. As the prostitute pulled Kate's chemise to cover her legs, Holliday and the man lifted her toward the door. From a table at the door Holliday grabbed two coats, despite their owners' objections, and covered Kate with them. "You'll get them back," Holliday shouted, pushing several other coats to the floor. His helper opened the door, and they carried Kate out into the bitter cold. Holliday kicked the door and shortly he heard another waltz. Damn it all.

They placed Kate in a wagon beside a pile of firewood that hadn't been unloaded. Except for Holliday's directions and Kate's occasional moans, only the crunching noise of horse hooves and wagon wheels breaking through the frozen glaze of the snow interrupted the awesome stillness of Christmas night. The landscape in its shroud of white reflected the beaming moonlight, casting a sickly pallor over everything.

The cold pricked at Holliday's face like a thousand icy needles and he rubbed his hands together to keep the stiffness from setting in. When the wagon stopped in front of Kate's crib, the whore jumped down to open the door as Holliday and the man unloaded Kate. Anticipating at least the warmth of a low burning fire, Holliday moved inside. As the whore lit a lamp, Holliday realized it was no less cold inside than outside. He stepped to the stove and dropped his bare hand upon it, shivering at the cold metal and cursing the empty woodbox by its side.

"Her fire's out," he said. "I'm buying your firewood. Bring it in." The man assisting stared a moment, then shrugged and retreated to the wagon. After the first load, Holliday pulled a double eagle from his pocket and pressed it into the man's hand.

The whore tucked Kate under her quilts and newspapers, then carried the borrowed coats back to the wagon. Holliday stepped to Kate's bed and felt her feverish head. She shivered at the touch of his cold hand, which came away wet with her perspiration. Holliday looked for a cloth to wipe her face, seeing but one, hanging half out of her washbasin. He tugged at the stiff cloth, but it was trapped in the basin by the icy grip of frozen water. "Damn." He knew he must warm the cabin.

As the man and the whore left, Holliday started a fire, feeding it newspaper and kindling. He mothered the flame with more wood, listening as he did to the retreat of the wagon, cracking through the glazed snow. Grabbing the washbasin, he set it on the stove, the water gradually melting and releasing the cloth that had frozen in it. After squeezing the rag of its excess moisture, he moved to Kate's side, humbled by the presence of sickness. Gently he wiped away the fevered beads of sweat, cringing as he rubbed the cloth across her dried, cracked, and bleeding lips. Her tongue darted from behind her parched lips and lapped at the slight moisture left by the cloth. Then her eyes opened, little slits gradually widening, then blinking constantly. "Water," she whispered, her voice as faint and dry as a desert breeze. Her eyelids batted away the confusion until her eyes finally focused on Holliday. "You came." She sighed. "Water."

He glanced about the room for her water pail, spotting it by the door. Leaving the moist cloth across her forehead, he retrieved the pail, half-full with ice. He placed the pail atop the stove and tossed another log into the fire. The pail's cold metal sizzled and popped as it absorbed heat and the ice began to puddle. Holliday found a tin cup on the table and filled it with the first of the melted ice, then carried the drink to Kate's side. Lifting her head with one hand, he offered her ravenous thirst slight sips. The water revived her senses and she twisted toward Holliday as he lowered her head.

"What happened?" she whispered.

"You came to the Bee Hive."

"I remember walking through the snow and you dancing with some woman. Was I dreaming?"

"You've been delirious, Kate. Just rest."

Kate's parched lips strained to smile. "I'm glad you came, Doc. I'd about given up on you, but I knew you'd come." She twisted her head in the pillow and reached for his hand, holding it against her cheek. Holliday sat beside her on the bed until her hand fell away from his and she sank into sleep.

Holliday raised himself wearily from the bed and suddenly he was tired, the dancing, the cold finally taking their due. He fell into one of the stiff rawhide-bottomed chairs and pulled at his boots. As he struggled out of the second boot, a pain like a river of ice raced down his back and suddenly he was shivering. Damn consumption. His nightly agony was gathering force and he felt

137

feverish. A deep husky cough exploded from his lungs and left a wad of bloody mucus into his mouth. He spit the phlegm into the woodbox, then undressed quickly. He trimmed the lamp, then crawled stiffly into bed beside Kate.

Through her fevered haze, she sensed his nearness and moved to him. Holliday put an arm around her, drawing her even closer. He shivered with his own fever. Kate had the odor of sickness about her, but even so, her nearness was stirring within him a rising urge that would not abate. Their hands groped for one another and then their two bodies were one, shoving against each other until they were spent of all but their fevers.

TWELVE

Kate flitted around Holliday's faro table, pesky as a fly too nervous to alight. Humming to the tune of the barroom piano, she circled behind Holliday, strode by him, running her fingers along the spine of his frock coat, then slid away, lifting her skirt to expose her calf and her availability. With just four customers, Holliday dealt a leisurely game, but damn how Kate grated his nerves, like a wheel on an ungreased wooden axle.

Since her recovery, Kate had pestered Holliday with her foolish favors like a virgin after her first kiss. Holliday knew few dangers the equal of a whore with marriage on her mind. He coughed with disgust as Kate passed quickly by, dragging her hand across his back. He twisted his head to curse her, but Kate was beyond him, the profanity trailing in her wake. His customers snickered until Holliday's jaw tightened. He slapped a card atop the discard stack, glaring from customer to customer until he spotted Chancey ambling toward him, his crooked nose contorted by the wide grin beneath it.

"Damn you. You think it's funny, don't you?" Holliday growled. "That woman's gonna cost the Cattle Exchange money by distracting your dealers. And you think it's funny!"

Chancey clapped his two massive hands and cocked his head. "She's not costing me anything tonight, business being poorest since Christmas. And I ain't heard anyone at this table yelling to raise the house limit, so she's not doing me much damage. It's you she's causing all the pain."

Holliday slid a card out of the dealing box and exposed a winning seven that no one had bet on. "Bad business when your whores bother your dealers and customers all the time."

Cracking his knuckles one by one along a balled fist, Chancey pursed his lips, as if cogitating the mysteries of womanhood. "Since she took a shining to you, Doc, I don't recall her giving me any trouble." Chancey's popping knuckles punctuated his laugh. "Fact is," Chancey said, flashing his tobacco-stained teeth, "only reason I hired you was to keep her out of my hair. I'll be damned if you haven't done just that."

"Crap, Chancey," Holliday started, then convulsed in a cough, "you should throw her butt out on the street."

The saloon owner tugged at his sagging ear lobe, then attacked the knuckles on his other hand, each joint exploding with a pop. "It entertains me to see a man of your nerve fidget over a woman. You can't shoot a female like you can a man."

"Damn," Holliday said, surveying the bets and drawing another card from the dealing box. A red queen came into view, losing the Cattle Exchange ten dollars to one of the customers. "Dammit, Chancey, you've flapped your tongue so much you've soured my luck."

Chancey reached for his smoke fixings in his tobacco tin and watched Kate, now dancing around the floor with a lame partner. "Yessir, if she don't put an edge on you like a double-bit ax, then I'm President Grant, Ulysses S.," he drew the ess out into a long smug hiss, then turned toward his office.

"Ulysses shit." Doc slapped the table as Kate, her arms around a club-footed buffalo hunter, winked at him from across the dance floor. Holliday nodded to his customers. "Twenty dollars for the one of you that'll screw her the rest of the night. She's not bad." In unison the four heads twisted around to judge if the prize matched their lusts.

Kate stopped instantly in her tracks, the cripple almost falling to the floor. "You best quit your staring, fellows," she yelled over the piano music. "It's bad manners and you're ruining my partner's concentration." She jerked the bewildered hunter's arm.

140

"Hell, you might rattle him so he'd miss my feet a time or two." As suddenly as she had stopped, she resumed her dance, the cripple lurching after her around the floor as fast as his lame foot could follow.

The faro players turned back to Holliday. "The offer still stands, any one of you want her?" Doc dug into the pocket of his frock coat and flipped a double eagle onto the table, the gold piece spinning, then settling onto the green felt. "There's twenty dollars. Enough there for all of you to line up outside her door at three dollars a turn."

Reconsidering the offer, each man took a second look, then one by one turned to Holliday, three shaking their heads, the fourth pausing, then glancing back over his shoulder at Kate. "Twenty dollars," he mused, spitting a stream of tobacco toward a spittoon and missing by a foot. "Does she have to get it all?"

"If your aim's as bad at screwing as spitting," Holliday paused, ". . . she won't get any."

"The money, dang it." The ruddy-faced cowboy pulled his hat low over his embarrassed eyes. "The money."

Holliday tugged on the stiff cuffs of his ruffled white shirt. "If you can keep her from pestering me for less than twenty dollars, the difference is yours."

Nudging the brim of his hat high enough to peek at Holliday, the cowhand nodded. "I reckon I've got a better chance making a profit in her bed than at your table," he said.

"Don't count on it," Holliday answered.

The cowhand grabbed the double eagle, tucked the gold coin in his britches pocket, then watched Kate until the music stopped. After she shoved the cripple away, the cowboy stepped toward the dance floor.

"Remember your aim, fellow," Doc whispered. "Kate don't take kindly to misfires."

The cowboy moved cautiously. Taking off his hat with one hand, he offered Kate the other.

"If you wanna dance," she yelled, "it's gonna cost you extra. That lame fellow stomped my toes into mush." The cowhand cleared his throat and half announced, half coughed out his intentions. Kate clapped her hands. "Screwing's a damn sight safer than dancing with you heifer herders." She grabbed his still proffered hand and, looking at Doc, shouted across the room. "At least somebody here appreciates good companionship." She jerked her lover-to-be's hand and started toward the door, with each step her ample behind swaggering from side to side as if saying, "So there, so there, so there."

Kate grabbed her coat from a peg at the door and slipped it on without help from her customer. Then she scurried ahead of him out the door and headlong into an entering customer. The customer shoved her back, but Kate swung her fist for his head. Though he ducked, the glancing blow knocked his hat to the floor. "You goddam, ill-mannered chickenshit," she screamed. "I'm a lady, so watch out."

To a chorus of laughter, Kate disappeared into the darkness as her victim bent over his deformed hat and mumbled under his breath. Brushing the dust off his derby and molding it back into shape, Ed Bailey threw back his shoulders like he had been the victor in the encounter and scowled toward Holliday's table. Holliday's eyes locked on Bailey's and sparks of hate flew between the men. Bailey mumbled words too low for Holliday to decipher, then spit on the floor as he turned to the bar. Bailey slapped his thigh and whistled at the bored bartender. Pulling a towel from a hand rack and wiping the chill from his fleshy jowls, Bailey asked for a drink.

Holliday warily watched Bailey's reflected glare in the back-bar mirror. When he reached hock in the dealing box, Holliday slipped his hand off the table and unbuttoned his frock coat before reshuffling the deck. As Holliday slid the mixed cards back into the dealing box, he heard his name mingled among Bailey's curses. Holliday stretched, then wiggled his fingers of their stiffness. Just in case. Bailey downed another glass of whiskey and Holliday wondered how many it would take to fortify his courage.

Twice more, Holliday made it through the deck before Bailey finally slammed his glass down on the bar, looked at himself in the mirror, and wiped his puffy lips on the towel. Watching the reflection, Holliday eased his chair back from the table, then slipped another card from the dealing box. One of the players laughed that he'd finally picked a winner, and Holliday shot a quick glance that way before watching Bailey unbutton the coat covering his sidearm. Holliday paid off the winner. Across the room, Bailey twisted away from the bar and hiked his gunbelt up his watermelon gut. With exaggerated steps, he marched to Holliday's table and elbowed his way between two bettors.

"Goddam you, Bailey, learn some manners before you step up to my table."

"Why don't you teach some to that big-assed whore of yours?" Bailey answered.

Holliday shoved himself away from the table, his chair legs screeching an alarm across the room. The piano music died away to be replaced by the thud of boots retreating from the faro table. Pulling his frock coat apart at the waist without taking his eyes off Bailey, Holliday cleared his throat and hooked the coat behind the holster on his hip.

"You best apologize to my customers for interrupting their game or your only friend will be the undertaker," Holliday said, his words coming sharp and distinct like the retort of a gun.

Bailey's eyes darted from side to side.

"Goddam you," Holliday challenged, "give them an apology or go for your gun, you bastard."

The words hit Bailey hard, his watery eyes batting at the insult which seemed to echo through the room's stillness. Holliday watched Bailey, knowing the challenge would go unanswered.

Bailey swallowed hard. "Pardon me, boys." He shrugged in their direction. "Didn't aim to offend your sensibilities."

"Then just what in hell did you aim to do, Bailey?" Holliday shot back. "Show off the manners of a rooting hog?"

Bailey's fleshy hand flinched over his sidearm, his face growing white with uncertainty.

"Goddam you, go for your gun, you son of a bitch," Holliday baited him. "And when you pull the trigger, make sure it's a good shot because I don't make a third the target you do."

Bailey caught his breath. "You cost me my table here and I don't aim to forget it. Won't no other saloon take me after the Cattle Exchange cut me loose, Holliday. You'll pay for that."

Holliday laughed, then fell silent, deathly quiet. "If I'm gonna pay," he said, a growl in his throat, "then call in your debt right now."

Bailey considered the offer. "I lost my work because of you."

"Way I hear it, Bailey," Holliday answered, "you were cheating the house. No wonder you can't get work."

"That's a lie you started."

Holliday jerked his Colt free, a glint of terror flashing across Bailey's face. "You calling me a liar?" Holliday thumbed back the hammer on his Colt, then heard the click of twin hammers nearby. Chancey had emerged from his office with his shotgun. "You calling me a liar, Bailey?"

"What you said is a lie." Bailey stepped back.

"Is it? You've cheated with that goddam reflecting pipe. You tried to cheat me the first night I ever put eyes on your pathetic face."

"I was good for Chancey," Bailey said, backing another step away from Holliday. "Brought him a lot of business, I did."

"Both of you cool off." Chancey's deep voice bellowed across the room, startling Bailey. "Now let's everybody keep our heads. I've got a load of shot here that'll put an end to both your complaints. Ed, you just let your coat fall over your gun there, and Doc you ease that revolver back home to its holster." Chancey stepped toward them, the shotgun at belt level.

For a moment the only noise in the room came from the slamming of the front door and a squeal Holliday recognized as Kate's. What in the hell was she doing back? As Bailey let his coat fall over his gun, Holliday eased his Colt into its holster.

"That's better," Chancey told them, releasing the hammers on the shotgun. "I don't want any killing in my place. It's bad enough to sweep up the floor without having to mop up your blood. Now, Ed, you know I don't like anyone disturbing my dealers. Why'd you come?"

"A drink, Chancey," Bailey answered. "That's all."

"Like hell, you've got a thorn in your butt about something. What do you want other than Holliday's hide?"

"My table back, that's all. I don't want any trouble," he said, eyeing Chancey for a moment, then turning to Holliday, "though I'm not running away if it comes."

"You could've come to me. You didn't have to cause Doc any trouble, now did you?"

"He's the one that cost me my table, taking a lesser split. You told me that yourself."

Chancey nodded, then grinned at Holliday. "That's what I told you, but it was a business decision."

"Still cost me my job. And Holliday's been spreading stories I was a cheat."

"Perhaps, Ed," Chancey said, pausing a moment to weigh his next words, "perhaps I can give you a table back."

Holliday slammed his fist into his palm. "Now wait a minute, Chancey. Giving him a table will lead to trouble. Me and him in the same room? Or are you letting me go this time?"

"Neither," Chancey answered gruffly. "You fellows don't do something that'll cause anybody grief. I may acquire another saloon."

Bailey whistled. "Another saloon? Which one, Chancey?"

"When the time's right, you'll know, Ed. Until then, you just stay away from here. If you cause any trouble, I'll guaran-damn-tee you won't ever work for me again, Ed. Think you can hold up that end of the proposition?"

"You know I can, Chancey," Bailey said, backing farther away from Holliday's faro table. "You know for sure that I can."

"See to it or you won't pass through the door of any saloon that I own."

Bailey nodded.

"Doc," Chancey said, "you'll get an explanation later. Just don't cause any trouble."

"You're the boss, Chancey."

"Okay, Ed, step to the bar for one on the house. Then I'll see you out the door," Chancey ordered. "Doc, you settle with your customers and we'll close the table for the night. Not enough business to merit a shooting. Maybe tempers will calm." Chancey turned to the idle piano player. "Dammit, get your hands out of your pockets and tickle the ivory, something easy."

The piano player jumped to his stool and started clacking out a popular tune. Bailey cast a final malevolent gaze toward Holliday, then stepped to the bar. Their grudge wasn't settled, just postponed, Holliday thought as he made right the bets of his customers. When Bailey leaned into the bar, Holliday's taut body relaxed with a cough. Glancing over the fist wadded at his mouth, Holliday saw Kate at the bar, a bottle of whiskey tilted to her lips. Damn if his twenty-dollar gold piece shouldn't have

145

bought him more time than this. Kate lowered the bottle, staring across the room at him, then swaggered toward him, choking the bottle by its neck.

"Chancey saved your hide, Doc," she smirked, then swigged at the liquor.

Holliday wiped his lips with the back of his hand. "I can take care myself."

Kate slid up to the table and slapped her bottle hard upon it. Holliday smelled the heavy odor of liquor upon her breath.

"Why'd you pay that cowhand to keep me the night, Doc? That's what I wormed out of him." From behind her full lips her voice sputtered like a lit fuse before it reached the charge. "And don't deny it, he told me you did."

Holliday ignored the question, staring beyond her at Bailey.

"Let's dance, Doc," Kate said, walking around the table to his side. "I hear you're a good one to waltz. I'd like to dance with someone that misses my toes." She grasped his fingers.

Jerking his hand away, he spoke. "You're a pest, Kate. It tires me."

She retreated slowly around the table to her bottle. Holliday could see the hurt flooding in her eyes and could feel his own anger rising. Kate lifted the bottle as gently as she would a newborn child and drank slowly from it. She looked at him with pleading eyes. "Please, Doc, just one dance?" Her voice was still soft.

"As long as Bailey's here, I'm keeping an eye on him."

"Then when he leaves?"

Holliday waved her aside, waiting for Bailey to slake his thirst. Kate slinked to the nearest table and nursed her hurt feelings with the bottle. Bailey seemed to enjoy prolonging his free drink, but finally he eased away from the bar, Chancey walking step for step with him and then opening the door like a jail guard. Both men stepped outside, the door closing behind them. Holliday could feel the tension draining from him. He took a deep breath that singed his lungs, then leaned back in his chair, rocking slightly on the rear legs.

And then Kate was beside him. "Now the dance you promised, Doc." Her voice carried the invitation of her extended hand.

"Go away, Kate, I'm tired," Doc answered.

146

"Tired? You lying polecat. I'm not good enough to be your dancing partner?" Her voice rose with her temper.

Holliday rocked in his chair, offering Kate the smug smile of a fat man after a huge meal. "I made no promises. You seem to have thought that up yourself."

"That's not right, is it?" She looked around with widening eyes, as if someone might come to her defense, second her story of his unfulfilled promise. But no one else paid her any mind.

"Dance, dammit," she yelled.

"Not tonight, Kate."

"What's the matter? I'm not good enough for you? You screw me every time you get the itch. Dammit, even when I'm fevering sick. But you won't take a dance with me. You snake. You'll dance with that Deno woman, won't you? But not me," she screamed. "I don't remember what happened Christmas night at the Bee Hive, but I heard tell. You carrying on with that woman, you and her dancing alone around the room. The hell with her, she's a card slut, no better than me, she is, but I'm only good enough to sleep with, not dance with."

Kate kicked at Holliday's legs, striking the seat of his chair, knocking him off balance. His chair teetered a moment as Holliday's flailing arms and legs almost regained his equilibrium, then toppled backward, crashing onto the floor and bringing another abrupt halt to the piano music.

"Damn you, Kate," Holliday sputtered, rolling over from the chair and crawling onto his hands and knees.

"Damn you, too, Doc Holliday," she said with a spray of spit. She spun around and darted to the door. By her hand, the door swung full open and banged against the wall, rattling the windows. "Nobody's gonna come between us anymore," she screeched. "Nobody."

She disappeared into the night, screaming indecipherable profanity into the pit of darkness. Good riddance, Holliday thought as he picked himself up and dusted the sawdust off his fresh suit. Kate was as unpredictable as a wounded wildcat and twice as dangerous. He was as glad to be rid of her as he would be to lose tuberculosis. As Holliday righted his chair, Chancey burst through the door, his eyes wild and his lips agape.

"Doc," he yelled, gesturing wildly with his arms. "come quick. Kate's gone to kill Lottie."

Her hands moved deftly over the cards, cradling them, then tossing them from palm to palm, her customers transfixed by her motions as if they were watching a coiled rattler. Lottie wore a pale blue dress with ballooning sleeves which narrowed into frilly laced cuffs, plenty adequate to hide a card or two. As she shuffled the cards they would at times disappear into a haze of lace and reappear again before passing under the shadow of her hand. Lottie mixed the cards without looking at them, glancing instead at the faces surrounding her table. They were mostly a quiet, modest collection of bashful cowhands between jobs, unbathed buffalo hunters back from the plains, and tipsy merchants whose wives thought them at a lodge meeting. Among them, there probably wasn't enough money to cover the bottom of a narrow-headed stump preacher's hat at collection time.

After inserting the shuffled deck into the dealing box, she fluffed the lace cuffs. "A fresh deck and a fresh start for you gentlemen." She smiled and they grinned back, dropping their meager bets all over the layout.

As Lottie slid soda from the box and uncovered the first card, a female shriek, a pantherlike cry, cut through the downstairs noise. A stream of profanity rolled off a female tongue. Another jealous whore, Lottie thought, as she listened to the footfall of someone running up the stairs. A second rabid scream echoed off the staircase wall. Lottie glanced up from her dealing box. Big Nose Kate stepped into view, her eyes thick with savagery, her nostrils flared from the hate in her heavy breath. Slowly, Kate lifted her hand. In it she carried a gun, pointed straight at Lottie's table.

"Lottie Deno," Kate screamed, "I'll kill you." Lottie's customers scattered.

Lottie stood slowly from her chair, her right hand brushing the folds in her dress. Pulling her hand away from her bodice, Lottie steadied her own revolver at Kate's heart. "You know whores aren't allowed up here, Kate."

Kate advanced, her gait deliberate and menacing. Two men with outstretched arms inched toward her, but she swung her hand at them, the gun exploding and a bullet splintering the plank floor at their feet. "Come closer and I'll plug you." Then she looked at Lottie. "I'll kill you," Kate said, waving the gun around the room, before pointing it unsteadily at Lottie, "if you don't stay away from my man."

"Which one, Kate? You've had so many," Lottie answered as she heard heavy footsteps on the stairs. Chancey, Holliday, and Fogle appeared at the top of the steps behind Kate.

"Doc Holliday. He's my man, and you stay away from him. You try to take him away from me, you even dance with him again, and I'll kill you."

"You've tried once. I'm losing my patience. Let's settle it now." Lottie cocked the hammer on her revolver.

Kate steadied her gun with her left hand and thumbed the hammer back. Holliday lunged for her arms, striking her hands as the gun roared, then coughed smoke. The bullet plowed into the floor. Kate screamed like a wounded panther, her arms flailing at Holliday, striking him on the cheek with her gun. Holliday wrestled with her. The acrid powder smoke from a bullet meant for her burned in Lottie's eyes as she watched Chancey jump for Kate's arms. Kate's wrath turned to him and his strong hands long enough for Holliday to wrench the gun from her hand. Kate screamed profanities at Lottie. "Leave him be, dammit. I love him."

"Why you low-down slut," Lottie shouted back, "if I should step in soft cow shit, I wouldn't even clean my shoe on that bastard."

"He not good enough for you, you faro whore?" Kate called, struggling against Chancey.

"I'll show you," Lottie said, stepping around the table toward Kate.

"Grab her, Fogle," Holliday called, and instantly the owner of the Bee Hive lunged toward her, wrapping his arms around her. Lottie struggled briefly against his manacle hold, then saw the futility of it. "Mike Fogle," Lottie shouted in his ear, "you make sure that whore stays out of this place or she'll be sleeping with the worms and maggots instead of every two-legged skunk that'll lower himself to her bed."

Kate lifted her knee sharply into Chancey's groin. Groaning, he released his grip. Kate slid free and broke for Lottie. Holliday shoved her to the floor as she darted by.

Chancey recovered enough to pounce upon her, squeezing at

her wrists and dragging her to the stairs. "A couple of you fellows take her downstairs before I kill her myself." Several helped carry Kate, screaming, away.

"Trouble's over," Holliday told Fogle. The owner of the Bee Hive spit at the sound of Kate's curses. "Damnedest whore in the Flat."

Fogle released Lottie. "Get back to your game." He turned to Chancey. "Obliged for your help. Kate's a troublemaker," he said, then paused for a moment, running his hand through his disheveled hair. "Chancey, I've been needing to talk to you. You have time to visit on the way out?"

Lottie looked at Fogle and his eyes averted hers. She slipped her gun back into her bodice, wondering why Fogle needed to visit with Chancey. She glided back to her table, smiling at her customers. "Okay, gentlemen, our interruption is over. Please excuse my language, but it was the only type that vile woman would understand," Lottie said, perplexed by the joint departure of Fogle and Chancey.

THIRTEEN

Two horsemen raced along Griffin Avenue shooting holes in the night sky. Their tongues and revolvers loosened by too much rye, they galloped up and down the deserted street, shouting obscene verses of "Don't Drink Tonight, Boys," the latest temperance song popular among sober women.

Inside the Cattle Exchange by a window stood Chancey, his double-barreled shotgun broken at the breech and hanging in the crook of his left arm. "Damn sheriff," he called out. "What's he think this is, the Fourth of July?" Chancey's boot tapped impatiently on the floor. He had rolled a cigarette but had forgotten to light it. Now the cigarette hung from his drawn lips, gradually darkening from soaked spit until it would never take to flame.

On break from his faro table, Holliday leaned into the bar with his elbow and watched Chancey. To attract the bartender, Holliday slapped the bar with his palm, the pop resounding inside the saloon. Chancey slammed the hinged barrel against the breech block and spun around behind the menacing stare of the shotgun's gaping black eyes. Realizing the danger only imagined, Chancey stared hard at Holliday, who shrugged his apology, and then turned back toward the street. Chancey was as nervous as a bull at steering time, Holliday thought.

Would their horses ever wear out? Or would the riders ever exhaust their ammunition? Holliday wondered. Kate was somewhere out there with her latest customer. Holliday estimated the odds of Kate taking a bullet and wondered if the revelers would accept a free case of ammunition for Kate's return. Hell, the two rowdies would probably lose an encounter with Kate, unless someone unloaded her tongue. Holliday knew no man the equal to that task, so he motioned for a bottle of Monarch bourbon. The bartender, conditioned by habit, obeyed his wordless command.

With his bottle, Holliday strolled to the window beside Chancey. He turned the container to his lips, threw back his head, and gulped a few hard swallows. Finished, he held the bottle by the neck in front of the window. "Wonder if they can hit this at a full gallop?"

Chancey shoved Holliday's hand away from the window as the racing hooves neared, then passed. Accepting Chancey's rebuff as an invitation to drink, Holliday sipped again at the bourbon. When the bottle slid from his lips, he took a big breath. "You're too edgy tonight, Chancey. Those fellows are just having a good time. They'll probably end their celebration in the Bee Hive, not here."

"That's what's bothering me, Doc."

"Hell, Chancey, you've never cared what happens in Fogle's place."

"It ain't just Fogle's place anymore, Doc," he whispered. "It's half mine now."

Holliday whistled. "I pick up conversation at my table, but your winning the Bee Hive is the best-kept secret in the Flat."

"Didn't win it, Doc," Chancey said, as the cowboys' winded mounts galloped past the Cattle Exchange again.

"Fogle didn't just give it to you."

"True," Chancey answered without elaboration.

Holliday leaned against the wall and unbuttoned his frock coat. "I've got all night."

Chancey stepped in front of the window, then pressed his cheek against the glass, looking for the riders. The firing had stopped. "Damn, Doc, I don't know where they went. Or where in the hell Sheriff Vernon Trickus has been. I may have to bribe him just to protect this damn town." Chancey slipped to the door, opened it slowly, and eased his head outside, glancing both ways down the street. "Looks clear, Doc, come on back to my office." The saloon owner turned and walked away.

Waiting at his office door for Holliday, Chancey groped at a match in his tobacco tin, then tried without success to light the spit-soaked cigarette disintegrating in his mouth. Cursing, he spit the wet tobacco on the floor, extracted the tobacco pouch and papers from his tin, and started a new cigarette. Doc entered the office as a match flamed in Chancey's hand. Chancey touched the fire to his cigarette and the ball of match light illuminated the trouble etched in Chancey's face. Chancey shook the match out and stared into the low burning flame of his kerosene lamp. He drew deeply, then exhaled twin serpentine clouds of smoke from his nostrils and waited for Holliday to close the door.

"Doc," he started, "I figured I'd own the Bee Hive one day, win it from Fogle in a game of cards. Hell, you made one run at it for me and would've had it if Lottie hadn't scrambled your card sense like broken eggs."

Holliday shook his head. "Dammit, she didn't beat me, she just had a lucky run at cards."

A strained grunt of a laugh escaped Chancey's lips with another ribbon of smoke. "Didn't think you believed in Lottie's Luck, Doc. I wanted that saloon so bad I'd challenge Lottie's Luck, so bad I could've whipped every man in town and the troops up on the hill to boot. Now I own half of it without ever turning a card."

"Now that you've got half a sack full, what's the goddam problem, Chancey?"

"It's the way I got it, Doc. The money I'd been saving to make another run at it I used to buy half the goddam place. Ever since I paid Fogle, my flesh's been crawling like a barrel full of snakes."

For a moment, Holliday jiggled the bottle, staring at its turbulent amber contents. "Hellfire, long as you got what you wanted, Chancey, what's the difference? Fogle didn't sell 'cause he's your buddy."

"He got in debt over his head — it's hard to figure as much money as the Bee Hive brings in — and needed some quick money for his debts."

Holliday jerked the bottle to his lips and downed an angry sip of bourbon. "So this is how you'll put Ed Bailey back to work for you and against me? Seems your luck is running better than mine, Chancey."

Chancey's dark eyes narrowed for an instant. "I wanted to whip Fogle for the Bee Hive. In my younger days, I did a little prize fighting. Once I'd readied for a match against a fellow I sure as hell wanted to beat, but wasn't so sure I could. Night before the fight, he got wise with a skinny little runt that packed this peashooter of a derringer. By damn if that runt didn't tattoo him with one of the smallest bullet holes you've ever seen, but when the smoke cleared my opponent was one of the deadest men alive. I'd just a soon been whipped all around the ring the next day than never know how I would've stood up against him. Same way here, I may never know if I could beat him. That bothered me so I told Fogle one day when he was ready we'd play for each other's half."

"Damn fool thing to do, Chancey, splitting the pot with a man you've practically beaten. What about Bailey?"

"I heard you the first time, Doc. Bailey'll start tomorrow at the Bee Hive."

"That's what should worry you, dammit. That man'll bring you bad luck. What about Lottie?"

"She stays where she is."

"If she likes," Doc nodded. "As long as she deals for you, and you keep an eye on Fogle's take of the winnings, you'll do okay." Holliday wiped his lips.

"Can't explain it, Doc, just a feeling that this has come too easy to bring anything but bad luck."

"Hell, Chancey, any bad luck you have will probably rub off on me," Holliday said, holding up his bottle. "Just talking about it has run me half-dry."

"It don't matter what you do, you're always running dry. How you put away that much liquor and still stay on your feet is beyond me."

"Like cards, Chancey. It takes practice."

"Then you ought to be as fine a bottle sharp as found anywhere," Chancey drew on his cigarette until the fire reached his fingers. He crushed the cigarette between his fingertips and

154

dropped it, grinding it into the floor with his boot. "If you could just play cards as well as you can drink."

"If you were to drink a little more, maybe you wouldn't be as worried." Holliday stroked his mustache, pulling a grin across his lips.

Chancey's lips parted to speak, then froze in a grimace at a shout in the saloon. The piano music died, chairs screeched to life, and fleeing boots pounded outside. At the sharp rap on the door, Chancey reached for his shotgun and Holliday jerked his Colt from its holster.

"Open easy," Chancey said, and the head of a bartender slid through the widening crack.

"There's been a shooting at the Bee Hive," the bartender started. "A couple dead."

Holliday glanced at Chancey, a grimace clouding the saloon owner's face like he'd expected the news. Swallowing hard, Holliday stared at the bartender. "Was Lottie hurt?"

Trouble was coming as sure as lightning on the horizon foretold a thunderstorm's approach. Lottie could feel it in the air. And then the firing had started outside, a couple of cowhands from the Millett Ranch catching up on their entertainment by shooting the darkness along Griffin Avenue. In her customers she sensed the tension, saw it in their tight-lipped faces as their bets came awkwardly, slowly, and in some cases on cards the casekeepers showed had all been played.

Finally, the gunfire outside died away and she watched the faces of her customers relax at the quiet, then stiffen at the yelling and screaming downstairs. Lottie could feel her fingers growing tacky from perspiration. Trouble had entered the Bee Hive with the two cowboys. For an instant, the downstairs noises died away, then the shooting started. Eleven maybe twelve shots exploded below and echoed up the stairs, followed by the heavy odor of gunpowder. Then a moment of total silence was quickly drowned in the wails of a whore, the cries of the wounded, and the shouts for help. Lottie's customers broke for the stairs.

"Don't let a little shooting scare you gentlemen away," she called. "If someone's hurt, there's nothing you can do about it. If it's just a cowboy showing off, he might not enjoy you interrupting him."

Her effort was as futile as a school marm trying to round up schoolboys after the final bell. Even the fascination of Lottie Deno, she thought, could not bring them back to the faro table tonight, not with the sound of groaning wounded and a whore who wailed like every potential customer in Texas had been killed.

Quickly, Lottie counted her winnings, seventy-nine dollars and some change. Bad night and it wouldn't get any better with the shooting, she thought, dividing out her twenty-five percent of the take. Twenty dollars beat a loss, but not by much. Maybe Griffin was nearing the end of its string. If the prices on prime buffalo hides this spring dropped much below a dollar, as had been rumored, business might not even improve when the buffalo hunters returned. Then, hiding behind a new name, she might move on. She didn't know where, but a town like Griffin would spring up in the middle of nowhere, grow like a weed, and die like one too.

After depositing the money in her small carpetbag, she headed for the stairs, the odor of acrid gunsmoke growing stronger with each step, stinging her nose and watering her eyes. Descending halfway down the stairs into a ghostly haze, she saw men and women kneeling over four blood-stained forms. One wore a cavalry uniform and twitched feebly as people attended him. Another — a cowboy by his garb — writhed in the sawdust, struggling for each breath. A circle of men backed away from yet another downed man; they left a towel over his face and the darkening stain from his forehead showed he would never arise. Against the far wall a fourth victim sat propped up, men tearing away his coat and pressed shirt. Lottie recognized the county attorney, a serious wound to the upper chest. Damn fool cowboys that started this.

From the foot of the stairs she waded into the edgy crowd and angled for Fogle's office behind the bar. Elbowing against the human tide, she reached Fogle's door, her path converging with a big man who towered over her. Glancing up, she looked into Chancey's dark eyes. Beside him stood John Henry Holliday.

"You okay, Lottie?" Holliday asked.

"Be better if these yahoos wouldn't shoot up what little business there is. You come to laugh at Fogle's misfortune?"

"Don't you know, Lottie?" Chancey interrupted, folding his broad arms across his chest. "Fogle's misfortune is mine, too, from now on."

She felt her stomach tighten at Chancey's words and at the insincere smile spreading across his face. "What are you talking about?"

Chancey just laughed, walked past Lottie, and shoved open Fogle's door. Holliday coughed. "Chancey is Fogle's new partner. He's got half interest in the Bee Hive."

Lottie's heart pounded like an angry hammer against an anvil. She stared from Doc to Fogle's open door. Holliday extended his arm, but she spurned his offer, her anger burning white. She strode into the office, past Chancey to Fogle, and slammed her satchel on his desk. Fogle lunged from his chair for a lamp that tipped over. Lottie saw the surprise in the corners of his blinking eyes as he righted the lamp, stood straight, and shook his fingers of the burn. She aimed her finger like a gun at his chest. "Is it true that Chancey's got half interest in the Bee Hive now?"

Fogle threw up his arms. "Damn killings outside," his voice trembled with defeat, "and now this. My partner," the word sliced through the room like a razor, "breaks the news to you. I had planned to tell you tonight, Lottie." Fogle dropped his arms and walked behind his chair.

Lottie's finger fell away and her chin slipped down, her fury receding because she believed him. He had never lied to her before. "How'd you lose? I'd played your hand."

Fogle pried his paper collar away from his neck and cleared his throat. "I sold him half. I had debts. I needed the money. My gambling luck's not as good as yours."

Glancing at Chancey, she felt her face flame with anger at his smug grin. "I'd loaned you money, Mike."

"I just couldn't ask that of a lady, Lottie, not even you. I'll have a chance later to win it back and I'll want you to play my hand when that day comes."

"If I'm still around," Lottie answered.

Chancey stepped beside her, his obsequious grin straining

his cheeks. "I want you to stay on at whatever your present arrangement is. Whatever differences we've had in the past are forgotten."

"Perhaps by you," Lottie started. "If I stay, I work for Mike, not you." Lottie unhooked her satchel and dropped Fogle's take of the night's winnings on the desk. Taking the carpetbag, she frowned at Fogle. "I'm sorry for you, Mike." She moved slowly toward the door, slipping her hand through Holliday's proffered arm. "My luck just turned bad, John Henry," Lottie said as he accompanied her through the saloon. Gazing around at the carnage on the floor, Lottie felt a queasiness in her stomach and knew it wasn't from the blood. "I don't like the way the cards fell this time. It can't lead to anything good."

"Chancey said the same thing, Lottie," Holliday answered as he steered her through the crowd. "Called it bad luck, him buying the Bee Hive instead of winning it."

"Hah," Lottie retorted. "As long as I was in Griffin he'd never have won it. Neither he nor you would ever have beaten me when Mike's Bee Hive was at stake."

They squeezed to the front door and outside into the cold winter wind which pricked at Lottie's face. She shivered and felt Holliday draw her closer to him.

"You've never cared much for Chancey?"

"He didn't take me for a lady when I came to the Flat. He offered to let me whore in his saloon, even offered to be my first customer."

"A lot of men in this town, myself included, have taken a fancy to you, Lottie."

"The answer's still no, John Henry, I'll not tell you my name, but at least you've been a gentleman about it. Chancey wasn't."

"Ashamed of your past?" Holliday asked as they walked deeper into the darkness toward her cabin.

"A lot of people in this country don't dwell on their past. I don't either," Lottie answered.

"Most of those folks have something to hide."

"We all run from our past. It's called aging, John Henry."

"I keep thinking maybe there was more in common between us than gambling."

"We're from the south, John Henry, so we have something in common but nothing more than that."

Holliday coughed, once, twice, three times hard, wrenching his arm loose from Lottie's. He was a sick man, she thought. He might have a past, but not much of a future. Holliday gasped for breath, then heaved more before controlling himself.

"I'll not give up," Holliday said. "You're too pretty to forget."

"Gamblers never give up, John Henry, they just go broke. Don't bet on me. You're better off wagering on Big Nose Kate."

"You hold her against me? I'm not saying I'm a pure man."

"Nor I a pure woman, John Henry, so sleep with your pleasure. I just don't take to Kate. What looks I have I want to keep without her altering them with a knife."

"She was delirious."

"Delirious, John Henry? She was jealous. She cares more for you than you'd ever admit. Marry her, if you want to become a husband. She might make a good wife. A lot of saloon women have turned respectable. So marry her, if you can walk away from your gambling table and hang out your shingle." Lottie was glad when they reached her cabin. She opened the door and left it ajar long enough to light a lamp, the glow of the yellow light slowly filling the room. It was cold and the night had been a bad one. "Come in for a moment, John Henry."

He obliged as she moved into the back room and put kindling into the stove, building a slow flame that she fed more wood. Looking over her shoulder, she saw Holliday standing just inside the door, his hat in his hand. Maybe she shouldn't have invited him inside. When the fire took hold, she searched for the whiskey bottle she kept for medicine. After finding it, she joined Holliday in the front room. "Maybe this will warm you up enough for the return trip, cut into that cough."

"Bad, isn't it?" He accepted the bottle.

Lottie nodded.

Holliday gulped the liquor down. Lottie flinched. No person could take liquor like Holliday. He was like a horse at a trough after a long, hot ride. He eased the bottle down and looked at Lottie. "With this cough I won't last many years. Maybe if it weren't for this consumption, things might be different between us." He took another swig.

159

"You're persistent, John Henry, I'll give you that."

"I'm a gambler, as you said. I took a gamble that I could change your mind. I lost. Most men do when they come up against you."

"I don't beat them. They beat themselves."

"You give them every opportunity to lose. Maybe that's the way it should be with a woman running a gambling table."

"I'm no different than a man running a table."

"Are you going to stay at the Bee Hive? I've sort of lost track of whether you gave me an answer on that one."

"I don't like working for Chancey."

"You'd still be working as much for Fogle as much as Chancey."

"It's not the same."

"Maybe not. But Griffin's still a good place for our type, and the Bee Hive is the best spot in Griffin."

"There are other towns on the rise. This one may be going down."

Holliday nodded and offered the bottle to Lottie.

"You keep it, John Henry, you need it more than I do."

Holliday nodded.

"Good night, John Henry . . . good night."

FOURTEEN

The pounding on the door cut through the haze of his sleep. Holliday turned over once, as if it were a bad dream, then shot up from the mattress and grabbed for his holstered gun hanging on the bedpost.

"Open up, you goddam polecat," screeched an unwelcomed voice. It was Kate, beating the door like a bass drum. "Dammit open up."

Holliday coughed and crawled out of bed, his bare foot brushing against the bottle, now empty, that Lottie had given him. He cocked the hammer on his Colt and slipped to the door.

Kate screamed. "Open this door 'fore I knock the bastard down, you varmint. Doc, do you hear me? Open it up. I gotta talk to you and I ain't waiting. Do you hear me?"

Doc nodded to himself. Half the hotel heard her and boarders cursed from adjacent rooms, the thuds of boots thrown against walls punctuating their demands for quiet.

Shaking his head of sleep's rust, Doc whispered through the door. "You alone Kate?"

"Damn right I'm alone, you snake," she screamed. "Are you?"

"Not so loud, dammit."

"Not so loud? You sick fool. Telling me to hold my voice.

You don't own me, you snake. Hell, you never even pay for me. Telling me to be quiet, you . . ."

Holliday unlatched the door and eased it open a hair, then wider until he stared at Kate in the dim hall light, her brown hair disheveled as if a West Texas wind had combed it, her breath strong enough of cheap liquor to light a match. She swayed like a tree in a strong breeze. Holliday pulled the door open long enough for her to stumble in. After closing and latching the door behind her, he released the hammer on his revolver.

"Thank you, Doc," Kate said meekly, then she dropped on his bed in a shaft of moonlight that angled in through the window. For a moment she glanced around the room as if trying to locate Doc. Then she propped her elbows on her thighs and dropped her head into the palm of her hands. "You've been to see her again, haven't you?"

Holliday moved to the bed and shoved his revolver in its holster, thinking how much more tranquil it would be if he just shot her before she started babbling again about marriage. "What if I did? No concern of yours, is it?"

Kate sobbed and lifted her head to Holliday, standing impassively over her. "I keep thinking one day you might like me for more than a good screw."

"Like a wife?" He spit the word out. "I play cards and I travel light." Holliday walked around the bed and slid under the covers opposite Kate. "When I leave town, there's no time for extra baggage."

"Baggage! Is that all I am? By god, you'd marry that Lottie if you had a chance." Kate's voice turned hard, her crying ceased. "Why not me, you son of a bitch?"

Holliday lunged for her. Grabbing a fist of her hair, he jerked her head backward into his lap. He heard her teeth snap from the sudden jolt and he twisted her long hair around his hand, pulling on it, as if he were cinching up a saddle. He heard her whimper, then grit her teeth. "Never call me that," he demanded.

"Son of a bitch, son of a bitch, son of a bitch," she gasped, as Holliday drew tighter on her hair.

"Keep it up, you'll be bald."

"Son of a bitch, son of a bitch, son of a . . ."

Doc knew he would sap his strength before he broke her resolve. He released his grasp.

". . . BITCH," she screamed.

Holliday shoved her away, swatting at her face, and fell back on his pillow.

Kate rolled to the foot of the bed, then scrambled to her hands and knees. "I'd take care of you, Doc. She never would. Did she ever get a patent medicine for your sickness? Why won't you give me a chance? I'm not ugly. Maybe she is prettier, but I'm not bad. Enough men pay for me that I know I've still got some looks about me."

"Gamblers and consumptives don't need wives, Kate. You know that. Gamblers can't afford to be tied down and consumptives are headed nowhere but to an early grave."

"You'd marry her, I bet, least that's what I've heard people say. You pay her plenty of attention, dancing with her while I was dying in my cabin. You'd marry her if she let you, but she's not right for you."

Kate wriggled off the bed and into the shaft of moonlight where Holliday could see her. She unbuttoned her coat and let it fall to the floor. She undid the back buttons of her dress and it joined her coat on the floor. Quickly in the cold room, she slipped out of her undergarments and into bed with Holliday. She ran her hand over his long johns. "Maybe this is what you need."

"What I need, Kate, is to be left alone and to gamble and die when the day comes. Nothing more, nothing less."

"Then turn me down, like Lottie's done you all these times," Kate said, slipping her hand under the long johns and rubbing his chest. "You are warm."

He flinched to her touch. "And your hands are cold," Doc answered.

"Not as cold as Lottie's heart. All she's ever held was a deck of cards."

"Don't bring her up again."

"Can she get to you like this?" Kate said, dragging her hand from his chest to his groin. "You can't turn me down, can you?"

"I could."

"But you won't. You want me. You wouldn't admit it, but you want me."

Holliday tried to turn over, his mind willing but his body suddenly under Kate's control.

"I'd do more for you than Lottie ever could, if you'd just let me prove it to you."

"No more talking, Kate," Holliday said, putting his arm around her and drawing her closer to him.

Fogle jumped from his office chair and extended his hand to Lottie. "I'm glad you came, Lottie. I was worried you might not return."

"I'm staying with you, Mike, for the time being." Lottie took Fogle's hand and shook it softly.

Fogle threw back his head and stood akimbo, reminding Lottie of a rooster announcing sunrise. "I'm encouraged you're staying, Lottie."

"I'll stay until I win the Bee Hive back for you. After that, who knows?"

"I'd appreciate the favor."

"My pleasure. Another chance to even a grudge with Chancey."

Fogle nodded. "And with Holliday?"

She smiled. "No, he's too good a dancer."

"He might die dancing, at the end of a rope someday, temper like his. At least Chancey doesn't fancy moving him over here from the Cattle Exchange, though I'm not sure I don't prefer him to Ed Bailey."

"What about Bailey, Mike?"

"He's working upstairs. Chancey made me take him on. He's a cheat, damn poor one at that, and he probably shorts the house more than his friends — and he has plenty of them."

"Except John Henry Holliday," Lottie said.

"That's why Chancey sent him over. Chancey had promised Bailey a job, but Holliday didn't cotton to the idea of working the same saloon as Bailey. Holliday doesn't forget a grudge."

"Nor a card trick," Lottie answered. "Chancey'll have Doc play for him when we make our play to regain the Bee Hive."

"We'll be ready that day, won't we?"

Lottie nodded. "But don't underestimate John Henry. He's

a money player and he'll be a hard one to hoodwink, unlike a lot of the men that play at my table. John Henry may be a gentleman, but he's a gambler first."

"That day is a ways off, Lottie, but now let me escort you back upstairs to your table. I've put Bailey on the opposite side of the room to lessen the distractions." Lottie followed him out into the saloon. "Lottie's staying," he called to the bartender. "Our luck is on the way up."

The stairs creaked and Fogle hummed beside Lottie as they climbed toward the gambling room. At the top of the stairs, Fogle cleared his throat loudly and most patrons turned to stare. "I have an announcement, gentlemen. Lottie's back!"

The men cheered and Lottie smiled, grabbing the folds of her dress and curtsying for them.

"Now you fellows," Fogle shouted, "can lose your money without feeling so bad." He laughed.

Lottie glanced about the room. Bailey held court for a pair of patrons at a back table. Good place for him, she thought. As the gamblers finished acknowledging Lottie's presence, they returned to their business, several gathering around a table in the center of the room. As Lottie moved to her table, Fogle accompanying her step for step, she stared at the crowd.

"What's the attraction there, Mike?"

"Pair of gamblers trying to prove who's best. You ever heard of Smokey Joe from Central Texas? He's one of them. Other fellow calls himself Monte Bill, says he's out of Arizona."

"Too many observers for it to be a friendly game, Mike. Could be trouble."

"They took an immediate dislike to one another. Decided cards'd settle their differences."

At her table, Lottie sat down behind the layout and Fogle cleared the casekeeper. "Gentlemen," he called, "Lottie is now ready for business. See if you can buck the tiger and this pretty lady as well."

Beneath the tiger gazing from the wall poster over her shoulder, Lottie shuffled the deck from hand to hand, a careless nonchalance about her. Some men abandoned other tables to join Lottie, but many remained at the central table where the simmering words between Monte Bill and Smokey Joe drifted with the smoke above the other noise.

"Maybe you should cool that game off, Mike. Doesn't sound too good to me."

"They're big boys, Lottie. Let's get your game going."

"You're the boss, Mike." Lottie smiled at the men scattered about her table. "Please don't clean me out or Mike may not keep me at the Bee Hive." She inserted the cards in the dealing box. "Place your bets."

The game moved fast, the bets stayed small, the distraction remained the game between Monte Bill and Smokey Joe. Gradually, the crowd around the table backed away, giving a wider berth to the gambling antagonists. Lottie saw between the spectators the two men, their posture stiff, their faces drawn with hate.

"You better break that game up, Mike," Lottie said. "It'll get out of hand when one loses a big pot."

"Last night was our run of bad luck for the month, Lottie. Now that you're back, things'll go better."

Lottie gathered the discarded deck from the layout and reshuffled the cards. "My feelings tell me we're not over our bad luck yet. This is eighteen seventy-seven, isn't it?"

"What's the year got to do with it?"

"Odd-numbered years have always been unlucky for me."

"You're too superstitious, Lottie."

"Name me a gambler that isn't." She inserted the cards in the dealing box.

"Ed Bailey, for one."

"He's not a gambler."

"Thinks he is, Lottie."

"Being's one thing. Thinking's another," Lottie said, then started through another deck until the noise from the nearby table turned to shouts. Lottie paused and stared toward the poker game. The voices were growing louder, hotter.

"Go on, Lottie, don't let them annoy you," Fogle offered, restacking a pile of chips on the table.

"Raise that," Monte Bill shouted at Smokey Joe.

"I'm betting every last dollar to my name," Smokey Joe challenged.

The spectators backed further away and Lottie could see several hundred dollars in the pot.

166

"Full house, aces over queens! Beat that."

Smokey Joe threw his cards on the money. "Bunkoed by a sneaking coyote who brings in a cold deck and marked cards. I'll take this pot." Smokey Joe reached with his left hand for the pot, his right hand dropping off the table.

"You're not bluffing me out of my fair winnings," Monte Bill yelled. His hand fell for his revolver.

Both men jerked their guns above the table. Spectators scrambled backward over each other and chairs. Simultaneous bolts of Colt lightning flashed across the table. Men throughout the room dropped to the floor. The thunder of the pistols reverberated off the walls. Some spectators scrambled on hands and knees for the stairs. Two clouds of white smoke mingled together, like the blood of Smokey Joe and Monte Bill.

For a moment, only Lottie stood. Then others picked themselves up from the floor, Fogle among them. "Damn fools. Looks like you were right, Lottie."

Lottie stared at Monte Bill, slumped along the edge of the table, his lifeless head leaking onto the floor. Smokey Joe had fallen to the floor, a chest wound gushing blood into the growing puddle from Monte Bill. In a moment, even the blood stopped. "They're dead or dying, Mike. They'll never make that mistake again."

Fogle pushed himself away from Lottie's table and moved tentatively toward the disputed table. He picked up Bill's hand and dropped it, then bent over Joe. "They're both dead." Other men eased over to look at death's work, one man reaching for the disputed pot.

"Back away, all of you," Fogle commanded. "Clear the room until the sheriff can get here. Somebody go fetch him." The men lingered a moment too long. "Move, dammit."

Lottie gathered her cards. "Game's over for tonight, fellows. Go on downstairs like Mike said."

Mike herded the men to the staircase. "You don't want to be here when the sheriff arrives. Let him figure it out. Drinks are on the house until we get the mess cleaned up."

Lottie put her deck of cards in her satchel. When the room cleared, she walked to the table with the dead men. She counted and stacked their final bets. More than five hundred dollars. Even so, not a pot worth dying over. She folded the paper money and gathered the double eagles, adding all to the satchel.

Fogle returned up the stairs and stood at the head, staring from the cleared table to Lottie.

"My price for staying on," Lottie said before being asked.

Fogle nodded then turned around at the sound of heavy boots behind him. "Had a shooting, sheriff."

"You've had a spate of bad luck here last two nights," answered Sheriff Trickus, coming into Lottie's view. He was a small man behind a big badge, freshly shined. His clothes were oversized, fitting his estimation of himself more than his narrow frame. His chin jutted forward with so much authority that his arrogant eyes looked down on everyone. He wore the responsibility of the job as poorly as he wore his duck britches and hickory shirt, but his sidearm glistened with the same pride as his badge. You couldn't buy justice from Trickus, but money always lined his pockets from those who had tried.

Lottie backed away from the table, catching a glint in the sheriff's haughty eyes as he stared at the table. Trickus stopped beside her, toeing both bodies with his scuffed boots. "Shame to die over a card game without a pot, wouldn't you say, Lottie? Why didn't you get out like the rest when these two peckerwoods started shooting?"

"By then it was too late."

"Downstairs, they say you stood like a tree. That so?"

"They weren't aiming my way. No sense in dirtying a dress in that case."

"You have nerve, old girl, and savvy, waiting until everybody left, then lifting the pot. It's something I wouldn't expect from Lottie Deno."

"Perhaps not, sheriff, but you are not a desperate woman."

Confident that both men would not arise to challenge him, the sheriff grew bolder, kicking both bodies, Monte Bill's toppling over like a rag doll onto the floor beside Smokey Joe. "If they don't groan, they ain't living." Trickus looked up from the table at Lottie, extending his hand, palm up. "Lot of vinegar over a game with no pot."

Lottie nodded, then shook her satchel, giving the heavy gold coins a chance to slip further to the bottom. "I put the money in here for safekeeping."

Trickus smiled. "That's the job of the law, Lottie. A couple hundred dollars I heard." His hand reached toward the satchel as Lottie unhooked it.

She slipped her hand in the narrow opening and pulled a wad of bills from inside, his hand there to meet and relieve hers of the load. "That all?" he asked. Lottie dipped inside for a few more bills to feed the sheriff's greedy palm. "That's better." He spoke to the money more than Lottie. "If there was more, keep it," he sneered. "Just call it Lottie's Luck." He grinned, his smile as ill-fitting as his clothes and his badge. "Maybe you'd better clear out, Lottie, 'fore someone other than me starts asking too many questions."

"Certainly, sheriff. You're the law."

FIFTEEN

The tall stranger stood flagpole straight, his blue eyes missing nothing in the saloon, not even the slight movement of Holliday's hand to brush his coat away from the ivory grip on his Colt sidearm. Holliday could feel the stranger's cold stare like ice upon his flesh and once as he glanced over his poker cards, Holliday's eyes met the flint of the stranger's. Neither man flinched. The stranger's unbuttoned overcoat, dusted from a long ride, was swept behind his sidearm. His square face was anchored by a handlebar mustache under a defiant nose which dared to be challenged. The stranger stood beside the bar without leaning against it. When his hands weren't lifting a drink to his lips, the stranger kneaded his knuckles and flexed his fingers, not in a nervous way, but in the calm, professional manner of a gambler. Or worse, a lawman.

This stranger sought neither a card game nor a woman. He was looking for a man. Holliday wondered if the law was catching up with him for murdering the Jacksboro soldier.

As Holliday took two cards, Chancey strode by the bar, glanced at the stranger, then stopped suddenly. Chancey and the lawman stared at each other until the stranger's lips twitched into a slight smile and he stopped flexing his fingers long enough to extend his hand to Chancey. The saloon owner grabbed it with his own massive paw and slapped the man's back, neither saying a word. Chancey motioned toward his office door. The stranger, with a backward glance over his shoulder, disappeared with Chancey into the office.

Distracted from his poker hand, Holliday tossed his cards on the deadwood and blamed his weak luck for withdrawing from the game. Coughing as he rose from the table, he called for a bottle of Monarch bourbon, then moved to an empty table, wondering if it were time to abandon Fort Griffin — and Lottie. After the bottle arrived, he enjoyed the feel of the liquor coursing down his throat. Shortly, the office door cracked open long enough for Chancey to stick his head out, scan the room, then call to a bartender. Holliday watched as both men stared at him. Then the bartender nodded and started for Holliday's table as Chancey retreated into his office. Drawing up beside Holliday, the bartender whispered, "Boss wants to see you."

Holliday stood up slowly, slipping his hand inside his coat pocket for a handkerchief. He wiped perspiration from his mustache and returned the handkerchief, his hand brushing against the Smith and Wesson in his shoulder holster. He moved quickly across the room to Chancey's door, rapped lightly on the wood, and pushed open the door. He entered, coughing into his fist, then slipping it inside his coat as his eyes adjusted to the dim light of Chancey's office and to the stranger standing in the corner shadows by the stacked liquor crates. Eyeing the man, Holliday pulled his handkerchief and coughed again into it.

"Doc," said Chancey, arising from his chair, "got an old friend here I'd like you to meet."

The stranger leaned forward out of the shadows, brushing his jittery fingers through his light brown hair, then offered Holliday a gaunt smile and his broad hand.

"Wyatt Earp, meet John Henry Holliday. Most folks around these parts just call him Doc."

Holliday coughed as he grabbed Earp's powerful hand.

"On July Fourth of sixty-eight," Chancey said, "Wyatt refereed a fight in Cheyenne, me and Mike Donovan. Donovan beat the hell out of me and might of killed me except for Wyatt."

"Good to meet you, Holliday," Earp said slowly, carefully. "Chancey wasn't that bad for a kid his age. Donovan just had several years ring experience on him."

171

"Donovan gave me all the experience I wanted that day," Chancey said. "He beat some sense into this thick skull. There had to be easier ways to make a living."

"How you earn your keep, Wyatt?" Holliday interrupted.

"A little gambling, a little star toting."

Holliday broke off their grip and backed away from Earp. "You carrying a badge now?"

"Nothing to worry about, Doc," Chancey intervened. "Wyatt needs some help. Thought you'd be in a position to assist."

"Not the first time the law's come after me," Holliday grinned, "but the first time for help."

Earp took a seat on a pair of wooden liquor crates and crossed one leg over his knee. Holliday's tense muscles softened. A man looking for a fight didn't take a seat.

"I'm working for the Santa Fe," Earp started. "I'm looking for a man named Dave Rudabaugh. He's been robbing Santa Fe trains. Chancey says you might recognize someone on the run or odd comings and goings here in Griffin. You heard of Rudabaugh?"

"Perhaps, but I'm not accustomed to working with the law."

Chancey interrupted. "You can trust Wyatt, and you'd be doing me a favor, Doc. I owe Wyatt a chip or two."

Holliday nodded.

"Don't consider this anything to do with the law, Holliday," Earp said, standing again. "It'd be a personal favor to me. And I won't forget it."

Doc stuffed his handkerchief back into his pocket. "Give me three days. Don't come to me unless you're willing to throw a couple dollars bucking the tiger at my table. I don't want my customers knowing I'm working for the law."

"You're working for me, not the law," Earp reminded.

"Won't look much different either way if word gets out, now will it?"

Earp nodded.

"Three days from now, come to my table and I'll tell what I've learned. Do you know anything else about this fellow?"

"The trail's a couple weeks cold by now. Rudabaugh rides

with a man named Mike Roarke and a handful of other ruffians. They've taken a liking to robbing railroad construction camps and pay trains. They'll be carrying money, some gold, but mostly paper with a lot of it Santa Fe script. If you see any floating around, chances are those boys dropped it here."

"What makes you trust me? What's to keep me from earning a few dollars pointing you out to them, if I find them?"

"I can do more for you than they can," Earp said.

"But they'd pay more."

"You're a man that weighs the odds, Holliday. The odds are always with me."

Holliday nodded. "Just don't spoil those odds by hanging around me during the next three days."

"You do your job and I'll do mine."

"Then I'll be leaving," Holliday answered. "Best we not spend enough time together for anyone to get suspicious. Good day, gentlemen." Holliday turned and grabbed the doorknob.

"And good luck," Earp called.

"We won't need any luck if the odds are always on your side, now will we, Earp?"

Kate traced the bony ridges of Holliday's back until they disappeared between his buttocks. He lay on his side motionless, his heavy breath puffing in the cold of the room. As Kate snuggled closer to him, pressing her breasts against his back, she slipped her hand down his front, beyond his stomach, and below his waist. She stroked him, then tickled him with her spider-walking fingers, but Holliday spurned her, even after his body could no longer ignore her nimble hand. Kate hated this mood which came over him from time to time. His flashes of anger and even his rebuffs at lovemaking she could tolerate because the causes were evident. But his moods of indifference were borne somewhere within, somewhere beyond her reach, deep in his consumption-wracked body. He would brood for days, despite her efforts, until he resolved the problem himself. Given a choice, she'd have preferred him angry, but Doc rarely gave her a choice.

Kate flopped back over on the bed and stared at the ceiling lit by the flickering lamp on the bedside table. It was no use, she thought, jerking the blankets around her neck. "If I bother you, I'll leave."

"You're not bothering me. Now." Holliday sighed.

"Something's bothering you."

"It's not you. Now."

"Meaning it was me a moment ago." Kate harrumphed. "Doc, you sorry ass. After what I've done for you these last five months, I ought to kick your skinny butt out of bed and slap you around. Hell, I could've retired in the best house on Nob Hill in San Francisco if I'd charged you for every time we screwed."

"Kate, go soak your head or your crotch and cool it down. If you had enough customers, you wouldn't waste your time with me."

Kate reached for Doc and pulled him on his back without a struggle. "Look at me," she said, and for once he obeyed. "It's Lottie Deno again, isn't it? You're still mooning over her, dammit. Want to marry her and she won't say yes and she never will. She's too good for you. Now, isn't it her?"

Holliday coughed hard into his fist. "Don't insult Lottie."

"I knew it. Damn you. She'll never marry you. I'm the only one foolish enough to marry a dying runt like you."

"Kate," Holliday paused, "it's times like these when I wish consumption would finish me so I wouldn't have to listen to your ravings."

"It's Lottie, isn't it?"

"Dammit, no. I need to do a favor for a friend and I haven't had any luck."

"Doc, I'm the only friend you've got. Won't you ever believe that? Nobody around here, not even Chancey, cares for you. Once you get in trouble, then see who your friends are."

"This isn't Chancey and it isn't Lottie. He isn't even from around here. Comes from Kansas."

"Damn, Doc, you're not the type that people take to, except a fool like me."

"A whore like you, right Kate?"

Kate shot up from her pillow and twisted around in bed. She slapped him. Doc sat up, rubbing his cheek. "You dare to call me a whore? Maybe that's what I am, but don't you ever call me a whore again when I'm in bed with you, you cheap bastard.

You can go to hell." Kate flung and kicked the covers away. "Let your goddam Kansas friend sleep with you when you're coughing and let him try to keep you warm. I've had it with you."

Doc scrambled for the blankets. "You walk out on me, Kate, and you'll never walk back in."

"And if I leave, you'll never get between another woman's legs for free. If I'm not getting the customers I did before I took up with you, it's because the other girls are spreading stories I'm contagious with consumption from you. Try to get one of them to sleep with you."

Kate jumped out of bed on the cold floor and struggled on her undergarments. "You've had me for the last time, Doc Holliday, unless you want to pay like everybody else."

"I can afford better than you!"

"Then pay for it." Kate pulled her dress over her head and began to button the back. "I'll even pay for your first screw. You've cost me money every time I've laid with you, so this won't be any different. Where's my shoes . . ."

"No telling. As anxious as you always are to rut, you probably kicked them off in the hall."

Walking around the bed, Kate scanned the floor. "Damn you." In the dimness, she spotted her shoes, hiding under Holliday's boots. As Kate bent to put them on, Holliday slapped her rear. "Damn you again, Doc. I hope your pecker withers away."

"I'll manage."

"But you'll manage without me to give it to you free."

"You'll be back, Kate, you always return."

"Just see about it this time. And come tomorrow or the next day when you get horny, don't be prowling around my cabin unless you've got money to spend, say three hundred dollars."

"A hundred times your going rate? You won't get that kind of money from me. Even a buffalo hunter without a female for a year wouldn't pay that kind. No, sir."

Kate jerked her coat on and shoved her hand inside the pocket. She pulled out a fist full of bills. "I'll give you some of this funny money to buy you a woman. It's probably worthless anyway. She flung the paper at his bed and the bills fluttered about the room. Holliday snatched at the air for one which landed on the covers at his chest.

"Take this," he said, wadding the bill up, "and shove it up your money hole." He drew back to toss it at her, then stopped. "Just a moment, Kate." Quickly, he unwadded the money.

Kate stepped toward the door and twisted the handle. "Bye, Doc, it was good while it lasted." She turned to see if he wanted her back, but he stared at the bill like he'd never seen funny money before. "Bye," she repeated, and against her will she opened the door and stepped into the hall.

"Wait. Come back, Kate," she heard him call as the door shut. He must do more, Kate thought, than just call her back. Now Holliday must come after her. Halfway down the hall, she heard the door open behind her.

"Kate, don't leave," his voice pleaded. She felt a tear sliding down her cheek, but she fought the impulse to run to him as she twisted tentatively about, hoping, praying for his arms to be outstretched. He held up a bill. "Where'd you get this?"

Another tear dropped from her watery eyes. Her voice came as a whisper. "Do you want me or that goddam funny money?"

"Both." Holliday gestured for Kate to return.

"When you come to me, Doc." She dabbed at the tears as she waited. Holliday, wearing but his long johns, looked both ways down the hall, then stepped to her. When she felt his hand upon her arm, she started to say how much she loved him.

But he spoke first. "I must know where you got this." He held the bill before her flooding eyes.

"What is it?" She walked with him to the room, but only after shutting and latching the door did he answer.

"It's Atchison, Topeka and Santa Fe Railway scrip — what the railroad uses to pay its people."

"No railway around here, there's not."

"Just where'd you get it?"

"A man, tall, scraggly beard. Smelled like he hadn't taken a bath since the war."

"You get a name?"

"None, though I heard some others call him Dave."

"How many?" Holliday crawled back in bed under the covers.

"Are answers all you want, or are you going to apologize?"

Holliday threw back the covers for her. "Take off your clothes and answer my questions. How many men? When?"

"Three, maybe four of them, two or more weeks ago. How come you're so interested in my customers all of a sudden?"

"Are you gonna start taking off your clothes?"

Kate slipped out of her coat, letting it drop to the floor, then began to unbutton her dress.

"Now the men, are they still around?"

"Pals of yours?"

"They still around?"

"No."

"Dammit." Holliday coughed in disgust.

Kate's dress slid to the floor on top of her coat. As she fiddled with her long underwear, Kate laughed at Holliday. "I know where they are . . ." She smiled as her fingers undid the final button.

"Well, where are they?"

"At least I know where they said they were going."

Holliday sat up in the bed and stared at her body unveiled before him. "Hell, are you telling the truth or playing games? If you've lied . . ." The threat went unfinished.

Kate slid into bed beside Holliday. "Rub my back, Doc." She turned away from him.

"The names?" Holliday asked as he stroked her back.

She waited, moaning softly. "That feels good, Doc. I'll do your back in a moment."

"Dammit, the names."

Kate turned over. "Your turn." She pulled back the covers and slid her hand from his shoulder to his buttocks. Suddenly, she drew back and slapped his butt.

Holliday spun over, entangling himself in the covers. "What the hell, woman? No more games."

"Doc Holliday, you want the goddam destination of your pals, they looked about your ilk, then you treat me like a lady, not a soiled dove. It don't matter what I am, you can act like you don't know any better and stay civil or you'll never get another screw out of me or the location of your damn friends."

Kate rolled away from Doc onto her back and slipped her hands under her head on the pillow. "Now screw me like you mean it or you'll never find out a thing."

When Holliday reached for her, she did not respond. He

moved against her body and Kate tingled at his touch. Though he moved as nonchalantly as if he were shuffling a deck of cards, at least he was caressing her, at least he was touching her. His movements were routine, his lust uninspired, his purpose purely mercenary. Kate understood this and wished it were different. But still, he was touching her and from his occasional moan, she knew he was enjoying her as much as his frail frame would allow.

When it was done, Holliday rolled off her and lay staring at the ceiling. "Where were the men going, Kate?"

"Do you love me, Doc?"

"Dammit, no marriage talk!"

Kate stared at Holliday. "Overheard them say they'd lay low around Fort Davis."

"Thank you, Kate. All this folderol and you could've told me a lot quicker and ended my curiosity."

"Now will you marry me?"

Holliday laughed, then coughed. "Now I'm gonna pick up all this funny money you scattered around the room and find me a woman tomorrow."

Kate shook her head, then buried it under the pillow.

"Let's go to sleep, Kate." Holliday leaned over and blew out the lamp, then put his arm around her.

Holliday slipped the cards into the dealing box. "Place your bet, mister."

Wyatt Earp slid a double eagle on the black lady. "I always trust the lady when a gentleman is dealing."

Holliday touched the brim of his derby, acknowledging the compliment, then turned to his casekeeper. "Take a break, I can keep up with a single customer for a while." When they were alone, Holliday spoke to Earp in a normal voice. "This cousin you're looking for, would he happen to have a shaggy beard and maybe stink to high hell?"

Earp nodded. "With a better nose, I could smell him out."

Holliday reached slowly into his coat pocket and pulled a half dozen paper bills. "You ever see any of this before?"

Reaching across the table, Earp pinched the paper with his long, nimble fingers, then examined it. "Santa Fe scrip. Seems Cousin Dave's been leaving his earnings along the way."

"Railroad men have lots of money."

"Sure would like to find my cousin Dave," Earp answered. "Got a debt or two I owe him."

"My source may not be the most reliable," Holliday paused as another midafternoon customer strolled by, "but from what I hear, he headed for Fort Davis, out in far West Texas toward El Paso."

Holliday pulled a pair of cards out with no result. Earp left his coin on the queen. "Any idea how much lead time my cousin has on me?"

"A couple weeks, maybe three."

"Not a good sign." Earp shoved the Santa Fe scrip back across the table. "At least I know I'm on his trail."

"Keep it to show your cousin if you catch up with him."

"Obliged."

Holliday pulled another pair of cards from the box without result. "Staying with the lady?"

Earp nodded. "I always stay with a good lady."

"If they decide to stay with you, though, they're sure hard to get rid of," Holliday answered. "Maybe you should trust the lady less and yourself more. I can't guarantee the information about your cousin, remember?"

"Better than information I had been getting. I'm not one to complain when a man delivers what he promises."

Holliday nodded. "Me neither."

Earp pulled his bet from the lady about the middle of the deck. "I feel my luck's changing. You can only trust the ladies for so long."

"My shuffling getting that bad, or have you played a game or two for more than just fun?" Holliday coughed.

"When I don't have more pressing matters, I do from time to time deal a hand of poker and rub a faro box."

"Then we both know the face cards are stacked heavy toward the bottom of this deck."

Earp nodded. "You handle the pasteboards pretty well. Maybe we can sit down in an honest game sometime."

"Professional courtesy."

Earp pushed his chair back from the table and stood up. "We should try that sometime, but this is not the place, not with Santa Fe paying me."

"Pass back through, stop and look me up."

"I'll do it, Holliday. And if you're ever up Dodge City way, I'll cheat you at my own table."

"Sounds like a good promise."

"In Dodge City, you'll have a friend."

In a bed never shared, Lottie lay on a feather pillow moistened from her tears. For two days now, ever since George Wilhelm had delivered with her supplies a letter from San Antonio, rest had been as scarce as blossoms in January. Without opening it, she knew by the ostentatious handwriting the letter's author. Immediately, she had asked George to get a message to the one man she could trust — Jack Jacobs. Jack was a decent man, and now she needed a good man. She would have lingered in bed except that Jack might arrive, so she dressed without enthusiasm, waiting in the cool dimness of the house, staring blankly at the letter left on the table where her tears had stained it. The letter's words haunted her every thought, its unexpectedness shaking her, though she knew it had been inevitable. Finally, she lost track of time, understanding only that the hazy light of an ashen gray day came from a western sun. A knock on the door startled her.

Quickly she stood and glanced in the mirror over her dresser, wincing at what she saw. Her face was drawn tight around her cheeks and lips, her eyes bloodshot, her hair mussed. A pitiful excuse for a woman, desired by so many and available to no one, she thought. Then she remembered the letter. Almost no one. She stood inspecting herself, knowing it was too late to redeem her appearance.

A second, harder knock sounded at the door. "Lottie, are you home?"

It was Jack Jacobs. She grabbed a brush from her dresser and rushed it futilely through her hair. "Just a moment, Jack," she answered, rushing to the door and shaking her auburn hair until it hung freely past her shoulders. Opening the door, she spoke. "I'm not much to look at, Jack, but thank you for coming."

Jacobs smiled as he came into her view. Taking off his hat, he stared at her for a moment and Lottie could see the smile sliding away as the shock rose in his eyes. He bit his lip.

180

"I've aged these last few days, Jack." She smiled. "I'm plain when I'm not fixed up."

He shifted his weight from foot to foot as he rolled up the brim of his hat with his hands. "I've never seen you," he stammered for the right words, "with your hair down before."

Lottie remembered differently. Jacobs was too decent a man to make a good liar, she thought. She motioned for him to come in. "Thank you for coming, Jack."

"Lottie, have you been well?" He stepped inside, shutting the door behind.

Lottie turned away from Jacobs and walked to the table. Picking up the letter, she folded it and inserted it back in the envelope. "I've not been sick, if that's what you're asking."

Jacobs eased beside Lottie as she turned to face him. "Something's troubling you. Even in the poor light I can see you've been crying."

"I'll not light a lamp or you'll see how bad I really look, Jack, but I've received this letter." She offered it to him.

Perplexed, Jacobs took it.

"Jack, I must tell someone I can trust of my problem."

"Nothing you'll say will change my opinion of you, Lottie. There's not a finer woman in these parts."

"A gambling woman?" Lottie broke away from Jacobs so he would not see the tears. "What I tell you, Jack, must remain secret as long as I am in Griffin."

Jacobs nodded as she turned around to face him.

"My real name is Charlotte . . ." She paused. "This you must tell no one as long as you live."

He nodded again.

"My name is Charlotte . . ." she began her story. For an hour she told him of her father, mother, and sister, their life in Kentucky before the war. It had been a prosperous life, a good life. Trips throughout the south and even to the hated northeast and on into Europe. Long riverboat rides and sitting on her father's lap while he gambled. Dances and balls and young men wooing her. It had been a magnificent life, as the daughter of a prosperous landowner, a state senator, a man known throughout the state. And a slave owner. Then came the war. Everything changed. Kentucky stayed in the Union, but her father aligned himself with the South, even though he was too old to fight. Lottie was just coming to the age when she was taking young men seriously and so many were dying.

And then the war was over and there was nothing left of that life. The land no longer belonged to southern sympathizers. The boys who had marched off to war hobbled back crippled of body or mind, if they returned at all. And, she told Jacobs, when she had needed her father's advice the most, she had refused to heed it. She had made a grave mistake going against his wishes. How it had broken her father's heart. And how she had missed his burial. Her mother and sister were without support then and she'd taken up gambling, with good instruction, and supported them, her sister in an eastern boarding school and her mother in Kentucky until her death. And then when her sister had finished her education, she had abandoned her older sister, ashamed of her occupation. Finally, there was the letter, reopening the past wound.

"Read the letter, Jack, it explains the rest."

Jacobs pulled folded paper from the envelope, holding it up to catch what light seeped in the window. He read slowly and shook his head when he finished. "I'm sorry, Lottie."

Lottie walked around the table, her hand clutching her neck. "I must win the Bee Hive back and then leave the Flat before he finds me, Jack."

"He'll just catch up with you somewhere else. Women gamblers are few and far between. He'd just find out wherever you went. Could be he's bluffing. Sometimes it's best to quit your running."

"But I can't trust him to stop chasing me. I found out too late. It could be tomorrow or he could already be in town. Who can say?"

"Or never?" he added.

She shrugged.

Jacobs stood. "I best be going before this starts tongues a wagging. Some think you entertain men here."

"Rumors were probably started by that evil woman John Henry Holliday consorts with."

"Something's been bothering me, Lottie. I know it's not my place to ask, but are you fond of Holliday?"

"In a way, Jack," Lottie brushed the hair back over her shoulder. "He reminds me of men before the war and the days before my life changed. He can be a gentleman. But there is no one in Griffin I am as fond of as you, Jack." She reached for his calloused hands and held them tightly. "Maybe it could have been different, Jack, but people like me aren't always what they seem to be."

"I'm sorry, Lottie, I truly am." Jack released her hands and put on his hat. "But you shouldn't run away this time. Promise me you'll not leave without telling me."

"I'll stay, Jack," she answered, raising on her toes and kissing him gently upon the cheek. "I'll stay."

SPRING

SIXTEEN

Pete Haverty flung a bit mouthpiece at a rafter near the stable door. "Damn rat." He spit the words out with a stream of tobacco juice that splattered against a stall wall. Haverty, his shirt sleeves rolled up, scratched his elbow, then snatched a curry comb from a nail. His impatient jaw furiously worked over his chaw and his watery eyes, as brown as the tobacco juice trailing out both corners of his mouth, stared restlessly at Holliday. "What was it you wanted?" he asked, then hobbled on a gimpy leg to a rear stall.

Removing his derby, Holliday fanned his face to drive away the beading sweat, then coughed into his hat as he followed Haverty through the stable. Though the stalls could use a carpet of hay instead of tobacco splatterings and the droppings, the horses in them were sleek from good feedings. Haverty slipped into the last stall by the rear door and attacked the splotched coat of a frisky pinto with the curry comb. Drawing up beside the stall, Holliday took in the paint, the stall floor covered with hay, and the water trough on the stall's back wall. Leaning against a post brushed by the slight breeze wafting in from the back door, Holliday refitted his hat. "Special horse?"

"I like him. Now what was it you wanted, fellow?"

"Did you rent a buggy to Lottie Deno?"

Pausing in his chore, Haverty scratched his elbow as he stared uneasily over the paint's back at Holliday. Running his calloused fingers through a mop of hair the color of rotting straw, Haverty cocked his jaw and fired a squirt of tobacco through his brown-stained teeth. "I ain't telling what nobody rents of mine unless they say to. It's bad business."

"I like a cautious man," Holliday said, stepping away from the post into Haverty's full view. He unbuttoned his frock coat and swept the right side behind his gun holster. "Yes, sir, I appreciate a cautious man, but nobody's gonna get hurt if you answer me. I can't make any promises, if you don't." Holliday's hand slipped over his Colt's ivory grip.

Haverty choked on his tobacco, then jumped when the pinto blew into the water trough. "Yeah, I rented her a buggy just like I do each Sunday afternoon when the weather's good."

Stroking his mustache, Holliday leaned back into the post. "Where'd she go?"

"Up Government Hill to get that pregnant woman, the officer's wife. They cut off the road this side of town like they were heading toward the river bend. Ballgame's in progress there." Haverty hung the curry comb on a nail and crossed his arms over his chest.

Holliday nodded. "Now can you rent me a good horse? This paint'll do."

Haverty stammered, shifting his weight from foot to foot, scratching harder at his elbow. "I don't, I mean, I . . . this horse is my runner. I . . . uh . . . he's saved for races."

"You're saying I can't have him for the afternoon."

Shrugging, Haverty nodded. "I don't let the paint out of this building without me. I've won enough money off folks with paint here," he slapped the pony on the rump, "that some might want to harm him or doctor him up and try to beat me in a race."

"I admire a cautious man," Holliday said slowly, "but I —"

"Fellow, I'll tell you what. Pick any mount in the stable and I'll loan him for the afternoon. No charge. Deal?"

Holliday slipped between Haverty and the paint. "This deal's not helping your business any."

"But it's not hurting my racing. Sporting is more fun than

business. I'll just take a loss here, long as it don't hurt my racing."

Slapping the horse solidly on the rump, Holliday grinned. "Fine, I'm not too fond of paints anyway. They're ugly."

"This one gets prettier each time he races. He ought to be gold as much money as he's won. Now, which horse you want?"

Holliday shook his head. "No matter as long as it looks decent with a good saddle on it. I'll wait outside."

After Haverty brought him a saddled bay, Holliday mounted and rode into the wind, away from the Flat and toward the cheers and laughter drifting on the breeze from downstream. From the sound, many Flat residents were spending Sunday afternoon away from the smell of Griffin, the buzzing flies, and the dusty streets. Holliday rode beyond thousands of buffalo hides from the winter kill. Like festering sores on the face of the land, the baled hides reeked of rotting flesh singed by the spring sun.

Riding easy in the saddle, Holliday scanned a distant copse of cottonwoods that fanned out in a vee from a broad crook of the Clear Fork. Two lines of buggies and wagons intersected at right angles under the shade of the trees, where spectators rooted for the local team against the boys from Albany, seventeen miles to the south.

The land had infected the spectators with a spring laziness. Men and women sat leisurely in their wagons or reclined on quilts in the thick grass, their children running about, disappearing behind the steep bank and moments later coming back in sight a distance away. Holliday rode by the spectators and down the embankment to water his horse. Twisting in his saddle, he studied the river, noting where the serpentine summer flood waters had bitten a wagon-size chunk of bank from under a great cottonwood tree anchoring the river bend. Though the ground at its base appeared solid, the undermined tree tilted slightly toward the river, its exposed roots straining against gravity to carry the load. A handful of boys used the convenient, if dangerous, hiding place to sneak a smoke away from their parents.

When the horse finished watering and blowing, Holliday directed the animal up the bank and among the spectators. The horse shied away from the darting kids playing tag. Holliday's nose perked to the aroma of fried chicken, and he coveted a wishbone as he passed one wagon. Holliday heard from the rough-hewn baseball diamond a thud drawing cheers from those around him. He turned in the saddle to see a local favorite racing from one towsack base to another. Holliday glanced at the crowd and shook his head, the game's fascination escaping him, though it seemed popular among merchants and cowhands, gamblers and wives, husbands and whores, hunters and children, soldiers and teamsters. Maybe they had bet money.

On the far side of the field, Holliday finally spotted Lottie, seated elegantly on a pallet beside her buggy. Rachel, now very pregnant, was sprawled beside her. As Holliday aimed his mount toward Lottie, he saw Rachel point her finger at him, her back going as stiff as her expression. He could see Lottie nodding her head at Rachel, then looking toward him and back to the game. Holliday guided his horse to her buggy and stopped, turning in the saddle and lifting one leg over the saddle horn.

"Afternoon, ladies."

"Good day, John Henry Holliday." Lottie smiled and brushed an auburn curl back in place. "You remember Rachel?"

Holliday nodded at Rachel's forced smile which quickly disappeared behind a cloudy brow. "You look well," he told her.

"John Henry," Lottie said, "I did not realize you enjoyed baseball so. Have you a bet on the outcome?"

"I don't bet on child's play." Holliday slid off his horse and, after tying the reins to a buggy wheel, he walked to the pallet and squatted in front of Lottie.

Lottie touched her index finger to her chin. "Does your lady friend Kate know about this?" She smiled softly.

"You're the only lady I know, Lottie," Holliday said, then pursing his lips without emotion, "excepting Rachel, of course." He tipped his hat toward her. "Spring, being what it is, Lottie, I thought you might reconsider my offer." He looked at Rachel. "In private."

"John Henry has asked for my hand," Lottie said to her companion. Rachel gasped, then flushed in embarrassment. "The seasons have changed, John Henry, but my answer has not."

"My run of bad luck with you will change one day, Lottie," Holliday responded.

"If your luck changes, Mister Holliday," Rachel interrupted, "then surely Lottie's will have worsened."

Holliday tipped his hat to Rachel again. "Perhaps I am in the company of only one lady after all." Holliday enjoyed the flush of Rachel's cheeks.

"The two of you are acting like children," Lottie scolded. "Let's act like ladies and gentlemen. John Henry, you may join us, if you avoid a sharp tongue." Lottie gathered her skirt and made more room on the quilt.

As Holliday stepped to the pallet, Rachel struggled against her enlarged stomach to get up. Holliday extended his hand to her. Rachel refused it, but despite her effort, she could not arise. Her shoulders drooping from exertion, she finally sighed and surrendered to Holliday's still offered hand. "I think I shall walk while you two visit."

"Don't stray far, nor strain yourself, Rachel." Lottie ordered. "Don't take chances with that baby." As Rachel walked away, Lottie turned to Holliday. "She's a good woman."

"Marriage does her well," Holliday said, sitting in Rachel's vacated spot. "Perhaps you should consider it."

Lottie tossed her head, a soft laugh slipping between her lips and a curl of auburn hair dropping over her ear. She patted her ear for the wayward curl and ushered it back in place. "Maybe I'm not cut out to be a wife, John Henry."

"It's Charlotte, isn't it, your name? You're a gambling lady, perhaps some evening we can play a hand of cards on it. I win, you tell me your name. You win, I'll not mention it again."

"But John Henry," her eyes fluttered, "it's no bother. I'm flattered, me well past my youth and receiving enough attention to make me giddy."

Holliday plucked a pair of wildflowers within reach and handed them to Lottie, enjoying the smile she returned.

She studied the orange, red, and yellow petals. "Thank you, John Henry, it has been years since anyone's given me flowers." She twirled the plant stems between the tips of her fingers. "They call these Indian blankets or firewheels?"

Holliday leaned over and plucked another to examine.

"They're pretty," Lottie said, "If I could only make a living picking them instead of men's pockets, I could be happy."

Holliday nodded. "Seven groups of petals, three petals each cluster, twenty-one total — a flower even a gambler can like."

"Some of the petals have fallen off." Lottie lifted her hands to a blue ribbon in her hair and slipped the two flowers under it. "Always thinking of business, John Henry. You'll never be the type to marry."

"Care to bet?" He laughed.

Lottie covered a chuckle with her hand at her lips. "See what I mean? Always gambling. You'd bet on anything."

"Not this infernal game," Holliday answered, gazing at the playing field. "What people get from this escapes me, Lottie."

"They get away from the smell of Griffin."

Holliday tossed his flower in the direction of the Flat and stood up. "It doesn't bother all of us. Every town has its own smell, but I could take you away from this one."

"And I could take myself away, if I desired to go."

"Someday tell me your name. I'd try dentistry. We'd give up the saloons." He stepped to his bay.

"I'll not dishonor my family name. It was a proud name in Kentucky before the war and before I became a gambler."

Holliday untied the bay's reins. "It would still be a proud name!"

"But the answer would still be no."

Holliday spotted Rachel staring at him from behind a nearby wagon. "I will leave. Your friend is tiring herself."

"She's a good woman, John Henry. You worry her, but she's a good woman."

"You're a good woman, too, Lottie. If you ever walk away from the game, I'll walk with you." He stepped to the bay.

"There you go, John Henry, though I'm not sure if all this flattery is for my hand or if you're trying to distract me."

He swung into the saddle. "Distract you from what?"

"Mike Fogle's asked for a shot to win full share of the Bee Hive. I figured Chancey would have mentioned it to you."

"First word I've had of it. Maybe you're trying to distract me, Lottie." Holliday smiled. "Make me question whether Chancey is gonna use me as his dealer."

"For a man that has all but proposed, you are certainly suspicious of the woman you would take for a wife."

"When it comes to gambling, Lottie, I can't take too many precautions."

"Nor when it comes to marriage, can I, John Henry."

Holliday tipped his hat. "Good day, Lottie. I hope your friend Rachel does not find your quilt too soiled by my touch to take the load off her feet."

Holliday nudged his horse forward, across the baseball field instead of around it. Spectators jeered and Holliday enjoyed their catcalls.

He rode the horse straight for Griffin, leaving the animal at Haverty's and hurrying to the Cattle Exchange. He barged into Chancey's office without knocking and found the proprietor hunkered over his strong box, counting Saturday's take. "Has Fogle hit you up for a game yet?"

"Not a word about it, Doc. Seems Fogle's forgotten."

His legs crossed on the bed, a bottle of Monarch between them, Holliday shuffled the cards and dealt around the bed four hands, bottom dealing some cards, second dealing others, and occasionally taking the top card. In turn, he uncovered each hand, a pair in the first he expected, three of a kind in the second he didn't, and nothing in the third. His own hand was two pair. Discarding as an opponent might, he then dealt replacements, his hand becoming a full house which topped the hands of his imaginary partners. Five card draw — he practiced it again and again against three imaginary opponents. In his mind they all were Lottie. He worked to take the chance out of chance. But how to set her up? She would be too shrewd to take a simple set hand. It would be too obvious. Then again, it just might fool her. Maybe the most blatant way would be the safest. Just deal her a pat hand and draw to his own hand, a higher one. Lottie could be taken, no gambler being unbeatable, but she would be no pushover. Holliday dealt two hands, himself against Lottie, manipulating the cards to his advantage, thinking out a ploy for the game that would count, a game that he suspected would come sooner than Chancey expected.

There was a knock on his door. Holliday pulled the pistol from his shoulder holster and set his bottle on the floor.

"What do you want?"

"Me, Doc, Kate. I want in."

192

Why did she always interrupt? He moved to the door and slid the latch open. Kate pushed her way past him. "Now that you're in, Kate, what do you want?"

She screamed, "What were you doing with Lottie yesterday?"

"Damn you, Kate, you're always jealous. Talking, that's all we did."

"If you wanted to talk, you could've come to me. I'd a talked to you."

"Ball, this baseball, I enjoy watching a game now and then and getting away from the stink of this place."

"Oh, hell you don't like foolishness like that, just cards and whiskey and guns and screwing. That's all."

"Kate, we've gone through this a hundred times. There was better than two hundred people there. What could I have done?"

"But you're still seeing her, still waiting for chances to visit her. Damn you, Doc."

Holliday marched back to the bed and card practice, Kate trailing him with her hands on her hips. "You'll walk away from me one too many times, Doc."

He glanced up from the cards, glared at her, his eyes flashing. "Then get out. I didn't invite you."

"You never do, Doc, you just invite yourself to take what you want. You never give a damn about anything. Maybe I should just leave you, get away, make something of myself instead of throwing my life away with you."

"Stages leave Tuesdays and Saturdays, Kate. I'll buy your fare. I still owe you for the money you gave me to buy a whore."

"Hell, Doc, I was in this town before you ever got here. Why in the hell don't *you* leave?"

"Same reason you don't. There's money here for the taking. I'm not through taking."

"You only take, Doc, you never give."

"Sure I give," Holliday said, squeezing the cards in his hands together. "Take this." He threw the deck at her.

Kate jumped back, but several cards hit her. She drew her arm to slap him and rushed for the bed, but before she reached him, he began to cough, hard, like he was expelling his lungs in great chunks. He lay back in the bed, scrunching up his face as the cough assaulted his body. Her hand flew to her mouth, then fell limp at her side as she bent over him. "I'm sorry, Doc, I didn't mean for this to happen to you. Forgive me." She reached for the bottle on the floor by the bed. "Take this."

Holliday grabbed the bourbon, but was coughing too hard to take a swallow. He sat up, his eyes wild and uncertain. Kate pounded him on the back.

"Please, Doc, don't die on me," Kate whispered as she hit his back. "You're all that I've got in Griffin. You might not be much, but you're all I got."

"Maybe a little happiness. Maybe I could give that to you." She ran her fingers through his hair, then rubbed his back.

Holliday twisted around and began to caress her through her clothes. She rubbed back until he began to unbutton her dress. "Please not today, Doc," she whispered. "I'm sore from too many customers last night."

He grabbed her face and twisted it around to his and kissed her wildly, then he shoved her away. "Then get out. You want marriage, then maybe there are some other things you should give up. I'll not have a wife everybody in Texas gets it from."

Kate slapped Doc and he grabbed her. "All you care about me is a place to relieve yourself."

"You're the one that wants to get hitched."

"Then take me, damn you," Kate said, unhooking the buttons on the back of her dress. "That's all you care about satisfying yourself, not about me. Goddam you." She let her dress fall to the floor and then pulled off her undergarments until she stood before him, naked but out of reach. "If you want me, Doc, then come take me. I'll not give myself to you this time."

Holliday eased off the bed and toward her, extending his hand to her, but Kate did not respond. She crossed her hands under her breasts and with each step Holliday advanced, she backed away a step until she was against the wall.

"You've come across the room for me, Doc, but you never rented a horse and rode out of town to find me like you did her. Am I not as good as Lottie, is that it? Bet she's never sore."

Holliday grabbed her and pulled her toward the bed. Aching for her flesh, he quickly undressed, then mounted and rode her savagely. She moaned from mixed pain and pleasure until

194

Doc was done and he rolled off. They lay beside each other for a long time without speaking until a hard knock on the door startled them. Holliday bolted from bed and grabbed his gun.

"Doc, you there?"

Holliday recognized Chancey's voice. "What's bothering you, Chancey?"

"Need to talk."

Holliday jerked on his pants, then opened the door.

"You were late coming in and I wondered if something was . . ." Chancey stepped in, saw Kate naked, and hushed.

She looked up, her legs leaking, and smiled unashamed without reaching for the sheet.

"Climb aboard, Chancey," Holliday offered, "everyone else has."

"She's the reason you're late into the saloon. I should of known," Chancey shook his head and started rolling a cigarette.

"I've been late before, Chancey."

"Not on a day I really needed to talk to you."

"Kate slowed me down."

"Hellfire, Doc, if you weren't always so horny nothing would slow you down, not even consumption."

Kate got up, walked around the bed, and picked up her clothes to put on. "Don't mind me, gentlemen, if you can be called that." She started to dress.

"Doc, Fogle's called in his chips. Tomorrow night we play."

Lottie wasn't bluffing after all, Holliday thought.

SEVENTEEN

The water rippled through a rock-bottomed shallow where Holliday nudged his horse into the Clear Fork. He saw downstream an orange-hued blanket of flowers hugging the bank in the afternoon shade of a cottonwood. A twist of his wrist on the reins sent the bay in that direction, prancing as briskly as the breeze. Here away from the Flat, the air smelled of spring's sweetness. The land promised more green than scanty summer rains would fulfill, and a rainbow of wildflowers seemed trapped between earth and sky, waving their violet, yellow, blue, red, and orange petals as if they could fly were they freed of stem and root.

As Holliday suspected, the patch of flowers that was his destination was dominated by the firewheels Lottie had admired at the baseball game. Dismounting, Holliday pulled a towel from under a leather saddle strap and carried it to the creek. Stepping easy so not to sink his boot in the water's muddy fringe, he bent and soaked the towel, then wrung it as he retreated to the flowers. Looking first to see that no one spied him, he then searched for firewheels with twenty-one petals. Finding many, he plucked more than four dozen and swathed them in the moist towel to preserve the bouquet until nightfall, until he and Lottie would play for the Bee Hive.

Though he suspected a wagonload of flowers would never

change her feelings for him, perhaps these few would fluster her concentration tonight. He wished the flowers were more than a gambling ploy. Standing by the bay as it nibbled among the green strands of fresh grass, Holliday enjoyed the shade's coolness and wished Lottie were at his side, her arms around his waist, her head upon his chest. The breeze through the cottonwood blew white wisps down from the trees, coating the ground in places with a carpet of white, the color of a virgin's bed, a bed he would like to share. Ironic, he thought, these emotions for a woman he planned to cheat in a few hours.

Holding the flowers gingerly in the crook of his arm, he mounted the bay and rode a half mile downstream to the bend where the baseball game had been played. For a while, he let his horse graze as he stared at the giant cottonwood somehow suspended above the creek in spite of the bank undercut beneath it. Then riding on beyond the great tree, Holliday saw in the distance a cloud of dust marking another cattle herd following the American Trail toward Dodge City. Hundreds of thousands of cattle had passed over it, leaving no grass but plenty of fertilizer. As he listened, Holliday heard the bellows of the balky cattle carrying, like a muted cacophony across the land, a haunting lullaby.

By the lengthening shadows, Holliday knew he must return soon or Chancey would fret. He rode away from the creek, eventually hitting the trail for Griffin and riding leisurely toward the Flat. His sporadic cough occasionally spooked the rented horse. Checking his pocket watch, he noted three hours of leeway, plenty of time for a hot bath, a good shave, and a change of clothes before the game.

Nearing the Flat, he watched three men approaching him from the creek crossing. One rode tall in the saddle, his shoulders thrown back and his head erect, his chin jutting forward. Holliday recognized Wyatt Earp, the Santa Fe operative.

Coming within talking distance, Holliday waited for Earp to signal that their acquaintance could be acknowledged. Earp rode silently toward him, Holliday detecting a glint of recognition in his eye. As their horses met, Earp drew back on the reins.

"Pardon me, mister," Earp said, as Holliday pulled up his horse. Earp's partners slowed. "You wouldn't happen to know a Shawn Chancey back in town, would you?"

Holliday nodded and Earp motioned to his two companions. "Ride on and I'll catch up. I want this gentleman to take a message to Chancey." The two riders moved wearily on and Earp smiled, extending his hand. "How are you, Holliday?"

"Still winning more than I'm losing," he replied, grasping Earp's hand firmly, then feeling a flush of foolishness at the flowers he carried. "You find your lost cousin?"

Earp eyed the flowers. "Missed him, dammit, though your information was good. He stayed in Fort Davis awhile then cut out for New Mexico Territory. Damn if I'm gonna chase him there, but maybe this'll get him out of Santa Fe's hair."

"I'd buy you a drink if you had time," Holliday offered.

"Appreciate it, Holliday, but I'm on my own time now and best keep riding for Dodge. You're welcome to join me."

"Can't. There's a card game tonight. Chancey's got half a saloon at stake, and I'm playing his cards for him."

"Don't let it get out of hand."

"Not tonight. I'm up against Lottie Deno."

"Heard she's a looker. That who the flowers are for?"

Holliday reddened. "Quite a looker, she is. And she's an even better card player. Let's move down in the shade of the trees, Wyatt, talk a little more."

"The cottonwoods spook me. Found a man hanging in one west of town."

"I hadn't heard."

"Seems there was a shooting in town last night. Sheriff took this fellow into custody, kept him overnight in one of the hotels for some reason, and was to take him to the Albany jail today. Vigilantes broke in and relieved him of his charge. I'll be damned if it wasn't me that found him, air dancing. Sheriff didn't seem a mite upset about any of this when I reported the body. Just shrugged and said he'd look into it."

"Vigilantes were active last spring," Holliday said. "A few cow thieves were hanged then and another fellow was hanged in the fall about the time I arrived."

Earp nudged his horse on along the trail and Holliday turned his bay around to accompany him. "Take care of yourself. Don't overturn a barrel of trouble with those folks."

"I keep the odds on my side, Wyatt."

"Can't always depend on the odds, Holliday, not in a town like Griffin. It's been around long enough now that the upstanding citizens want to get rid of the seedy types that made them and the town prosper. Griffin's at its peak, maybe on the downslide, and when the fine local citizens get nervous about our kind, they organize as vigilantes to make their town respectable."

Holliday coughed. "Damn if this consumption won't kill me before the vigilantes do."

Earp stuck his hand out to Holliday. "You ever get in trouble or need a friend, look me up in Dodge City."

"I'll do it, and I'll hello Chancey for you."

Earp laughed. "Chancey's a good one, except in a tight. He looks after himself first."

"I'll remember what you say, Wyatt. Maybe I'll look you up someday when business slacks around here."

Earp slapped his horse's flank and rode into the distance.

"I don't like it," Chancey said with a sigh that bloomed into a cloud of cigarette smoke. The stairs groaned at his heavy steps. "The killing last night, the vigilantes, the hanging. Damn it's not a good sign."

"You worry too much," Holliday said, following him up the stairs of the Bee Hive. Holliday smelled of soap and tonic water, his shirt was new, his suit laundered and his derby brushed. Walking at Chancey's side, Holliday shielded the bouquet of firewheels behind Chancey's broad back.

"Maybe I'd worry less if you'd ever beaten Lottie's Luck, Doc! It's my saloon and money you'll be playing for."

"You want to play the hand yourself, Chancey? Hell, I can remember you groaning over buying half the Bee Hive instead of winning it outright. In a few minutes, you'll own the whole damn thing. Lottie's Luck be damned."

"If you don't believe in Lottie's Luck, Doc, then why in hell are you all gussied up and carrying her flowers?" His voice was as pointed as newly stretched barbed wire.

Holliday didn't like the tone. "Are you behind me or not?"

The question hung in the air until they reached the top of the stairs. Chancey drew deep on his cigarette, then flicked it at

199

a spittoon by the top landing. "I am," he exhaled smoke with his words, "if you cheat her."

Holliday touched his freshly waxed mustache. "Then you're behind me." As Chancey laughed, Holliday spotted Lottie across the room and she never looked better. Beneath the tiger snarling out of a gaudy broadside on the wall, she stood near her faro table, wearing a pale yellow dress with a high neck that buttoned up the front and set off her auburn hair like the flame from a candle. Her face was powdered, her cheeks delicately rouged, her lips lightly tinted. When his eyes met hers, Holliday tipped his hat, then pulled the bouquet from behind Chancey's back. Seeing the flowers, Lottie smiled weakly at him.

He heard Chancey. "Just remember whose money you'll be betting, Doc."

Lottie moved as softly as a yellow cloud from her table toward Holliday, raising her hand as she neared. Holliday took it, lifting her fingers to his lips and kissing them. Then he wrapped her fingers around the bouquet of firewheels. "For the lady of the evening," he said, tipping his hat.

"Every lady loves flowers, John Henry. I must credit your persistence," Lottie spoke with a coolness as she lifted the flowers to her nose. "You forget that tonight I am no lady."

"Others should be the judge of that."

"Tonight," Lottie said, "the cards will be the judge of everything." She released the flowers and they tumbled to the floor as useless as broken promises.

Chancey stepped beside Holliday. "You dropped your flowers, Lottie."

Lottie's soft features turned hard, her jaw like chiseled granite until she spoke. "Mike was a fool to ever get tied up with you."

Pointing his finger at her breast, Chancey matched the venom in her words. "You just be sure, Lottie Deno, that your partner Fogle brings enough cash with him to cover his losses."

"I'll back him with every cent I've got against you or any other man that takes me for a whore, Chancey."

"Good women don't frequent saloons." Chancey wadded his fingers into a fist and pounded his hand.

"And good men respect women," she said, her words simmering. She glanced at Holliday. "You are in the employ of a low man, John Henry. It'll bring you bad luck." She offered Holliday her arm, and together they walked to a vacant table.

Chancey called as Holliday pulled a chair out for Lottie. "Just remember, girl, gamblers shouldn't make enemies among their own kind because they'll accumulate enough among the suckers. Make this quick, Doc, show her it's a man's game."

"Enough chatter," Holliday said taking his seat and waving Chancey away. In his coat pocket, Holliday carried a rigged deck and an honest pack. "Five card draw, my cards," he told Lottie. She would ask to inspect the cards, so he withdrew the straight deck from his pocket, broke the seal on the box, removed the cards, then unwrapped them from their brown paper shroud. "Your money?" he asked Lottie, and instantly Mike Fogle stood beside her, dropping a packet of bills on the table.

Chancey slapped an envelope of his own in front of Holliday. "There's more money where that came from."

Holliday shuffled the cards, tossing them from hand to hand, slowly at first, waiting for Lottie to ask to inspect the deck, then faster and harder when he realized she had forgotten the precaution. The argument with Chancey had distracted her. Disgust knotted in Holliday's stomach for not risking the rigged deck. Unknowingly, she had already outwitted him.

A ring of observers pressed around the table as Holliday left the cards for Lottie to cut. Holliday glanced at the faces as Lottie split the deck, his gaze stopping at a fleshy mug that made his own face tighten into a scowl. Behind Lottie stood Ed Bailey. Damn. Now he must keep up with Bailey as well as the cards. Holliday picked up the two stacks from Lottie's cut. "No betting ceiling. Five card draw. Ante a hundred dollars."

Lottie nodded and tossed her wager on the table, Holliday quickly matching it. With the fresh deck the deal didn't matter, so Holliday dealt straight, then placed the deck on the table and corralled his cards, lifting them to his chest, fanning the corners, an ace and two deuces appearing. Holliday would spar with these early hands, stacking the deck and setting Lottie up for the big hand. The ace would come in handy later. Holliday rearranged his cards, the ace with the two discards, then looked into Lottie's impenetrable gray eyes, her emotionless face.

"I'll go another hundred. Two cards," she said, tossing a pair to the middle of the table.

Holliday matched her bet and replenished her cards. "Lady takes two," he called. Perhaps she had three of a kind, with her luck. "Dealer takes three," he said, collapsing his three discards into a pile — the ace on top — and dropping them diagonally across the deadwood. He dealt himself a trio; a pair of fives appeared to reinforce his weak deuces. Still, they would be useless against her three of a kind, Holliday guessed.

Lottie bumped the pot another hundred. "You staying?"

Holliday rearranged his cards, deuces and fives, until the deuce and five of clubs were together. "Dealer folds," he said. As he closed his cards, his hands screened them for an instant, just long enough for the two clubs to slide up his sleeve. His other discards he placed atop the deck, not the deadwood.

Lottie smiled and threw her cards into the deadwood with enough force to scatter Holliday's neat stacks. Damn, Holliday thought. Now he couldn't be sure which one was the ace he had hoped to save. When she reached for the pot, Holliday nicked with his thumbnail the corner of the suspected ace of hearts. As he straightened the deadwood, Holliday slid the marked card to the bottom of the deck. Lottie stacked her winnings, oblivious to the cheating. She was growing careless.

So was Ed Bailey with his boisterous talk, saying how quickly Lottie would clean out Holliday. Holliday felt the anger rolling in his throat and his breath whistling between his teeth. He must control his temper, Holliday thought, or Lottie would thrash him.

"Chancey," he called, "see that I get a bottle of whiskey and a jigger." Chancey grunted and snapped his finger at one of the roving Bee Hive barkeeps. The bottle and glass arrived as Holliday finished shuffling. Putting the deck down, he poured a drink, spilling a puddle the size of a quarter eagle on the table, then downed the liquid. As he reclaimed the deck, he angled it in his hand as he dealt. From the reflection in the spilled bourbon he confirmed the ace of hearts was on the bottom. Holliday manipulated the cards through three more hands, claiming two pots and Lottie winning the third. All were puny pots. So far, Lottie and Holliday were running even — except for the ace on the bottom of the deck and the two clubs up his sleeve. Holliday tossed another hand across the table to Lottie.

"You're forgetting your ante," Lottie smiled.

Holliday matched Lottie's bet, then poured himself another drink before picking up his cards and fanning them out. "Maybe this is my hand, Lottie."

"Three cards." She tossed an unwanted trio onto the table.

Holliday ignored her.

"Three," she repeated.

She was getting edgy, Holliday could feel it. Would she make a play before he dealt her the rigged hand? Holliday stared at two kings, two worthless cards, and the seven of clubs. He needed the seven to build the straight flush he was saving up his sleeve. He separated his cards, stacking two on the deadwood and leaving the seven of clubs on the bottom of his three keepers. After picking up the deck, he tossed three cards to Lottie. "Dealer takes three," Holliday said, and dropped three more on his keepers. He straightened the cards between his fingers, then laid them in his palm, coughing as he pushed the extra card, the seven of clubs, into his sleeve. He studied Lottie and her eyes seemed oblivious to his swindle, then he spread his cards. He had lucked out on the draw, the pair of kings being joined by two nines. He nodded toward Lottie. "You in?"

Lottie bumped the pot two hundred dollars. "I'm with you."

Holliday grinned. "I'll raise you another hundred and call your hand." He shoved the money toward the middle of the table.

Lottie matched him, then revealed her cards. "Aces and fours."

Shaking his head, Holliday tossed his cards onto the pile, sorry to have lost, but glad two more aces had turned up. "You beat my kings, Lottie."

As Lottie pulled in the pot, Holliday heard Ed Bailey laughing loudest among all the spectators. Holliday glared from the table to Bailey's puffy face. Their eyes met and Bailey's laugh died in his throat. When Holliday glanced back at the cards, Lottie had already added hers to the deadwood. Holliday damned Ed Bailey for distracting him long enough to lose her two aces in the deadwood. Holliday bit his lip. The aces? He should have forgotten Bailey and kept his eyes on the aces. He must find them. His hand reached for the discards, his fingers picking them up just as a cough ripped out of his lungs, three cards falling from his fingers and overturning on the felt table. Two were the aces of spades and clubs. His cough improved instantly. He mixed the cards, manipulating the two aces to their mate on the bottom of the deck. Now he needed the ace of diamonds.

He shuffled the cards, tossing them from hand to hand. "Ante, Lottie." Around her the crowd seemed restless. Holliday shared their impatience, needing the ace of diamonds and three more clubs. He dealt another hand, finding in his the diamond ace and two clubs — the three and six — he wanted. Lottie called for two cards without raising the pot. He obliged her, then she folded without comment. Damn her! Though he had won the pot, she had made it harder for him to sleeve the clubs. Instead, he slid them with the ace to the bottom of the deck.

"You're giving up too easily, Lottie."

"I'm ahead in the play."

"But the Bee Hive's still half Chancey's."

"We're still playing," she said, matter-of-factly.

Holliday finagled the cards again, but too many were accumulating on the bottom. Six keepers there. He held the deck in the palm of his left hand as a cough screamed out of his lungs, then another, and he raised his right hand to Lottie. "May I get . . ." he coughed again, ". . . my handkerchief?"

Lottie nodded. Holliday shook his head, trying to throw the cough. Then in one fluid motion, he screened the cards from Lottie by twisting his left palm toward his chest. With his right hand he extracted the deck — except for the bottom two cards — and placed it on the table. As Lottie watched his right hand disappear into his coat for the handkerchief, his left hand flicked the two additional clubs up his sleeve. Now only the four of clubs was lacking, he thought as he coughed into the clean handkerchief.

"Your cough, John Henry, strikes at the oddest times."

She knew something was amiss. "Way it is with consumption," he answered.

Holliday, growing impatient for the four of clubs, split the next two hands with Lottie. The following hand, he took with a full house over Lottie's three fours, including the four of clubs. He pulled the pot in, then the deadwood. As he drew the discards to the deck, his thumbnail nicked the edge of the four. Rearranging the deck, Holliday slipped the four to the bottom of the stack with the four aces. He evened the deck and as he placed it on the table he palmed the top three cards in his right hand. His left hand moved catlike from his money stack to the table's center for the ante. "Your ante," he told Lottie as he jerked his left hand away from the pot, the sleeved cards sliding into his palm. As he picked up the deck, he dropped the sleeved cards on top, then covered them with the three palmed cards in his right hand. He began his series of false shuffles, tossing the cards in batches from hand to hand, but always preserving the order at the top and bottom. As he shuffled, Lottie asked Mike Fogle to send for an iced glass of lemonade.

Finally, Holliday set the deck on the table.

Lottie tapped the cards with her finger and for a moment, Holliday sat disbelieving. She had declined a cut and instead sipped at the just arrived lemonade. Could she know more than he had figured out? Holliday picked up the cards, looked at Lottie, then shook his head.

He dealt her the top card from the deck. He didn't know what it was; it didn't matter. From the bottom of the deck, he dealt himself the four of clubs. From the bottom, he passed her an ace. From the top he took an unknown card for himself. Another ace from the bottom for her hand and another unknown from the top for him. Another ace for her from the bottom. He watched her but she betrayed no emotion. Then from the top, he took the first of the stacked clubs. From the bottom he passed her a final ace and from the top he dealt himself his third club.

Holliday dropped the deck and watched Lottie spread her cards apart. Her face never quivered, but behind her, Ed Bailey craned his neck for a glimpse of her cards. His mouth widened. Bailey's eyes glanced to Holliday and his mouth drew out into a knowing grin.

Then studying his own cards — four, five, and seven of clubs, along with a ten of spades and queen of hearts — Holliday realized a mistake. Damn, he hadn't placed the clubs in good

205

order! Without the six of clubs, he might not draw into his straight flush. He might lose the saloon yet. Damn it all, the three of clubs would ruin him, too, if he didn't get it. He must get both the three and six and not the two of clubs to beat her. His throat went dry and tight. He grabbed for the bottle, this time unintentionally spilling liquor as he filled the jigger.

Lottie closed her cards and exchanged them for a stack of bills in front of her. Thumbing through the money, she spoke. "I'll up the pot five hundred, John Henry. You in?"

"I'll see you and raise you another five hundred."

"I'm in." She sipped at the lemonade, then spoke again. "And I'll bet Fogle's half of the Bee Hive against Chancey's."

The trap was sprung, Holliday thought, as Fogle edged toward Lottie. She leaned forward over the table, waiting for an answer. Reaching to her neck, she undid the top two buttons on her high collar.

"A lady shouldn't undress in the presence of gentlemen." Holliday nodded.

Lottie cleared her throat. "I make no claims tonight to be a lady. Are you in or not?"

"I'm in. How many cards?"

Now Lottie stalled, re-examining her cards. Holliday knew she didn't want to appear too anxious. With four aces, you don't have much to consider except whether to discard for a higher off.

"Having second thoughts about your bet, Lottie?" he asked.

Her gray eyes stared over the top of her cards. "Might I ask one thing of you, John Henry, before I take my cards?"

"Ask."

"Pass the cards without picking up the deck this time."

Damn, he thought, he couldn't say no without being accused of cheating. If he said yes and Lottie got the three or six of clubs, his straight flush was ruined. She had a two out of three chance of beating him. Goddam it, now he believed in Lottie's Luck. He hoisted the jigger to his lips and savored the liquor's taste as he figured his chances. "Odd request, Lottie. You suggesting I'm cheating?"

Lottie's eyes fluttered and she answered softly. "Certainly not, John Henry. Just wanted to make sure you wouldn't try something that foolish now that the saloon's on the line."

He swallowed hard. "On one condition I will agree, Lottie."

Lottie closed her cards. "That being?"

"We have a side bet — between you and me this round."

Lottie hesitated a moment, lifted her hand to her chin, and tapped her lips with her index finger. "Okay, how much?"

"Not money, Lottie, not money," he answered. "I win, you tell me your name, your real name."

"And if I win, John Henry?"

"I'll never ask again, nor think you would ever tell me."

Lottie picked up her cards, fanned them out again, then collapsed them into a single pile. "It's a bet, John Henry, but a hand of cards will not mean a change of heart."

"Fair enough. How many cards you want?"

She raised her hand to her chin again and tapped her lips with her fingers.

"How many cards, Lottie?"

She fanned her cards out. "Three, John Henry, three."

Maybe Holliday was one step ahead of her, Lottie thought. But his jaw went slack and his eyelids blinked when she said three cards. He sat in motionless disbelief. "Three cards, John Henry. Three cards," she repeated. Behind her Ed Bailey gasped. The son of a bitch had been watching her cards, she thought. At least she could be sure he wasn't in cahoots with Holliday.

Four aces and a nine. Wasn't much room to improve upon that, but John Henry had been manipulating the cards since the game started, false shuffles, false cuts, and maybe even slipping cards up his sleeve when he coughed. Consumption allowed a man some liberties at the card table for which a healthy man might be shot. Holliday had been playing to set her up. Only a straight flush would beat four aces. Holliday wouldn't dare deal her and himself set hands. He must draw for cards, otherwise it would be too obvious a setup. He would take two, maybe three cards. Two most likely. He would be playing her to hold her four aces and maybe discard the fifth card for a higher one. If she ruined his straight, she could win with a lesser hand than she had been dealt. Taking two cards would leave her three aces, but if Holliday had stacked enough in the deck he might still be able to pull out a straight flush. If she discarded the nine and two aces, she'd still have a pair and it would beat any pair Holliday could come up with.

Then perhaps Holliday had figured she'd be suspicious of a pat hand and was playing her to think just as she was, then he'd pull in three of a kind to win over her pair of aces. Maybe he had even stacked both sides of the deck so he could play either way. So, she had asked him to leave the deck on the table. If he had two options then, now he would have but one. She'd just have to hope he wasn't a step ahead of her.

Holliday reached for the deck.

"Remember our bet, John Henry. Leave them on the table."

Holliday's scowl surprised Lottie and she knew by his emotion that she had beaten him. He snapped each card from the deck and tossed it across the table as she threw her three discards to the center and gathered the new cards. Slowly, she fanned them open. Ace of spades, ace of hearts, six of clubs, three of clubs, two of clubs. Holliday had been going for a straight flush on clubs. Unless he had lucked into three of a kind or two pair from the unrigged cards, she had beaten him.

"Dealer takes three," Holliday called. He eased them off the deck on the table and added them to his good cards. His face was etched in the stone of defeat. Then he folded his cards together and stared blankly at Lottie.

"I'll raise you two thousand," Lottie said, rubbing it in. She counted out the bills. "Are you in, John Henry?"

Holliday squeezed the cards between his fingers, then threw them atop Lottie's discards. He touched his finger to the brim of his derby. "Dealer folds, Lottie."

Beside Lottie, Fogle shouted, "God bless Lottie's Luck." And the other spectators applauded.

Ed Bailey laughed, a smirk of hatred not pleasure, of mockery not admiration on his face. "Lottie's Luck, my ass," he called. "Doc's stupidity had more to do with it than luck."

Lottie heard the words and she knew by the flash in Holliday's eyes that he had too.

EIGHTEEN

Uncle Billy Wilson's Eatery was deserted when Holliday shoved open the door and seated himself at the table running the length of the room. Wilson sprawled over a stool beside a rear window, fanning away the midafternoon heat with a folded copy of last week's *Frontier Echo*. He arose slowly and started toward Holliday, stopping briefly to catch his breath and stare into the kitchen. "Hot weather be rough on a fat man," he said as he wiped the sweat from his brow with his apron. "Wish't I was a thin man like ya. Heat don't bother ya?"

"Take up gambling for a living, Uncle Billy," Holliday glanced across the table set with tin plates and utensils but barren of food. "You'd sweat more and eat less."

Wilson chuckled as he drew up opposite Holliday. He lifted a ham of a leg upon the bench and leaned forward, resting his arms on his knee. "Mrs. Wilson wouldn't like me bein' near the saloon girls. I'm not the best-lookin' husband in Shackelford County, but I'm hers and I'll be damned if she'll share me."

"Food, Uncle Billy, what you got?"

Wilson lifted his hands from his knee and recited what would be ready in another hour. "Buffalo stew left from yesterday is all I can offer now. This is me slowest time, between dinner and supper. Fresh food'll be ready in an hour maybe."

"A bowl of that stew, if it's safe to eat."

Wilson grinned and retreated to the kitchen, where Holliday could hear him giving orders to his wife. Shortly, he returned with a bowl of stew and a mug of coffee, his sweat dripping into both. He placed them before Holliday, then took a seat.

Holliday dipped his spoon in the hot stew and shoved it in his mouth, grimacing at the saltiness. The pasty conglomeration had simmered too long on a hot stove and his scalded portion had been scraped from the bottom of a burnt pot. Holliday could see specks of char in the second bite that went ungently down his gullet. As bad as it was, he ate it in the hope Wilson wouldn't jaw at him so much. But Wilson let no customer eat in peace.

"Ya read the *Frontier Echo?*" Wilson queried, fanning himself with the folded copy.

Holliday shook his head.

"Pete Haverty got's an answer to his advertisement. Yes, sir, all the way from San Antone, the answer came."

Enduring another bite of stew, Holliday grunted. If the conversation was coming anyway, why force himself to eat more? He lingered over the meal, not caring to head for the Cattle Exchange this early, not after losing the Bee Hive last night.

Wilson unfolded the paper and pointed to a small box on the front page. " 'Pete Haverty of only Livery, Feed and Stage Stable in town will swap or run horses,' " Wilson read, then refolded the paper and fanned himself. "Fellow all the way down in San Antone wrote challengin' Haverty to race horses sight unseen. Crazy fool that Haverty is, he's gonna run his pinto against this fellow, come Saturday. Be a lot of money thrown around the Flat on that one, eh? Haverty's pinto's never been beaten around here. Damn fools in the Flat will bet on anything, but I can't understan' them throwing their money away on an animal as dumb as a horse."

"Horse's ain't as dumb as you think, Uncle Billy." Holliday washed the stew's salty sediment down with a sip of coffee. "You don't see any of them betting on people."

Wilson laughed, then noticed Holliday's dwindling coffee. "Let me bring a pot over." He waddled to the kitchen.

Enjoying the quiet in Wilson's absence, Holliday toyed with the spoon in his stew. He tried another bite, his tongue rebelling against the taste, and gave up on eating.

Wilson shuffled back to the table, a steaming coffee pot in his mitted hand. "Yes, sir," he said as he filled Holliday's cup, "I'd place me money on the pinto in most cases, but I'd sure like to see what he's running against." He sat the coffee pot on the table near Holliday.

"Damn ugly horse like a pinto deserves to be beaten." Holliday spit the words out as if they were the stew.

Wilson lifted his foot and dropped it on the bench beside Holliday. "No, sir, it's not a pretty horse, but it's got a good heart. Reminds me of an animal I saw in Californy during the spring of fifty, during the rush, I tell ya. This horse was the scrawniest, ugliest critter I ever seen with less than six legs. Blind in one eye, walked with a damn limp, at least that's what he'd been trained to do, we figured out later. But damn if he didn't outrun by six lengths the best-lookin' horseflesh I ever seen. Taught me a lesson about horses, it did. Ya can't judge a horse by his color. Same way with a woman. Ya gotta see the heart to know what's it really like. Take Mrs. Wilson. She's not much to look at compared to some of those saloon girls I see walkin' around bringin' outlandish notions to me mind, but by damn, she's got a good heart and she's a good worker and she'd do any man proud. Only one other woman in these parts with as good a heart and that's Lottie Deno. Course, ya'd know that, Mister Holliday, 'cause every man in these parts has taken a fancy to her."

Holliday nodded, staring into his empty cup, remembering last night.

"A fine woman, that Lottie is. She don't put on no airs over everybody. And I hear she's as good a judge at pickin' winnin' horses as she is at winnin' cards," Wilson said, leaning forward and crossing his hands over his knee. "Like last night, I hear."

Holliday started to speak, but a pain shot through his lungs and he grabbed instinctively at his throat as if to choke the agonizing spasm. Then he coughed and the sharpness dulled.

Wilson continued. "Lottie splittin' up four aces and beatin' ya, but ya know 'bout that." His voice lowered to a whisper. "What 'bout the latest hanging, Mister Holliday?"

Holliday gazed up from the stew, his eyes watering with pain, his appetite dulled by the throbbing in his lungs. He shook his head and it seemed to rattle like trace chains on a runaway wagon.

Wilson nodded. "Vigilantes are putting a scare in the bad element that's botherin' this town."

The words settled on Holliday as poorly as the stew on his stomach. He shoved his bowl to the center of the table. "Weren't for the bad element, Uncle Billy, you'd be a damn sight poorer. I'll be damned if the better element would put up with this slop. Bet a hog wouldn't eat it." Holliday pitched the coffee cup after the bowl.

"Didn't mean no harm, Mister Holliday."

"You one of 'em, Uncle Billy?" Holliday said, pushing himself away from the table.

"Huh?"

"One of the vigilantes that's making the laws as they see fit? You make this town respectable, Uncle Billy, and you'll kill it as sure as you bleed a hog at butchering time." Holliday spit on the floor and walked out, Wilson's sputtering apologies trailing in his wake.

Chancey took quick puffs on his cigarette as he glanced through the open door of his office into the saloon. He walked around Holliday, who pounded his balled fist into his open palm.

"Dammit, Chancey," Holliday repeated, punctuating his words with a rap in his palm, "not Bailey, not here."

"I heard you the first time, Doc." Chancey slammed the door. "If you'd just won the Bee Hive, Doc."

Holliday felt his face pucker. "Would you have broken up four aces on the chance of ruining a straight flush? You'd have to be crazy!"

"Or maybe shrewd, Doc. You ever think she outsmarted you?"

"Luck, Chancey, Lottie's Luck."

"Ha!" Chancey took a final drag on his cigarette, then dropped it on the floor and crushed it with his boot. "You laughed at Lottie's Luck going into the game. Now you're blaming your losses on it. Seems you want it both ways."

Holliday clenched both fists, the rage throbbing in his temples. "And you can't have it both ways, Chancey. Me and Bailey here'll mean trouble."

"You're a good dealer, Doc, among the best." Chancey paused, pulling the makings of another cigarette, his eyes avoiding Holliday's. "But the fact is that Bailey has more friends in this town than you do. Some come in to play that wouldn't bet a dollar against anybody else. You may make me more profit, but Bailey adds the extra that nobody else gets."

"Chancey, he'll treat his friends better than you, dammit. Fact is, he enjoyed me losing the Bee Hive. He's too dumb to figure it might mean his job."

Chancey licked the tobacco-loaded cigarette paper and looked down at Holliday. He jammed his cigarette into his mouth and from his shirt pocket jerked a match, which he flicked into a flame with his thumbnail. He touched the cigarette until he breathed smoke, then shook the match to death. "There's no loyalty in the gambling business, just money."

"Then cut him lose or you'll lose money, Chancey."

"I did once, Doc. It cost me some business. I keep telling you, he's got too many friends, and Lottie's such a draw at the Bee Hive, I need the men Bailey'll bring in. Doc, you rile too many people for your own good and mine. People play you for spite. With Bailey, they play for fun. Fewer sore losers come out of Bailey's games."

"And less money for the Cattle Exchange. Hell, Chancey, you know he's too spineless to stand up for the house's share."

"The answer is no, Doc, I'm not getting rid of Bailey this time, and you're welcome to stay as long as you forget your differences with him. I'm not saying I like him either, but dammit, just forget about it."

"We're heading for trouble, Chancey." Holliday turned away.

The saloon owner exhaled a dejected cloud of smoke. "If only you'd won the Bee Hive. Damn Lottie's Luck, Doc."

Holliday grabbed the knob on the door and jerked it open.

"Hell, Doc, you're the better dealer," Chancey said. "Just that this town may not last many more years and I intend to suck all the money out of it I can. Maybe have something for my old age. If I chose my own company, I'd take you over him any day."

"You can have him tonight, Chancey, I won't be in to play my table." Holliday closed the door on Chancey and stepped into the saloon. For a moment he stood surveying the revelers until he spotted Kate in the playful grasp of a buffalo hunter. Holliday marched over, grabbed Kate's hand, and pulled her away.

The hunter jumped up, his lean, six-foot frame rising menacingly over Holliday. "I was playing with her."

"Find yourself another whore," Holliday told him.

Kate shook her hand free from his, her eyes flashing. "Don't call me a whore."

The buffalo hunter stepped toward Holliday. "Show some more manners, you goddam slick-eared gambler."

Holliday reached for his holster. Before the hunter could react, he jerked his gun and pointed it at the buffalo hunter's face. "Take another step, big man, and you can wipe your nose off the rear wall."

The hunter halted as Holliday backed away.

"Come on, Kate, I need a woman."

Kate crossed her arms over her chest. "Dammit, I need a customer."

"I'll pay," Holliday answered. "Now get to moving before your acquaintance here tries to pull something foolish and there's one less customer for you later."

Kate stormed past Holliday and out the swinging doors. Holliday eased back toward the exit. "No offense, big man," Holliday said, reaching with his free hand into his pocket. He pulled out a ten-dollar gold piece and flipped it at the hunter's muddied boots. "That'll buy you a woman and a round of drinks. Enjoy them both."

As Holliday stepped outside and reholstered his pistol, Kate greeted him. With a gun pointed at his head. "Now, Doc, if you don't want to wipe your nose off the street, you apologize for calling me a whore."

"I told him to buy a whore. I didn't call you one."

"Then don't insinuate," she said, sticking her pistol back under her blouse.

Holliday slipped his hand inside his pocket and extracted a twenty-dollar gold piece. "Professional deal, no blabbering about anything, especially marriage. Agreed?"

Kate started down the walk without taking the gold coin.

"Agreed, Kate?"

"I should of shot you."

"Agreed?"

"You could have saved your money, Doc, if you'd a just brought me flowers like you did Lottie. I wouldn't have dropped them on the saloon floor."

"It was a gambling ploy. Thought it might ruin her concentration."

"Hell, Doc, you're the one that can't think straight when the two of you are together." There was dejection in her voice.

"It was just a ploy."

"No, Doc, you've always had an eye out for her. You even bet to learn her name. You've never once asked about my name. You've never cared about mine, never asked. I've got a real name. I'd of told you, I'd of told you anything you wanted to know. And if she'd told you her name, what would you have done then? Asked her to marry you? I've heard talk, that you'd proposed to her. Damn you, sleep with me until you're limp and then propose to her. Doc, why don't you care about me? Sure, Lottie's pretty, but am I that bad to look at?"

Holliday left the question unanswered. He held up his hand again. "Here's twenty dollars. That's as much as you'd make honestly in one night. No more blabbering. Understand?"

"I'm glad she beat you, Doc, 'cause it's made you miserable. Means you and Ed Bailey are almost partners. You deserve each other. And Lottie, one day her own luck will sour as bad as week-old milk."

"Twenty dollars, Kate."

She held out her hand for the money.

215

NINETEEN

"Where the hell you going, fellow?"

Holliday backed away from the stable door, gauging the man standing there with a shotgun across his arm. Holliday eased his frock coat clear of his holstered revolver. "Lift that scatter gun an inch, you're a dead man," he said softly, his fingers drifting easily to the ivory grip on his Colt.

"Who is it?" Pete Haverty's familiar voice stammered from inside the stable.

"Don't know," answered the shotgun-wielding guard as Haverty limped from the shadowy depths of the stable.

"Afternoon, Pete," Holliday said. "Business so good you're chasing customers away?"

Haverty cleared his throat, cast a quick glance toward the back of the stable, then looked at Holliday. "It's okay."

"I never seen this fellow before," said the man tapping his fingers on the breech of the shotgun.

"He's a gambler. Doc Holliday's the name. He works at the Cattle Exchange."

"I don't frequent those dens of iniquity."

Haverty stepped between the two men. "Go on back inside," he said to the guard. "Mister Holliday, we've all been a bit edgy since we flushed someone out of the stable last night tampering with the pinto. Lot of money's been bet, and somebody was trying to better his chances in the race today. We're just jumpy."

"Your guard may jump to an early grave if he pulls down on me again," Holliday said.

Haverty nodded. "We're all nervous. My opponent came into town yesterday, all alone. Usually, there's more than one, if they're serious about horses, so this fellow may have had a partner slip into town. Crafty bunch these horse racers."

"Like gamblers?"

Haverty nodded, then grinned. "Now what is it you want?"

"Rent me your best buggy and animal. I may bring a guest to the race."

"I'll give you the rig Lottie always hires out. It's best."

Holliday stepped toward the door and the narrow shade the stable offered from the midafternoon sun, but Haverty raised his hand. "I'd feel better if you stayed out here, Mister Holliday. With the race just an hour away, too many people inside make the pinto nervous."

"Remind me never to give you a break in a card game if you're ever fool enough to visit my table." Holliday grinned.

"My foolishness is horses, not cards, Mister Holliday. I'll have your buggy fixed up."

"Do that. Just don't send your shotgun friend back out."

Haverty disappeared and Holliday paced in front of the stable. Toward Griffin Avenue he could see the Saturday crowd gathering, already jockeying for good positions along the race course from the Clear Fork to the edge of Government Hill. While some men cleared the streets of wagons and horses, others blocked off the main paths converging on Griffin Avenue. A pair of men were dumping a sack of flour across the street for a finish line. The street pulsed with the rapid movement of excited people. A horse race always drew a crowd. Even the pious bunch that shunned saloons wagered on horses. After all, it was quite different to bet on one of God's noblest creatures, the horse, instead of one of man's lowest inventions, the deck of cards.

Shortly, the stable door swung open and a hand led the buggy outside. "Haverty said you could have this rig for the day with his compliments."

Taking the reins, Holliday grunted, "Tell him I hope his ugly horse loses."

He climbed into the buggy, which shone black from a fresh dusting, then slapped the reins against the bay's flanks. After making a U-turn in front of the stable, he guided the rig around the outskirts of town and toward the creek and a lonely cabin beneath a giant cottonwood. As the buggy neared his destination, the rattling trace chains signaled his approach and for an instant Holliday thought he saw the flash of a face behind briefly parted curtains. Drawing to a halt outside the cabin, he shouted a woman's name. "Lottie Deno, I know you're in there."

The door opened slowly, Lottie coming behind it, her hair falling gently across the shoulders of her blue cambric dress, her arms folded across her breast, her lips lifting gently at the corners with amusement. "John Henry Holliday, I am surprised."

"Good day, ma'am, I have come to escort you to the event of the year in Griffin." Holliday tipped his hat, then jumped from the buggy. "Everyone in the Flat plans to see Pete Haverty's horse lose today, and I thought you should too."

"John Henry Holliday," Lottie shrugged, "you are worse than a schoolboy."

"My motives are not so innocent, ma'am. I need to beat you at something for my reputation."

Lottie walked out beside Holliday. "I'm not sure you'll help my reputation," she said, a smile in her eyes.

"Name your wager and your odds and you can have Haverty's pinto," Holliday offered. "I'll take whatever he's racing against, sight unseen."

"But can you be trusted?"

"No question about it, Lottie, I can be trusted."

"As long as you're betting on horses instead of cards, maybe you can be trusted, John Henry." She smiled again. "But we've played our last card game."

Holliday shrugged. "The Bee Hive should be Chancey's, Lottie. Nobody should break up four aces."

"And nobody should deal me a pat hand."

"Had to. I was keeping up with too many cards to risk going around on the draw. I wanted to beat you."

"And to learn my real name?"

"I lost, so I'll forget that. There's a horse race about to start in the Flat and I bet you're not as good a judge of horses as cards."

Lottie smiled, then frowned. "Thank you, John Henry, but I really shouldn't."

"I almost got killed renting this rig for you," Holliday complained.

"And both of us could get killed if Kate finds out." She stared at the buggy. "Looks like Haverty's rig to me."

"It is. They're mighty jumpy at the stable, carrying shotguns and not letting anyone in. They say someone tried to tamper with the pinto during the night."

"Odd, John Henry. Last night I could have sworn I heard someone prying around outside my place here. Must of been a drunk, but he was sure a quiet one, if it was."

Holliday extended his hand toward Lottie. "Come with me. No questions about anything but horses and gambling, promise."

She nodded. "But let me put my hair up and change."

Shaking his head, Holliday spoke. "Your hair looks fine, just as is. Your dress too. If we want a place near the finish line, then we better go."

"Okay, John Henry. Then we'll do as you say. I'll take the pinto and you the other horse. Just give me a moment." She retreated into her cabin and emerged shortly, tying the blue ribbon of a broad brimmed white hat under her chin. Holliday helped her into the buggy, then brushed against her as he climbed in and took the reins. The rig dashed away to the Flat.

The murmur of an excited crowd drifted out to them as they neared town and then parked the buggy behind the Cattle Exchange. Other latecomers scurried like busy ants for places along the dusty street and Holliday navigated Lottie through them, finally stopping under the shade of a pecan tree as a cheer rose from both sides of the street.

The spectators had seen Haverty's pinto stepping out into the middle of the street, Haverty beside it, a smaller man astride the bareback paint. The animal skittered at the crowd noise until Haverty patted its neck. The jockey rode Indian-style, without a saddle's extra weight, his legs hooked in a rawhide loop around the horse's middle. Jutting his chin forward, a scowl upon his face, the rider slapped the pinto's flank and the animal danced away from Haverty. The crowd cheered again and the horse seemed to understand, lifting its legs higher and tossing its head forward and then up. When the jockey nudged the animal with his heels, the pinto lurched ahead in a lope, seeming almost to stumble before quickly regaining its balance. As the horse ran by, the spectators cheered or booed by betting preference. Holliday studied the ugly animal, then turned to Lottie beside him. "I'm glad my money's on another mount."

Lottie moved forward for a better glimpse of the pinto. "Doesn't look like a speed horse, but Haverty keeps him well fed and exercises him considerably."

A clamor came from down the street and Holliday turned to the noise. A chestnut horse pranced forward, as confident as the rider on his back, a monkey of a man in a gaudy red silk shirt, a riding cap, and baggy white britches. As the rider came nearer, Holliday could see him sitting astride an English riding saddle. "I like the looks of my horse better," Holliday pointed out, "but I can't say I favor the dude that's riding him." Holliday watched the animal, waiting for an answer from Lottie, but none came. Even her breath seemed lost. He looked at her, taking in a paleness he had not noticed before, a wideness in her eyes that seemed as frightened and confused as they appeared transfixed by the rider coming slowly down the street on the chestnut.

"I don't like that rider's looks," Holliday said, still without receiving an answer.

As the horse drew opposite them, Lottie spoke. "You say someone tried to tamper with the pinto last night, John Henry?"

"That's what I hear."

Lottie shook her head. "It figures."

"What figures?"

"No matter, John Henry."

Holliday stared at the horse and rider as they passed. Blond tufts of hair tumbled from under his cap over the dark complexion of his face, his eyes shifting from side to side as he alternately loped and walked the animal toward the finish line. A pointed nose gave his face the look of a predator, and he sat in the saddle like a hawk in the tree ready to swoop down upon innocent prey. Even so, his face was cut from a handsome cloth that must appeal to women. By the fancy clothes he would be taken for a dandy, but a hardness in his eyes seemed brittle with experience and in the set of his shoulders was an unconquered cockiness. Though not imposing physically, Holliday figured he carried enough hidden weapons to make up the difference with a bigger opponent.

"Wish I could trade riders with you, Lottie," he said, glancing to his side, but Lottie had slipped behind him, her head dropping behind the shield of her hat. Holliday lifted her chin with his finger and stared into her gray eyes, seeing something he had never before seen there — fear. "You're getting awfully worried over a race, Lottie. What are we betting? Fifty dollars?" He put his arm around her narrow waist and pulled her beside him. He could feel her body stiffening with tension.

Holliday watched her, noting her eyes glazed with the morbid fascination of a woman watching a snake, her face still ashen, her breath now irregular and heavy. Holliday held her waist gently, not understanding why he felt he must not let go. The rider passed, reached the finish line and turned around, loping down the side of the street where Holliday stood. As he passed again, the rider stared into the spectators under the pecan tree and Holliday felt Lottie draw closer into him, like a chick under its mother's wing. The rider stopped and twisted in his saddle, looking toward Holliday, then circling his horse back around in Holliday's direction.

The frisky animal pranced at them until the rider jerked hard on the reins, stopping an arm's length away. The rider lifted his hat with a hand that carried a quirt, then ran the fingers of his other hand through his curly blond locks. He nodded toward Holliday. "Good day, sir," he said as he stared at Lottie. "Not a woman's hat I passed the last eight years without looking under it for you, Lottie. It's been a long time."

"Not long enough, Johnny." Her words were iced with regret.

"Your hair is as long and pretty as I remember, though you still cover it too often with your hats. Did you get my letter?"

"I did."

Holliday felt the discomfort in her terse words.

"You did," Johnny replaced his cap. "Surprised you're still around, then, but I would have eventually found you anyway."

Holliday released Lottie and stepped between her and the rider, the horse moving forward from the flinch of the rider's

221

heel. "I'm escorting Lottie," Holliday challenged, "and I'm not certain she wants your company."

"May not matter what she wants." The rider laughed.

Holliday threw back the frock coat and hooked it over his pistol. "Nothing funny to my way of thinking, mister."

"Johnny Golden's the name, Lottie could tell you that." He glared at Lottie. "A lot of things she could tell people, about her past. It would surprise them, wouldn't it, Lottie? There was a time when she wanted my company, right Lottie?"

Lottie's voice came with renewed strength. "Like you said, Johnny, that was a long time ago."

"Not that long, Lottie."

Holliday lifted his arm with a snakelike motion and slapped the chestnut on the nose. The horse reared and Johnny grappled for a saddle hold. "You bastard," Johnny shouted as he rode out two bucks of the horse, then struck savagely at its neck with the quirt, drawing a bead of blood. The horse settled down, backing away from Holliday. Golden pulled his hat down low over his brow. "Damn you, mister," Golden called to Holliday.

"Step off that horse, you son of a bitch," Holliday dared him, "and you'll have so many bullet holes you'll whistle when the wind blows."

"Mister, I don't know your name but —"

"John Henry Holliday. Some folks call me Doc. You want to look me up after this is over, I'll be waiting."

"It's Lottie I want to look up after this race." The rider jerked the reins of the horse and turned him toward the starting line at the creek. "I got no problem with you, Doc. But don't come between me and Lottie again. I won't stand for it." The rider hit the horse's flank with a quirt and the chestnut galloped down the street to the spectators' cheers.

Holliday turned to Lottie. "Who's your friend, Lottie?"

"Just a man I knew once," she answered.

"Wish I had bet on another man," Holliday offered.

Lottie nodded. "I wish I had too," she said quietly.

Holliday strained to hear her over the spectators cheering as the pinto raced by. All around them people made bets with one another and the crowd thickened under the pecan tree. The local favorite pinto pleased the crowd, but the lines of the chestnut

222

looked stronger, faster. Those who cherished their wallets more than their local chauvinism backed the chestnut and Johnny Golden. The others favored the pinto. The crowd lining the street fanned out from the walks to watch the horses line up at the creek for the starter. Holliday craned at the starter who held a gun in the air. A white puff of smoke followed by the muffled retort of the pistol sent the horses lurching forward and the crowd retreating to the walk.

The pinto stumbled and the chestnut shot ahead. For the split second it took the bareback rider to control the pinto, the chestnut had leaped ahead two lengths. Golden flailed at the chestnut with the quirt and the horses nostrils flared and its eyes widened with fear. The animals lunged wildly forward, the chestnut's big strides slinging dust and clods at the pinto. The smaller animal churned at the street like a dust devil darting across the distance. At the midpoint along the street, the pinto had pulled within a length of the leader and Johnny Golden, glancing over his shoulder at the gaining rider, beat his mount's flank savagely.

All around, the people yelled in a frenzy. The pinto was gaining, though the chestnut still commanded the race. Reaching the three-quarter mark on the course, the pinto made up another stride on the chestnut and was only a neck behind as they neared Holliday.

"Come on, you damn pinto," Holliday shouted, "beat that son of a bitch."

His eyes as wild as his mount's, Golden looked to his side, where the pinto came within reach. Golden struck the chestnut with the quirt and, as the pinto drew even, lashed out at the other rider. The bareback rider ducked and the whip's sting drained painlessly into the air. The pinto stuck its nose even with the chestnut, its stride faltering as Golden reached out to swing again at the pinto's rider.

"Did you see that?" Holliday shouted at Lottie. "Your friend's a mean one." Holliday moved out into the street as the animals shot by, only twenty yards from the finish line. Other spectators surged around him like waves around a shore rock. At the finish line, the two crossed together, the rider on the pinto drawing his animal to a walk at the same pace as Golden. When the animals halted, the pinto rider leaped from his horse to the chestnut, knocking Golden to the ground, then falling atop him. The two started rolling in the dirt, tossing punches at one another as Sheriff Vernon Trickus raced toward them. If there was anything better than a good horse race, it was a fight, and the crowd pressed forward around the combatants.

"Your friend deserves a beating, Lottie," Holliday said, turning around. She was gone. He looked about, then pushed his way through the throng back to the pecan tree. The crowd was thick, but not so heavy that she couldn't have stayed up with him had she wanted. Damn her, Holliday thought.

While he looked, the crowd gathered impatiently for Sheriff Trickus to break up the fight so a winner could be announced. Finally, Uncle Billy Wilson mounted the water wagon and held his hands out for quiet. Gradually, the murmuring dwindled until Wilson's voice could be heard.

"Folks," he called, "we had quite a race here today."

The crowd mumbled agreement.

"Best us on the finish line could see, it was a dead heat."

The crowd groaned.

"But a winner has been declared. Pete Haverty's pinto will remain undefeated because of the other rider's poor judgment in lashing out at our rider."

The crowd responded with a mixture of shouts and boos. Wilson held up his hands for a brief moment and signaled for silence. "A rematch has been set up for next Sunday. Give all of ya a chance to look the horses over and decide if ya want to change your bets." Wilson, now that he had the crowd's attention, kept on talking, but Holliday weaved his way through the people and jogged back to the wagon behind the Cattle Exchange, the exertion straining against his lungs until every breath was ringed in pain.

Lottie wasn't at the buggy. Holliday climbed in and slapped the reins against the animal. Making a big swath behind the saloon, the buggy turned toward the street, still crowded with spectators. It would take too long to get through there, so Holliday circled the wagon around again and headed out behind the buildings lining Griffin Avenue and turned toward the creek and Lottie's cabin. As he passed behind the buildings and a great stack of buffalo hides, he saw Lottie in the distance, holding her skirt up and running toward her cabin. When she spotted Holliday, she lifted her skirt higher and raced the final fifty yards to her cabin door. Her white hat blew off, but she left it and slammed the door behind her.

Holliday reached the cabin too late. "Lottie, what's wrong?"

"Just go away, John Henry. I don't feel well," she gasped with winded breath.

"I owe you fifty dollars. The horses finished a dead heat, but my rider was disqualified. I'm here to pay up."

Lottie did not answer again. After five minutes of waiting, Holliday turned the buggy around and started back to town, leaving her white hat where it had fallen on the grass.

TWENTY

Across the room Ed Bailey was a jigger shy of drunk. Holliday shrugged.

It was Chancey's money Bailey was squandering — and doing it loudly. Bailey blubbered for another bottle, then giggled from the effects of its predecessors. Circled at his table like a pack of hungry wolves around a wounded buffalo, his card players feasted on a dwindling stack of money, Cattle Exchange money.

Holliday played solitaire at his faro table, his customers long drained away by the easier takings at Bailey's table. In the yellow light diffused by smoke, Holliday pulled his watch from a vest pocket and opened the cover. "One-forty," he said to himself, returning the watch to his pocket, then gathering his cards for another round of solitaire.

When a bartender suggested Bailey had had too much to drink, glass shattered at Bailey's table. Holliday leaped to his feet, his Colt cocked and ready to fire. He watched Bailey wave a broken bottle at the bartender.

"Dammit," Bailey yelled, wobbling up from his chair, "bring me another bottle, quick."

Chancey's office door flew open and the saloon owner emerged, accompanied by his shotgun trained at Bailey.

226

"No trouble, boss," Bailey stammered, "just dropped my bottle." He placed the jagged bottle neck on the table.

"Busted it, is more like it," Holliday said.

Bailey leaned forward over the table, propping his teetering frame with his hands. His eyes blinked at Holliday. One hand lifted from the table toward his sidearm, then fell away as Bailey's eyes focused on Holliday's malevolent gun pointed at his gut. Bailey aimed his index finger at Holliday. "You stay out of this, Holliday. The damn bottle slipped out of my hand." Bailey swept his arm grandly over the table. "This is my table and you've no right interfering with my dealing."

"You're so drunk you're costing the Cattle Exchange money I have to make up. What about it, Chancey?"

"Put your gun up, Doc. Damn if I want my dealers killing each other, sorry lot though they may be."

"You're gonna push me too far, Holliday," Bailey shouted. "I'll remember your interference."

"Shut up, Bailey, and put that goddam gun up, Holliday," Chancey said, twisting the shotgun in Doc's direction.

Holliday eased his Colt back into its holster.

"Where's my whiskey?" Bailey shouted. "Damn if I don't need a drink to get my mind back on the cards. That bastard better not fool with me . . ."

Holliday's hand dropped back to his gun.

"Don't do it, Doc," Chancey called. "Come in my office."

Holliday marched across the room, his eyes locked on Bailey, who still insisted on a fresh bottle.

"Get in there and sit down, Doc," Chancey said at the door.

"I told you, he'd bring you nothing but trouble. That's all it's been. My winnings can't cover his losses forever."

"Doc, shut up for a minute and let me think this one out. Damn if this isn't a powder keg you two jackasses are intent on blowing up." Chancey stepped inside, closing the door.

Holliday faced Chancey. "Put the goddam shotgun away." When Chancey obliged, Holliday resumed. "It's either me or him."

Chancey scratched his chin, then fidgeted for the cigarette fixings in his tobacco tin. Quickly he put one together, flared a match, and sucked the flame down into the cigarette. He exhaled a heavy breath. "There'll be less trouble if I get rid of you."

"Then do it, dammit."

Chancey paced across the room, finally stopping in front of his strongbox. "But if I don't cut him loose, I may not need this." He kicked the strongbox.

"You should've never hired him back, Chancey."

A knock came at the door.

"Go away," Chancey ordered.

One of the bartenders replied. "Someone here to see you."

"Tell him I'll see him later."

"You'll want to see this lady."

Chancey grunted and strode to the door, his massive frame blocking Doc's view outside as he swung the door open. Chancey drew deep on his cigarette. "President Grant himself couldn't have surprised me more," he said, then backed away.

Into the room walked Lottie Deno.

"Lottie!" Doc could not hide the shock in his voice.

"John Henry, I . . ." she started, then paused.

Holliday moved to her and in the flickering lamplight saw her gray eyes glistening with tears. Her hair was mussed and her dress seemed oddly wrinkled and ill-fitting. Holliday sensed her discomfort before Chancey. She rubbed her hands together, staring more through than at the saloon owner.

"I've come to ask a favor of you, Chancey."

Chancey crossed his arms. "I thought you were too much of a lady to be asking me any favors, Lottie."

Lottie stared blankly through Chancey. "Me too. But things change. I . . . I . . ." the words seemed trapped in her, "I want to deal for you. I'm through at the Bee Hive."

Chancey laughed. "Your luck go bad, or did Fogle proposition you?"

"Go easy on her, Chancey," Doc said, stepping between them. "This have anything to do with that fellow, Johnny Golden?"

Lottie nodded. "He started bothering me at work. My luck went down. He was spending enough money that Fogle wouldn't throw him out."

"And now," Chancey gloated, "you're in trouble and want protection in the Cattle Exchange?"

Lottie's nostrils flared and she shoved past Holliday.

228

"You've insulted me before." She drew her hand and slapped him. "You know I can draw business without whoring. Like you would say, it's a business deal. Nothing more."

Chancey rubbed his cheek. "If a whore'd slapped me, I'd throw her ass out."

"I'm no whore, Chancey, and you're no gentleman. We both know that from past experience, don't we?"

Holliday reached for Lottie's hand. "Chancey, either say she can stay or tell her to go looking for another place, but give her an answer, dammit."

Chancey spit his cigarette to the floor. "Maybe you can solve a problem of mine, Lottie." He rubbed his chin. "I've not been too satisfied with the help I've had around here. I don't have a vacancy," he said, "but I'll make one for you."

"My cut of the winnings?"

"Same as your friend Holliday." Chancey said.

"That's acceptable. When do I start?"

"Sundown tonight, Lottie. It'll give me time to spread word around town where you're working now."

Lottie shook her head. "No . . . please . . . he'll just find me sooner."

"Lottie," Chancey shot back, "I'm hiring you and I'll be damned if I'm gonna keep it secret. I want the business you'll draw, or you can go back to the Bee Hive."

"But —" Lottie started.

Holliday interrupted. "If it's Johnny Golden that's got you buffaloed, we'll watch out for you, Lottie." Holliday stared at Chancey. "At least I'll look out for you."

"You won't be harmed in my saloon, Lottie," Chancey reassured her. "Of course, Doc is gonna have to watch out for himself."

"I always do."

"You'll have more cause to now, Doc," Chancey checked the load in his shotgun. "Lottie, tonight you can have Ed Bailey's table."

Holliday's thin lips twisted into a hollow smile beneath his malevolent mustache. He tipped his derby to Lottie. "You just helped rid this saloon of a skunk."

Chancey started for the door. "Doc, you best be on guard

from now on. Bailey's gonna blame you." Chancey stepped into the gambling area.

"Bailey," he called, "you've had enough to drink tonight and enough to lose. End your game, I'm cutting you loose." When Bailey didn't seem to understand, Chancey repeated his decision.

Then it soaked in and Bailey exploded from his chair toward Chancey. He stopped cold when he realized the shotgun was pointed at his gut. "Damn, it's Holliday, isn't it?" Bailey screamed. "I'll get you for this, you son of a bitch!"

Holliday grabbed for his gun, but Lottie caught his hand, then shoved the door shut.

"I'll get you, you son of a bitch, I'll get you!" he heard Bailey shouting at the door.

Business was slow for Holliday, but across the room a table was buzzing with activity. Word of Lottie's new roost had spread through the Flat and men had come out in numbers to play at her table. Around midnight Holliday pulled his last card from the dealing box and quit his table. As he counted his earnings, Kate strode up and sat down opposite him. Holliday glanced at her, noticing her misbuttoned blouse and the whiskey bottle she carried.

"Well, Doc, you happy now that you can keep Lottie under your eye? Seems she cost you more business tonight than you would have allowed from Ed Bailey." Kate guzzled the liquor.

"She's brought you enough business that you can't button your blouse straight, Kate."

The whore looked down at her blouse, undid the top three buttons, and spread the blouse far enough apart for Holliday to see the pale white flesh converging at her breasts. "Seven men've had their hands inside here tonight, Doc. I've made close to twenty-five dollars honest, and half that again picking their pockets."

"Then you've no reason to trouble Lottie tonight, Kate." He studied her a moment. "What I see in you, I'll never know."

"A free screw," she said matter-of-factly.

Holliday scraped the remaining change from the table and

into his hand. "Free? That's a laugh. Cost me my peace and quiet. At least when I buy a whore, when I'm done, I'm done."

Kate's lips pouted. "All this sweet talk's making me horny, Doc. Lottie ever get horny? Or does she let you close enough to find out?"

Picking up his cards and dealing box, Holliday stood. "She doesn't talk about that, Kate," he scowled. "She's a lady."

"Maybe she's a lady," Kate shot back, "but is she a woman?"

Without answering, Holliday turned away toward the bar, depositing his cards and dealing box and casekeeper behind it, then carrying his money into Chancey's office.

Chancey was hunched over his desk counting the evening's early winnings. He glanced over his shoulder at Holliday, then turned back to the money stacked before him.

"Here's my take for the night, Chancey," Holliday said, laying the money near him. "Not much. Lottie's getting all the business."

Chancey huffed. "You wanted me to shuck Bailey and I did, so don't be bellyaching about your bad luck. Hell, Lottie's on a streak now. Few of her customers are winning anything, and even the big losers aren't complaining so much. How's she do it?"

"She cheats, Chancey."

Chancey held up a fistful of paper and coins. "She does it well. You ought to watch her and learn something."

"Chancey, you have a way of getting on people's nerves."

"And a way of making money, Doc. Yes, sir, I do my best."

Holliday left Chancey to his money, returning to the bar for a bottle of Monarch. Then he slipped behind Lottie. He watched her lithe movements and her grace over the cards; she played quickly, bantering lightly with the men. Holliday moved into her view and her smile widened to acknowledge him. For half an hour Holliday stood equally transfixed between her beauty and her gambling skills. He nursed on his bottle and was about to leave when a man in a green bowler elbowed his way among Lottie's customers to the edge of the table. Johnny Golden, the sneer of a hungry wolf across his face, had arrived. He carried a cane with a golden deerhead and he slapped it into the table. Lottie jumped with a start, looked at Johnny Golden, and seemed to lose her concentration.

"I'm placing a hundred dollars on the knave, the man that never gets the lady, Miss Deno." Johnny sneered. "It is Miss Deno, is it not, Lottie?" He pulled coins from his pocket and stacked five gold double eagles atop one another. With his cane, he pushed the pile over the jack.

"House limit is fifty dollars, Johnny." Her eyes avoided his. "I play by the rules here."

Johnny laughed like a coyote, then slammed his cane into the table, scattering his money along with the bets of others. Holliday pushed among the grousing customers to the table.

"Leave the lady alone," Holliday commanded.

Golden twisted his head slowly, his teeth barred in a snarl of contempt, toward Holliday. "Well, lookahere, if it isn't Miss Deno's escort to the races." Golden's words, like his eyes, were contemptuous. "Or should I say her husband? She always has been fond of gamblers and their easy money."

As Holliday unbuttoned his frock coat, Golden laid his cane across the playing board on the table and dropped his hands to his own waist. Warily, he opened the front of his coat to expose his hips. "I'm unarmed, mister."

Lottie shot up from her seat. "Don't believe him, John Henry," she said calmly, "he carries a derringer in his pocket and a bigger gun under his arm."

"Make a move either place and it'll be your last, fellow," Holliday said, putting his bottle on the table. Lottie's patrons backed away as a hush filled the room. Holliday watched Golden's hawkish eyes and was about to make his play when he heard Chancey.

"Damn!" Chancey exploded. "Now Holliday's causing me trouble." He barged up to the table near Golden. "What's the problem, Lottie?"

She pointed to Golden. "This man interrupted my game."

The accused laughed. "Pretending you don't know my name, Lottie? Such a shameful woman."

"Shut up," Holliday ordered.

Golden stared back. "You keep butting in where you have no business, mister. I don't take kindly to meddling."

Chancey grabbed Golden's arm. "Now, mister, you must understand this is my saloon and Lottie and Doc are my dealers. I

232

don't want any trouble, so why don't you just slip out the door and we'll all forget this ever happened."

Golden spit on Lottie's table. "Some things a person just can't forget. That's true, isn't it, Lottie?"

Pale and her lips quivering, Lottie nodded. "It's true, Johnny, no matter how hard I've tried."

"Now, mister," Chancey said, "before I send for the sheriff, perhaps you should just go on." With his free hand, Chancey picked up the cane from the table, admiring the golden stag. "This belong to you?"

Golden nodded.

"Good-looking stick, yessir," Chancey said, holding the cane in the middle and staring at the heavy knob. As Golden started to speak, Chancey drew his hand back and slammed the heavy end of the cane against the side of Golden's head. The powerful blow resounded with a sickening thud.

For an instant, Golden's eyes stared blankly ahead, then his eyelids collapsed over them and he tumbled down onto the table, atop his spittle and his unwanted wager.

"Get him out of here," Chancey ordered a bartender.

Holliday stepped beside Lottie. "You okay?"

She nodded.

As two men pulled Golden from the table, Holliday reached for the five double eagles Golden had wagered on the jack. "He won't be needing these, will he?"

Chancey stared at Lottie. "You up to continuing?"

She nodded again.

Throwing out his chest, Chancey took a step toward her. "See how much better we take care of you than Fogle ever did? Who is this guy?"

"He's Johnny Golden," Holliday answered, "the one that tried to horsewhip Haverty's rider in the race on Sunday."

Chancey whistled. "You know this fellow?"

"A long time ago," Lottie whispered, turning away from Chancey to her customers. "Okay, gentlemen, straighten your bets and let's see if we can pick up where we left off."

Holliday eased away from the table and felt a hard tap on his shoulder. Turning around, he saw Kate, fire in her eyes, a bottle in her hand and too much liquor in her belly.

233

"You'd never stand up for me like that. Just go to hell, Doc Holliday." She turned around and marched for the door.

Holliday jerked his gun from its holster. "You goddam whore," he called after her. He took aim and squeezed the trigger. The gun exploded, carrying in its wake the sound of tinkling glass and a thud. Kate screamed. Holliday had hit his target. All Kate now held was the neck of a bottomless liquor bottle. She ran from the saloon into the night.

"Damn you, Doc," Chancey called. "No need for that."

Holliday reholstered his pistol.

Chancey shook his head and walked away. "You're gonna cause me more trouble than I want to handle."

Holliday settled in at the bar with his bottle and watched Lottie finish a run through the deck. She lost heavily. Her luck had changed, and Holliday wondered if perhaps his had too.

TWENTY-ONE

"You gonna take me or not, Doc Holliday?"

He rolled away from Kate and pulled the bedsheet over his head, even though the room was oven hot.

Kate jerked the cover from him. "Dammit it, Doc, are you gonna take me?"

Holliday growled. "I'm not interested in seeing a damn puppet show."

She slapped his bare back, then turned over and reached for the floor. Retrieving a spread-eagled copy of the *Frontier Echo,* she said, "Let me read this to you again, Doc."

"The answer's no, no matter how many times you read it."

Sighing, Kate rolled up the newspaper and popped his naked buttocks. "It's not like I'm asking you to take me to church." She unrolled the paper. "Now listen to this, 'Thursday and Friday Nights, June 4–5. Great Carnival of Fun! Grand Opening of the Fashionable Drawing Room Soirees of Signor Silvano, Aided by the Wonderful Royal Marionettes (17 in Number) from the Theater Royal and Princess Theatre, London.' "

"Wonderful," Holliday said.

"But there's more," Kate continued. " 'Best Combination Traveling, A Large Stage will be erected handsomely fitted with appropriate scenery, curtains, carpets and the room will be brilliantly lit by 30 patent safety illuminators.' Now doesn't that sound exciting?"

Holliday grunted. "Like a good horse race."

Kate threw the paper at Doc. "Damn you for taking Lottie to a horse race. You can't forget her." Kate sat up, bending her knees and resting her chin on them. "It'd cost you a dollar for the both of us to see the marionettes. It cost you more than that to rent the buggy for Lottie."

Doc coughed, sitting up at the pain streaking through his lungs. The words sputtered from his mouth. "I should of shot you instead of your bottle last night." He dropped his legs off the bed and grappled with his pants. "It's too damn hot to stay in here. And way too noisy for a man to get any shuteye."

"Fifty cents, that's all I'm asking you to spend on me, Doc. If Lottie asked you to take her, you'd go."

"She didn't ask."

"And she won't," Kate said. Triumphantly, she lifted her chin from her knees and folded her arms across her bare breasts. "I hear Jack Jacobs is taking her. So, any notion you had about asking her isn't worth a damn."

Holliday wrestled his shirt on and then struck the bedpost for his sidearm. "I'll be gone thirty minutes, Kate. When I come back, you be gone."

"No, sir. You've been talking so damn high and mighty, so just shoot me like you want to . . ."

"Don't be an ass, Kate."

". . . and then you can dump me anywhere you want to."

"It was just talk, Kate."

"Mean talk over fifty cents of your money and a couple hours of your time. By damn, I've given you more than that."

Holliday coughed. "Okay, Kate, you win. I'll take you to watch the marionettes. Just leave me alone for some peace and quiet."

Kate leaped up from the bed, dancing around the floor. "I knew you'd do it, Doc. You won't admit it, but you care for me." She waltzed to him. Wrapping her arms around him, she pulled him into her naked body and pressed her lips against his and against the cough that fought to escape his mouth.

Holliday convulsed for breath, broke her grasp, and backed

toward the door, grabbing his boots. "You just be gone when I return, Kate."

"Like I said, Doc, you really care for me."

Holliday escaped out the door.

Kate nodded to herself. "One day, Doc Holliday, we'll be man and wife." She gathered her clothes and dressed quickly and was gone before Holliday returned.

The line stretched from the locked doors of the Southern Hotel east along the street almost to the Cattle Exchange. Holliday shook his head as he emerged from the saloon, Kate's arm interlocked in his.

"Knew there were a lot of fools in the Flat, Kate, but not this many." Holliday motioned toward the end of the line with his free hand. "No way people at the end of that line can be packed into the Southern. A lot of fools."

Kate smiled coyly and brushed an imaginary speck from the waist of her new yellow dress. "And one weasel, Doc Holliday."

"What?"

"I knew you'd try to weasel your way out of this. You waited until the line got too long before coming over here. Ain't it a fact, Doc?"

Holliday felt his face flush. "Damn if that isn't a good idea. Wish I'd thought of it." Holliday stopped at the end of the line. "I'll wait with you, but the Southern can't handle this many folks in one sitting."

For a moment, Kate stood motionless except for full red lips which quivered into a smile. Then she tugged at his arm. "Come with me, Doc."

Along the heat-warped planks, Kate pulled Holliday.

"I knew you'd come to your senses, Kate, when you saw the line like it was."

Better than halfway to the hotel door, they passed Lottie, standing in the heat with Jack Jacobs. Like Kate, she wore yellow, but it seemed more becoming on Lottie. Doc tipped his hat as he marched by. Looking over his shoulder, he saw Lottie smile, but he felt Kate's pace quicken and her fingernails dig into his arm.

Pulling up within a dozen people of the door, Kate turned to Doc. "We'll wait in line here," she said, pointing to two youths. Behind the boys, several people grumbled.

Doc took off his derby, then addressed Kate. "I'm not about to step ahead of these fine folks in line."

Laughing, Kate pulled her arm from Holliday's and stepped up to the two youths. "Thank you, boys," she said. "I told you this skunk would try to renege on me."

The two youths sniggered, then swaggered from the line. "The pleasure was all ours," the taller one said.

Kate tugged Doc into line. "The pleasure will be yours tomorrow," she told them.

The boys laughed, bringing a gasp behind Kate from a drab-faced woman in a drab but proper dress, and strolled away down the walk, one looking back over his shoulder at Kate and winking. Kate leaned toward Doc and rested her head on his shoulder as he replaced his derby. "Don't take it wrong, Doc, I just wanted us to get good chairs, near the front."

Holliday coughed and broke away from Kate's grip long enough to extract a flask from his coat. Fumbling with the cap, he coughed again. "Did you promise those boys time in the sack?"

She nodded, drawing another gasp from the respectable woman behind her. "At no charge."

Holliday touched the flask to his lips and eased his head back. The warm liquid dulled the fire in his chest. He wished he had brought more to assuage the embarrassment of standing in line to see a damn marionette show. The afternoon heat heightened his discomfort and he shifted his weight from foot to foot, his obvious boredom displeasing Kate.

She jerked at his arm. "You're jumpier than a kid in church, Doc. You promised you'd come. Don't make me feel like you're under sentence to be hanged."

Holliday turned to Kate, the flask at his lips. He swallowed hard, then capped the bottle and hid it in his coat pocket. "I promised I'd come. As best I recall, we didn't agree that I had to enjoy it."

For a moment, she stared blankly at Holliday as a gauze of betrayal covered her face. Clasping her hands around the sash of her dress, she turned to the street to watch the passing parade of people and horses. Holliday leaned his back against the wall of the Southern Hotel and waited, tapping his boot against the plank walk to annoy Kate.

At length the door to the hotel opened and Holliday stepped away from the wall, motioning for Kate to step ahead of him. Grabbing her skirt and lifting it enough to expose the white of her calf, she marched sullenly ahead, never looking his way. Holliday lingered a moment, spawning impatient murmurs from those behind him in line. Kate waited at the door long enough for Holliday to catch up and pay the overweight puppeteer with rouged cheeks, spotless white shirt, and broad red suspenders. "The show will begin in thirty minutes," he told Holliday. Lingering a moment, Holliday lost Kate among the people scurrying ahead of him toward the front seats. More than a hundred and fifty chairs were crammed into the room around a narrow aisle leading up to a brightly lit miniature stage. People pushed past Holliday as he searched for Kate. Finally, he spotted her in the third row, second seat from the aisle. Approaching the empty chair beside her, he pointed to the seat. "For me?"

"Who gives a damn, Doc Holliday? Either sit down and shut up or go on back to your table. You don't care about me," she said, her voice rising in anger. "Shit, if all you want out of me is free screws."

Grimacing at her indelicate public words, Holliday sank to his seat, placing his hand on Kate's leg. "You're taking this all wrong."

Kate shoved his hand from her knee and twisted her legs as far away from Holliday as she could. "Don't touch me," she said, her words carrying the chill from her lips. "Get out of here, if you can't consider my feelings. You're as selfish a man as I've ever known. I regret the day I met you, Doc Holliday."

Holliday fumbled for the flask in his coat pocket, almost dropping it on the floor. His knuckles turned white as he twisted the stopper loose. Before this night was over, he thought, he'd need a case of bourbon. The flask at his lips, he drained all the amber liquid it offered. Though the bourbon's wetness helped douse the growing anger within him, it could do nothing to abate the sweltering heat building in the crowded room. Holliday looked at the open windows, but the the breeze was too little to go around. While all about women fanned at the blush of their faces, Kate sat motionless, sweat running like tears down her face. Another sip at the flask drew air only, so he stoppered the flask, shoved it in his coat, and removed his derby, placing it in his lap, over his genitals. He pulled his watch from his vest, popping the cover and squirming at the twenty-five minutes remaining until showtime. He glanced at Kate just as she looked at him. Her eyes glistened.

"You can go on, Doc." She spoke softly, the anger dissipating as occasional tears mixed with the sweat birthing on her face. "I've read too many books, wanted something I could never have. I just wanted to love you and be loved a little. But you're no good. You don't love yourself so you make it impossible for anyone else to love you. I want you, you want Lottie, and she — who could have any man in this town — wants none. Just go on, Doc, don't stay for me."

She buried her head in her hands and cried softly, vulnerably while around her women fanned themselves, men discussed politics, and the children fidgeted for the show to start. Holliday draped his arm on her chairback and dropped his hand to her back, patting her gently. She flinched at his touch, then flung her head up and turned to Holliday. "Don't get yourself horny, Doc, unless you want to pay for it this time."

Holliday's arm retreated. "You're as unpredictable as a skunk with hydrophobia, Kate. Damn if you can't perplex a man more than a deck with fifty-three cards."

A wave of laughter washed through the audience as a puppet stuck its head out from the maroon curtains of a miniature stage and called, "Just minutes from showtime," then darted back inside. The children giggled or stood on their chairs for a better glimpse of what they missed. A girl behind Holliday lost her balance and fell into Holliday's back. "Tell the man you're sorry," her dour mother ordered. The girl stepped around beside Holliday and offered her shy apology, holding her skirt with her hands. Holliday scowled at her and she jumped back for her chair. "He's a mean man," she told her mother and was rewarded with a slap to the cheek.

"Don't talk about strangers that way," her mother scolded. The girl cried.

Kate twisted around in her seat. "That's okay, darling, you're right about this man."

Shocked by Kate's comment, the girl's mother gasped, then caught her breath. "You don't talk to my daughter, you — you hussy."

"Momma, what's a hussy?" the girl asked between her tears.

Holliday would have laughed, except for a commotion at the back of the room.

"Dammit, let me in. I'm not staying. Now where is she?"

Holliday recognized the voice and slapped his hat to his head, turning around in his seat to see Johnny Golden shove the moneytaker into the back row of chairs. Women screamed and gathered their children together like hens brooding over their chicks.

"Lottie, where are you?" Golden called.

Holliday felt Kate's hand grab his as he stood and glanced quickly around the crowd for the yellow dress that would be Lottie. He missed her until Jack Jacobs rose from a seat. Kate's hand squeezed tighter against his as Holliday slid into the aisle.

"Someone's with her. It's not your worry, Doc. Please stay with me." Her voice seemed to break.

Shaking free from the grasp that could never hold him, Holliday unbuttoned his coat and moved toward Johnny Golden.

Lottie stood up beside Jack Jacobs, looking from Golden to Holliday, her eyes rimmed with fear. "Please, Jack, stop them or they'll fight. They both have tempers."

"So there you are," yelled Golden, his speech slurred from too little thought and too much whiskey. "It's time you came with me. Have you told folks in these parts about me? About us?" He staggered for a moment, stopped to regain his equilibrium, and then stepped from row to row, holding onto the back of chairs for support.

Jacobs moved toward the aisle, tripping over feet and legs. "Hurry, Jack," Lottie called after him.

"Golden," Holliday shouted, "stop where you are."

The slight man halted and looked around until his eyes met Holliday's. "It's you again, is it?" Golden challenged. "By damn if you haven't taken too much of a liking to my Lottie."

"Hurry, Jack," Lottie pleaded, a growing urgency in her voice.

241

Holliday pulled his gun easily from his holster, Golden too drunk to notice or to care.

"Don't shoot him, John Henry, he's drunk and out of his mind." Lottie's hand flew to her face as Holliday pointed the gun at Golden. "Hurry," she implored Jack Jacobs.

Jacobs stumbled past the cowering spectators and lunged into the aisle, holding his hand up toward Holliday. "No shooting, Holliday." He stepped between the men. "This is not a saloon. Don't frighten the women and children like this."

"Who the hell are you?" Golden lunged toward Jacobs, releasing his grip on a chairback and tumbling forward.

Jacobs reached out for him.

"Get your damn hands off me," Golden commanded.

Jacobs stood him up straight and drew back his fist.

"Now get out of my way you goddam . . ."

Jacobs plowed a balled fist into Golden's nose and he crashed to the floor. "Don't use that kind of language in the presence of women and children."

Sprawled across the aisle, Golden struggled to raise himself, then his eyes rolled upwards and he tumbled backward onto the floor, his arms twitching, then turning limp.

Jacobs spun around to Holliday. "Put up your gun and help me get him out of here so decent people can see the show."

Holliday holstered his pistol as the crowd applauded Jacobs.

Lottie stepped into the aisle and bent over Golden. "Why?"

She could say no more before Jacobs motioned her away with a sweep of his arm. "Back to your seat, Lottie, we'll remove him."

For a moment, Lottie stared at Holliday. Fear was in her eyes. "Your gun can't solve everything, John Henry."

"It'll keep him from bothering you, Lottie." She turned away toward her seat and Holliday bent to grab a booted leg. "You helping, Jacobs, or are you leaving this to me?"

When Lottie took her place, Jacobs answered sharply. "I'll help. You're too puny to drag him out of here yourself."

Holliday scowled. "That's why I carry a pistol."

"Or two?"

"Brother Colt," Holliday continued, "made all men equal."

Jacobs grabbed Golden's other leg and the two men dragged

242

him past the spectators, now crowding into the aisle, and out the door into the street. They left Golden by a horse trough amid a circle of the curious.

"Roughest puppet show I ever saw," Holliday growled at a couple of persistent starers. Holliday kicked Golden's leg, then addressed Jacobs. "What about this fellow's acquaintance with Lottie?"

"Thank you, Holliday," Jacobs answered, "but I must be getting back to Lottie."

"What's his connection?" Holliday persisted. "He know her from somewhere?"

Jacobs started back for the hotel and Holliday grabbed his arm, feeling the muscles go taut and dangerous.

"They had some bad dealings in the past." Jacobs scratched his head. "What Lottie told me, I promised to keep to myself. If she wants you to know, it'll be up to her to tell." Jacobs broke from Holliday's grasp and headed back inside.

Holliday pulled the flask from his pocket, unstoppering it until he remembered it was empty. He took a step toward the hotel, then halted. The Cattle Exchange was just down the street and as long as he was this close, he'd get his flask refilled. He'd need it before the damn puppet show was over or before Kate was through yapping and crying for the night.

Quickly, he was at the saloon, staring over the batwing doors, noting the dearth of patrons. The puppet show had cut into the crowd. Chancey was behind the bar, polishing glasses. Holliday pushed inside to the bar and placed his flask solidly in front of Chancey.

"Why you working the bar?"

"One of my barkeeps is out sick and another wanted to see the damn puppet show. Hell, that damn Signor Silva or whatever his name is, is stealing my customers and my workers. I thought you were escorting Kate to the show."

"Give me a refill," Holliday shoved the flask at Chancey. "I got sidetracked by Golden bothering Lottie again."

"Golden?"

"Yeah, he's out there by a horse trough. Jack Jacobs cold-cocked him."

Chancey pulled a fresh bottle of Monarch bourbon from the

backbar and uncorked it. "Somebody needs to take care of Golden. Lottie was a hell of a dealer until he broke up her game the other night. Since then I've been lucky if she's broken even. Damn Lottie's Luck! It's that damn Golden that's ruined her." Chancey stuck a flask funnel in Holliday's container and poured the bourbon inside.

"Damn if somebody doesn't need to do something about him, Chancey."

The saloon owner wiped the lip of the bourbon bottle, then the flask. "I've been considering the same thing."

"If Jacobs hadn't interfered I might have had him at the puppet show. I'd pulled my gun on him. He was so drunk he'd gone to hell with a blank look on his face, if Jacobs hadn't stepped between us and unloaded on him."

Shaking his head, Chancey shoved the corked flask toward Holliday. "You wouldn't have killed him in front of the decent folk, women and children, would you?"

"Makes no difference to me."

"Maybe not, but it would to the vigilantes. They'd likely give you a good necktie party for that."

"You got any better ideas, Chancey?"

Chancey began building a cigarette, lit it, propped his elbows on the bar, and leaned toward Holliday. "The sheriff owes me a favor. Maybe I could get him to put enough of a scare into Golden that he'd leave town for good. When's he racing Haverty's horse again?"

"Sunday."

"You can always find something about horse racers that'll concern the law." Chancey grinned.

Holliday smiled back. "I'd take pleasure in killing him."

Chancey leaned closer to Holliday until Doc could feel the heat of the cigarette point. "You're a fool, Doc. The vigilantes won't tolerate that anymore. This town's changing."

"Maybe I should change towns."

"I've thought the same thing for myself. Buffalo can't last forever the way they're carting hides in by wagon trains. And the cattle trailing will be shot to hell when the railroad arrives."

"Then what's keeping you here, Chancey?"

"It's hard to move a saloon, but what's keeping you around, Doc? Is it Lottie or Kate?"

Holliday grabbed the flask and tucked it into his pocket. "There's money to be made."

"Lottie or Kate?"

"Lottie, dammit."

Chancey drew away from Holliday and grabbed a towel to wipe the bar. "You're a loner, Doc, not the type for a wife and a home. First time Lottie and you had a spat, you might just haul off and shoot her like you would a mangy old dog."

Holliday headed for the door, calling over his shoulder at the bar. "Chancey, you're better at dispensing drinks than advice."

He made his way slowly back to the hotel. The line once outside the hotel had jammed inside, and Holliday squeezed through the packed bodies toward his seat. After Holliday cleared the clump of people standing at the back, he fought his way down the aisle cluttered with people, answering with curses their grumbles as he tripped over them. He finally reached the third row, but a man was in his seat.

"You're in my place, fellow," Holliday said, none too quietly.

The man looked up at Holliday and shrugged.

"I escorted this woman." Holliday pointed to the next seat, then stopped. It wasn't Kate. He shook his head and stared at the woman again. She was old and matronly. He looked up and down the adjacent rows. Kate wasn't there. The bitch had abandoned him. Holliday turned abruptly away.

"Down in front," someone yelled at him.

"Just a minute, you son of a bitch," Holliday mumbled. He groped back down the aisle, wanting to strike out at the aggravated spectators he stepped on.

Finally, he reached the door and emerged into the evening heat. He walked straight to Kate's crib, but she was not there. Nor was she in his room when he returned to the Planters House.

TWENTY-TWO

Holliday unfastened his sweat-softened paper collar and dropped it to the floor by the tub of ice. In the smoke and heat of the Cattle Exchange the garrote of a collar had distracted him from his poker hand. The cards, tacky from the sweat of gambling fingers, clung together like a stain to cloth. Manipulating sticky cards marked a fool, so Holliday played five card draw as an equal with his opponents. It was a low stakes game, maybe earning Chancey enough money to buy another tub of ice but never enough to cool the Cattle Exchange. There wasn't that much money — much less ice — in all of Griffin. Holliday had heard that three women passed out from the heat at the puppet show the night before. Maybe one of them was Kate. He had not seen her since then, nor inquired about her.

Holliday played five card draw because Lottie had siphoned all his faro business away. But Lottie's Luck, to Chancey's chagrin, had indeed soured since Johnny Golden had interrupted her game in the Cattle Exchange. The ante at his table was so small, Holliday would have given up for the night, but there was only the hotel to go to and his room would be as hot as the saloon.

At the cackle of Lottie's laugh, Holliday glanced up from his cards. All he saw of Lottie among her customers was a bobbing, beribboned leghorn hat of lavender, hazy through the smoke. After an opponent raised the pot, Holliday evaluated the measly merit of his own cards, then matched the dollar raise and called the hand. Grinning, the customer exposed a full house. Holliday grimaced. He should pay more attention to the game and less to Lottie. Holliday folded his cards and nodded for the winner to claim the pot. Damn the heat. On a cooler night with a good deck of cards, the son of a bitch smiling across the table from him would have been cleaned out by the sixth hand.

Collecting the cards without enthusiasm, Holliday looked around the room for a bartender, but all had disappeared just when he needed a fresh bottle. Holliday's head felt listless from the oppressive heat and his mouth tasted of cotton. He needed more bourbon. Out of boredom he tossed the cards from hand to hand more times than required for an honest deal. Still searching for a bartender as he dealt the cards around the table, Holliday saw Kate swagger into the saloon, a man on her arm. Holliday swallowed hard against the dryness in his throat and felt a burning rage singe his cheeks. Kate walked arm-in-arm with Ed Bailey, the son of a bitch.

Kate stared back, smiling as smugly as the winning bastard across the table. Holliday folded his hand without examining his fresh cards. Kate, puckering her mocking lips at him, strolled to the bar. Bailey let his fleshy hand slip from her arm and down her thigh as he ordered drinks.

Damn Kate, Holliday thought, shoving the cards to the middle of the table. "Somebody deal for me," he commanded.

Kate and Bailey lifted their drinks, tilted their heads, and drained the liquor. Finishing, Kate dropped her jigger on the counter and bent over, lifting her skirt above her knees and adjusting the garter halfway up her thigh, then letting the cloth fall over her leg again. As she straightened her frame, suddenly quite appealing to Holliday, she waved at him. Holliday's hands tightened into fists and slammed into the table.

Kate snapped her fingers at the barkeep, who lifted a whiskey bottle to refill her glass. She snatched the bottle by the neck, then grabbed Bailey's hand from her thigh and pulled him toward Holliday's table. Holliday felt his muscles tighten like an overwound spring. Kate was unpredictable, and Bailey shared his mutual grudge.

247

Kate stomped to a halt across the table from him and hoisted the bottle of Monarch bourbon above her head. "I drink the best when I celebrate, Doctor John Henry Holliday."

"Kate, you're bothering my customers."

Kate nodded. "But not them as much as I'm annoying you. I'm celebrating, Doc Holliday. Care to know why?"

Holliday unfolded himself from his chair, his fingers wiggling with trigger anticipation as he stood. "I don't give a damn, you whore."

"I've found someone to replace you, Doc Holliday, and he's a damn sight better than you in bed. I ran into him after I left the puppet show. He showed me what a man could be."

Holliday said, "I came back for you, Kate."

"You shouldn't have left, Doc. You know Ed Bailey?"

"Get away, you goddam whore," Holliday answered.

"Just a minute." Bailey stepped beside Kate. "Apologize to the lady or answer to me."

Holliday laughed, his fingers touching the ivory grip of his Colt. "Make me apologize, big man. See if you're as big as your mouth."

The gamblers at the table scrambled from their seats and toward the walls. A stifling silence filled the room.

"Go ahead," Holliday dared, "prove what a big man you are!"

Bailey backed away. "Okay, I'll . . ." he started.

"Stop it, both of you." It was Chancey. "There'll be no shooting in my saloon tonight."

Kate swung around to Chancey. "Holliday started it."

Chancey moved his shotgun in a slow arc from Bailey to Kate. "Doc was dealing, Kate. You jerked Bailey here for no good."

Holliday eyed Bailey with venom. "Bailey and I just as well settle our differences, Chancey. It'll come one day. Today's just as good as another."

"No day's a good day in my saloon, Doc," Chancey replied. "I don't want any gunplay here. Now back away, Bailey, and you with him, Kate." He waved the shotgun at them.

The two lovers retreated from the table like it was rabid.

"Another thing, Kate," Chancey said. "You're through

248

working my saloon. You can drag up your customers from somewhere else. Did that message get through your thick skull, Kate?"

"Doc started it, Chancey. You'll be sorry you kicked me out. This place'll lose business. You watch because it'll happen. I draw customers for you."

Chancey laughed. "Kate, all you draw is flies."

"You'll be sorry, Chancey." She stormed toward the door. Suddenly, she stopped and turned around. "Doctor John Henry Holliday," she shouted, "you're a Georgia son of a bitch!" She hurled the bottle at him. "Go screw yourself."

Doc dodged the glass shattering at his feet like a broken romance. Holliday pulled his gun from its holster, but Kate was out the door before he could fire.

Chancey clucked his tongue. "You wouldn't shoot her in the back, would you?" He lowered his shotgun.

"I've thought about it."

"So have I," Chancey answered. "Maybe you should take a break, Doc. I'll have someone else finish up your table."

The breeze was warm and gentle and agonizing. Holliday coughed up the staleness of the saloon into the darkness of night. Just in case Bailey was waiting to ambush him, he avoided the puddles of light which seeped out the windows around the Flat. But he suspected Kate had snared Bailey in her crib and was giving him a good ride. Holliday wondered if she were charging him for the opportunity.

Without a moon, the night sky was sharply punctuated with a smattering of stars, more stars than Holliday could ever remember seeing. A meteor trailed across the sky and disappeared in a shower of flaring sparks that glimmered in the sky for an instant then was gone forever. Down Griffin Avenue toward Government Hill more sparks were flying; a cowboy with more liquor in his gut than sense in his head was firing his pistol at the stars and missing. Between his shots, a bawdy woman cried from somewhere about a missed lover; the strains of a harmonica carried from upwind; and the people hurried down the street, seeking refuge from the stink of festering buffalo hides.

For half an hour, Holliday walked cautiously from building to building along the street, his right hand riding easily on the butt of his sidearm. Returning to the Cattle Exchange, he clung to the darkness away from the rectangles of light bleeding out windows, then stopped to reconnoiter the men lingering in the street. His eyes strained to penetrate the darkness where sudden assassins might be poised. By a front window he saw a slight figure staring into the Cattle Exchange and swigging on a bottle of liquor. Holliday recognized him and smiled, fingers gripping his pistol butt. Johnny Golden was surveying the saloon. Suddenly, Golden flung the bottle beneath the horses at the hitching rack and strode boldly to the Cattle Exchange door.

Holliday jerked his revolver. If he hurried, he could kill Golden. He pointed the Colt, pulling the hammer back for the kill and aiming for Golden's heart. His finger tightened on the trigger, but two men stepped between Holliday and his target. By the time they moved, Golden had disappeared into the Cattle Exchange. Slowly, Holliday lowered the gun and eased the hammer down, angered he had missed the opportunity. As Holliday slipped up to the door, one of Chancey's bartenders scurried out, running down the street. In the bartender's wake, Holliday stepped inside.

Golden stood at Lottie's table, his hands on his hips. "You're coming with me this time, Lottie. I got the right to make you do it."

Lottie shook her head. "I'm never leaving with you."

By Lottie's side stood Chancey, puffing on a cigarette. As Holliday lifted his revolver, he felt Chancey's hard gaze upon him. Chancey shook his head. "Put it away, Doc. I told him he could speak to Lottie, if he made no trouble."

"Last time you saw him, you told him to stay out of your saloon. You going soft, Chancey?"

"Shut up, Doc. This will be taken care of in due time. Like about now," Chancey said, nodding toward the door.

Holliday turned around.

Chancey's bartender had returned with the sheriff and two deputies at his side. The huffing barkeep pointed toward Golden, still arguing with Lottie. The sheriff drew his pistol and stepped toward Lottie's table.

"Johnny Golden," Sheriff Trickus called out, "turn around slow and easy."

Golden lifted his hand from his waist toward his armpit.

"Don't try anything, Johnny, you're dealing with the law and I've got two deputies with me."

Golden's hands relaxed. "Did you do this, Lottie?"

"No, Johnny." She sighed.

Golden turned slowly around to face the sheriff. "What's the problem, sheriff? This some scheme of Haverty's so I can't race my horse against his tomorrow?"

The sheriff laughed. "I've received word from San Antone that the chestnut you've been racing was stolen."

Golden stepped hard toward the sheriff, "That's a lie, dammit! Haverty did put you up to this. It won't work, sheriff, 'cause I've got the papers on that horse."

"Maybe you'd best come with me, Johnny. We'll inspect your papers and see if your story matches San Antone's." The sheriff waved his gun at Golden and the deputies circled him.

"He carries a gun under his shoulder, a knife in his boot, and a derringer in his coat pocket, sheriff," Lottie said softly.

Golden raised his arms. "You goddam traitor, Lottie. That's no way for a man's —"

Trickus struck him across the side of the head with his gun barrel. "Shut up, dammit."

Staggering backward, Golden almost fell, but caught himself against Lottie's table. He spit at her. Instantly, Chancey lunged past the circling deputies, grabbing Golden's arm and twisting it behind his back. Golden screamed from the pain. Trickus moved in and slipped his hand inside Golden's coat, removing a revolver, then the derringer from his pocket while a deputy searched his boot for the dagger.

"Now back away, Chancey," Trickus called. "Let the law handle this as it should be."

Chancey wrenched Golden's arm upward a final time, then shoved the arm down free. "Don't spit at my dealers, you skunk."

Golden's eyes watered from the pain in his arm and shoulder. "You're all against me," he stammered. "There isn't any law in this stinkhole."

"You're talking to the law, Johnny. Word's gotten around you've been treating Lottie poorly, so you won't find many friends here," Trickus answered.

"But she's —"

"Oh, Johnny," cried Lottie. "I'll never be again."

Trickus grabbed Golden's limp arm and jerked him toward the door. "Until our jail's finished, we detain our prisoners in the Southern Hotel. It's better than you deserve."

"No," Golden grimaced, jerking his arm free, his eyes flaring with pain and hate. "I'll get even with all of you. Lottie," he sneered, "just see how much longer our little secret remains untold."

"Shut up and move along." Trickus pushed him toward the door. "You try anything with these folks and you'll have the law to deal with."

The two deputies grabbed Golden by each arm and tugged him out the door. Holliday followed the sheriff outside, watching the law officers and their prisoner disappear into the darkness toward the hotel down the street.

When Holliday re-entered the saloon, he marched to Lottie's table. She was counting her money to split with Chancey.

"There's still a couple hours good playing time, Lottie," Chancey implored her. "Every time Golden comes here he shakes you up too bad to continue."

Lottie kept counting.

"Must be quite a secret he has on you, Lottie. What is it?" Chancey asked without response. "I daresay he won't be bothering you again in the Cattle Exchange after tonight."

Dropping a handful of money on the table, Lottie looked up for the first time. "What do you mean, Chancey?"

Now Chancey ignored Lottie.

Lottie stepped around the table. "What have you done, Chancey? By damn, you answer me or I'll never turn another card in your damn saloon."

"When you left the Bee Hive and started for me, Lottie, you damn sure didn't do it because you liked me. You've made that plenty plain," Chancey said. "You did it because this Golden was pestering you. You figured me and Holliday offered better protection against him than Fogle did."

Lottie drew back her arm, but Chancey's hand flew to her wrist before she could slap him. "Did you arrange for the sheriff to arrest him?" she asked.

"Dammit, I sure did. The sheriff owed me a favor and I told him to persuade Golden it'd be healthier to leave the Flat and never return." He squeezed her wrist until she squealed, then he pushed her away.

"You bastard."

"That's what you wanted, wasn't it? Now, dammit, it's done. If you're dissatisfied, it's because you misplayed your hand, Lottie."

For a moment, Lottie stood with her hands on her hips, her eyes laced with anger.

Holliday stepped between them. "Calm down, both of you. Let the dust settle."

Neither answered, but both heard two muffled gun retorts from down the street. Lottie's hand flew to her mouth. "Oh, my God, what have they done?"

Holliday took Lottie's hand "I was out earlier and it's probably the same cowboy shooting off a drinking bout."

Then came the clatter of boots on the plank walk outside and Sheriff Trickus burst through the door. "Need some men quick, Chancey, to help find Golden."

"What happened?"

"He made a break for it. We fired at him. Deputy thinks he hit him. May have, from the sound of whatever the bullet hit."

"Come on, some of you men," Chancey called, "let's see if we can find the body."

Lottie whimpered, tears rolling down her cheek. Then she cried softly.

"If he's wounded, we may be able to save him," the sheriff said. "Hurry."

A dozen men answered the call, Chancey among them, and headed out the door behind the sheriff.

"Why," Lottie sobbed, "did Chancey have him shot, for God's sake?"

Holliday helped Lottie to her chair and she almost fell into it. "Chancey wouldn't have a man killed," he answered. "Like he told you, he just wanted to scare a little sense into Golden, make him leave you alone."

"I should never have come to the Cattle Exchange, but I had nowhere else to turn."

"Dammit, Lottie, that's why you need a husband. Someone to look out for you."

She laughed almost uncontrollably, her laughter mingled with sobs. "It's that simple, is it John Henry?" She reached for his hand. "Husband'll take care of everything, will he?"

"He'd be by your side when you needed him."

Dropping Holliday's hand, she cackled like a madwoman until her laughter turned into an almost uncontrollable coughing fit.

"You need a drink, Lottie." Holliday motioned for a barkeep to bring a bottle to the table. When bottle and glass arrived, Holliday poured her a shot. "Why let a gambling tinhorn like Golden upset you so?"

Lottie downed the drink in a single gulp. "He's my husband."

"Damn Lottie's Luck," Holliday mumbled.

TWENTY-THREE

Lottie's hand trembled against the door latch, the hinge moaning as morning's brightness rushed in. If only she had left the Flat when she had received Johnny's letter. But now, it was too late; she had tested her luck once too often. Jack Jacobs stood at the door, straight as a soldier, his hat over his heart, his gentle blue eyes suggesting the worst.

"They found him." He stopped, biting his lip.

"Dead?"

Jacobs nodded. "I'm sorry."

Lottie looked beyond Jacobs to the Flat. "Why all night to find him?"

He reached out for her hand. "You don't want to know."

"Maybe not, but I should hear it."

Jacobs pointed with his hat to the couch. "Then sit down." She clung to his arm as Jacobs walked her to the seat. "He hid in the buffalo ricks. He was hit hard but didn't bleed much or leave a trail. Come midmorning someone noticed a pack of dogs gathered around a stack of hides. That's when they found him."

Lottie looked up into Jack's eyes, discomforted with sympathy. "Was he mauled?"

"He wasn't a wholesome sight," Jacobs admitted, "but he was beyond pain by that time."

Dropping her face to her hands, Lottie sobbed. She felt his tentative arm around her shoulder, the awkward pat of his hand.

"I should have left when I received his letter." She spoke through her fingers and struggled weakly as his hand pried hers from her face.

"You couldn't run forever, Lottie. He would have caught up with you someplace else. Cry for him, but not for yourself." His hand squeezed tightly around hers.

Hot tears streamed down her cheeks. "I'm crying for Father," she stammered. "He told me nothing good would come of this marriage, but I was young and foolish and knew everything and Johnny was adventuresome and monied and handsome and —"

"And a cheat," Jacobs interjected.

"The war was ending, Father was broke, landless. Our betrothal seemed to ease so many problems, but it only created more, breaking Father's heart and, by Appomattox, his will to live." Lottie shook her head. "Father was right, and I a fool."

Jacobs released her hand and stood. "I'm not much good at this, Lottie, dealing with grieving women, I mean. Nothing I can say will change things."

Lottie pulled a handkerchief from her sleeve and dabbed her eyes. "I'm being a fool now. I ran away from him. I never loved him, so why should I be upset? But you don't care to hear about that. There is something you can do."

Wiping her eyes, she stood up and walked to the window. "I owe Johnny a decent burial, at least. Buy a good suit of clothes and coffin. See that he gets a gravestone. Have the hearse stop by here on the way to the cemetery. Dispose of what belongings he had. And if that chestnut horse was his, sell him to Haverty."

Nodding, Jack Jacobs took his hat from the couch. "I'll be glad to, Lottie."

"I need a new trunk for my belongings and my money," she continued. "Have Frank Conrad give you all my winnings and buy a trunk from him."

"I've a trunk I'll give you, Lottie. It might look obvious if I get your money and a new trunk. Anything else?"

"Jack, don't tell anyone about these arrangements. I have paid my rent through Saturday. Tell the sheriff no one is to disturb my place until six o'clock."

"If there is more I can do, Lottie . . ."

She snickered through her tears a moment. "I keep thinking of things. Yes, later I'll give you something to take to my friend Rachel at the fort."

The curtains blocked the midmorning light. Lottie sat on her bed. Dressed in black, a veil covering her face, she counted the money and restacked it in the leather trunk with Jack Jacobs's initials carved over the latch. She took five hundred dollars in paper money and looked for something to put it in. She had but one envelope, the one addressed to her in Johnny Golden's hand. Finding a pencil, she obliterated her name and replaced it with Rachel's. She removed Golden's letter and read it aloud.

"My Charlotte," — the word "my" was underlined — "so you go by the name Lottie Deno now. Shouldn't it be Lottie Golden? Running out on me wasn't the smartest thing you ever did because I will find you and we will live together as man and wife. That's my right. My luck was running mediocre until I overheard a saloon conversation about a red-headed woman gambler in Fort Griffin. I knew they meant MY Lottie. Do not run away from me again because I will find you and you will be most sorry you ran out on me more than once. Johnny."

No mention of love. Johnny had never loved her, she thought. He just wanted to possess her, to own her, to control her like he did the chestnut racehorse. She wadded up the letter and dropped it on the table. Tears moistened her eyes. She lifted the veil and dabbed at them with a silk handkerchief, a gift from her father when she was but a girl. Why hadn't she listened to him? She might be living a decent life now, not working as a gambler in a festering Texas frontier town.

Outside she heard the sound of a wagon and the monotone of low male voices. She stepped to the window and cracked the curtains with her black-gloved hand. A somber hearse was approaching, the sunlight glistening off its polished wood and brass fittings. She felt her throat tighten as she stared at the dark coffin, peeking, like her, from behind curtained windows. She dropped the curtain and walked to the table, picking up the wadded letter and the envelope she had addressed to Rachel.

A horse nickered as the hearse stopped opposite her door. Lottie gritted her teeth and stepped outside. The men removed their hats. Jack Jacobs nudged his horse toward her, and Lottie looked behind him. There was the sheriff, a deputy, John Henry Holliday, Mike Fogle, Pete Haverty, Billy Wilson, George Wilhelm from Conrad's store, and the undertaker.

"I didn't know, Jack," Lottie said, forcing a smile, "that Johnny had so many friends here."

"They're your friends, Lottie, not his."

Sheriff Trickus eased his horse up beside Jacobs. "Ma'am, we're terribly sorry. We didn't know he was your husband."

Lottie nodded. "He wasn't much of a husband."

"We didn't mean for it to turn out this way." Trickus turned his horse toward the hearse.

"You've made good arrangements, Jack," Lottie offered. "It's better than he deserved."

"I did it for you, Lottie, not him."

Lottie stepped to his horse and extended the envelope. "Give this to Rachel up at the fort in two days." Then she handed him the wadded letter from Golden. Throw this on his coffin when they cover it up. I don't want to keep it and something won't let me destroy it."

"Sure, Lottie."

She moved closer to his horse and motioned for him to lean over. "Come by in the morning, about six," she whispered. Lifting the veil from her hat and standing on her toes, she kissed his cheek. "Thank you, Jack, for everything." Beyond him, she could see Holliday's jealous stare and she felt sorry for him. "Goodbye, until tomorrow, Jack."

Jacobs nodded to the undertaker and the hearse inched somberly away. As the riders passed, Holliday tipped his hat. For many minutes Lottie watched the procession move upstream to the cemetery. Then, for the last time in her life, she turned her back on Johnny Golden.

Holliday grinned. "Business has been down since the shooting."

"Hell," Chancey answered, "it'd help if she came back to

work. She can't stay in her cabin and mourn his passing forever. She'd be better off coming back to work and forgetting it. Hell, she must not of loved him, running out on him like that. Reckon she left town?"

Holliday closed the office door and ambled to Chancey's desk. Lifting his booted foot atop two stacked beer crates, he grinned. "I thought about that, Chancey, and watched the stage yesterday. She wasn't on it and she hasn't bought a rig from the stables. Even Golden's chestnut is still in Haverty's."

Chancey coughed up a laugh with his cigarette smoke. "Doc, you beat all. Now that her husband's out of the way, you think you've got a chance with her?"

Tapping his boot against the crate, Holliday answered without words.

"Damn, Doc," Chancey said, "I thought you had more sense than that. Lottie thinks she's too damn good for our type."

Holliday was spared answering with a sharp rapping on the door. "Boss," called a bartender.

"Yeah," Chancey answered.

"Kate's outside with Ed Bailey," the bartender replied. "You want me to get rid of them?"

Chancey rose from his chair. "Let me get my shotgun."

Holliday moved toward the door.

"Stay in here, Doc," Chancey ordered. "You'd just flame the fire." He checked his shotgun's load. "Now Kate, she's the one for you. She'd give you more than most women."

Holliday growled. "If she wasn't sharing it with everybody else in the county."

The shotgun's twin barrels clicked into place. "If you'd marry her, Doc, it'd save me a lot of problems."

"Yeah, but I'd have a living hell." Holliday fell in line behind Chancey, the bartender backing out of Chancey's way.

Glancing over his shoulder, Chancey stopped in the door and scowled at Holliday. "I thought I told you to stay in here."

"You did, Chancey."

"Well, dammit, do it! I don't want you shooting anybody in my place."

"I just want to watch," Holliday replied.

"Just see that that's all you do, Doc." Chancey barged ahead

259

into the saloon. "Kate, I told you to keep your butt away from my saloon. Do you understand English, woman?"

Ed Bailey stepped toward Chancey. "Now just a minute, Chancey, she's with me. She's causing no harm and she's not luring away your business." Bailey glanced behind Chancey toward the office. Holliday could see Bailey's eyes explode with hate. "She's better than some of the people you let work here."

Holliday emerged from the room.

Without looking around, Chancey issued orders. "Back in the office, Doc. You two jackasses can't leave well enough alone, now can you?"

Kate eased to Bailey's side, slipping her hand in his. "Let's leave, Ed, I've got better things for us to do." She ran her free hand up the front of his thigh.

The movement of her hand stimulated a grin across Bailey's face. "I'm taking Kate with me, Chancey, and I'll keep her out of this place. But am I welcome here from time to time?"

"I'll take any fool's money just as long as he doesn't cause me any trouble, but you're not welcome with her."

Bailey said, "Come on, Kate, let's head to your place."

Kate winked at Holliday and he could feel his blood heating. "I always enjoy men that make a woman feel wanted," she said.

"You just like to feel, Kate." Holliday spit out the words and retreated back into the office.

"Get going, Bailey." Chancey waved the shotgun at him and Kate. "Think you can find it within your limited brain, Kate, to remember you are not welcome in the Cattle Exchange again?"

She cackled, her laugh exploding in short bursts. Waving her arm around the room, she spoke. "Hell, Chancey, looks like your business is down since I left. If you had a brain, you'd be begging me to come back and attract a few more customers."

"It's Lottie, Kate. She was the Cattle Exchange's biggest draw, not you. It'll pick up when she gets back."

Bailey tugged on Kate's arm. "Let's go, Kate."

She shook free. "Maybe Lottie's out looking for another husband she can run out on. The bitch! And her calling me a whore when she had run out on her husband." She cupped her hands to her mouth and yelled. "Did you hear that, Doc? Lottie's a damnable bitch, leaving her husband, dancing with you and whatever else you did. Show your hide, you runt of a man."

Holliday burned from her words. He stepped from the shadow of the office, his lips drawn tightly across his face, his eyes narrowed and dangerous.

"Doc Holliday," she said as he moved into view. "You're a Georgia son of a bitch." Kate spun around and grabbed Bailey's hand. "Let's get out of here."

Slowly, Holliday pulled his pistol from his holster. He took careful aim, his trigger finger pressing snugly against metal.

Chancey yelled, "No, Doc, not in here."

The gun exploded in a cloud of white smoke. The bullet thudded into its target. Ed Bailey dropped to the floor. Kate stopped, looked down at Bailey, then at the doorjamb beside her where the bullet had struck. She turned slowly about to face Holliday.

"Crap like that's why nobody in the Flat cares a damn about you, Doc Holliday. You're a fool if you think any woman better than me could ever fall for you."

Bailey raised up, his hand slipping toward his holster.

"Don't try it, Ed." Chancey flourished the shotgun at him.

"Get off the goddam floor," Kate scolded Bailey, her hands on her hips. "If he'd meant to kill you, you'd be deader than business in this saloon."

Bailey picked himself up like he would a bit of trash, disgusted and reluctantly.

"Hurry up about it before he does plug you." She tapped her foot on the floor.

"Shut up, Kate," Bailey said, dusting his britches off and staring at Holliday.

Holliday waved his Colt. "Just try something, Ed Bailey, give me the excuse I've wanted to settle our differences."

Though he said nothing, Bailey's message was clear from the hardness in his eyes. He backed out of the saloon, a shrugging Kate marching after him. "You fool," she shouted once they were outside, then her words were lost in the street noises.

Chancey cursed Holliday. "Damn you. No cause for that."

As he holstered his revolver, Holliday nodded. "Shows you Kate's got more grit in her craw than that bastard Bailey."

"Oh, hell, Doc, I'm tired of both of them. I should have told Ed to stay away too."

"You'd never do that," Holliday smirked. "It'd be bad for business." He marched to the bar, the bartender automatically setting up a bottle of Monarch for him. "Thanks."

Chancey headed for his office, pausing by Holliday. "Doc, just don't shoot Bailey in my saloon."

"I won't shoot him here!" Holliday picked up the bottle. "On the house?"

"Sure," Chancey said, "business ain't worth a damn and you're downing more free whiskey than ever here."

Nodding, Holliday stepped for the front door.

"Where you going?"

Holliday didn't answer.

Chancey marched stride for stride with Holliday, grabbing his arm at the door. Chancey's grip was viselike until Doc's fingers fell on the ivory grip of his Colt. Chancey's hand dropped away. "Don't cause any trouble or it'll make business worse here. Tell me where you're going."

"To see Lottie."

A man knocked at Lottie's door. Holliday recognized but could not place him. The tall, lean fellow wore overalls. He shifted back and forth on his feet, toeing at a wooden crate beside the door. He saw Holliday approaching and a wave of relief seemed to wash over him.

"You coming to see Miss Deno?"

Holliday nodded.

"I can't get her to answer. It's not like her. She's too much of a lady not to answer."

Holliday rubbed his chin, looking at the grocery-filled box, then back at the bibbed fellow beside it. "Who the hell are you?"

"George Wilhelm, Mister Holliday. I remember you from Miss Deno's Christmas party. You danced so well with her until, you know, that crazy woman came in." Wilhelm stepped aside.

Holliday knocked four times on the door. "Why're you here?"

"I bring Miss Deno supplies every week," Wilhelm answered. "I work at Conrad's store."

262

"Lottie, are you in there? George has your supplies. Don't worry us by hiding." Holliday waited for an answer. None came.

George took off his slouch hat and fanned himself with it. "Hot afternoon, isn't it?"

Nodding without caring, Holliday moved to a window. "Did you try looking inside for anything amiss?"

"Well, no sir. I hadn't been here long when you came up."

Holliday walked around the cabin, stopping at every window, peering each time into the backs of tightly pulled curtains. "She'll roast in there without fresh air. Lottie, you okay?"

"Maybe she's staying in a hotel a few days," George offered. "Word I hear is she had Jack Jacobs take all her money from Mister Conrad's safe. Some say it's as much as twenty thousand dollars. You think that's possible?"

Holliday stopped. "You say she took all her money out?"

Wilhelm nodded.

"Damn!" Holliday went and beat on the front door again. He tried the handle. It was locked. He fought the urge to shoot it open. "If you knew, other folks knew too."

For a moment Wilhelm caught his breath, then stammered. "You don't . . . you mean she could . . . you don't think someone maybe did her some harm, do you?"

"Fetch the sheriff so he'll be here in case there's been trouble," Holliday commanded.

Wilhelm's face turned dark. "You don't think anyone would have hurt her, do you?"

"Twenty thousand is a lot of money. Now be quick and gone." Wilhelm moved to pick up the supplies until Holliday propped his boot on the crate's edge. Then Wilhelm scampered away.

Behind the cabin, Holliday leaned into the wall's narrow shade. Had Lottie left? The possibility tore hard at his stomach. He feared more that she was gone than that she might be hurt or dead. He wondered if he would ever again find her. Mired in his thoughts, he lost track of time until he heard the noise of approaching men. Walking around to the cabin front, he saw George gesturing wildly at the sheriff. When they came within speaking distance, Holliday overheard George. "He won't believe me, that's why you must tell him."

Holliday, waiting at the cabin door, nodded at the six approaching men, then spoke. "Sheriff, figured you'd need to be here before we opened up Lottie's place."

"No, sir, we won't be interfering with her cabin."

Holliday stepped toward Trickus, pointing his finger at the sheriff's badge. "She could be in trouble. Word's around she had her money on her."

"I've heard the rumors, Holliday, but I've also gotten instructions from Lottie by way of Jack Jacobs. Her place is not to be disturbed until Saturday afternoon at six o'clock. Her rent's paid through Saturday and that's how she wanted it. I plan to oblige her. Least I can do since the shooting."

"You did her a favor, sheriff."

"Way I hear it, it may have been you that I favored."

Holliday stepped to Trickus. "What do you mean by that?"

"Just gossip I heard about you being soft on her, throwing card games to her."

"Don't believe that." Holliday scowled.

"Didn't say I believed it, Mister Holliday, just that I'd heard it. But by damn you can believe that Jack Jacobs told me at Golden's burial that Lottie had asked not to be disturbed until Saturday. That's the way it's going to be."

Holliday shrugged and marched past the sheriff toward town. Until dusk, he checked the hotels and the livery stables for clues on Lottie. After dark, he watched her cabin for two hours in hopes of seeing a light or smoke from her cookstove. He saw nothing but a crescent moon and the stars.

As he knocked on the door, Jack Jacobs enjoyed the cool of the evening shade on the long porch which faced out across the vast parade ground separating the officers' quarters from the enlisted men's hovels. He patted his shirt pocket, assuring himself the envelope was still there, then he took off his hat and wiped the sweat from his brow just as a tall officer wearing a captain's uniform stepped to the door.

"My name's Jack Jacobs," he introduced himself. "I'm here to see your wife. Lottie Deno sent me."

The officer nodded and opened the door. As he stepped inside, Jacobs recognized Rachel's voice coming from the same direction as the aroma of fresh baked bread. "Who is it, Richard?" Her flour-smudged face peeked out from the kitchen door. "Oh, Mister Jacobs, what a pleasant surprise."

"I wasn't sure you'd remember me, ma'am, us meeting only at the Christmas party and at the . . ." Jacobs stopped.

"The lynching," she finished his sentence and smiled. "You are one of the pleasant memories I have of that day." She wiped her hands on an apron that hung like a shroud over her belly bloated with child. "I am always glad to see a true friend of Lottie's." She stepped toward him.

Richard spoke. "Mister Jacobs says Miss Deno sent him."

Rachel lowered her head. "I am so sorry, Mister Jacobs, if what I heard about Lottie is true. Was it her husband that was killed Saturday, the one that was racing those horses?" She motioned to a new rocker. "Please be seated."

"Ma'am, it's true, I fear."

She seated herself and reached for Richard's hand. "I am most sorry for Lottie, Mister Jacobs."

"And she was most ashamed, too, for fear you'd think less of her, so she sent me to apologize and say you were her only woman friend in Griffin."

"I wanted to see her when I heard, Mister Jacobs, but," she patted her enlarged abdomen, "in my condition I must not travel, even so short a distance. But she is always welcome in my home. Tell her that please."

Jacobs swallowed hard. "I wish I could, ma'am, but Lottie's gone. She left town on the first stage after the burial."

"I wish she had come to see me."

"She wanted to, but her shame was too great, you being a decent woman and all. She did ask that I give you this, though." Jacobs pulled the envelope out of his pocket. He stared at Lottie's handwriting and the blotches obliterating Golden's hand. The captain retrieved the envelope for his wife. "She was fond of you and wanted to see the baby, but she just couldn't stay in Fort Griffin anymore. Not with what happened."

Rachel took the envelope from her husband. As she lifted the flap, her eyes widened. She gasped. "It's money, Richard." She counted it. "Five hundred dollars in all. It's more money than I ever held at once. Did she have any left for her needs?"

Jacobs smiled. "Enough. She just thought a mother-to-be living on army pay could find a good use for a little extra.

"I wish I could thank her, Mister Jacobs, in person, but I will write her instead."

"I wish you could, ma'am, she'd have liked that. But she told no one, not even me, where she was going."

TWENTY-FOUR

Holliday arrived at Lottie's cabin a half hour ahead of the others and checked the door still locked and the windows still curtained. Then he walked to the cottonwood tree behind the dwelling and paced in the lengthy shade of late afternoon. Had Lottie left the Flat? She hadn't ridden the stage or bought a rig from the stables. Perplexed, he kicked at a dull gray patch half hidden in the grass and a receptacle tumbled on the turf.

Bending to pick up his find, he recognized it instantly. It was a dealing box, the rigged faro box Lottie had saved for him. Holliday brushed off the small ants scurrying upon it, then knocked the box against the heel of his boot, the collected dirt and plant matter tumbling to the ground. He remembered how Lottie had sent for him to give him the dealing box, how she had spurned his proposal, and how in anger he had tossed the dealing box away. The memory seemed to attack his chest and he coughed and wheezed until he spit a chunk of bloody mucus onto the grass. He tried to rub away the decay of the box, but it had been too long ignored to give in to such caresses now.

Hearing the approach of others, Holliday ambled around the side of the cabin, carrying the corroded dealing box with him. He watched Sheriff Trickus, George Wilhelm, Jack Jacobs, and a half dozen others, curious of Lottie's fate, walk up to the cabin. Their voices lowering reverently the closer they came, they gathered in a clump at the door. Without a word, Jacobs handed a key to Sheriff Trickus, who inserted it in the lock and opened the door, the stuffy heat escaping.

Trickus stepped inside. "Give me a minute."

The men crowded at the door until Trickus returned. "She's not here," he said.

Holliday pushed with the other men inside, one calling, "Lookahere, a note on her bed." He handed it to the sheriff.

"Read it," several called.

Trickus cleared his throat. "It says 'Sell these belongings and give the money to someone in need.' That's all," Trickus scratched his chin. "Well, who's in need?"

Jack Jacobs spoke first. "The family of the little girl, Sophie, could use the money. Her father's taken too much a liking to the bottle to work."

Several nodded and the sheriff gave his assent. "But what happened to Lottie?"

"She caught the stage Tuesday," Jacobs answered.

"That's not right." Holliday stepped forward. "I watched the stage and she didn't get on."

Jack Jacobs nodded. "I carried her outside town and we stopped it there. The driver'll confirm it on his next trip."

"Well, boys," said the sheriff, "I reckon we've seen the last of Lottie Deno."

Collapsing into a chair, Holliday slammed the corroded dealing box on the table. As a cough ripped through his body, he lifted his hand for the bartender. "A bottle of bourbon," he demanded. The bottle and Chancey arrived the same time.

Chancey hitched his britches up, then leaned over the table, picking up the dealing box, running his fingers over its pitted surface, then toying with the ruined springs inside. "Not in very good shape, Doc. Reminds me of you. Right now, you don't look too good yourself."

Holliday dropped his derby on the table and ran his fingers through his hair. "Put it down, Chancey."

For a moment longer, Chancey held the rigged box.

"Maybe you didn't understand me, Chancey," Doc said slowly, his words buzzing like a coiled rattlesnake. "Leave it be."

Chancey let the box slide from his fingers and crash into the table. Holliday flinched, his tongue flicking across his lips.

"You're jumpy tonight, Doc, and late."

Holliday uncorked his bourbon bottle and drank heavily from it. "Lottie's left."

"It's just as well. Her luck had gone to hell," Chancey replied. "Are you dealing tonight, Doc, or just drinking?"

"I can hold my liquor."

"Better than any I ever saw, Doc." Chancey leaned forward, staring into Holliday's eyes. "But can you hold onto my money with your mind on Lottie? You're a powder keg ready to explode."

"You're the match that's gonna make me go off, Chancey." Holliday coughed hard into his fist, then snapped his palm toward the floor to rid it of the slimy residue from his lungs. He lifted the bottle toward his lips, but Chancey grabbed his wrist.

"No trouble or shooting, Doc. It's bad for business."

"I won't start any! My word — I won't shoot anyone."

The manacle of Chancey's grip loosened and Holliday completed the bottle's trip to his lips. After several swallows, he came up for air. "I'll deal poker, but not faro, Chancey."

"It would never have worked, you and Lottie," Chancey said with as little compassion as if he paid for it by the ounce. "Just forget her, Doc. No woman's worth that much."

"Lottie was a lady," Holliday said softly. He brushed the weather-beaten dealing box aside. "Bring me a fresh deck and pass the word I'm dealing draw, Chancey." Slowly after Chancey returned with cards and chips, the table filled with Saturday night gamblers. Holliday played card after monotonous card, too bored to cheat, too indifferent to win big, too accomplished to lose much. The deck may have been readers, but Holliday never looked for markings. Occasionally, he would glance at an empty table nearby. Until Golden was killed, Lottie had dealt there.

As he raked in his nicest pot of the evening, Holliday spotted Ed Bailey, making his way from the door to the bar. For maybe thirty minutes, Bailey downed his liquor and stared back at Holliday. Finally, Bailey gulped a jiggerful down hard and broke away from the bar toward Holliday. Holliday eased his chair back from the table to meet Bailey's approach.

Bailey stood by the table, his bloodshot eyes wide over doughlike cheeks. "Deal me in, Holliday," he commanded.

"Go rut with Kate, Bailey. No matter how bad you screw, you're bound to be better at it than at cards."

Bailey's fleshy fingers curled into fists and he planted them on his wide hips. "I left her satisfied back at her shack. Way she tells it, that's more than you ever did for her."

"She's got a short memory."

Smirking, Bailey unwadded his hands and clapped them together. "Memory's not what she told me you were short on."

"You wanna play, Bailey? Then sit down and shut up," Holliday answered, just as Chancey stormed to the table.

"Just a minute, you two," he called. "No trouble tonight."

Bailey's face bloated like a toad frog. "I'm not looking for trouble, Chancey, just a little game. You're not throwing me out, Chancey. I didn't bring Kate, like you said."

Chancey rubbed his chin. "You gave me your word no shooting, Doc. Bailey, I don't like this."

"You afraid I'll break your dealer, Chancey?"

"Oh, the hell with both of you," Chancey shrugged.

"If you're playing, Bailey, take a seat." Holliday scowled as two customers gathered their chips and pushed away from the table. "If you're jabbering with Chancey, take it some place else." Holliday pointed at a chair on the opposite side of the table. "Sit and shut up."

Bailey frowned. "I pick my own chair." He pointed to the just vacated seat at Holliday's right. "That's my seat."

Chancey growled. "Goddammit, you two bastards are picking a fight. I'm getting my shotgun." He turned toward his office.

Bailey moved tentatively first, then boldly toward the chair beside the dealer. Holliday's two remaining customers shook their heads and stood up.

"Dammit, Bailey, you're running off my business."

Bailey threw a stack of bills on the table. "I came to play, not listen to you bellyache. You gonna deal?"

Holliday grabbed the cards and shuffled them from hand to

hand, leaning slightly back and twisting his chair around for a better angle at Bailey. Holliday didn't like his position to the left of Bailey. If he drew his sidearm, Bailey could deflect the barrel with his left hand while drawing his own gun. Holliday would go for his shoulder gun, if it came to that. Holliday stacked the cards neatly on the table between himself and Bailey. "Cut," he said softly, "unless you trust me."

Grabbing the stack of pasteboards with his pulpy paw, Bailey eased the top half of the deck away, then dropped it from about six inches off the table, the cards hitting the green felt and fanning out into a messy stack.

Holliday nodded at Bailey. "Cocky, aren't you? Fifty-dollar ante! See how long that stack of bills lasts." Holliday tossed his chips out in the middle of the table, but Bailey tarried. Holliday gathered the cards, then snapped the top one from the deck. "You'll not get another card until the pot is right, Bailey. You do understand how the game is played?"

Bailey drew his arm across his mouth, wiping the droplets of sweat on his coat sleeve. "What's your hurry, Doc?" Bailey said, throwing bills on top of Holliday's chips. "This game'll last until one of us is finished. Let's enjoy it. All right if I smoke?" Bailey pulled his silver-inlaid pipe from his coat pocket and clenched it between his teeth.

"As long as you're not dealing." Alternately, Holliday tossed cards between himself and Bailey.

Bailey toyed with his cards, viewed them, then placed them on the table. Under Holliday's suspicious eye, he eased his hand into his coat pocket and slowly drew out a packet of tobacco. He fingered tobacco from the pouch, sniffed at the weed, then stuffed it into the pipe. His hand retreated to his coat pocket, trading the pouch for a box of matches.

His eyes never leaving Bailey until the match flared, Holliday saved a pair of nines from his hand and prepared to throw the others away after Bailey adjusted his cards. The delay in play was having its intended effect. Holliday could feel the anger rising explosively in him. And he enjoyed it.

Sucking his pipe to life as he shook the match out, Bailey glanced at Holliday. "Two cards. Honest cards. Raise you a hundred dollars." He tossed his money into the pot.

"Separate your throwaways from the others, Bailey, if you want any cards." Holliday matched his raise and discarded three.

On his pipe Bailey drew deep, then emitted the smoke in short shots from between his puffy lips. Picking up his cards, he casually tossed the discards between himself and Holliday, who then pitched two cards in front of him.

"Dealer takes three," Holliday dropped a trio in a stack by his keepers, then mingled the replacements with them. Holliday played square with Bailey. In this game, cheating did not seem so important. As long as Bailey lost.

Bailey was slow and precise with every move, his hand going again inside his coat, reappearing with a pocket watch. He stared at the time. "It's getting late, Holliday."

"Rate you're playing, it'll be late tomorrow night before we finish this hand."

Bailey responded with a puff of smoke toward Holliday. "I'll go another fifty dollars."

"I'll match you and go fifty more. You still in?"

Bailey smiled. "I'm not taking down my tent this hand, no matter how much you bet."

"Then raise me, if it's so damn good."

"I'm fine."

"Then show your cards."

Fanning his hand out in an exaggerated arc, Bailey revealed them as slowly as a banker okays a loan. "Full house. Deuces over jacks."

Collapsing his cards, Holliday tossed them on the deadwood.

Bailey laughed heartily. He reached out to rake in the money with his hands like he would pull a woman to him, then retreated to the deadwood, picking up the top five cards before Holliday could stop him. "Two pairs, fours and nines," he grinned. "My three little deuces would've beaten that."

A river of rage flowed through Holliday. "You don't monkey with the deadwood, Bailey, or see my discards unless I show you."

Bailey leaned back in his chair and laughed. "Worried I'll break you? I've got your woman and now I'll get your money, Doc." He slurred the nickname with disgust. "Deal, damn you."

Nodding, Holliday tossed a hundred dollars out in the pot. "The ante's going up, Bailey. A hundred dollars to start."

Bailey laughed and counted out enough from the last hand's winnings to match Holliday's bet. "I'm in and staying in." Bailey laughed again and called to spectators. "You're about to see Doc Holliday eat his cards."

A smile with the wicked curve of a bowie knife flicked across Holliday's face as he corralled the cards and remixed them. He shuffled without watching the cards, staring intently at Bailey, then glancing once up into the crowd. Chancey was there, cradling his shotgun in the crook of his arm. Holliday gave Bailey the cut, then dealt the cards. Slipping the deck on the table, Holliday picked up his hand and fanned the cards apart. It was miserable — a pair of sixes and junk — but by damn he would teach Bailey a lesson with these cards.

"The bid's to you, Bailey."

"I'll up it fifty dollars, Doc."

Holliday smiled. "I'll see your fifty and raise you two hundred." The spectators whistled.

Bailey fidgeted with his cards, stared at them doubly hard, then reluctantly pushed the money onto the pot. "I'll take three cards," he said.

Three cards, Holliday thought. Indeed he would teach Bailey a lesson this time. Best he could have was a pair. When Bailey started a stack of deadwood, Holliday passed him a trio and gauged Bailey's reaction to the new cards. There was little pleasure in his eyes. Holliday laughed to himself.

"The dealer takes," then Holliday paused until Bailey gazed behind bloodshot eyes at him, "one card." Without picking up his hand from the table, Holliday shoved the top card to the deadwood. He dropped the new card atop his other four, picked up his refurbished hand, and spread the cards apart. Knowing Bailey was watching, he arched his eyebrow for a brief instant. "You good, Bailey?"

Bailey pondered for a moment, started to nod his head, then seemed to lose control of his fingers, which put another fifty dollars in the pot. "I'm upping you fifty."

"I'll see that and I'll raise you five hundred dollars." Spectators moved closer to the table.

Bailey squirmed in his seat, looking from his hand to the spectators as if waiting advice on what to do. There was none. He collapsed the cards in his hand and tossed them atop the deadwood.

Holliday grinned. "Shame to win that much money on a little pair of sixes."

Bailey clenched his fist until it whitened.

Holliday drew in the deadwood and picked up the top five cards, Bailey's hand. One at a time, he turned them over. A pair of jacks and three discards. "What do you have to say for yourself, Bailey, letting my sixes scare your jacks?"

"Leave the deadwood alone, Doc. That's what you told me."

"You saw my last hand. We're square, now that I've seen yours."

Bailey's hand moved toward the table edge.

"Don't try it, Bailey," Holliday ordered. "Keep your hands in sight." Holliday started shuffling the deck.

Bailey's hand returned to his stack of money.

"That's better," Holliday chided. "Now it'll cost you a hundred dollars to start this hand. Can you manage that, Bailey, or do you need a loan?"

"I can manage." He shoved the money to the middle of the table. "Deal straight."

"You accusing me of cheating?"

"I'm just making sure you understand me."

"You'd do better, Bailey, if you played a little smarter." Holliday shuffled, then passed the cards to Bailey for the cut.

Bailey sliced but a dozen cards from the top. "Cut thin and win, I always say."

"Just cut without the goddam blabbering, Bailey."

Bailey clenched his teeth against his pipe stem, sucking on it until the tobacco glowed and smoke balls rose in the air.

Holliday pitched cards to Bailey and himself. Bailey drew hard on his pipe as he eased his cards apart. Holliday squared his cards between his fingers, staring intently at Bailey. As Bailey's demeanor accustomed to the cards in his hand, Holliday looked at his own. Three clubs. A chance at a flush, but little else. This wasn't a good start for a heavy betting hand. He watched Bailey pull one from his hand and drop it on the table. Holliday was playing him for two pair. That would be a winner, Holliday guessed, looking at his own hand and figuring the odds of drawing into a flush.

"I'm raising you two hundred dollars, Doc, and taking one card." Bailey picked up the money and held it over the pot, letting the money drop as he loosened his fingers.

It was as Holliday feared; Bailey thought he had a good hand. Maybe he could bluff Bailey again. "I'll see your two hundred and raise you three hundred more, Bailey."

"You bluffed me once, Holliday, but not again. I'll see you and add another fifty dollars to that."

Holliday matched him.

"Now give me my card, Doc."

Holliday obliged. "Hope it was worth the extra fifty dollars, Bailey." Holliday looked at his cards once more, then tossed two atop the deadwood. By keeping three, he could go for his flush and perhaps mislead Bailey that he had three of a kind. That would beat two pair, if that was indeed what Bailey had. It was worth a try. "I'll take two." Holliday dropped two new cards atop his keepers. He fought to hide the disappointment when he spread them apart. He had lucked into a single pair, a new card matching his jack of clubs, but nothing more. Bailey would win this hand sure as the devil, but he couldn't back down, not now, and he was uncertain if he could bluff Bailey again.

Holliday looked up at Bailey. "Now show me how valuable those cards are."

"Three hundred," Bailey said, throwing money onto the table like it was worthless.

"I'll see your three hundred, Bailey, and match you two hundred more."

Bailey paused, working the pipe from one side of the mouth to the other, clamping it tightly between his teeth at its new destination. His cards he folded, then fanned out again, looking from them to Doc and back. As his hand dropped toward his money, he stared at the pile, then back at Doc.

"You in, Bailey?"

"I'm thinking."

"Make it quick."

With his free hand, Bailey reached for the deadwood.

"Leave them alone, Bailey."

Disregarding the warning, Bailey bent up the corners of the top two, Holliday's discards. "This doesn't tell what you have."

Holliday dropped his cards on the table. "But you know what I don't have."

As Bailey eased his hand away from the deadwood, Holliday reached with his left for the pot.

"What goes, Holliday?" Bailey's voice was high with fright.

"You lose, Bailey!"

"Not without seeing your cards I don't," he shouted.

Bailey jerked his hand away from the tabletop and to his side. He was going for his revolver. His mouth flew ajar and the pipe dropped in his lap, scalding ash burning into his britches and leg. He screamed as his free hand slapped at his lap.

Holliday jammed his hand inside his coat. His fingers slipped between the gun under his shoulder and the knife in his pocket. His instinct said gun, but his fingers wrapped around the dagger. In Bailey's eyes Holliday saw a glaze of terror magnified by a cloud of doubt. Bailey's arm was rising. Holliday jerked at the dagger, but the leather sheath seemed to come with it. He pressed his left arm against his ribs and pulled. The knife cleared the sheath, then his coat lapel. "You son of a bitch," he yelled.

Bailey lifted his gun. The barrel struck the edge of the table. A gunshot exploded into the floor, a cloud of white smoke engulfing both men. Bailey regained control of his gun and twisted his arm toward Holliday.

In a deadly arc the dagger flashed toward Bailey. Their weapons came together with a clang. "Oh, my god!" Bailey screamed. His revolver fell on the table. So did his thumb.

The dagger, bloodied, could not be stopped. It sank into Bailey's chest. Bailey's eyes bulged out and his uncomprehending mouth widened further at the knife. His face turned suddenly ashen, the ghostly paleness heightened by the cloud of smoke around him. His lips parted for him to speak, but nothing came out — except blood. And from his nose, a pink foam bubbled. A gurgling in his throat preceded the quietness of death. Then Bailey tumbled sideways onto the floor.

With the knife, Holliday brushed Bailey's thumb from atop the cards and onto the floor. He gathered the pot, taking Bailey's stake as well. Looking up toward Chancey, Holliday grinned. "I didn't shoot him, Chancey."

Leaning over in his chair, Holliday wiped the bloody blade on Bailey's pants leg, then sat up to count his money.

"You went too far this time, Doc," Chancey said.

Doc stared at Chancey and the gaping black eyes of the shotgun pointing at his neck. "Bailey was cheating. Put your gun away, Chancey, it makes me nervous."

"You went too far, Doc! Count your winnings but don't lift a hand off the table or I'll shoot. Somebody fetch the sheriff. I can't have killings in my saloon. It's bad for business."

TWENTY-FIVE

"You gotta help him, Chancey."

The breathless voice surprising and angering him, Chancey jerked around in his chair. "How in the hell did you get in here, Kate?" Chancey gauged the distance between himself and the shotgun propped in the corner. He eased up from his chair.

"You gotta help him, Chancey."

"Kate, you fool, Bailey's dead."

"Doc, dammit. I never cared for that bastard Bailey. Doc's the one I wanted."

"Fine way of showing Doc your affection," Chancey answered, inching toward the corner, "but that's to be expected of a whore." He took a bold step to the shotgun, stopping cold at the sound of a metallic click. He turned to Kate, his eyes focusing on the cocked revolver in her hand.

"Step an inch closer to that shotgun and I'll kill you, Chancey." Kate waved the revolver as her witness.

Chancey retreated to his desk. "What do you want, Kate?"

"I need help to free Doc."

Chancey laughed, then slid into his chair, stroking his chin and propping his feet on the desk. "Free Doc? The law's got him now, and I'm not interfering with the law."

"The law," Kate screamed. "You know where they took

him? The Southern Hotel, dammit. Last time they had someone under guard there, the vigilantes treated him to a necktie party."

"Ain't it a shame, Kate." Chancey calmly built a cigarette. "I warned Doc. Now he deserves what he gets."

"He thought you were his friend. I ought to kill you."

"Go ahead, Kate, maybe they'll hang you two together."

Kate spit at Chancey. "You bastard, making money off both Doc and me, now turning against us."

"Doc was stewing for trouble 'cause Lottie left."

"Noooo," Kate's voice turned deep and menacing. "He didn't like her. He was jealous of Bailey having me. Doc killed him for me. It was me Doc did it for."

Chancey smiled behind a veil of cigarette smoke. "Believe what you like, Kate. But it was Lottie."

"He did it for me, Chancey. He loves me. You wouldn't know about love, would you? It might be bad for business."

Again Chancey smiled. Then the door creaked and Kate spun around. Instantly, Chancey bolted from his chair and grabbed her arm before she could shoot the entering bartender. His massive hands strangled her gun wrist, the revolver falling to the floor.

Kate screamed, "Let go of me," and pummeled Chancey's broad chest with her free fist before the bartender finally muzzled her flailing hand.

"What are we gonna do with her, boss?" he asked, a grimace blooming on his face from a shoepoint planted on his shin.

"We'll escort her out. If she ever returns, kill her." Her wrists clamped in one hand, Chancey bent over to pick up her gun. Then he and the bartender herded Kate out of the office, through the saloon, and beyond the swinging doors. At the edge of the plank walk, they shoved her into the street.

"You bastards," Kate shouted as she tumbled into the dirt.

Chancey yelled, "Remember my warning, Kate. You come back, I'll kill you." He pitched the gun over her head into the street. "You're bad for business."

Kate scrambled for the revolver as Chancey scurried back inside. "You son of a bitch," he heard her shout. "I hope your business withers away first. Then your pecker."

"Where you been, sheriff?" Holliday spoke before Trickus could shut the door. "Meeting with the vigilantes?"

Trickus flexed his arm and the door flew open with a crash. "Shut up, Holliday."

"Take me up to the fort. They've got a stockade." Holliday struggled feebly against the ropes binding his legs and arms to a chair.

Turning to his two deputies, Trickus motioned toward Holliday. "Check the rope and tighten it."

"Your record for protecting prisoners in the hotel isn't too good, sheriff."

"And gag him, if he doesn't shut up." The deputies moved cautiously about Holliday, as if he might suddenly wrench free.

Trickus strode about the room, stopping on each revolution by the window, holding the curtains back and staring into the darkness. As the deputies finished checking Holliday's bindings, the tall one plopped on the bed.

"Get your butt up and stay on guard," Trickus ordered.

"But he can't get loose," the deputy answered.

"His type is slippery as an eel, so be careful."

The deputy snickered, dropped his feet to the floor, and stood. "We won't have to watch him much longer, though."

Trickus averted his eyes from Holliday's. And then Holliday stared at the window, the thought of what awaited beyond the darkness stabbing deep into his brain.

"No sense in delaying justice with a judge and jury, is there, sheriff? Even if I killed in self-defense."

"Bailey was a popular man," Trickus answered.

"Bailey was a pig."

"I've been out trying to calm some of the men down that called Bailey a friend."

"That shouldn't have taken long."

"Holliday, shut your damn mouth." Trickus spun around and marched by the washstand, stopping to inspect the two guns, the dagger, and a weather-beaten faro dealing box beside the washbasin. "You dumb sons of bitches, which one of you left your weapons here?"

The tall deputy nodded. "Me."

"I tell you, don't leave nothing around he could grab. Stick them in your gunbelt."

"Damn, you're jumpy," the tall deputy said as he joined Trickus. He shoved both revolvers in his belt and slipped the dagger in his boot. "I'll be glad when this night is over."

"Me, too," Trickus said, sitting on the bed, facing Holliday.

Though Holliday stared in Trickus's direction, his eyes focused behind him on the window. For an instant he saw a specter pass before the pane, his body tensing as if he had seen the face of death. Then between the parted curtain, he caught a brief glimpse of a familiar face, disappearing the moment Trickus twitched his head around.

It was Kate. What in hell could she want?

Kate saw him bound behind the sheriff, then jerked herself away from the window as Trickus had turned her way. She wasn't sure how many deputies were with him, and she didn't have the time to check again. Down the street a crowd of men gathered quietly in the deep darkness between buildings where no light from illuminated windows could seep. And toward that black chasm, Kate had seen one man carrying a rope.

Kate had tied the horses by the Cattle Exchange. She carried in one hand Doc's valise, half-filled with his clothes and half with her own, and in the other his medical bag bulging with his dental tools, his marked cards, and her favorite book, *Tom Sawyer*. Now she needed coal oil. She should have thought of it before. Without a distraction, she had no hope of springing Doc. And dammit, she didn't have much time to improvise, not with those men smoldering for his neck.

She stepped around the corner and onto the plank walk in front of the hotel. Catching her breath, she pushed open the door and struggled her way inside. A spindly clerk with jerky motions and nervous eyes stood up suddenly from a chair behind the desk. He watched Kate carry her bags across the room. It was the same room where the puppet show had been held, but now it seemed too small for such a crowd. Two couches squeezed between mismatched end tables bordered the threadbare carpet leading from door to desk. And on each table sat an unlit lamp.

Kate dropped the valise and medical bag at her feet as she leaned over the counter. A head taller than the clerk, she peered down on him. "A gentleman would've given a lady a hand!"

The clerk sniffed his upturned nose. "A lady wouldn't be out on the street this time of night!" He backed away from the counter as Kate lifted her hand.

"The pen." She smiled at the inkwell and writing instrument by the register. "I'd like a room."

"We don't do business with your type, madam."

Damn it to hell, a cocky son of a bitch. She didn't have time to waste arranging a room with this puny specimen of manhood. Again she smiled, but her voice was a deep, dark whisper. "Mister, a lot of men have been treated to the inside of my blouse. But besides my womanly charms there I hide a pistol." She paused, then yelled. "Now give me a goddam room or I'll put a tiny hole between your eyes."

The clerk froze as Kate's hand flashed toward her blouse. Down the back hall, a door banged open.

"Everything okay up there?"

Kate recognized Trickus's voice. She turned her head away from the hall in case the sheriff came to investigate. With the gun in her hand, she whispered to the clerk. "Tell him nothing's wrong."

"Everything's fine, sheriff," the clerk called. "Some drunk woman stuck her head inside 'fore I shooed her out."

Kate heard the door slam back. She sighed.

"A room'll be four dollars for the night."

"That's more like it, fellow." She stuck her gun back inside her blouse and exchanged it for four dollars. "Cash in advance. I know you wouldn't trust me to pay in the morning."

The clerk grabbed the money and held it up to the lamp.

"It ain't tainted."

He put the money in his pocket, then shoved the register and a pen toward Kate. "Last room on the left," he said as she signed. Then he tossed a key on the register, smudging Kate's still wet signature.

Kate pushed the key back across the counter at the clerk. "If you're not offering to take my bags, least you can do is unlock my room, light the lamp, and open a window."

Muttering beneath his breath, the clerk shook his head. "What's a woman like you got to fear from the dark?"

"Men like you. Now move, so I can get a good night's sleep."

"Alone, I suggest." The clerk primly straightened his shoulders.

"As always." Kate curtsied as the clerk grabbed the key, fished for a tin of matches beneath the counter, and marched down the hall.

"You coming?" he called, without looking over his shoulder.

"Soon as I get my bags." When he disappeared, Kate ran across the room. At the end table nearest the door, she choked the lamp between her hands, then jerked them away. The lamp was still hot; it must have been blown out only minutes earlier. The clerk's footsteps stopped and she heard him fumbling the key in the lock, then the door swinging open on oil-starved hinges. She didn't have much time. She wrapped her hands in the folds of her skirt and gingerly picked up the lamp, only then noticing the emptiness of the glass bowl that should hold the coal oil. The lamp had burned itself dry. She slid it brusquely back on the table. Jarring the chimney off, she caught it with her bare hand, then clenched her teeth as the hot glass seared her palm. Hearing the clerk opening the window, she realized she had too little time to worry about the pain. Twisting around to look at the other three table lamps, she cursed at the sound of the approaching clerk. She grabbed another lamp, scurried to the door, and wrestled it open. The footfalls sounded closer. She leaned out the door, half placing, half dropping the lamp on the rough plank porch. She straightened up to close the door just as the footsteps turned silent behind her.

"What the devil are you doing?"

"Wind blew the door open." She lied and knew he knew it. She closed the door softly.

Folding his arms across his chest, the clerk stopped at the lampless table, lowered his arms, and placed the tin of matches there, as if he realized something were amiss but couldn't quite figure it out. "Likely story," he said, moving to her side.

Kate held her breath and rubbed her hands together, the friction aggravating the pain in her palms.

Staring at Kate, the clerk nodded, a smile spreading across his face like sunshine breaking through a cloud. "You're trying to slip a fellow in here." He lunged for the entry, pushed Kate

283

aside, and wrenched the door open. He stuck his head out, looking around. "He's gone, dammit."

Kate eased away from the door, stationing herself between the clerk and the table minus the lamp. Backing up, she slipped one hand behind her and groped for the tin of matches. Feeling it, her hand closed tightly around the tin.

"Woman," the clerk said, shutting the door, then glaring at Kate, "you'll not conduct yourself as a harlot in this hotel."

Kate harrumphed, then nodded compliantly. "This is not what you think." Her lying lips smiled.

The clerk stepped past Kate, and she moved closely on his heels, the clerk heading for the counter, Kate grabbing her bags and going down the hall.

"The key's on the bed," he called in her wake.

Kate struggled against her feet to keep from running. Reaching her room, she kicked the door to and tossed the bags on the bed, taking in the room as she did. It was a corner room with two windows, both open. She flew to the side window and stuck her head out long enough to see the mob of men crawling out of the dark holes of night into the street. Quickly, she pulled the window down and jerked the curtains together. Racing to the back window, she raised it as high as it would go, then shoved a leg outside, worked her head and torso out, and pulled the other leg out behind her.

Kate crouched low as her eyes adjusted to the dark. Gradually, buildings took shape. Not forty paces from the hotel was a small barn. It would do. As she stood up, the match tin slipped from her hand. She caught a glimmer of it from light coming out her window, but as she stepped forward to pick it up, her foot kicked it into the darkness. She fell to her knees, groping madly for the tin, slapping the ground with her burned hands. The noise of the mob was growing louder. Time was growing shorter, Kate thought. Then she felt the tin and her fingers closed around it. For a moment she clutched it to her breast, then she shoved it inside her blouse and ran around the opposite side of the hotel to the front.

She stuck her head around the front corner of the hotel. The mob, with two angry torches lighting the way like malevolent eyes, was coming. The lamp. She must fetch it before they got

284

here. She raced down the porch, grabbed the lamp, and dashed off the walk, stumbling as she turned the corner of the hotel, the lamp chimney tumbling to the ground and shattering like a crystal explosion. Startled by the breaking glass, a stray dog growled, then chased her, nipping at her heels until she spun around and kicked at the dark form behind her. The cur yelped and receded deeper into the darkness that was night.

What the hell else could go wrong? she wondered as she reached the small barn. Surely it would burn, she thought as she flung the door open, the clatter seeming to thunder across the Flat. She caught a glimpse of the mob as it advanced on the hotel. The vigilantes came like a giant growling bear, emboldened by its own noise. She hurried inside the barn, the sweet smell of hay tickling her nose. The lamp tucked under her arm, she pulled the tin of matches from her blouse and struck a match against the wormwood walls. It flamed just long enough for her to see the bed of hay scattered across the entrance, then died. This building would make a good fire.

Lifting the lamp over her head, she flung it to the ground. As the lamp splattered glass and coal oil against the hay, Kate was startled by a kicking and nickering in the back of the stall. Dammit, a horse. Kate jumped deeper into the barn and followed the noise to the animal. The horse flinched at her touch, but she patted him long enough to find the halter that bound him. Undoing it, she slapped his flank and the animal bolted for the door, darting outside and away from the advancing terror of the mob.

Kate hoped she wasn't too late. Moving to the shattered lamp, she scratched the match against the wall, a small flame erupting. She threw the match too quickly at the hay and it died before striking the ground. She stuck her fingers in the tin for another match and nurtured it to life against the wormwood wall. She bent over and held the flame to the hay. Slowly the match licked the hay, taking hold and beginning to assume a life beyond control. As the flames grew, she fed them more hay, then picked up a burning pile and tossed it further into the barn. She jumped back at the swoosh of flames taking to the coal oil. The hay seemed to explode, and Kate laughed as she dashed for the corner hotel room with the open window and the burning lamp.

At the window, she could hear around the side of the building the shouts of the vigilantes, screwing up their courage by their noise. She jerked up her skirt and shoved her leg through the window, following it with her torso. Before she could bring her other leg in, she was petrified by a voice.

"I knew it."

Her head twisted instantly toward the sound of the clerk's voice. "Don't you give your customers any privacy?" She pulled her leg in.

"Not," he gloated, "when they use this hotel as a brothel."

Kate stuck her head outside. "Run, cowboy," she yelled.

The clerk pushed Kate away from the window and stared into the night. "So I was right," he said, turning to Kate and folding his arms across his chest. "The sheriff's just down the hall. I'll get him to take care of you."

Kate pulled her revolver from her blouse and stepped toward the clerk. "We'll settle this without the sheriff."

"Oh my god," the clerk answered, his hands dropping to his side as he took a step toward Kate.

Cocking the revolver, she pointed it at his nose. "Another step and you're a dead man."

He pointed out the window, his skin turning pale. His lips mouthed a word twice before he mumbled, "Fire."

"Don't move."

"Fire. The barn. My horse." He lunged for the door and out into the hall. "Fire!" he screamed. "Fire out back! Everybody out to save the town!"

Kate ran to the door and watched as adjacent rooms emptied of half-dressed men. Toward the front of the hall, a door opened slowly and a man stepped out with a drawn gun. It was Trickus. Kate ducked inside, closing the door except for the inch-wide crack through which she spied. For a moment the sheriff surveyed the hall, then called for a deputy. Together they bolted toward the front of the hotel. She couldn't help but laugh. It had worked. She forced herself to count to fifty, then picked up the key from the bed and grabbed the medical bag and valise.

At the sound of a key in the lock, the deputy twisted his face to the door. He eased his gun out of his holster and slipped toward the noise. His hand reaching for the knob, the deputy called, "Who is it?"

"Aaaaghh!" a woman screamed.

Holliday recognized Kate's voice.

"Who is it?" the deputy repeated.

"Wilma Plunkett. You're in my room."

The deputy twisted the knob and cracked the door, which flew open, Kate barging in behind it, her head downturned, away from the deputy. She dropped the valise and the medical bag on the floor. Her arm flew out from her side and she handed the deputy the key. He took it as she cut her eyes briefly toward him. "Aaaaghh!" she screamed. "Don't shoot me just because you got the wrong room, sir. I . . . I feel faint." She lunged for a chair and plopped down, burying her face in her hands. Her mumbled voice muttered through the palm mask. "I'd paid for the room and the clerk was going to show me to it and then he started yelling fire and everybody started running out and I thought the building was on fire and I was going to burn to death and now you're in my room and pointing a gun at me to kill me." She sobbed.

Holliday watched the deputy holster his pistol and then shut the door. As the deputy examined the key, Holliday caught Kate observing him through her fingers as she mumbled incoherently.

"There's nothing to fear, ma'am," the deputy began. "Been a lot of excitement outside here in the last few minutes."

Kate sobbed louder. "And there's a mob of men outside and I thought they were going to kill me. Some of them were carrying a rope and a couple wearing hoods over their heads and I don't know what's to become of me. I shouldn't have been out on the street, but I thought we had some good law officers in town that would stop that mob. Guess I was wrong."

"You've made two mistakes, ma'am," the deputy coughed. "This isn't your room and the law will take care of you." The deputy sidled toward Kate and placed his hand upon her left wrist. "Just calm down and we'll get this straightened out. There's just been a simple mistake."

Kate nodded and leaned forward to stand up. She stumbled into the deputy and in one fluid motion her left hand jerked his pistol from its holster and her uplifted knee caught the deputy in the groin. He groaned. "No mistake, deputy."

"What the hell," the deputy gasped through the pain, looking full into Kate's face for the first time. "Why, Kate you bitch!"

His hand flinched toward his empty holster.

Kate cocked his revolver. "Raise your hands or you're dead." The deputy complied.

"In his belt, Kate," Holliday warned, "he's got my revolvers and in his boot my dagger."

Kate smiled coyly at Holliday. "Doc, aren't you gonna say you're glad to see me, you little shit?"

"Dammit, Kate, we don't have time for that."

Kate motioned with the revolver for the deputy to move toward the bed. "Let me correct you, Doc. You don't have time for this. If I hadn't fired that barn the vigilantes would already've hoisted you from a cottonwood. Now, you little shit, are you glad to see me?"

"Dammit, yes. Now set me free before your little fire burns out and we're both air dancing."

"Fall on the bed, deputy." He tumbled forward and she placed the gun at his temple. "If you so much as fart, I'll blow your brains out." She removed Holliday's guns from his belt.

"The knife in his boot," Holliday said, rocking toward the bed in his chair. "Get it and cut me free."

"Dammit, Doc, shut up. I'm in charge now." With Doc's guns under her arm, she backed away from the bed and turned the deputy's gun on Holliday. "Now, Doc, you tell me something. Did you kill Bailey 'cause you were mad about Lottie leaving? Or were you jealous Bailey'd been sleeping with me?"

"Why do you think I killed him, Kate?"

"You were jealous, Doc. That was it, wasn't it?"

"Sure, Kate, sure. Now untie me before the sheriff returns."

"Deputy," Kate called. "You get up easy off that bed and cut the ropes. You so much as draw a drop of his blood and I'll spill yours all over this floor."

The deputy slid off the bed and drew the knife from his boot as he eased toward Holliday. For a moment he held it menacingly over Holliday's spine.

"Do something foolish, you'll die, deputy. You're dealing with Doc Holliday's wife-to-be."

His lips twitching, the deputy lowered the knife to the bindings and freed Holliday's arms, then his feet.

Holliday flexed his arms and rubbed the circulation back into them. As the deputy finished slicing the rope around his boots, Holliday spoke. "Put the knife on the floor by my feet." As he obeyed, Holliday raised his boot and stomped the deputy's hand into the floor.

The man screamed and jerked his injured hand free, massaging it with his other.

"Now, you son of a bitch," Holliday said. "You'll feel what the ropes are like." He leaned forward and picked up the knife, then stood, his knees wobbly as a newly dropped calf. He staggered toward the bed. Kate steadied him and slipped Doc's sidearm back into its holster. She kissed him on the cheek, but he shrugged her off. "Not until I get this bastard tied." He shoved his knife back into its sheath and took the shoulder gun from Kate. Then he stepped around behind the deputy, grabbed him by the hair, and jerked him against the chair back. "Sit straight while I tie you. Kill him if he moves," he commanded Kate. Holliday held his pistol by the barrel and slammed it with all his might into the deputy's head. The deputy sat motionless for a moment, his only movement the upward roll of his eyes. Then Doc crashed the pistol butt against his head again and the deputy toppled over like a sack of flour onto the floor.

"We've gotta steal horses and get out of town, Kate."

"I've taken care of that. I've tied horses the other side of the Cattle Exchange." Kate grabbed Holliday's medical satchel.

Holliday motioned Kate to the door with his gun, but he lingered a moment by the washstand, fingering the corroded dealing box and shoving it inside his coat.

"What's that, Doc?"

"You're asking too many questions, Kate," he answered, picking up his valise. "Just lead the way to the horses."

Easing the door open, Kate surveyed the hall. It was vacant. Holliday cocked his pistol as he followed her down the hall, through the deserted lobby, and cautiously out on the walk. Everywhere men ran as if the city might not survive. Kate and

Doc moved against the stream, conspicuous by their cautious pace, but no one took time to watch. Nearby, men were directing a water wagon to the fire and sending another to the creek for re-filling. As Doc and Kate passed the deserted Cattle Exchange, she pointed to two mounts at an adjacent hitching post.

Holliday eyed the horses. "Damn, Kate, not Haverty's pinto and that damn Golden's chestnut!"

"Nothing can outrun them, Doc." She stopped on the walk. "You never approve of a thing I do for you."

"Haverty will have the sheriff out looking for them."

She pitched Doc's medical bag on the walk. "You don't like it, you get your own damn horses and get the hell out of my sight." She folded her arms across her chest and tapped her foot on the plank walk. "Burn the stinking town down, get the drop on a deputy so you won't hang, I do, and all you do is complain."

Footsteps on the plank walk behind them interrupted Holliday's response. Turning, he saw a bulky figure step from the shadows toward them. For a moment, Holliday paused as mutual recognition washed over himself and Chancey.

"Doc Holliday," Chancey called, "what are —" Then as he inched close enough to confirm Holliday's identity, Chancey broke toward the main street. His husky voice seemed to carry over the noise of the fire. "Holliday's escaped! Holliday's escaped!"

Kate laughed. "Now, you little shit, are my horses good enough for you?"

"Plenty, Kate, let's get out of here." He pitched his valise over the saddle and mounted the chestnut. Kate hesitated. "Dammit, you can't back out now," he shouted.

Kate picked up the medical bag and jumped toward the pinto, untying it from the hitching post and climbing unladylike aboard.

Holliday jerked his mount around and rode off toward the river, not by the main road but by a trail among the buffalo ricks. Cautiously, they wended their way through the obstacles, then clearing them, raced toward the line of trees, dimly visible three quarters of a mile ahead. Quickly, they were among the cotton-woods. Holliday drew up his horse and ordered Kate to stop.

"Maybe no one's taken up the chase." His voice was sharp, despite his breathlessness.

The seconds seemed to draw past as slow as years, and then, after an interminable time, it seemed that no one was giving chase. Holliday spent the time tying his valise to his saddle and Kate doing likewise with the medical bag. And when nothing emerged following them, Doc spoke, "I'm surprised Chancey turned against me."

"He never was with you, Doc. I'm the only one who's for you." She nudged her horse closer to his, just as Holliday heard the noise of pounding hooves.

"Damn, Kate," Holliday muttered. "They're after us."

Maybe twenty riders just coming into view from behind the huge buffalo ricks were aimed straight at them.

"Let's go, Doc," Kate implored, "but where can we hide?"

For a moment, Doc was silent. "The baseball field, the giant cottonwood."

"What?"

"Listen, Kate, just follow me. We'll make a wide circle away from the creek and head back into it upstream where they play baseball. Let's go."

He slapped the flank of the chestnut and splashed through the creek shallows, Kate behind him. And, in a few moments, the posse was too. Over the thundering hoofbeats of their mounts, Holliday thought he heard the shouts of riders and then the retort of their guns. Thank god, Kate had stolen the best horses. "We've got to put as much distance between them and us as fast as we can, Kate," Holliday yelled. "Don't save your horse for later. Just stay with me."

The two animals sensed the urgency. Their clean, even strides gave Holliday a sense of confidence that his plan would work, if only their speed bought enough time to hide when they struck the river again.

Whipping their horses forward, Kate and Holliday made for the ridge leading out of the valley, then turned sharply heading the direction the stream flowed. For maybe two miles they paralleled it, then arced back toward the Clear Fork. They had stretched the distance between themselves and the posse, but would the distance be enough? Holliday wondered.

Nearing the watercourse, Holliday shouted at Kate. "Hit the creek, then head back for town."

"Back to town?" Kate drew up on the reins, then slapped the pinto on the flank, the horse stumbling from the indecision. "You're a fool, Doc," he heard her yell.

The chestnut hit the water hard, then struggled to regain its stride as Holliday jerked the reins. Holliday cursed as the animal faltered, then dashed upstream, almost jarring Holliday from the saddle. Ahead, Holliday could see the bend in the creek that cradled the baseball diamond in its elbow. The huge tree at the stream's edge suddenly loomed ahead of him like a giant fortress. He twisted his head over his shoulder to see Kate approaching. The posse had yet to come into sight. If only Kate made it in time. In the darkness, he could gradually make out the somber bank. The giant hole gouged out from under the tree's roots by last summer's floods had not caved in.

Holliday aimed the chestnut for the space beneath the bank and between the gnarled roots. Reaching the hole, the animal shied away. Holliday jerked the reins taut, then beat the animal's chest with the slack. The horse eased cautiously forward, and Holliday dismounted to lead the animal into the chasm as the splashing pinto neared. Holding the reins of the spooked chestnut, he leaped from his hiding place to stop Kate.

She screamed, then recognized Holliday. "You scared me. I thought I'd lost you, Doc."

"No time for that," Holliday called. "Take cover." He grabbed the pinto's bridle, jerking it toward the undercut bank.

Kate slapped the pinto and he moved skittishly into the hiding place, which smelled of moist earth and rotten wood. She jumped off the horse and maneuvered it as deeply into the cut as she could. "Some damn spot you picked to hide, Doc Holliday."

"You got any better ideas? They may spot us if they come down the creek, but if they ride up the bank, we may get away with it."

Kate wrapped the reins around her hand. "This place gives me the creeps. If there are any snakes in here, I may scream."

"You do, you may hang the both of us." Holliday caught Kate's arm and squeezed it tightly. "Quiet." He poked his head out from a tangle of roots and stared down the creek. "They've stopped in the creek," he whispered. Barely he could make out milling forms in the distance.

Kate peeked toward the riders. Then the pinto spooked and bolted for the stream. Kate screamed as the horse jerked the reins tied around her arm. Holliday lunged for the saddle horn of the animal, missing it, then grabbing for the stirrup. He shoved his hand into the stirrup and pulled. For a moment, as the pinto broke for the open and the chestnut backed away, Holliday thought he would be torn in half, between the hand caught in the stirrup and the other wrapped in the chestnut's reins. But Kate jerked savagely at the pinto's reins, then slapped it hard on the nose. The horse whinnied, then retreated into the little cave.

Both horses under control, Holliday glanced downstream. The posse was coming toward them, moving at a canter.

"They're coming, Kate, stay quiet. Our lives depend on it."

Kate grunted. Holliday pulled his gun from his holster. "If there's shooting, Kate, you break for freedom. I'll cover you as long as I can."

"What about you, Doc?" She reached for his arm and squeezed it. "You'll get killed."

"I owe you one, Kate. There's little future for a gambler with consumption."

"Nor for this whore without you, Doc. I can use a gun." She released his arm and patted the pinto.

"Not this time, Kate. For once, you'll do as I say."

From down the river, they could hear the muffled sound of voices, words made indecipherable by distance and the splash of horses' hooves. The riders drew within fifty yards. Holliday cocked his pistol. "If I shoot, you mount and ride, Kate."

The distance between the quarry and the hunters halved. Holliday heard Kate's breathing between his own labored gasps for air and it seemed that even the posse would hear them too. Then the voices of the pursuers carried to the hiding place.

"They'd be fools to head back to town."

Holliday recognized Trickus's voice, but not the reply that answered him.

"But I know I heard a woman scream and maybe a horse."

Trickus spoke again. "Sound travels far on a still night. Probably a whore in the Flat. Let's head downstream."

They came within ten yards and Holliday felt himself backing against his horse, pressing it against the pinto. He grabbed for the horse's nostrils and covered them with his gun hand. Finally, the riders turned from the stream and up the bank. Holliday exhaled a heavy breath of relief. There was more conversation which he could not make out, then sheriff's voice.

"Okay, you two ride on toward town. We'll follow the stream until after dawn to see if we spot them or any trace."

Then the pinto kicked at the chestnut. Kate and Holliday shoved the nervous horses apart, but the noise was lost in the sound of the posse galloping away from the cottonwood tree. Slowly, Holliday twisted from his horse and looked downstream, raising his revolver. At least now, he and Kate would have a better chance against a pair of men instead of a whole posse. But had the other two ridden away at the same time?

"Kate," Holliday whispered. "Did they all leave?"

"I couldn't hear for my pounding heart," she whispered.

For several minutes the man, woman, and animals huddled together beneath the great cottonwood tree as rivulets of dirt shook loose upon them from the earthen roof, the seconds dragging by like minutes, the minutes like hours until Doc had no perception of actual time. His urge to flee battled his need for caution. Finally, he dared to ease his head out between a tangle of roots. He held his breath and looked both directions along the stream. As he lifted his hand to motion for Kate to emerge from hiding, his eyes spotted a silent pinpoint of light arc from the bank overhead into the creek. Someone had tossed a cigarette into the creek. He slammed his hand against Kate. Two mounted men lingered on the bank above them. Holliday caught a whiff of cigarette smoke and knew the wait must be longer. His heart seemed to pound as loud as a drum on the Fourth of July. He weighed the merits of killing the pair and making a dash for freedom until he heard one of them speak.

"Maybe Trickus was right, but I swear I heard something."

"Like the sheriff said," the other answered, "sound can play tricks on you on a still night. Let's let the sheriff catch up with this fellow. That's his job, not ours."

In a moment the hoofbeats of their mounts trailed away into the distance and all was silent, except for Holliday's and Kate's breathing and the pounding of their hearts.

Kate whispered. "What'll we do now, Doc?"

"We'll stay for a while." He eased the hammer down on his revolver and stuck it back into its holster.

And they waited. Gradually, they allowed their mounts a little more freedom and themselves chances to work the cramps out of their muscles. Painfully slow, the night continued until a hint of dawn rimmed the sky. "Get ready to ride. We'll have to make good time."

She smiled back. "I'll go anywhere with you, Doc."

He nodded, brushing the dirt from his coat. "I'll look around. You wait here." Holliday emerged fully from the dirty den. Slipping cautiously upstream, he crouched his way up the bank, lifting his head eye-level against the flatness that stretched to town. Like a prairie dog emerging from his den, he looked all around, then climbed out into the open. Nothing he saw ahead or in the surrounding country frightened him, but he bent over and ran to the cottonwood tree. Finding the lowest branch, he lifted himself aboard and climbed as high as he dared. As if he were in the crow's nest of a sailing vessel, he scanned all around the country. The Flat was awakening, but nothing seemed amiss there, and the posse was nowhere to be seen.

Quickly, he descended to the low branch, then dropped himself to the ground. He pitched forward as he fell and landed on all fours. Shaking his head, he stared at the ground. In the dimness his eyes slowly focused on a bed of Indian blankets strewn among the grass. The flowers were mostly dried up, having lost most petals to the summer sun, but Doc broke eight off anyway and formed an awkward bouquet. Standing, he felt his coat fall heavily against his hip and he remembered the corroded dealing box Lottie had saved for him. He pulled it from his pocket, shaking his head as he studied it. Then he turned toward the embankment and slipped down to the horses and Kate.

"Things seem calm, Kate," he called softly. A frail light reached the edge of the hiding spot, enough for Holliday to see Kate's features as she emerged. She wasn't a bad-looking woman, he thought, even with a dirt-smudged face and eyelids drooping from fatigue. He smiled at her. As she moved beside the horses, Holliday tossed the dealing box into the creek.

"What was that?" she asked with a start.

Holliday looked from the water up at her. "Something I

don't need anymore." Stepping beside her, Doc lifted his hand and extended the pathetic flowers to Kate.

"For me?"

"No, goddammit, for your pinto," Holliday shrugged. "Sure dammit, they're for you."

Gently, she took them from him and leaned against him to kiss his cheek.

He flinched at the touch of her lips. "We don't have time for that now. We've got to ride."

"But where to, Doc?" She handed him his reins and they both mounted.

"Kansas, Kate. I've got a friend named Wyatt Earp in Dodge City."

EPILOGUE

Doc Holliday rode from Fort Griffin into Dodge City and into legend. His acquaintance with Wyatt Earp became the single enduring male friendship of his life. Together Earp and Holliday would become myth and survive — at Tombstone's O.K. Corral — the most famous gunfight in the history of the Old West. A tumbleweed of a man, Holliday drifted among the boomtowns of the 1870s, most believed in search of a new card game or an old enemy. But those were people who never knew of Lottie.

Big Nose Kate Elder considered the following years in Dodge City as the happiest of her life and fancied herself the wife of Doc Holliday. Their tempestuous relationship was never sanctified by marriage vows, though Kate followed him from Dodge City to Tombstone. And when consumption finally caught up with Doc Holliday in Glenwood Springs, Colorado, in 1887, she was with him.

Keeping his promise, Jack Jacobs never revealed Lottie Deno's true identity. Lottie disappeared from history the day she carried her money-laden trunk aboard the stagecoach outside Fort Griffin. However, in 1934, Charlotte Thurmond, the widow of a one-time gambler named Frank Thurmond, died in Deming, New Mexico. Among the possessions of the devout eighty-eight-year-old Episcopalian was a leather trunk with the initials "J. J." over the latch.